LISTEN TO THE VOICE

Selected Stories

Iain Crichton Smith (1928) was born in Glasgow and raised by his widowed mother on the Isle of Lewis before going to Aberdeen to attend university. As a sensitive and complex poet in both English and his native Gaelic, he has published over twenty-five books of verse, from *The Long River* in 1955 to the *Collected Poems of* 1992. In his 1986 collection *A Life*, the poet looked back over his time in Lewis and Aberdeen, recalling a spell of National Service in the fifties, and then his years as an English teacher, working first in Clydebank and Dumbarton and then at the High School in Oban, where he taught until his retirement in 1977. Crichton Smith has been the recipient of many literary prizes, with Saltire Society and Scottish Arts Council Awards and fellowships, the Queen's Jubilee Medal and, in 1980, an OBE. He now lives in Taynuilt with his wife, Donalda.

As well as a number of plays and stories in Gaelic, Iain Crichton Smith has produced ten collections of stories, the best known of which are *Survival without Error* (1970); *The Black and the Red* (1973); *The Hermit and Other Stories* (1977); *Murdo and Other Stories* (1981); *Mr. Trill in Hades* (1984); *Selected Stories* (1990), and *Thoughts of Murdo* (1993). His novels are *Consider the Lilies* from 1968 (also in Canongate Classics); *The Last Summer* (1969); *My Last Duchess* (1971); *Goodbye, Mr Dixon* (1974); *An t-Aonaran* (1976); *An End to Autumn* (1978); *On the Island* (1979); *A Field Full of Folk* (1982); *The Search* (1983); and *The Tenement* (1985); *In the Middle of the Wood* (1987), and *An Honourable Death* (1992).

IAIN CRICHTON SMITH

Listen to the Voice

Selected Stories

Introduced by Douglas Gifford

CANONGATE
CLASSICS
49

First published as a Canongate Classic in 1993 by Canongate Press Ltd, 14 Frederick Street, Edinburgh EH2 2HB. Copyright © Iain Crichton Smith. Introduction © Douglas Gifford. All rights reserved.

'Survival Without Error', 'Adoration of the Mini' and 'On the Island' were first collected in *Survival Without Error* (1970). 'The Dying', 'An American Sky', 'The Wedding', 'The Black and the Red' and 'The Professor and the Comics' were first collected in *The Black and the Red* (1973). 'The Hermit' and 'Listen to the Voice' were first collected in *The Hermit and Other Stories* (1977). 'At the Fair' and 'Murdo' were first collected in *Murdo and Other Stories* (1981). 'What to Do About Ralph?' and 'The Play' were first collected in *Mr Trill in Hades* (1984). 'Napoleon and I', 'The Old Woman, the Baby and Terry', 'By Their Fruits' and 'Chagall's Return' were first collected in *Selected Stories* (1990).

British Library Cataloguing-in-Publication Data
A catalogue record for this book is available from The British Library.

ISBN 0 86241 434 2

CANONGATE CLASSICS
Series Editor: Roderick Watson
Editorial Board: Tom Crawford, J.B. Pick

The publishers gratefully acknowledge general subsidy from the Scottish Arts Council towards the Canongate Classics series and a specific grant towards the publication of this title.

Set in 10 on 11 Plantin by Hewer Text Composition Services, Edinburgh
Printed and bound in Great Britain by BPCC Paperbacks Limited, Aylesbury

Contents

Introduction

'Listen to the Voice' insists the title story of this collection, and Iain Crichton Smith, one of our finest writers, has always been engaged with the world of private and public voices. This has taken him from the existential bleaknesses of silence to the reviving and hilarious comedy which he finds in the oddness and banality of everyday speech. Some of his stories, like 'The Black and the Red' or 'The Professor and the Comics', suggest that following the promptings of an inner truth can lead to self-discovery and change. In others, however, as in the title story itself, the 'voice' listened to emerges as repressive, intolerant, or even mad.

All the evidence of Smith's poetry and fiction indicates an author deeply divided as to whether human experience has validity or not, and the reader of these stories will discover a disturbing and unsettled world. Lonely people in sterile relationships struggle with the bonds of monotony and 'duty'. Religion, culture and even daily village life, can suffocate, or make one an exile in one's own country. And beyond the village, the world at large all too often appears no better, a realm of bourgeois pretension, banal obsessions and the materialistic images of television. Significantly, for someone brought up on Lewis, (an island many would consider to offer beauty and tradition), Smith finds little consolation in landscape, in myth and legend, or in local culture. His are not the characters of a Neil Gunn or Grassic Gibbon, but of a bare, anonymous northern territory of unfriendly villages and dull towns, where, if nature intrudes at all, it is unknowable or alienating, as in the frequent imagery of an uncaring, heedless sea. If individuals triumph, it's not via the promptings of natural beauty, but through the assertion of self or the acceptance of fallen humanity.

The final hallmark of all Smith's work is his unremitting
emphasis on the need to recognise the ordinary, weak,
tragic, but vital nature of undistinguished people. This
did not come easily to him, with his Free Church background, his dominating mother's insistence on education,
his Aberdeen University study of Classics and English
Literature. The creative tension between a persistent respect
for an élitist and academic British tradition and an opposing
and radical love of the mundane is everywhere in these
disturbing short stories.

The collection also reflects the tension in Smith's fiction
and poetry generally, that is, between the Lewis and Gaelic
influences of childhood and the first half of his life, and
the concerns of his maturity with the wider world, and
particularly with issues of an existential and philosophical
nature. The stories range from mundane local community
concerns, where conformity matters so much, to fables such
as 'Chagall's Return', with its recognition that home and the
local may be a coffin as well as a nest to the artist.

'An American Sky', 'The Wedding', and 'The Black and
the Red' clearly define the claims and the failures of one's
home, village, island. 'The Black and the Red' was the
title story of a 1973 collection, and it is an important
semi-autobiographical account of Smith's university transition just after the war, from mother-dominated past to
involvement with ideas and issues radically alien to Lewis
and the Free Church. The story is cleverly constructed
so that it has a first part dominated by Black, with eight
sections or movements, conveyed through the letters home
to the mother, still tied up with concern for church and her
opinions, and the second, increasingly Red, with five rapidly developing sections/letters showing rebellion and final
epiphany and transformation. It is important, however, that
the reader does not fall for a simplistic Black/bad–Red/good
dichotomy. From the opening red rawness of the dawn sun
over Skye, redness is new life—but also associated with
the scavenging gulls, the uncertainty and vulnerability of
George the sceptical student, and the brittle assertiveness
and passion of Fiona. Yes, 'red' can be affirmative—it is
blood and life after all—but it can also be wounding and

pain. Even so, it is still immeasurably superior to the black, grey and ghostly deadness of the church bickering of Lewis, the mother's implied reproaches and complaints, the disillusioned academics with their dead ideas from disappointed teaching.

'An American Sky' offers a warmer balance of the two; John MacLeod returns at sixty from America to a changed Lewis, of TV and motor bikes and laconic youngsters who are disconnected from oral tradition, Gaelic culture, even family and village. Chinese restaurants and bingo jar with his memories, so that in the end neither past nor modern worlds dominate or offer value. The 'epiphany' of this story lies in the enigmatic and repeated imagery of the swarm of midges:

> They were rising and falling in the slight breeze. They formed a cloud but inside the cloud each insect was going on its own way of drifting with the breeze. Each alive and perhaps with its own weight, its own inheritance. Apparently free yet fixed, apparently spontaneous yet destined . . .

Doesn't the reference to predestined life, with its exact balance against freedom, tell us much about Smith's tension of Black and Red at this point? Similarly 'The Wedding' offers an initial downward estimate of island quality, in the way the father of the bride is shown up as clumsy, predictable and anachronistic amongst the young Gaels; but the story balances his banal wedding speech and the bride's embarrassment by allowing him to blossom in the later singing, when only he can sing with authority and memory of the old songs. Significantly, the 'I' author finds the wedding strangely 'authentic and false'—so that the nett effect of these Gaelic-based stories is to question both worlds. One can become an exile from the world as well as from one's home, and Smith finds his main tension between acceptance of the bleeding world and alienation from it.

Concomitant with these stories of roots are the many stories exploring duty towards bleak and authoritarian parents. 'The Adoration of the Mini' and 'The Dying' show a movement from simple repudiation of repressive bonds to complex evaluation of what exactly 'love' and 'duty' amount to. 'Hate' and 'fear' are interwoven with them; yet while Smith nearly always concludes that new life is unquestionably superior to custom-based servitude, he shows always the paradox of pain resultant from self-assertion and love. The pregnant daughter of 'The Adoration' says farewell to her dying father; but 'what she was included her father', and she pities her unborn child, knowing that life may repeat her father yet again. This refusal to allow unqualified human love is taken to its ultimate conclusion in 'The Dying', where the relationship of the dying person to the watcher is reduced to one in which the human body becomes 'the breathing', 'the grey hairs around the head', 'the voice'—and finally, 'the log', inert, dead matter, a cold factuality alongside a living grief. Death is unknowable.

This reduction of the human connection to the anatomised actuality pervades nearly all Smith's stories. In 'Survival Without Error', 'The Hermit', and 'Listen to the Voice' marriages are reduced to a grey failure to communicate, or to dubious memories in which the survivor can't quite decide whether love existed or not. Or they end up in a solipsistic loneliness in which, as in 'The Hermit', a whole community becomes an aggregation of separate, lonely, and selfish people. 'Survival Without Error' introduces Smith's concept of the final and necessary invention of the sick community, the scapegoat. His analysis of human complexity is profound here; the last turn of the introverted and loveless self and society is to create the 'other' who is nevertheless a version of the self and of the society. The lawyer of 'Survival' has to condemn Lecky, since to condone challenges him to see himself in Lecky and to deconstruct the defences he's built to save himself from the same self-destruction. Likewise 'The Hermit' (worked up from a much shorter story in *The Village*, 1976) demonstrates the underlying bond between the retired headmaster, alone and vulnerable in frustrated age, and the self-sufficient hermit who seems to need nothing from other humans. 'Survival' is the less profound of the two; clearly its lawyer is inhuman and warped by national service, ambition and selfishness. 'The Hermit', on the other hand, disturbs more because it has a residual sense that perhaps the actions of the headmaster are sadly right, and in getting rid of the catalyst who seems to destroy people's sense of themselves by simply being there, the web of the village has been preserved. Smith isn't approving; but beyond the obvious petty sordidness of village affairs he suggests the darker view that scapegoats allow us our complacency, just as in 'The Adoration of the Mini' the dying man obscurely consoles himself by creating an enemy in his daughter, or in 'Listen to the Voice', a long-suppressed revenge masquerades as appalling honesty.

'Survival', with or without error, is another dominating idea, with two opposite implications. Yes, some survivals seem like genuine epiphanies, with hitherto quiescent or repressed protagonists asserting themselves dramatically, from the pregnant daughter of 'Adoration' to the amiable yet ferocious retiring Professor, or the tentative communication of Ralph and stepfather. But beyond the Red-loving student of 'The Black and the Red' or the reconciliation of 'At the Fair', several 'survivals' seem much more inscrutable. For example, the Canadian uncle of 'By Their Fruits', with his crass prejudice and vulgar easiness; is he a testimony to colourful widowerhood or a monument to selfish survival? It is almost as if Smith were asking why certain types and individuals survive when the weaker have gone under. 'The Old Woman, the Baby and Terry' likewise implies the question, since the answer to the social worker's nagging speculation as to what links the aged parent, the unborn child which drains his wife, and Terry, who takes and takes again, biting the hand which helps him, is that all are survivors, instinctively taking from others, ruthlessly exploiting for survival. Often it's the selfish who triumph, and often the strategies for survival are weird and grotesque, as in 'Napoleon and I', with its typical love-hate relationship, its powerful symbolism of war and classic megalomania, and the sting in the tail that the old woman can outdo her husband in selfish madness.

'Napoleon and I' also represents a kind of story and strategy increasingly used by Smith to handle some of his deepest perceptions of the randomness and unrelated

nature of experience. It perhaps sounds odd after indicating
how bleak Smith's vision can be to celebrate his humour,
but if one recalls the essential paradox underlying his
work of tragi-affirmative co-existence, it may surprise less.
Smith can make his reader suddenly guffaw, as when
'Napoleon' tells the milkman to bring up five divisions,
'Touty sweet'. 'On the Island', with young Allan, Donny
and William crazily and self-mockingly wandering from
Louis Armstrong to 'The Hen's March to the Midden',
affecting accents, discovering Ossian (or was it Columba?) in
the incongruous figure of the upright, old bearded patriarch
in the rowing boat, or parodying philosophical and political
debate, has for all its zany humour a hint of 'the horror'.
'Nevertheless, it's got to be faced', says William, *a propos*
of nothing; and when asked what has to be faced, 'this
wilderness. Seas, rocks, animosity, ferocity. These waves
all hating us, gnashing their white teeth . . .', he replies.

> They looked at it but their hatred was not as great as its,
> not so indifferent. It was without mercy because it did not
> know of them. It was the world before man . . . It was
> what there was of it. Nothing that was not unintelligible
> could be said about it.

The great achievement of this strand is the long short
story 'Murdo'. Here is agony and hilarious grotesquerie
conjoined, the humour with its own bizarre *Verfremmsdung*
effect, as Smith measures the depths of Murdo's imminent
breakdown by the goonery of his actions and declamations
to astonished neighbours. Like the sad, humble, laughable
figure of Mr Trill who features in several of Smith's stories,
Murdo is an extreme way of seeing the pretentiousness of
culture, the naked quality of actuality, as well as being
another strategy for handling the unbearable.

Of course, Smith has an opposite utterance to this; in
which Art *does* matter, in which drama, painting, and
human struggle to give utterance and to communicate, is
seen positively. 'The Professor and the Comics', 'What to
Do About Ralph?' and 'The Play' all allow epiphany through
the value of therapeutic literature and art, as does the late
symbolic prose-poem 'Chagall's Return'. Smith has always

had two ways of seeing life: depending on the perspective, it can be coffin *or* nest, and homeland, native culture, community, and even Art itself can be equally ambiguous.

These are not perhaps the stories one might expect from one of the finest of our Gaelic poets. They are curiously un-Scottish in their un-identified and strangely de-contextualised villages and towns, with their 'Ralphs' and 'Marks'. But their very refusal to deal with conventional Highland life makes its own stark criticism of what has really happened to these peripheral places of once-different traditions. There's a great deal of oblique and implicit social criticism of what Britain has become behind the apparently localised action. Most of all, however, they are stories without parallel in their intensity of experience of the pain of loss of community, of belief in ideals, of acceptance of social value. The wonder is that Smith so often manages to discover in such pain moments of Grace, affirmation, communication, that, for all the bleakness of the human situation, there will always be a voice somewhere worth listening to.

Douglas Gifford

The Dying

WHEN THE BREATHING got worse he went into the adjacent room and got the copy of Dante. All that night and the night before he had been watching the dying though he didn't know it was a dying. The grey hairs around the head seemed to panic like the needle of a compass and the eyes, sometimes open, sometimes shut, seemed to be looking at him all the time. He had never seen a dying before. The breathlessness seemed a bit like asthma or bad bronchitis, ascending sometimes into a kind of whistling like a train leaving a station. The voice when it spoke was irritable and petulant. It wanted water, lots of water, milk, lots of milk, anything to quench the thirst and even then he didn't know it was a dying. The tongue seemed very cold as he fed it milk. It was cold and almost stiff. Once near midnight he saw the cheeks flare up and become swollen so that the eyes could hardly look over them. When a mirror was required to be brought she looked at it, moving her head restlessly this way and that. He knew that the swelling was a portent of some kind, a message from the outer darkness, an omen.

Outside, it was snowing steadily, the complex flakes weaving an unintelligible pattern. If he were to put the light out then that other light, as alien as that from a dead planet, the light of the moon itself, would enter the room, a sick glare, an almost abstract light. It would light the pages of the Dante which he needed now more than ever, it would cast over the poetry its hollow glare.

He opened the pages but they did not mean anything at all since all the time he was looking at the face. The dying person was slipping away from him. She was absorbed in her dying and he did not understand what was happening. Dying was such an extraordinary thing, such a private thing.

I

Sometimes he stretched out his hand and she clutched it, and he felt as if he were in a boat and she were in the dark water around it. And all the time the breathing was faster and faster as if something wanted to be away. The brow was cold but the mouth still wanted water. The body was restlessly turning, now on one side now on the other. It was steadily weakening. Something was at it and it was weakening.

In Thy Will is My Peace . . . The words from Dante swam into his mind. They seemed to swim out of the snow which was teeming beyond the window. He imagined the universe of Dante like a watch. The clock said five in the morning. He felt cold and the light was beginning to azure the window. The street outside was empty of people and traffic. There was no one alive in the world but himself. The lamps cast their glare over the street. They brooded over their own haloes all night.

When he looked again the whistling was changing to a rattling. He held one cold hand in his, locking it. The head fell back on the pillow, the mouth gaping wide like the mouth of a landed fish, the eyes staring irretrievably beyond him. The one-barred electric fire hummed in a corner of the room, a deep and raw red wound. His copy of Dante fell from his hand and lay on top of the red woollen rug at the side of the bed stained with milk and soup. He seemed to be on a space ship upside down and seeing coming towards him another space ship shaped like a black mediaeval helmet in all that azure. On board the space ship there was at least one man encased in a black rubber suit but he could not see the face. The man was busy either with a rope which he would fling to him or with a gun which he would fire at him. The figure seemed squat and alien like an Eskimo.

And all the while the window azured and the body was like a log, the mouth twisted where all the breath had left it. It lolled on one side of the pillow. Death was not dignified. A dead face showed the pain of its dying, what it had struggled through to become a log. He thought, weeping, this is the irretrievable centre where there is no foliage and no metaphor. At this time poetry is powerless. The body looked up at him blank as a stone with the twisted mouth. It belonged to no one that he had ever known.

The copy of Dante seemed to have fallen into an abyss. It was lying on the red rug as if in a fire. Yet he himself was so cold and numb. Suddenly he began to be shaken by tremors though his face remained cold and without movement. The alien azure light was growing steadily, mixed with the white glare of the snow. The landscape outside the window was not a human landscape. The body on the bed was not human.

The tears started to seep slowly from his eyes. In his right hand he found he was holding a small golden watch which he had picked up. He couldn't remember picking it up. He couldn't even hear its ticking. It was a delicate mechanism, small and golden. He held it up to his ear and the tears came, in the white and bluish glare. Through the tears he saw the watch and the copy of Dante lying on the red rug and beyond that again the log which seemed unchanging though it would change since everything changed.

And he knew that he himself would change though he could not think of it at the moment. He knew that he would change and the log would change and it was this which more than anything made him cry, to think of what the log had been once, a suffering body, a girl growing up and marrying and bearing children. It was so strange that the log could have been like that. It was so strange that the log had once been chequered like a draughtsboard, that it had called him into dinner, that it had been sleepless at night thinking of the future.

So strange was it, so irretrievable, that he was shaken as if by an earthquake of pathos and pity. He could not bring himself to look at the Dante; he could only stare at the log as if expecting that it would move or speak. But it did not. It was concerned only with itself. The twisted mouth as if still gasping for air made no promises and no concessions.

Slowly as he sat there he was aware of a hammering coming from outside the window and aware also of blue lightning flickering across the room. He had forgotten about the workshop. He walked over to the window and saw men with helmets bending over pure white flame. The blue flashes were cold and queer as if they came from another world. At the same time he heard unintelligible shoutings from the people involved in the work and saw a visored head turning to look behind it. Beyond it steadied the sharp azure of the morning. And in front of it he saw the drifting flakes of snow. He looked down at the Dante with his bruised face and felt the hammer blows slamming the lines together, making the universe, holding a world together where people shouted out of a blue light. And the hammer seemed to be beating the log into a vase, into marble, into flowers made of blue rock, into the hardest of metaphors.

The Adoration of the Mini

IT WAS AN old people's hospital and yet he wasn't old. As she stood at the door about to press the bell she looked around her and saw beside a shrouded wheelchair some tulips swaying in the white March wind. Turning her head into the cold bright sun, she saw farther down the road a fat man in blue washing a bright red car. She felt joyous and sad by turns.

She pressed the bell, and a nurse in white and blue came to the door. Visiting hours were two to three, but she thought she could call at any time now. The nurse was stony-faced and middle-aged and glancing at her quickly seemed to disapprove of the roundness of her body: it was not the place for it. She pushed back her blonde hair which had been slightly disarranged by the wind. She asked for Mr Mason, and the nurse showed her the door of the ward. Here and there she could see other nurses, but none of them was young; it would have been better if at least one or two had the expectancy and hope of youth. It would make the place brighter, younger, with a possible future.

She walked into the ward. The walls were flaked with old paint, and old men, propped on pillows, stared ahead of them without recognition or care. One old man with a beard, his eyes ringed with black as if from long sleeplessness, looked through her as though she had been a window pane beyond which there was no country that he could love or desire. By one or two beds—the bedside tables bearing their usual offerings of grapes and oranges, and bottles of yellow energy-giving liquids wrapped in cellophane—there were women talking in whispers.

She walked through the main ward, not seeing him, and then through into a smaller one. And there he was, on his own, sitting up against the pillows as if waiting. But he could not be expecting her. He might be expecting her mother or her brother or her other sister, but not her.

The smell of imminent death was palpable and distinct. It was in the room, it was all round him, it impregnated the sheets, it was in his face, in his eyes. She had seen him ill before, but not like this. His colour was neither yellow nor red, it was a sort of grey, like old paper. The neck was long and stringy, and the knotted wrists rested meagrely on the sheet in front of him.

She stood at the foot of the bed and looked at him. He looked back at her without energy. She said,

'I came to see you, father.'

He made no answer. It was as if he hadn't heard her or as if (if he had heard her) she wasn't worth answering. She noticed the carafe of water at the table at the foot of the bed and said,

'Do you want a drink?'

He remained silent. She began again:

'I came up by train today. It took me eight hours.'

She shook her yellow hair as if to clear her head and said,

'May I sit down?' He still didn't speak and she sat down on the chair. He spoke at last:

'How do you think I look?'

She replied with conscious brightness,

'I had thought you would be worse.'

'I think I'm dying,' he said tonelessly and almost with cunning, 'I've had strange visions.'

He shut his eyes for a moment as if to rest them.

'What do you want?' he asked without opening his eyes.

'I wanted to see you.'

'What about?'

'I . . .'

'You left a good job and went off to London and you're pregnant, isn't that right,' he said slowly, as if he were carving something with a chisel and hammer. 'You had a good brain and you threw it all away. You could have gone on to university.'

'We're married now,' she said.

'I know that. You married a Catholic. But then Catholics breed a lot, don't they?' He opened his eyes, looking at her in disgust, his nose wrinkling as if he could smell incense. She flared up, forgetting that he was dying.

'You know why I left, father. I didn't want to go to university. I'm an ordinary person.'

'You had an I.Q. of 135. I shouldn't be telling you this but I saw it on your school records.'

'I didn't want to go to university. I didn't want to do Science.'

'I didn't care. It didn't need to be Science. It could have been any subject. You threw yourself away. You went to work in a wee office. And then you got pregnant. And now you say you are married. To a Catholic. And you'll have to be a Catholic too. I know them. And your . . .' He couldn't bring himself to say that her child would be a Catholic.

She couldn't stop herself. 'I thought a scientist wouldn't care for these things. I thought a scientist would be unprejudiced.'

He smiled grimly. 'That's the kind of remark I would have expected from you. It shows that you have a high I.Q. You should have used it. You threw it away. You ignored your responsibilities. You went off to London, to see the bright lights.' She sensed envy in his voice.

After a while she said,

'I couldn't stand school. I don't know how I can explain it to you. The books didn't mean anything after a while. It was torture for me to read them. Can you understand that?'

'No.' His mouth shut like a rat-trap.

'I tried,' she continued. 'I did try. But they didn't mean anything. I would look at a French book and a Latin book and it didn't connect with anything. Call it sickness if you like, but it's true. It was as if I was always tired. I used to think it was only people in non-academic classes who felt like that. I was all right in the first three years. Everything seemed to be interesting. And then this sickness hit me. All the books I read ceased to be interesting. It was as if a haze came down, as if the words lost any meaning, any reality. I liked music but there was nothing for me in words. I'm trying to explain. It was a sickness. Don't you understand?'

'No, I don't understand. When I was in the upper school I wasn't like that. I read everything I could lay my hands on. Books were treasures. When I was in university it was the same. I read because I loved to read. I wanted to have as much knowledge as possible. Even now . . .' He paused.

She probed: 'Even now?'

But he had stopped speaking, like a watch run down. She continued,

'Yes, I admired that in you, though you were narrow-minded. I admired your love of books and knowledge and experiments. I admired you for thinking out new ways of presenting your subject. I admired your enthusiasm, though you neglected your family. And then too you went to church. What did you find in church?'

'In church? I found silence there.'

'It was different with us,' she continued. 'It wasn't that I didn't try. I did try. I would lock myself in my room and I would study my Virgil. I would stare at it. I would look up meanings. And then at the end of an hour I hadn't moved from the one page. But I tried. It wasn't my fault. Can't you believe me?'

'I don't understand.' Then he added mercilessly, 'It was idleness.'

'And there you would be in the other room, in your study, preparing your lesson for the following day, smoking your pipe, thinking up new ideas like the time you made soap. You were the mainstay of the school, they said. So much energy. Full of power, boyish, always moving, always thinking. Happy.'

A smile crossed his face as if he were looking into another world which he had once loved and in which he had meaning and purpose.

'Yes, I gave them a lot,' he said. 'A lot. I tried my best with you as well. I spent time on you. I wanted you to do well. But I couldn't make a favourite of you. And then you said you were leaving.'

'It happened one night. I had been doing some exercises in English. I think it was an interpretation passage. I was sitting at the table. There was a vase with flowers in front of me. The electric light was on, and then I switched on the radio and I heard this voice singing "Frankie and Johnny". It was Lena Horne. I listened to it. At first I wasn't listening to it at all. I was trying to do my exercise. Then, after a while, the music seemed to become more important than what I was doing. It defeated what I was doing. It was about real things and the interpretation wasn't about anything. Or rather, it was about the lack of trade unionism in Japan. I'm not joking: that's what it was. How the bosses wouldn't allow the workers any unions and how they kept their money for them. It had no meaning at all. It was like. . .It was like some obstacle that you pushed against. Like a ghost in a room. And I laid down my pen and I said to myself, What will happen if I stop doing this? And then I did stop. And suddenly I felt so free. It was as if I had lightened myself of some load. I felt free. I listened to the song and I didn't feel any guilt at all.'

He looked at her almost with hatred.

'If you didn't feel any guilt why are you here then? Why didn't you stay with your Catholic? By the way, what does he do?'

'He has an antique shop. Actually, he's quite scholarly. He's more scholarly than you. He knows a lot about the Etruscans. He's very enthusiastic. Just like you. He's got a degree.' She laughed, bubbling.

'In that case,' he said, 'why didn't you stay with him?'

'I came to ask you,' she said 'what it all means.'

He said, 'I remember one morning at a lecture we were told about Newton. It was a long time ago and it was a large lecture room, row upon row of pupils, students stretching to the very back and rising in tiers. There was sunlight and the smell of varnish. And this bald man told us about Newton. About the stars and how everything was fixed and unalterable and the apple falling to the ground in a garden during the Plague. Harmony. He talked about harmony. I thought the sky was full of apples. And that the whole world was a tree.'

There was a long silence. In it she felt the child turning in its own orbit.

'What use are the books to you now?' she said. The words

sounded incredibly naive almost impudent and inhuman but she didn't mean them like that. And yet. . .

'You mean,' he said, 'that my life was useless. That I spent my days and nights on phantoms. Is that what you want? Did you come to gloat?'

'No, I want to know, that's all. I want to know if it was something wrong with me. Perhaps it was something wrong with me all the time.'

She imagined him walking in the middle of the night, listening to the silence of the wards, watching the moonlight on the floor. She imagined him looking into the eyes of nurses for reassurance, without speech. She imagined him imagining things, the whispers, the rumours, the laughter. Sometimes a man would die and his bed would be empty. But there would always be another patient. She imagined him thinking: At what hour or minute will I die? Will I die in pain? Will I choke to death?

She thought of London and of this small place. She thought of the anonymity of London, the death of the rainy days. The lostness. The strangeness. Had she chosen well? She thought of Sean, with his small tufted beard, vain, weak, lecherous. He was her only link with that brutal city. All else flowed, she could only follow him, the indeterminate atom.

'You don't know what duty is,' he said at last. 'You live on romance and pap. I've seen you reading *Woman's Own*. You think that the world is romantic and beautiful.' (Did she think that? Was that why she had run away? Did she think that now? What had she not seen? Into the heart of the uttermost darkness in that room where at night the lights circled the ceiling, and nothing belonged to her, not even the flat, not the Etruscan soldiers with their flat, hollow sockets.)

'You don't know about trust and loyalty. You knuckle under whenever any difficulty crops up. Your generation is pap and wind. You owe allegiance to nothing. I have owed allegiance to this place. They may forget me, but I served. What else is there to do?'

She said in a low voice, 'To live.' But he hadn't heard her.

'To serve,' he said. 'To love one's work. Oh, I was no Einstein but I loved my work and I think I did good. You, what do you do?'

Nothing, she thought, except to live where the lightning is, at the centre where the lightning is. At the disconnected places. At the place where our truth is to be found on the rainwashed blue bridges. At the place without hypocrisy. In the traffic. Where she would have to fight for everything including her husband, not knowing that at least this she could keep, as her mother had known. In the jungle.

She stood up and said, 'Goodbye, father.'

Defiantly he said, 'You refused your responsibility.'

It was like standing on a platform waving to a stranger on a train. For a moment she couldn't make up her mind whether he was leaving her or she leaving him.

He relapsed into petulance. 'I shouted for the nurse last night but she was too busy. She heard me right enough but she didn't come.'

She thought to herself: There is a time when one has to give up, when nothing more can be done. When the connection has to be cut. It is necessary, for not all things are retrievable.

As she stood up she nearly fell, almost upsetting the carafe of water, herself full of water.

He had closed his eyes again when she turned away and walked through the ward head down, as if fighting a strong wind. She paused outside the door in the blinding March light where the tulips were.

The man she had seen before had finished polishing his car and was looking at it with adoration. She thought: The Adoration of the Mini, and smiled.

The child stirred. The world spun and took its place, the place that it must have as long as she was what she was. She had decided on it. And what she was included her father. And she thought again of her child, loving and pitying it.

At the Fair

THE DAY WAS very hot as had been most of the days of that torrid summer and when they arrived at the park where the fair was being held she found that there was no space for her car: so she had to cruise around the town till she found one, cursing and sweating. It was at times like these, when she felt hot and prickly and obscurely aggressive, that she wished Hugh could drive, but he had tried a few times to do so and he couldn't and that was that. It wasn't a big car, it was only a Mini, but even so there didn't seem to be any space for it anywhere, and policemen were everywhere waving drivers on and sometimes flagging them down to give them information. However after half an hour of circling and back-tracking, she did manage to find a place, a good bit away from the fair, and after she had locked the doors the three of them set off towards it. In the early days, before she had got married, she hadn't bothered to lock the car at all. Even if a handle fell off a door, like the one for instance that wound down the window, she didn't bother having it repaired, and the back seat used to be full of old newspapers and magazines which she had bought but never read. Now, however, it was tidy, as Hugh (though, or because, he didn't drive) kept it so. He also polished it regularly every Sunday, since he didn't do any writing on Sundays, finding that three hours a day for five days in the week satisfied whatever demon possessed him. She herself worked full-time in an office while he stayed at home writing and making sure that their little daughter who was not yet of school age didn't burn herself or fall down the stairs or do anything that endangered her welfare.

It was a Saturday afternoon and it was excessively hot, but in spite of the heat Hugh was wearing a jacket and this irritated her. Why couldn't he be like other men and go about in his shirt sleeves; why must he always wear a jacket even when the sun was at its most glaring, and how could he in fact bear to do so? She herself was wearing a short yellow dress with short sleeves which showed her attractive round arms, and the little girl was wearing a white frilly dress with a locket bouncing at her breast. She looked down at her tanned arms and was surprised to see them so brown since she had been working all summer at her cards in the office catching up with work caused by Margaret's long absence. But of course at weekends she and her husband and the little girl went out quite a lot. They drove to their own secret glen and sometimes sat and picknicked listening to the noise of the river, which was a deep black, muttering unintelligibly among the stones. The blackness and the noise reminded her for some strange reason of a telephone conversation which had somehow gone wrong, spoiling instead of creating communication. Sometimes they might take a walk up the hill among the stones and the fallen gnarled branches and very rarely they might catch a glimpse at the very top, high above them, of a deer standing questioningly among trees. She loved deer, their elegance and their containment, but her husband didn't seem to bother much.

The little girl Sheila was taking large steps to keep up with the two of them, now and again taking her mother's hand and gazing gravely up into her face as if she were silently interrogating her, and then withdrawing her hand quickly and moving away. She talked hardly at all and was very serious and self-possessed. In fact it seemed to her mother that she was more like what she imagined a writer ought to be than Hugh was, for he didn't seem to notice anything but wandered about absent-mindedly, never listening to anything she was saying and never calling her attention to any interesting sight in the world around him. His silence was profound. She had never seen anyone who paid so little attention to the world: she sometimes thought that if a woman with green hair and a green face walked past him he wouldn't notice. That surely was not the way a writer ought to be.

Anyway he wasn't a very successful writer as far as sales

went. He had had two small books of poetry published by printing presses no one had ever heard of except himself, and had sold one short story to an equally unknown magazine. She had long ago given up trying to understand his poetry. He himself wavered between thinking that he was a good poet as yet unrecognised and a black despair which made her impatient and often angry with him. In any case the people they lived among didn't know about writing and certainly couldn't have cared less about poetry: if you didn't appear on TV you weren't quoted. They lived in a council house in a noisy neighbourhood which seemed to have more than the average share of large dogs and small grubby children who stared at you as you went by.

The fair was really immense and she looked down at her small daughter now and again to make sure that she hadn't got lost. She sometimes worried about her daughter's silences, thinking that perhaps they were a protection against the two of them.

Hugh said to her, 'We could spend a lot of money here, do you know that? There are so many things.'

She was suddenly impatient. 'Well, we only get out once in a while.' She knew that Hugh worried about money because he himself hardly earned anything, and also because his nature was fundamentally less generous than her own. He had given up working two years before, just to give himself a chance to see if he could succeed as a writer. Before that he had worked in a library, but he complained that working in a library was too much like writing, and in any case he was bored by it and the ignorant people he met. As far as she could see nothing had in fact happened since he gave up writing, for when he wasn't writing he was reading, and he hardly ever went out. He would sit at his typewriter in the morning but most of the time he didn't write anything or if he did he threw it in the bucket. When she came home at five she would find the bucket full of small balls of paper. She herself knew very little about literature and couldn't judge whether such work as he completed was of the slightest value. She sometimes wondered whether she was losing her respect for him: his writing she often thought was a device for avoiding the problems of the real world. On the other hand her own more passionate nature dominated his colder one. Before she met him she had gone out with other men but her resolute self-willed character had led to quarrels of such intensity and fierceness that she knew they would eventually sour any permanent relationship.

As they walked through the fair, pushing their way among crowds of people, they arrived at a stall where one could throw three darts at three different dartboards, and if one got a bull each time would win a prize.

'Would you like to try this?' she asked him.

'Not me. You try it.'

'All right then,' she said. 'I'm going to try it.' She took the three darts from the rather sour-looking unsmiling woman who looked after the stall and stood steady in front of the board. She was always a little dramatic, wanting to be the centre of attention, though she didn't realise this herself. She didn't know about darts, but she would try to get the bulls, for she was very determined and she didn't see why she couldn't throw the darts as well as anybody else.

'Ten pence,' said the woman handing her the darts with a bored expression.

A number of other people were there, and she smiled at them as if saying, 'Look at me. I don't know anything about darts but I'm willing to try. Aren't I brave?' She threw the first dart and missed the board altogether. She laughed, and threw the second dart which this time hit the outer rim of the board. She looked proudly round but her husband's face was turned away, as if he was angry or ashamed of her. She drew back her round pretty tanned arm and threw the dart and it landed quivering in a place near the bull. She turned to him in triumph but he had moved on, little Sheila clutching his hand. There was some scattered ironic applause from the crowd and she bowed to them with a flourish.

When she came up to him, he said, 'You didn't do so badly. But these darts are rigged. Some of them don't stick in the board. All the fairs are the same. They cheat you.'

'Oh cheer up,' she said, 'cheer up. We came here to enjoy ourselves.'

Two youths carrying football scarves in their hands went past and whistled, and Hugh's face darkened and became stormy and set. She smiled, aware of her slim body in the yellow dress. She hoped that he wouldn't settle into one of his gloomy childish moods and spoil the day. He looked quite funny really from the back, as he had had a haircut recently: most of the time he wore his hair long like an artist's or a poet's but today it was much shorter, showing more clearly the baldish patches at the back.

'All fairs cheat you,' he repeated as if he were worried about the amount of money they might spend, as if he were busy adding a sum in his mind. For a poet, she thought, he brooded rather much on money, and far more so than she did. Her philosophy was a simple one: if she had enough for the moment she was quite happy. But today she didn't care, she actually wanted to spend money, positively and extravagantly, as if by doing so she was making a gesture of hope and joy to the world. As they were passing a machine which emitted cartons of orangeade when money was inserted she bought three and they drank them as they walked along. She threw hers away carelessly on the road, but Hugh and Sheila waited till they came to a bin before depositing theirs.

The heat was really quite intense and she was annoyed that he showed no sign of removing his jacket.

What had she expected from marriage? Was this really what she had expected? Before her marriage she had been lively and alert and carefree but now she wasn't like that at all. She was always thinking before she made a remark in case she said something that would wound her husband, in case he found buried in it a sharp intended thorn which he would turn over masochistically in his tormented mind.

They came to a shooting stall and she said, 'Would you like to try this then?'

'Well . . .' She put down the fifteen pence and he took the rifle in his hand, looking at it for a moment helplessly before breaking it in two. The woman gave him some pellets which he laid beside him, inserting one in the rifle after fumbling with it shortsightedly for some time. He snapped the broken rifle together and took aim: it seemed ages before he was ready to fire. She kept saying to herself, Why are you taking so long? Why don't you fire? Fire.

He sighted along the rifle and fired, and one fat duck in the moving procession fell down. Again he aimed steadily and carefully, at one point putting the rifle down in order to wipe the sweat from his eyes, but then raising it and firing. He looked extremely serious and concentrated as if there was nothing in the world he liked better than shooting down these fat slow ducks passing in procession in front of him. And again he knocked one down. So he had a talent after all—another talent, that is, apart from his poetry. He steadily aimed and again hit a duck.

'What do I get for that?' he asked the woman excitedly.

The woman pointed without speaking to a miscellany of what appeared to be undifferentiated rubbish but which on examination defined itself as clay dishes, cheap soiled brooches and a teddy bear.

'Take the teddy bear,' Ruth suggested and he took it, handing it over proudly. She in turn gave it to Sheila who gravely clutched it like a trophy.

'I didn't know you could shoot,' she said as they walked along together.

'I used to go to fairs when I was younger,' he replied, but didn't volunteer any more. She was proud that he had won a prize though it was a not very plush teddy bear and she put her arm momently in his. He seemed pleased, and relaxed a little, but she wished that he would remove his jacket.

'The prize wasn't worth the entry fee,' he commented as they walked along.

'That's true.'

'All these fairs are the same. They cheat you all the time.'

She knew that what he was saying was true but she thought that he shouldn't be repeating it so often: after all there were more things that they could talk about than the deceitfulness of fairs. When she had married him his conversation had been less monotonous and more enterprising than this, but she supposed that sitting in the house all day, every day, there wasn't much new experience flooding into his life.

A woman on toppling heels and wearing blue-rinsed hair walked past them.

'Did you see that woman?' she asked. 'Do you see her hair?'

'What woman? I didn't notice.'

'It doesn't matter,' she sighed.

Yet he had aimed carefully and with great concentration at the ducks as if more than anything else in the world he had wanted to shoot them down. He was pretty well as quiet as Sheila most of the time; she herself wasn't like that at all, she liked to talk to people, that was why she worked in an office. She liked the trivia of existence. She would take stories home to him at night but he hardly ever listened to her or suddenly in the middle of what she was saying he would talk about something else. He might for instance say, 'Do you think poetry is important?' And she would answer, 'I suppose so,' and immediately afterwards, 'Of course it is.' And she herself would have been thinking about her boss whose wife had visited him in the office that day and how he had shown her round as if she had been a complete stranger. Or about Marjorie who had told her how she had thrown a frying pan at her husband with the eggs still in it.

And he would say, 'It's just that sometimes I wonder. Sometimes I . . .' They had come to the Hall of Mirrors and she said, 'What do you think? It costs fifteen pence.'

'I don't know. What do you think?'

Why was he always asking her what she thought? She wished he would accept some responsibility for at least part of the time. But, no, he would always ask, 'What do you think?' If only once he would say what he himself thought.

She didn't know what a Hall of Mirrors would be like but she said aloud, 'Why not?' It was she who always walked adventurously into the future, throwing herself on its mercy without much previous thought.

'Come on then,' she said. 'Let's go in.'

Hugh and Sheila followed her into the large tent.

It was hilarious. When they entered they saw two people whom they assumed to be husband and wife doubled over with laughter in front of a mirror, the wife pointing at her reflection and unable to utter a word. The husband glanced at the three of them and at her in particular, raising his hands to the roof as if saying, 'Look at her.' Hugh stared at his wife angrily and she thought, 'To hell with him. Can't I even look at another man?'

Then she turned and looked in the mirror. Her body had been broadened enormously, her legs were like tree trunks, and her large head rested like a big staring boulder on massive shoulders. It was like seeing an ogre in a fairy story, in a world of glass, a short wide ogre so close to the earth that he might have been planted in it. She began to laugh and she couldn't stop. Even Sheila was laughing and crying: 'Look at Mummy she's so fat.' She looked so rustic in the mirror as if she had lived all her life on a farm and had only gained from it a disease which gave her eyes a staring thyroid look, and her body the appearance of someone suffering from advanced dropsy. The man smiled at her again—as if caught up in her simple laughter—and Hugh glowered at the two of them.

Then he himself turned and looked in an adjacent mirror. This particular one elongated his body so that he seemed very tall and thin and his head with its frail brow was like a tall egg on top of his stalklike body. He smiled without thinking and she laughed from behind him and so did Sheila, clapping her hands, and shouting, 'Daddy's so thin. Look at Daddy.' She moved from mirror to mirror. In one she was squat and heavy and lumpish, in another her legs were as thin as the stalks of plants, climbing vertically to her incredibly shrunken waist. And all the time Sheila was running from one to the other excitedly. Hugh wasn't laughing as much as she was, he seemed rather to be studying the reflections as if they had philosophical or poetical implications.

Most of the people in the tent were laughing so loudly and with such abandon that they were like occupants of an asylum, rocking and roaring and leaning on each other, hardly able to breathe. But though she laughed she didn't abandon herself as helplessly as they did. And Hugh gazed at the reflections gravely as if they were pictures in an art gallery which he was trying to memorise.

She looked down at her slim body in the yellow dress as if to make sure that she wasn't after all the distorted woman in the mirror, the gross heavy-rooted peasant with the swollen arms and the swollen legs. And all around her was the perpetual storm of laughter and the rocking red-faced people. And suddenly she too abandoned herself, doubled over, banging her fist on her knee, shrieking hysterically at the squat figure, making faces at her. Tears came into her eyes, she wept with a laughter that was close to pain, and in the middle of it all she saw the reflection of her husband, tall and incredibly thin, with the immensely frail tall egg perched on his shoulders, gazing disapprovingly at her.

She couldn't stop laughing, it was as if a torrent had been released in her, as if she were a river in spate. And beside her the man and his wife were doubled over with laughter, their faces red and streaming, the man making faces in the mirror to make his reflection even more macabre.

Finally she stood up and made her way to the door, Hugh following her with Sheila. He was silent as if he felt that she had betrayed him in some way.

'Didn't you like that?' she asked him. 'It was really funny.' And she began to laugh again, this time more decorously, as if at the memory of what she had seen, rather than at its present existence. Why on earth did he never let himself go? Ever? She was angry with him and gritted her teeth. She supposed that even when he had been working in the library he had been like that, sad and serious, gravely spectacled, a source of tall disapproval when women borrowed their romances or thrillers. But how on earth had he learned to be so dull?

The two youths who were wearing striped green and white scarves came back up the road again, shouting. Hugh pulled Sheila aside out of their way, turning his eyes from them.

Damn you, damn you, she almost shouted, why didn't you go straight on? But she knew that he shouldn't have done so and that she was being unreasonable, for after all the creatures she had just seen were quarrelsome, irrational, and violent. But was that what writing did for you, sitting day after day in your room and then drawing aside from the rawness of reality when you emerged into it? Oh my God, she thought, what is it I want? Joy, life . . . She listened to the steady beat of the music which animated the fair. In the old days she used to dance such a lot, now she didn't dance at all. She even knew some of the tunes they were playing, nostalgic reminders of her youth. Paper roses, paper roses, she hummed to herself, as she walked along. But why couldn't he take off his damned jacket? There were men passing all the time with bare torsos tanned to a deep brown and looking like gipsies, while by contrast Hugh seemed so pale even in this gorgeous summer because he never left his room. Damn, damn, damn. If only one was a gipsy, wandering about the world in a coloured caravan, without destination, without worry.

She wanted to dance, to sing, to shout out loud. But she didn't do any of these things and she merely walked on beside Sheila and Hugh looking as demure as any of the other women she met, a member of an apparently contented family, while all the time the beat of the music throbbed around her and inside her.

They came to a place where there were small cars for the children to drive and she asked Sheila if she would like to go on one of them. Sheila gravely nodded and then paid the man with the money her mother gave her, stepping with the same unhurried gravity into one of the cars which ran on tracks so that there was no danger. Ruth watched her daughter as the latter gazed around her with the same unsmiling serious self-possessed expression and when one of the other little girls began to cry Sheila gazed at her with a faint distaste. It worried Ruth that her daughter should be so unsmilingly serene and while she was thinking that thought Hugh said, 'She's cool, isn't she?'

'Isn't she?' Ruth hissed back and Hugh turned to her in surprise.

'I'm worried she's so cool,' Ruth continued in the same hissing tone. 'She never smiles. She's like a robot.'

'What's wrong with being cool?' Hugh asked her.

'I don't know. Maybe she's like you. Maybe she'll be a writer.'

'What do you mean by that?' said Hugh, his face pale.

'What I said. Maybe she should be a writer. Isn't that a good thing? Maybe a writer doesn't have to have emotions.'

'I don't understand what you're trying to say.'

'Oh skip it,' said Ruth impatiently and watched her daughter driving past with the same unearthly competence and composure as she had noticed before, self-reliant, never bumping into anyone, never making a mistake.

'Anyway,' she said aloud, 'what does your writing mean? This is the real world. What have you got to say about this? About the fair? You haven't said anything. I don't think you've noticed a thing.' She was hissing like a snake and all the time he was staring at her with his pale hurt face among all the tanned people. Perhaps he thought the fair vulgar, beneath him; perhaps he thought that the music which recalled her youth to her was indecorous, inelegant, raucous.

They watched Sheila driving round and round in her small yellow car.

'It's because I don't drive,' said Hugh.

'No,' she almost screamed. 'It's nothing to do with that. Nothing at all to do with that. It's your lack of feeling, your damned lack of feeling. She's getting like you. Look at her. She's like a robot, don't you see?'

'No I don't see. She's self-contained, that's all. But I don't think she's like a robot.'

'I don't care what you say, I know.'

'Do you want me to stop writing then?' he asked plaintively.

'You do what you want. Anyway I don't think writing is the most important thing in the world, as you seem to.'

And all the time there throbbed around her the beat of the music, heavy, sonorous, plangent. Her body moved to its rhythm. And her daughter revolved remorselessly in her small car.

'You're shouting,' said Hugh. 'People are hearing you.'

'I don't care. I don't care whether they hear me or not.'

The cars stopped and she leaned over and pulled Sheila towards her. She walked off ahead, Sheila beside her. It was as if she wanted to get into the very centre of the fair, its throbbing centre, in among the lights, the red savage lights, so that she could dance, so that she could feel alive, even in that place of cheating and deception, crooked sights, bad darts.

He was so dull, always asking her if poetry was important. And what should she tell him? Why was he doing it if he doubted its value so much? The fair was important: one could sense it: its brash reality had all the confidence in the world, its music was dominating and without inhibition. It was doing a service to people, even though the prizes were cheap and without substance. The joy of existence animated it, colour, music.

What's wrong with me? she asked herself. What the hell is wrong with me? She watched a girl and a boy walk past, arm in arm, and she felt intense anguish like the pain of childbirth.

She hated her husband at that moment, he looked so pale and anguished and out of place. If only he would hit her, say something spontaneous to her, but he looked so perpetually wounded as if he was always trudging home from a war he had lost. The only time she had seen a look of concentration on his face was when he had been firing at the ducks.

She saw a great wheel circling against the sky with people on it, some of them shrieking.

'I think I'd like some lemonade,' she said aloud, and they walked in silence to the lemonade tent.

While they were in the tent a drunk man pushed his way past them swaying on his feet and muttering some unintelligible words.

'Hey,' she shouted at him but he pretended not to hear.

'Did you see that?' she said to Hugh. 'He pushed past. He had no right to do that.' She was speaking in a very loud voice because she was so angry and Hugh looked at her in an embarrassed way. She wanted to stamp her heels into the man's ankles: but she knew that Hugh wasn't going to do anything about it and so she said, 'I don't think I want any lemonade at all.'

'That bugger,' she said, referring to the drunk man, hoping that he would hear her, but he seemed to be rocking happily in a muttering world of his own.

Before she knew where she was—she was walking so fast because of her rage—she found herself away from the fairground altogether and in an adjacent park where she sat on a bench, seething furiously. When her husband finally caught up with her and sat beside her she felt as if she could pick up a stone and throw it at him, so great was her frustration and her loathing. Sheila sat down on the grass, cradling the teddy bear in her arms and saying into its ear, 'Go to sleep now. Go to sleep.' Its unblinking eyes with their cheap glitter stared back at her. She seemed to have forgotten about her parents altogether and was in a country of her own where the teddy bear was as real as or perhaps more real than her parents themselves.

'Why didn't you want lemonade?' said Hugh.

'If you must know,' she replied angrily, 'I didn't take it because that man got ahead of us in the queue and you didn't do anything about it.'

'What was I supposed to do about it? Start a fight?'

'I don't know what you could have done. You could at least have said something instead of just standing there. You let people walk all over you.'

'What people?'

'Everybody.'

'Perhaps,' he said, 'I should get a job then. It's quite clear to me that you don't want me to be writing.'

'What on earth . . .' She gazed at him in amazement. 'What on earth has that to do with what I'm talking about? I don't care whether you write or not. You can carry on writing as long as you like. I don't care about that. It doesn't worry me.'

'You think I'm a failure. Is that it?' he asked.

'I don't know whether you're a failure or not. You're never happy. You're always thinking about your writing. And yet you never seem to see anything that goes on around you. I don't understand you.'

'And what about you? Do you see everything?'

'I see more than you. You don't care about the real world. You really don't. You didn't really want to come to the fair, did you? You think it's beneath you.'

'No,' he said, 'it wasn't anything like that at all. It's just that . . . Oh, never mind . . .'

Sheila was still talking to the staring teddy bear, quiet and self-possessed as she sat on the grass in front of their bench.

In the old days the two of them had gone out together and they would lie down beside the river that flowed through the glen and she would think that Hugh's silence was very restful. But they would talk too.

What did they talk about in those early days that passed so quickly? Days passed like hours then, now hours seemed as long as days. She didn't even know what he did with himself when she was out working, and even when she came home at night with her fragments of news he didn't seem to be listening or, if he was, it was to some inner voice of his own, and not to her. She knew that she was jealous of that inner voice that tormented and obsessed him, that it was a part of him that she would never know, deep and dark and distant. What inner voice was there anyway beyond the fair, beyond the passing people and the music? She stared down at the grass which was green in places and parched in others. If Sheila hadn't been there she might have walked away but she was there and she couldn't leave her.

Sitting beside each other on the green bench they stared dully down at the ground. Eventually she got up. 'We might as well go back and see the rest of the fair,' she said. 'After all that's what we came for.' Hugh got to his feet resignedly and followed her as did Sheila, cradling the teddy bear in her arms.

When they returned to the fair, she asked Sheila if she would like to go on the swings. She paid for her and watched her settle herself on one of them, she herself standing on the ground and watching her from below, while Hugh was silent at her side. Sheila sat on the swing turning round and round with the same unnaturally quiet self-possessed air. Sheila terrified her. She wondered if, while she was away at work, Sheila was learning to be like her father, distant, without feeling. Maybe Hugh was taking her away into his own secret unhuman world. She wanted to rush up to the swing and stop it and take Sheila into her arms and say to her, 'This is the real world. This is all the world there is. Don't you smell it? Don't you hear the music? Enjoy it while you can. This is your childhood and it won't come again.'

She turned and glanced at Hugh, but he was staring ahead of him, hurt and wounded, as if into a private dream of his own.

God, she thought, what is happening to us? Maybe I

should leave him. Maybe I should take Sheila with me and leave him. Maybe I should take her into the centre of the fair and teach her to dance.

The swing had come to a halt and gravely as ever Sheila stepped off and walked over to her parents still clutching her teddy bear. She stopped beside them, staring down at her brown shoes, shy and serious.

Ruth took her by the hand and in silence they moved forward.

'Would you like to go into the Haunted House?' she asked Hugh but he didn't answer. She didn't want to go by herself, as she was superstitious and believed firmly in ghosts.

What had that Hall of Mirrors meant? What had been the significance of it? She had looked so squat and earthbound there. Was that what she was really like who once had danced with such abandon and joy?

She thought, I'd like to go to a dance just once. Just once to a dance so that I would let myself go. But Hugh didn't like dancing. I should like to listen to music, she thought, the music of my early days when I had my freedom, before that silence descended. He has done more harm to me than I have done to him with his tall thin spiritual body and his brooding mind. If I had only known before my marriage . . . If only . . . But it was too late.

She was still alive but dying. The flesh—surely that was superior to the spirit, the soul.

There must be dancing in the world, joyousness and music.

But Hugh walking beside her was not speaking. She knew that he was hurt and angry, she could tell by the pallor of his face, by his compressed lips. What had he learned at the fair? Had he had any ideas for a poem? She didn't like his poems anyway, she didn't pretend to understand them, she was not a poseur as some people were. There were lots of people who would say that they liked a poem even if they didn't understand it, in order to be 'with it'. She, on the other hand, was the sort of person who would speak out, who had definite opinions.

She wasn't enjoying the day one little bit, she knew that: everything was so hot and sticky. She wanted to be at the centre of things just once, she wanted to do something dramatic, something that she would remember in later years. She wanted to throw perfect darts, hit a perfect target. . . . No, on second thoughts, she didn't even want to do that, she merely wished to laugh and enjoy herself and have a happy untidy day so that she could go home and plump herself on the sofa and say, 'Gosh, how tired I am.' But that wasn't likely to happen.

The three of them walked together but she seemed as far away from the other two as she could possibly be. And all the time Hugh remained wrapped in his silence as in a dark mysterious cloak.

They came to a tent outside which there was a notice saying SEE THE FATTEST WOMAN IN THE WORLD. She stopped and looked at the other two and said, 'I want to see this. Even if you don't,' she added under her breath. She paid forty-five pence for the three of them and they entered the tent. Sitting on a chair—she thought it must be made of iron to sustain the weight—there was the fattest grossest woman she had ever seen in her whole life.

The head was large and the cheeks were round and fat and there were big pouches under the treble chins. The breasts and the belly bulged out largely under a black shiny satiny dress. With her huge head resting on her vast shoulders the woman was like a mountain of flesh, and in close-up Ruth could see the beads of sweat on her moustached upper lip. The hands too were huge and red and fat and the fingers, with their cheap rings, as nakedly gross as sausages. Crowned with her grey hair and almost filling half the tent, the woman seemed to represent a challenge of flesh, almost as if one might wish to climb her. Ruth gazed at the immense tremendous freak with horror, as if she were seeing a magnification of some disease that was causing the flesh to run riot. Sunk deep in the head were small red-rimmed eyes, and in the vast lap rested the massive swollen hands. And yet out of this monstrous mountain, vulgar and sordid, there issued a tiny voice saying to Sheila:

'Do you want to talk to me, little girl?'

And Sheila looked up at her and burst out laughing.

'You're just like Mummy in the tent,' she shouted. And

she ran over and clutched her mother's hand, laughing with a real childish laughter. Pale and tall, Hugh was watching the woman and Ruth thought of the vast body seated on a lavatory pan in some immense lavatory of a size greater than she had ever seen, and as she imagined her sitting there she also saw her spitting, belching, blowing her enormous nose. She was sickened by her, by her acres of flesh, by the smell that exuded from her.

She imagined the fat woman dying in a monstrous bed, people bending over her as she breathed stertorously, beads of sweat on her moustache.

And Sheila was still laughing and shouting, 'She's just like you, Mummy,' and tall, with egg-shaped head, Hugh gazed down at her, ultimate flesh seated on its throne.

Ruth felt as if she was going to be sick; the image in the mirror had come true in the stench of reality; the legs like tree trunks, the large red hands, the sausage-like fingers were there before her. She ran out of the tent, the bile in her mouth, and Hugh followed her with Sheila. In the clean air she turned to Sheila and said, 'There's the Big Wheel. Do you want to go on it? Your father can go with you if you like.'

'All right,' said Hugh, as if some instinct had told him that she wanted to be alone.

She watched them as they got into their seats, and then from her position on the ground below she saw them soaring up into the sky, descending and then soaring again. She waved to them as they turned on the large red wheel. And Hugh waved to her in return but Sheila was staring straight ahead of her, cool and self-possessed as ever. Up they went and down they came and something in the movement made her frightened. It was as if the motion of the wheel was significant amidst the loud beat of the music, the crooked guns and darts. As she saw the two outlined against the sun she knew that they belonged to her, they were her only connection with reality, with the music and the colour of the fair. If something were to happen to them now what would her own life be like? She almost ran screaming towards the wheel as if she were going to ask the operator to stop it lest an accident should happen and the two of them, Hugh and

Sheila, would plummet to the ground, broken and finished. But she waited and when they came down to earth again she clutched them both, one hand in one hand of theirs.

'That's enough,' she said, 'that's enough.'

The three of them walked to the car. She unlocked the door and got into the driver's seat, Hugh beside her wearing his safety belt, and Sheila in the back.

Sheila suddenly began to become talkative.

'Mummy,' she said, 'you were fat in the mirror. You were a fat lady. You had fat legs.'

Ruth looked at Hugh and he smiled without rancour. They were sitting happily in the car and she thought of them as a family.

'Did you think of anything to write about?' she asked.

'Yes,' he said but he didn't say what it was he had thought of till they had reached the council estate on which they lived.

He then asked her, 'Do you remember when we were at the shooting stall?'

'Yes,' she said eagerly.

'Did you notice that the woman who was giving out the tickets had a glass eye?'

'No, I didn't notice that.'

'I thought it was funny at the time,' Hugh said slowly. 'To put a woman in charge of the shooting stall who had a glass eye.'

He didn't say anything more. She knew however that he had been making a deliberate effort to tell her something, and she also realised that what he had seen was in some way of great importance to him.

What she herself remembered most powerfully was the gross woman who had filled the tent with her smell of sweat, and whose small eyes seemed cruel when she had gazed into them.

She also remembered the two boys with the green and white football scarves who had gone marching past, singing and shouting.

She clutched Hugh's hand suddenly, and held it. Then the two of them got out of the car and walked together to the council house, Sheila running along ahead of them.

On the Island

THEY TIED UP the boat and landed on the island, on a fine blowy blue and white day. They walked along among sheep and cows, who raised their heads curiously as they passed, then incuriously lowered them again.

They came to a monument dedicated to a sea captain who had sailed the first steam ship past the island.

'A good man,' said Allan, peering through his glasses.

'A fine man,' said Donny. 'A fine, generous man.'

'Indeed so,' said William.

They looked across towards the grey granite buildings of the town and from them turned their eyes to the waving seaweed, whose green seemed to be reflected in Donny's jersey.

'It's good to be away from the rat race,' said Donny, standing with his hands on his lapels. 'It is indeed good to be inhaling the salt breezes, the odoriferous ozone, to be blest by every stray zephyr that blows. Have you a fag?' he asked Allan, who gave him one from a battered packet.

'I sent away for a catalogue recently,' said William. 'For ten thousand coupons I could have had a paint sprayer. I calculate I would have to smoke for fifty years to get that paint sprayer.'

'A laudable life time's work,' said Donny.

Allan laughed, a high falsetto laugh and added,

'Or you might have the whole family smoking, including your granny and grandfather, if any. Children, naturally, should start young.'

The grass leaned at an angle in the drive of the wind.

'We could have played jazz,' said William, 'if I had brought my record player. Portable, naturally. Not to be plugged in to any rock. We could have listened to Ella

Fitzgerald accompanied by her friend Louis Armstrong who sings atrociously, incidentally.'

'Or, on the other hand, we could have played Scottish Dance Music each day. "The Hen's March to the Midden" would not be unsuitable. I remember,' he continued reflectively, keeping his arms hooked in his lapels, 'I remember hearing that famous work or opus. It was many years ago. Ah, those happy days. When hens were hens and middens were middens. Not easy now to get a midden of quality. A genuine first class midden as midden.'

'The midden in itself,' said William. He continued, 'The thing in itself is an interesting question. I visualise Hegel in a German plane dropping silver paper to confuse the radar of the British philosophical school, and flying past, unharmed, unshot, uncorrupted.'

'I once read some Hegel,' said Allan proudly, 'and also Karl Marx.'

Donny made a face at a cow.

They made their way across the island and came to a pillbox used in the Second World War.

'Sieg Heil,' said William.

'Ve vill destroy zese English svine,' said Donny.

'Up periscope,' said Allan.

The island was very bare, no sign of habitation to be seen, just rocks and grass.

'Boom, boom, boom,' said Donny, imitating radio music. 'The Hunting of the Bismarck. Boom, boom, boom. It was a cold blustery day, and the telegraphist was sitting at his telegraph thinking of his wife and four children back in Yorkshire. Tap, tap, tap. Sir, Bismarck has blown the Hood out of the water. Unfair, really, sir. Bismarck carries too strong plating. Boom, boom, boom. Calm voice: "I think it'll have to be Force L, wouldn't you say, commander?" And now the hunt is on, boom, boom, boom, grey mist, Atlantic approaches, Bismarck captain speaks: "I vill not return, herr lieutenant. And I vill not tolerate insubordination." Boom, boom, boom.'

William looked at the pillbox, resting his right elbow on it.

'I wonder what they were defending,' he mused.

'The undying right to insert Celtic footnotes,' said Donny.

Allan said,

'I was reading a book about Stalingrad. You've got to hand it to these slab-faced Russians.'

The wind patrolled the silence. The green grass leaned all one way. There were speedboats out in the water plunging and rising, prows high.

'Oh well, let us proceed, let us explore,' said William. As they were walking along they came to a seagull's ravaged body, the skull delicate and fragile, lying among some yellow flowers. The carcass had been gnawed, probably by rats. Its white purity in the cold wind was startling. Its death was one kind of death, thought William with a shudder. Suddenly he placed the seagull's fragile skull on top of a hillock, and they began to throw stones at it. Donny stood upright, one hand clutching a stone, the other still in his lapel.

'Have I been successful?' he asked, after he had thrown the stone.

Allan went over. 'No,' he said shortly and took up position. In a frenzy, William threw stone after stone, but missed. It was Allan who finally knocked the seagull's skull from the knoll.

'All these years, like David, watching the sheep,' he admitted modestly.

They walked on and came to the edge of the water on the far side of the island. They were confronted by a seething waste, tumbled rocks, a long gloomy beach, a desert of blue and white ridged waves, a manic wilderness. As they stared into the hostile sea they saw a boat being rowed past by a man with a long white beard who sat in it very upright as if carved from stone. It was very strange and eerie because the man didn't turn his head at all and didn't seem to have noticed them. Donny broke the silence with,

'Ossian, I presume.'

'Or Columba,' said Allan.

'Once,' said Allan, 'I was entertaining two friends.'

'Ladies,' they both shouted.

'Let that be as it may,' said Allan, 'and may it be as it may. I, after the fourth whisky, looked out the window and there, to my astonishment, was a blanket, white with a border of black stripes, waving about in the air. I need not say that I was alarmed; nor did I draw the attention of the two people I was entertaining to it; nor did they notice it. At first, naturally, I thought it was the D.Ts. But better counsels prevailed, and I thereupon came to the conclusion that it must be the woman above engaged in some domestic activity which entailed the hanging of a blanket out of her window.'

'It was,' said Donny, 'the flag of the Scottish Republic, a blanket with . . .' He stopped as the bearded man rowed back the way he had come. They watched the white hair stirred in the cold wind and the man with his upright stance.

'The horrible man,' said William suddenly.

'The thing in itself,' said Donny.

'Scotland the Brave,' said Allan, cleaning his glasses carefully. 'I remember now,' said Donny. 'I saw these two green branches on a tree and, full of leaves, they were dancing about in a breeze just outside my window. I didn't pay any attention to them at first and then I saw that they were like two duellists butting at each other and then withdrawing, like, say scorpions or snakes, upright, as if boxing. Such venom,' he concluded, 'in the green day.'

He added, 'Another time I was coming home from a dance in a condition of advanced merriment and I was crossing the square, all yellow, as you will know. Thus I came upon a policeman whom I had often seen in sunny daylight. He asked me what I was doing, looking at the shop window, and I returned a short if suitable answer, whereupon he, and his buddy who materialised out of the yellow light like a fairy with a diced cap, rushed me expeditiously up a close and beat me furiously with what is known in the trade as a rubber truncheon. It was,' he concluded, 'an eye opener.'

'Once,' said William, 'I saw a horse and it could think. It was looking at me in a calculating way. I got out of there. It was in a field on a cold day.'

They stared in silence at the spray, shivering.

'There is a man who is supposed to live in a cave,' said William at last. 'It must be an odd existence.'

'Mussels,' said Donny.

'Whelks,' said Allan.

'All locked up for the night,' said William.

After a pause he said,

'Nevertheless, it's got to be faced.'

'What?' said the others.

'This wilderness. Seas, rocks, animosity, ferocity. These waves all hating us, gnashing their white teeth.'

'I think,' said Allan, 'we should do a Socrates.'

'Meaning?' said Donny.

'Meaning nothing. Irony is not enough any more.'

'It's the inhumanness,' said William, almost in a whisper, feeling what he could not say, that for the waves they themselves didn't matter at all, any more than the whelks or the mussels.

Donny stood facing the water, his hands at his lapels. 'Ladies and gentlemen,' he began, 'Mr Chairman, ladies and gentlemen, guests, hangers-on, attendants, servants, serfs, and tribesmen, I have a few words to say about a revered member of our banking profession: well-known bowler, bridge-player, account-keeper, not to mention the husband of a blushing bride who looks as good as new after clearing her fiftieth hurdle.'

'You're right,' said Allan. 'He's right you know, Willie.'

'Meaning?'

'He faces it. He faces the chaos. Without dreams, without chaos. Only without chaos is it possible to survive. The plant does not fight itself, neither the tiger nor the platypus.'

'You mean that that speech orders the waves,' said William. 'Let me think.'

After a while he said,

> If thou didst ever hold me in thy heart,
> absent thee from felicity awhile
> and in this harsh world draw thy breath in pain
> to tell my story.

'They have their purpose and their eyes are bright with it. Keats.'

'Meaning?' said Allan.

'Meaning vanity. If there were no vanity there would be

nothing. The flowers and the women all drawing attention to themselves. The signals. Have you not known, have you not seen, all the people around you, each with his own purpose staring out of his eyes and proclaiming "I am." "I am the most important. Look at me." "I must not be trifled with."? Have you not known it, have you not seen it, have you not been terrified by it? That each feels himself as important as you, that intelligence weakens, that the unkillable survive, the ones who don't think?'

A seagull swooped out of the stormy black and landed on a rock with yellow splayed claws, turning its head rapidly this way and that as if deliberating.

'Then,' said Donny, 'vanity prevails.'

'Without vanity we are nothing,' said William, 'without the sense of triumph.'

'And we have to pay for it with pomp,' said Allan. 'Out of the savage sea the perfected ennui.'

'From the amoeba to the cravat,' said Donny. The wind blew about them: it was like being at the end of the world, the crazy jigsaw of rocks, the sea solid in its strata, the massive power of its onrush, the spray rising high in the sky.

'Where action ends thought begins,' said William, almost in a whisper. 'Out of the water to the dais. And yet it is unbearable.'

'We rely on the toilers of the night,' said Donny.

'Is there anything one can say to the sea,' said Allan, 'apart from watch it?'

They looked at it but their hatred was not so great as its, not so indifferent. It was without mercy because it did not know of them. It was the world before man.

'Imagine it,' said William, 'out of this, all that we have.'

'And us,' said Donny, no longer clowning.

'To watch it,' said Allan. After a while he said,

'It would be fair if we threw stones at it too.'

'Yes,' agreed the other two, beginning to throw stones at the white teeth, but they sank without trace and could hardly be seen against the spray which ascended like a crazy ladder.

There was no ship to be seen at all, only the weird

rowing boat that had passed twice with the white bearded man in it.

They turned away from it, frightened.

As they were leaving, Allan said,

'There is nothing more beautiful than a woman when her long legs are seen, tanned and lovely, as she drinks her whisky or vodka as the case may be.'

They bowed their heads. 'You have found the answer, O spectacled sage of the west. Except that the battle there too is continuous.'

'Except that everywhere the battle is continuous,' said William. 'Even in the least suspected places. But you are right nevertheless.'

They took one last look at the sea. In the smoky spray they seemed to see a fish woman, cold and yet incredibly ardent, arising with merciless scales.

'I knew a girl once,' said Allan. 'We slept on the sofa in her sitting room.'

'Both of you?' said the others.

There was a reverent silence.

'I knew a girl once,' said William. 'I remember her gloved hands on the steering wheel, and the dashboard light was green.'

Their clothes stirred in the breeze. Their flapping collars stung their cheeks. They passed the place where the dead seagull was.

'We will bury it,' said Allan. 'It's only fair.'

'No,' said William, 'it would be artificial.'

'Agreed,' said Donny. 'Motion carried, seconded, trans-formed and retransformed in some order.'

They saw a rat. It looked at them with small beady eyes and scurried out of sight.

'Look,' said William. A cormorant dived from a rock into the seething water. They watched for it to emerge and then it did so like a wheel turning. Also, they saw three seals racing alongside each other at full speed, sleek heads and parts of the body above the surface.

'They say it is the fastest fish in the sea,' said William.

'They say seals turn into women,' said Allan, polishing his glasses. They watched the speedboats drilling through the water. The town with its spires, halls, houses, pubs, rose from the edge of the sea, holding out against the wind. It was what there was of it. Nothing that was not unintelligible could be said about it.

Napoleon and I

I TELL YOU WHAT IT IS. I sit here night after night and he sits there night. In that chair opposite me. The two of us. I'm eighty years old and he's eighty-four. And that's what we do, we sit and think. I'll tell you what I sit and think about. I sit and think, I wish I had married someone else, that is what I think about.

And he thinks the same. I know he does. Though he doesn't say anything or at least much. Though I don't say much either. We have nothing to say: we have run out of conversation. That's what we've done. I look at his mouth and it's moving. But most of the time he's not speaking. I don't love him. I don't know what love is. I thought once I knew what love was. I thought it was something to do with being together for ever. I really thought that. Now I know that it's not that. At least it's not that, whatever else it is. *We do not speak to each other*.

He smokes a pipe sometimes and his mouth moves. He is like a cartoon. I used to read the papers and I used to see cartoons in them but now I don't read the papers at all. I don't read anything. Nor does he. Not even the sports pages though he once told me, no, more than once, he told me that he used to be a great footballer, 'When I used to go down the wing,' he would say. 'What wing?' I would say, and he would smile gently as if I were an idiot. 'When I used to go down the wing,' he would say. But now he doesn't go down any wing. He's even given up the tomato plants. And he imagines he's Napoleon. It's because of that film he says. There were red squares of soldiers in it. He sits in his chair as if he's Napoleon, and he says things to me in French though I don't know French and he doesn't know French. He prefers Napoleon to his tomato plants. He sits in his chair, his legs spread apart, and he thinks about winning Waterloo. I think he's mad. He must be, mustn't he? Sometimes he will look up and say 'Josephine', the one word 'Josephine', and the only work he ever did was in a distillery. Napoleon never worked in a distillery. I am sure that never happened. He's a comedian really. He sits there dreaming about Napoleon and sometimes he goes out and examines the ground to see if it's wet, if his cavalry will be all right. He kneels down and studies the ground and then he sits and puffs at his pipe and he goes and takes a pair of binoculars and he studies the landscape. I never thought he was Napoleon when I married him. I just said *I do*. Nor did he. I used to give him his sandwiches in a box when he went to work and he just took them in those days. I don't think he ever asked for wine. Now he thinks the world has mistreated him, and he wants an empire. Still they do say they need something when they retire. The only thing is, he's been retired for twenty years or maybe fifteen. He came home one day and he put his sandwich box on the table and he said, 'I'm retired' (that was in the days when we spoke to each other) and I said, 'I know that.' And he went and looked after his tomato plants. In those days he also loved the cat and was tender to his tomato plants. Now we no longer have a cat. We don't even have a tortoise. One day, the day he stopped speaking to me, he said, 'I've been hard done by. Life has done badly by me.' And he didn't say anything else. I think it was five o'clock on our clock that day, the 25th of March it would have been, or maybe the 26th.

Actually he looks stupid in that hat and that coat. Anyone would in the twentieth century.

I on the other hand spend most of my time making pictures with shells. I make a picture of a woman who has wings and who flies about in the sky and below her there is a man who looks like a prince and he is riding through a forest. The winged woman also has a cooker. I find it odd that she should have a cooker but there it is, why shouldn't she have a cooker if she wants to, I always say. On the TV everyone says, 'I always say', and then they have a cup of tea. At the most dramatic moments. And then

I see him sitting opposite me in his Napoleon's coat and I think we are on TV. Sometimes I almost say that. But then I realize that we aren't speaking since we have nothing to speak about and I don't say anything. I don't even wash his coat for him.

In any case, how has he been hard done by? He married me, didn't he? I have given him the best years of my life. I have washed, scrubbed, cooked, slaved for him, and I have made sandwiches for him to put in his tin box every day. The same box.

And our children have gone away and they never came back. He used to say it was because of me, I say it's because of him. Who would want Napoleon for a father and anyway Napoleon didn't spend his time looking after tomato plants, though he doesn't do that now. He writes despatches which he gives to the milkman. He writes things like 'Tell Soult he must bring up another five divisions. Touty sweet.' And the milkman looks at the despatches and then he looks at me and then I give him the money for the week's milk. He is actually a very understanding milkman.

The fact that he wears a white coat is neither here nor there. Nothing is either here or there.

And sometimes he will have forgotten that the day before he asked for five divisions, and he broods, and he writes 'Please change the whole educational system of France. It is not just. And please get me a new sandwich box.'

He is really an unusual man. And I loved him once. I loved him when he was an ordinary man and when he would keep up an ordinary conversation when he would tell me what had happened at the distillery that day, though nothing much ever happened. Nothing serious. Nothing funny either. It was a very quiet distillery, and the whisky was made without trouble. Maybe it's because he left the distillery that he feels like Napoleon. And he changed the chair too. He wanted a bigger chair so that he could watch the army manoeuvres in the living-room and yet have enough room for the TV-set and the fridge. It's very hard living with a man who believes that there is an army next to the fridge. But I think that's because he imagines Napoleon in Russia, that's why he wants something cold. And on days when Napoleon is in

Russia he puts on extra clothes and he wants plenty of meat in the fridge. The reason for that I think is that the meat is supposed to be dead French soldiers.

He is not mad really. He's just living in a dream. Maybe he could have been Napoleon if he hadn't been born at 26 Sheffield Terrace. It's not easy being Napoleon if you're born in a council house. The funny thing is that he never notices the aerial. How could there be an aerial or even a TV-set in Napoleon's time, but he doesn't notice that. Little things like that escape him, though in other ways he's very shrewd. In small ways. Like for instance he will remember and he'll say to the milkman, 'You didn't bring me these five divisions yesterday. Where the hell did you get to? Spain will kill me.' And there will be a clank of bottles and the milkman will walk away. That makes him really angry. Negligence of any kind. Inefficiency. He'll get up and shout after him, 'How the hell am I going to keep an empire together with idiots like you about? EH? Tell me that, my fine friend.' Mr Merriman thinks he is Joan of Arc. That causes a lot of difficulty with dresses though not as much as you would imagine since she wore men's armour anyway. I dread the day Wellington will move in. I fear for my china.

Anyway that's why we don't speak. Sometimes he doesn't even recognize me and he calls me Antoinette and he throws things at me. I don't know what to do, really I don't. I'm at my wits' end. It would be cruel to send for a doctor. I don't hate him that much. I think maybe I should tell him I'm leaving but where can you go when you're eighty years old, though he is four years younger than me; I would have to get a home help: he doesn't think of things like that. One day he said to me, 'I don't need you. I don't need anyone. My star is here.' And he pointed at his old woollen jacket which had a large hole in it. Sometimes I can hardly keep myself from laughing when I'm doing my shells. Who could? Unless one was an angel?

And then sometimes I think, Maybe he's trying it on. And I watch out to see if I can trap him in anything, but I haven't yet. His despatches are very orderly. He sends me orders like, 'I want the steak underdone today. And the wine at a moderate temperature.' And I make the beefburgers and coffee as usual.

Yesterday he suddenly said, 'I remember you. I used to know you, when we were young. There were woods. I associate you with woods. With autumn woods.' And then his face became slightly blue. I thought he was going to fall, coming out of his dream. But no. He said, 'It was outside Paris and I met you in a room with mirrors. I loved you once before my destiny became my sorrow.' These were exactly his words, I think. He never used to talk like that. He would mostly grunt and say,'What happened to the salt?' But now he doesn't say anything as simple as that. No indeed. Not at all.

Sometimes he draws up a chair and dictates notes to me. He says things like, 'We attack the distillery at dawn. Junot will create a diversion on the left and then Soult will strike at the right while I punch through the centre.'

He was never in a war in his life. He was kept out because of his asthma and his ulcer. And he never had a horse in his life. All he had was his sandwich box. And now he wants a coronet on it. Imagine, a coronet on a sandwich box. Will this never end? Ever? Will it? I suffer. It is I who put up with this for he never leaves the house, he is too busy organizing the French educational service and the Church. 'We will have pink robes for the nuns,' he says. 'That will teach them the power of the flesh which they *abominate*,' and he shouts across the fence at Joan of Arc and says, 'You're an impostor, sir. Joan of Arc didn't have a moustache.' I don't know what I shall do. He is sitting there so calm now, so calm with his stick in his hand like a sceptre. I think he has fallen asleep. Let me put your crown right, child. It's fallen all to one side. I could never stand untidiness. Let me pick up your stick, its fallen from your hand. We are doomed to be together. We are doomed to say to the milkman, 'Bring up your five divisions', for morning after morning. We are doomed to comment on Joan of Arc's moustache. We are together for ever. Poor Napoleon. Poor lover of mine met long ago in the autumn woods before they became your empire. Poor dreamer.

And yet . . . what a game . . . maybe I should try on

your crown just for one moment, just for a short moment.
And take your stick just for a moment, just for a short
short moment. Before you wake up. And maybe I'll tell
the milkman, We want ten divisions today. Ten not five.
Maybe that would be the best idea, to get it finished with,
once and for all. Ten instead of five.

               And don't forget the cannon.

What to Do About Ralph?

'WHAT ON EARTH has happened to you?' said his mother. 'These marks are getting worse and worse. I thought with your father teaching you English you might have done better.'

'He is not my father,' Ralph shouted, 'he is not my father.'

'Of course, having you in class is rather awkward but you should be more helpful than you are. After all, you are seventeen. I shall have to speak to him about these marks.'

'It won't do any good.'

How sullen and stormy he always was these days, she thought, it's such a constant strain. Maybe if he went away to university there might be some peace.

'He has been good to you, you know; he has tried,' she continued. But Ralph wasn't giving an inch. 'He bought you all that football stuff and the hi-fi and the portable TV.'

'So I could keep out of his road, that's why.'

'You know perfectly well that's not true.'

'It is true. And anyway, I didn't want him here. We could have been all right on our own.'

How could she tell him that to be on your own was not easy? She had jumped at the chance of getting out of teaching and, in any case, they were cutting down on Latin teachers nowadays. Furthermore, the pupils, even the academic ones, were becoming more difficult. She had been very lucky to have had the chance of marrying again, after the hard years with Tommy. But you couldn't tell Ralph the truth about Tommy, he wouldn't listen. Most people, including Ralph, had seen Tommy as cheerful, humorous, generous, only she knew what he had been really like.

44

Only she knew, as well, the incredible jealousy that had existed between Jim and Tommy from their youth. Almost pathological, especially on Tommy's side. It was as if they had never had any love from their professor father who had been cold and remote, hating the noise of children in the house. They had competed for what few scraps of love he had been able to throw to them now and again.

She couldn't very well tell Ralph that the night his father had crashed his car he had been coming from another woman, on Christmas Eve. She had been told that in the wrecked car the radio was playing 'Silent Night'.

Of course, in his own field Tommy had been quite good, at least at the beginning. He had been given a fair number of parts in the Theatre and later some minor ones on TV. But then he had started drinking as the depression gripped and the parts became smaller and less frequent. His downfall had been his golden days at school when he had been editor of the magazine, captain of the rugby team, actor. What a hero he had been in those days, how invisible Jim had been. And even now invisible in Ralph's eyes. And he had been invisible to her as well, though she often recalled the night when Tommy had gate crashed Jim's birthday party and had got drunk and shouted that he would stab him. But he had been very drunk that night. 'I'll kill you,' he had shouted. Why had he hated Jim so much even though on the surface he himself had been the more successful of the two? At least at the beginning?

She should have married Jim in the first place; she could see that he was much kinder than Tommy, less glamorous, less loved by his father, insofar as there had been much of that. But she had been blinded by Tommy's apparent brilliance and humour, and, to tell the truth, by his more blatant sexiness.

Of course he had never had any deep talent, his handsomeness had been a sort of compensatory glow, but when that faded everything else faded too. She herself had been too complaisant, declining to take the hard decision of leaving him, still teaching in those days, and tired always.

To Ralph, however, his father had appeared different. He had been the one who carried him about on his shoulders, taught him how to ride a motor bike, how to play snooker (had even bought a snooker table for him), taken him to the theatre to see him perform. Even now his photograph was prominent in his son's room. She had been foolish to hide from him the true facts about his father's death, his drunken crash when returning home from one of his one-night stands. She should have told him the truth, but she hadn't. She had always taken the easy way out, though in fact it wasn't in the end the easy way at all.

And then Jim had started to visit her, he now a promoted teacher, although in the days when Tommy had been alive not often seen except casually at teachers' conferences, but very correct, stiffly lonely, and certainly not trying to come between her and his brother, though she knew that he had always liked her. She had learned in the interval that kindness was more important than glamour, for glamour meant that others demanded some of your light, that you belonged as much to the public as to your wife. Or so Tommy had used to say.

She remembered with distaste the night of the school play when she had played the virginal Ophelia to his dominating Hamlet, off-hand, negligent, hurtful, almost as if he really believed what he was saying to her. But the dazzled audience had clapped and clapped, and even the professor father had turned up to see the theatrical life and death of his son.

But how to tell Ralph all this?

That night she said to Jim in bed,

'What are we going to do about Ralph?'

'What now?'

'You've seen his report card? He used to be a bright boy. I'm not just saying that. His marks are quite ridiculous. Can't you give him some help in the evenings? English used to be his best subject. In primary school he was always top.'

'I can help him if he'll take it. But he won't take it. His English is ludicrous.'

'Ludicrous? What do you mean?'

'What I said. Ludicrous.' And then, of course, she had defended Ralph. No one was going to say to her that her son's intellect was ludicrous which she knew it wasn't. And so it all began again, the argument that never ended, that wasn't the fault of anyone in particular, but only of the situation that seemed to be insoluble, for Ralph was the thorn at their side, sullen, implacable, unreachable.

'I'm afraid he hates me and that's it,' said Jim. 'To tell you the truth, I think he has been very ungrateful.'

She could see that herself, but at the same time she could see Ralph's side of it too.

'Ungrateful?' she said.

'Yes. Ungrateful. You remember the time I got so angry that I told him I had after all brought him a television set and he shouted, "You're a bloody fool then."'

'You have to try and understand him,' she said.

'It's always the same. He won't make the effort to understand. His father's the demi-god, the hero. If he only knew what a bastard he really was.' Always making fun of him with his quick tongue, always taking girls away from him, always lying to his distant father about him, always making him appear the slow resentful one.

That night she slept fitfully. She had the feeling that something terrible was happening, that something even more terrible was about to happen. And always Ralph sat in his room playing his barbarous music very loudly. His stepfather would mark his eternal essays in his meticulous red writing, she would sew, and together they sat in the living room hearing the music till eventually he would tell her to go and ask Ralph to turn it down. She it was who was always the messenger between them, the ambassador trying hopelessly to reconcile but never succeeding. For Ralph resented her now as much as he resented Jim.

She couldn't believe that this could go on.

Ralph sat at the back of his stepfather's class, contempt-uous, remote, miserable. Quite apart from the fact that he thought him boring, he was always being teased by the other pupils about him. His nickname was Sniffy, for he had a curious habit of sniffing now and again as if there was a bad smell in the room. But, to be fair to him, he was a good, conscientious teacher: he set homework and marked it and it really seemed as if he wanted them all to pass. But there was a curious remoteness to him, as if he loved his subject

more than he loved them. Nevertheless, he was diligent and
he loved literature.

'This, of course, was the worst of crimes,' he was saying,
sitting at his desk in his chalky gown. 'We have to remember
that this was a brother who killed another one, like Cain
killing Abel. Then again there is the murder in the Garden,
as if it were the garden of Eden. There is so much religion
in the play. Hamlet himself was religious; that, after all,
was the reason he didn't commit suicide. Now, there is a
very curious question posed by the play, and it is this' (he
sniffed again),

'What was going on between Gertrude and Claudius even
while the latter's brother Hamlet was alive? This king about
whom we know so little. Here's the relevant speech:

> 'Aye that incestuous, that adulterate beast,
>   with witchcraft of his wit, with traitorous gifts,
>   won to his shameful lust
>   the will of a most seeming virtuous queen . . .'

The point was, had any of this happened in Hamlet's
lifetime? He meant, of course, King Hamlet's. Had there
been a liaison between Gertrude and Claudius even then?
One got the impression of Claudius being a ladies' man,
while Hamlet perhaps was the soldier who blossomed in
action, and who was not much concerned with the boudoir.
After all, he was a public figure, he perhaps took Gertrude
for granted. On their answer to that question would depend
their attitude to Gertrude.

The voice droned on, but it was as if a small red window
had opened in Ralph's mind. He had never thought before
that his mother had known his stepfather before the marriage which had taken place so suddenly. What if in fact
there had been something going on between them while his
father was still alive? He shivered as if he had been infected
by a fever. He couldn't bring himself to think of his mother
and stepfather in bed together, which was why he had asked
for his own bedroom to be changed, so that he would be as
far away from them as possible.

But suppose there had been a liaison between them.
After all, they had both been teachers and they must

have met. True, they had been at different schools but it was inconceivable that they hadn't met.

O God, how dull his stepfather was, in his cloud of chalk. How different from his father who inhabited the large air of the theatre. What a poor ghostly fellow he was in his white dust.

But the idea that his mother had known his stepfather would not leave his mind. How had he never thought of it before?

That night, his stepfather being at a meeting at the school, he said to his mother,

'Did you know . . . your husband . . . before you married him?'

'I wish you could call him your stepfather, or even refer to him by his first name. Of course I knew him. I knew the family.'

'But you married my father?'

'Yes. And listen, Ralph, I have never said this to you before. I made a great mistake in marrying your father.'

He was about to rise and leave the room when she said vehemently, 'No, it's time you listened. You sit down there and listen for a change. Did you know that your father was a drunk? Do you know that he twice gave me a black eye? The time I told everybody I had cut myself on the edge of the wardrobe during the power cut, and the time I said I had fallen on the ice? Did you know where he was coming from when his car crashed?'

'I don't want to hear any more,' Ralph shouted. 'If you say any more I'll kill you. It's not true. You're lying.'

For a moment there he might have attacked her, he looked so white and vicious. It was the first time he had thought of hitting her; he came very close.

Her face was as pale as his and she was almost swaying on her feet but she was shouting at him,

'He was coming from one of his innumerable lady friends. I didn't tell you that, did I? I got a message from the police and I went along there. He had told me he was going to be working late at the theatre but he was coming from the opposite direction. He was a stupid man. At least Jim is not stupid.'

He raised his fist as if to hit her, but she didn't shrink away.

'Go on, hit me,' she shouted. 'Hit me because you can't stand the truth any more than your father could. He was vulgar, not worth your stepfather's little finger.'

He turned and ran out of the house.

Of course it wasn't true. That story was not the one his mother had told him before. And for all he knew the two of them might have killed his father, they might have tampered with the brakes or the engine. After all, a car crash was always suspicious, and his father had been a good if fast driver. His stepfather couldn't even drive.

He went to the Nightspot where some boys from the school were playing snooker, and older ones drinking at the bar. He stood for a while watching Harry and Jimmy playing. Harry had been to college but had given it up and was now on the dole. Jimmy had never left town at all. He watched as Harry hit the assembled balls and sent them flying across the table. After a while he went and sat down by himself. He felt as if he had run away from home, as if he wanted to kill himself. He was tired of always being in the same room by himself playing records. And yet he couldn't bring himself to talk to his stepfather. The two of them were together, had shut him out, he was like a refugee in the house. He hated to watch his stepfather eating, and above all he hated to see him kissing his mother before he set off for school with his briefcase under his arm. But then if he himself left home where could he go? He had no money. He loathed being dependent on them for pocket money, which he used buying records.

He hated his mother as much as he hated his stepfather. At other times he thought that they might have been able to live together, just the two of them, if his stepfather had not appeared. Why, he had loved her in the past and she had loved him, but now she had shut him out because she thought he was being unfair to her husband. He was such a drip: he couldn't play snooker, and all he did was mark essays every night. The house felt cold now, he was rejected, the other two were drawing closer and closer together.

'How's old Sniffy,' said Terry as he sat down at the same

table, Frank beside him. They, of course, were unemployed and Terry had been inside for nicking stuff and also for nearly killing a fellow at a dance.

Then they began to talk about school and he had to sit and listen. Terry had once punched Caney and had been dragged away by the police. No one could control him at all. Frank was just as dangerous, but brighter, more cunning.

'Have a whisky,' said Terry. 'Go on. I bet you've never had a whisky before. I'll buy it for you.'

The snooker table with the green baize brought unbearable memories back to him, and he said,

'Right. Right then.'

'I'll tell you another thing,' said Terry. 'Old Sniffy's a poof. I always thought he was a poof. What age was the bugger when he got married? Where was he getting it before that?'

Frank didn't say anything at all, but watched Ralph. He had never liked him. He had belonged to the academic stream while he himself was always in one of the bottom classes, though he was much brighter.

'A poof,' Terry repeated. 'But he's having it off now, eh, Frank?' And winked at Frank. Ralph drank the whisky in one gulp, and tears burned his eyes.

'Old bastard,' said Terry. 'He belted me a few times and I wasn't even in his class.'

The two of them took Ralph back to his house. Then they stood around it for a while shouting at the lighted window, 'Sniffy the Poof, Sniffy the Poof.' And then ran away into the darkness. Ralph staggered to his room.

'What was that? Who was shouting there?' said his mother. 'Some of your friends. You're drunk. You're disgustingly drunk.'

But he pushed her away and went to his bed while the walls and ceiling spun about him and the bed moved up and down like a boat beneath him.

He heard his mother shouting at his stepfather, 'What are you going to do about it then? You can't sit here and do nothing. He's drunk, I'm telling you. Will you give up those exercise books and do something?'

Later he heard his mother slamming the door and heard the car engine start, then he fell into a deep sleep.

At breakfast no one spoke. It was like a funeral. He himself had a terrible headache, like a drill behind his right eye, and he felt awful. His mother stared down at the table. His stepfather didn't kiss her when he left for school: he seemed preoccupied and pale. It was as if the house had come to a complete stop, as if it had crashed.

'You have to remember,' said his stepfather when talking about *Hamlet* that morning, 'you have to remember that this was a drunken court. Hamlet comments on the general drunkenness. Even at the end it is drink that kills Hamlet and Claudius and Gertrude. Hamlet is at the centre of this corruption and is infected by it.'

His voice seemed quieter, more reflective, as if he was thinking of something else. Once he glanced across to Ralph but said nothing. 'I'm sorry,' he said at the end of the period, 'I meant to return your essays but I didn't finish correcting them.' A vein in his forehead throbbed. Ralph knew that he was remembering the voices that had shouted from the depths of the night, and he was wondering why they had been so unfair.

'Something's wrong with old Sniffy,' said Pongo at the interval. Ralph couldn't stand the amused contempt the pupils had for his stepfather and the way in which he had to suffer it. After all, he had not chosen him. His stepfather never organized games, there was nothing memorable about him.

When he went home after four, the door was unlocked but he couldn't find his mother. She was neither in the living room nor in the kitchen, which was odd since she usually had their meal ready for them when they returned from the school.

He shouted to her but there was no answer. After a while he knocked on her bedroom door and when there was no response he went in. She was lying flat out on the bed, face down, and was quite still. For a moment his heart leapt with the fear that she might be dead and he turned her over quickly. She was breathing but there was a smell of drink from her. She had never drunk much in her life as far as he knew. There was a bottle of sherry, with a little drink at the bottom of it, beside her on the floor. He slapped her face but she only grunted and didn't waken.

He didn't know what to do. He ran to the bathroom and filled a glass with water and threw it in her face. She shook and coughed while water streamed down her face, then opened her eyes. When she saw him she shut them again.

'Go way,' she said in a slurred voice, 'Go way.'

He stood for a while at the door looking at her. It seemed to him that this was the very end. It had happened because of the events of the previous night. Maybe he should kill himself. Maybe he should hang or drown himself. Or take pills. And then he thought that his mother might have done that. He ran to her bedroom and checked the bottle with the sleeping tablets, but it seemed quite full. He noticed for the first time his own picture on the sideboard opposite the bed where his mother was still sleeping. He picked it up and looked at it: there was no picture of his father there at all.

In the picture he was laughing and his mother was standing just behind him, her right hand resting on his right shoulder. He must have been five or six when the photograph was taken. It astonished him that the photograph should be there at all for he had thought she had forgotten all about him. There was not even a photograph of his stepfather in the room.

And then he heard again the voices coming out of the dark and it was as if he was his stepfather. 'Sniffy the Poof, Sniffy the Poof.' It was as if he was in that room listening to them. You couldn't be called anything worse than a poof. He heard again his mother telling him about his father. A recollection came back to him of a struggle one night between his mother and father. She had pulled herself away and shouted, 'I'm going to take the car and I'm going to kill myself. I know the place where I can do it.' And he himself had said to his father, 'Did you hear that?' But his father had simply smiled and said, 'Your mother's very theatrical.' For some reason this had amused him.

She was now sleeping fairly peacefully, sometimes snorting, her hands spread out across the bed.

And his stepfather hadn't come home. Where was he?

Had something happened to him? At that moment he felt terror greater than he had ever known, as if he was about to fall down, as if he was spinning in space. What if his mother died, if both of them died, and he was left alone?

He ran to the school as fast as he could. The janitor, who was standing outside his little office with a bunch of keys in his hand, watched him as he crossed the hall, but said nothing.

His stepfather was sitting at his desk on his tall gaunt chair staring across towards the seats. He was still wearing his gown and looked like a ghost inside its holed chalky armour. Even though he must have heard Ralph coming in he didn't turn his head. Ralph had never seen him like this before, so stunned, so helpless. Always, before, his stepfather appeared to have been in control of things. Now he didn't seem to know anything or to be able to do anything. He had wound down.

Ralph stood and looked at him from the doorway. If it weren't for his mother he wouldn't be there.

'Should you not be coming home?' he asked. His stepfather didn't answer. It was as if he was asking a profound question of the desks, as if they had betrayed him. Ralph again felt the floor spinning beneath him. Perhaps it was all too late. Perhaps it was all over. It might be that his stepfather would never come home again, had given everything up. His gaze interrogated the room.

Ralph advanced a little more.

'Should you not be coming home?' he asked again. But still his stepfather retained his pose, a white chalky statue. It was his turn now to be on his own listening to his own questions. Ralph had never thought of him like that before. Always he had been with his mother, always it was he himself who had been the forsaken one. On the blackboard were written the words, 'A tragedy gives us a feeling of waste.' Ralph stayed where he was for a long time. He didn't know what to do, how to get through to this man whom he had never understood. The empty desks frightened him. The room was like an empty theatre. Once his father had taken him to one in the afternoon. 'You wait there,' he said, 'I have to see someone.' And then he had seen his father talking to a girl who was standing face to face with him, wearing a belted raincoat. They had talked earnestly to each other, his father laughing, the girl looking at him adoringly.

No, it could not be true. His father hadn't been at all like that, his father had been the one who adored him, his son. What was this ghost like when compared to his father?

He couldn't bring himself to move, it was as if he was fixed to the floor. There was no word he could think of that would break this silence, this deathly enchantment.

He felt curiously awkward as if his body was something he carried about with him but which was distinct from his mind. It was as if in its heaviness and oddness it belonged to someone else. He thought of his mother outstretched on the bed, her hair floating down her face, stirring in the weak movement of her breath. Something must be done, he couldn't leave this man here and his mother there.

Slowly his stepfather got down from his desk, then placed the jotters which were stacked beside him in a cupboard. Then he locked the cupboard. He had finished marking them after all and would be able to return them. Then he began to walk past Ralph as if he wasn't there, his gaze fixed straight ahead of him. He was walking almost like a mechanical toy, clumsily, his gown fixed about him but becalmed.

Now he was near the door and soon he would be out in the hall. In those seconds, which seemed eternal, Ralph knew that he was facing the disintegration of his whole life. He knew that it was right there, in front of him, if he couldn't think of the magic word. He knew what tragedy was, knew it to its bitter bones, that it was the time that life continued, having gone beyond communication. He knew that tragedy was the thing you couldn't do anything about, that at that point all things are transformed, they enter another dimension, that it is not acting but the very centre of despair itself. He knew it was pitiful, yet the turning point of a life. And in its light, its languageless light, his father's negligent cheerful face burned, the moustache was like straw on fire. He was moving away from him, winking, perhaps deceitful. He saw the burden on this man's shoulders, he saw the desperate loneliness, so like his own. He felt akin to this being who was moving towards the door. And at that moment he found the word and it was as if it had been torn bleeding from his mouth.

'Come on home,' he said. 'Jim.'

Nothing seemed to be happening. Then suddenly the figure came to a halt and stood there at the door as if thinking. It thought like this for a long time. Then it turned to face him. And something in its face seemed to crack as if chalk were cracking and a human face were showing through. Without a word being said the ghost removed its gown and laid it on a desk, then the two of them were walking across the now empty hall towards the main door.

Such a frail beginning, and yet a beginning. Such a small hope, and yet a hope. Almost but not quite side by side, they crossed the playground together and it echoed with their footsteps, shining, too, with a blatant blankness after the rain.

The Play

WHEN HE STARTED teaching first Mark Mason was very enthusiastic, thinking that he could bring to the pupils gifts of the poetry of Wordsworth, Shakespeare and Keats. But it wasn't going to be like that, at least not with Class 3g. 3g was a class of girls who, before the raising of the school leaving age, were to leave at the end of their fifteenth year. Mark brought them 'relevant' poems and novels including *Timothy Winters* and *Jane Eyre* but quickly discovered that they had a fixed antipathy to the written word. It was not that they were undisciplined—that is to say they were not actively mischievous—but they were thrawn: he felt that there was a solid wall between himself and them and that no matter how hard he sold them *Jane Eyre*, by reading chapters of it aloud, and comparing for instance the food in the school refectory that Jane Eyre had to eat with that which they themselves got in their school canteen, they were not interested. Indeed one day when he was walking down one of the aisles between two rows of desks he asked one of the girls, whose name was Lorna and who was pasty-faced and blond, what was the last book she had read, and she replied,

'Please, sir, I never read any books.'

This answer amazed him for he could not conceive of a world where one never read any books and he was the more determined to introduce them to the activity which had given himself so much pleasure. But the more enthusiastic he became, the more eloquent his words, the more they withdrew into themselves till finally he had to admit that he was completely failing with the class. As he was very conscientious this troubled him, and not even his success with the academic classes compensated for his obvious lack of success with this particular class. He believed in any event that failure with the non-academic classes constituted failure as a teacher. He tried to do creative writing with them first by bringing in reproductions of paintings by Magritte which were intended to awaken in their minds a glimmer of the unexpectedness and strangeness of ordinary things, but they would simply look at them and point out to him their lack of resemblance to reality. He was in despair. His failure began to obsess him so much that he discussed the problem with the Head of Department who happened to be teaching *Rasselas* to the Sixth Form at the time with what success Mark could not gauge.

'I suggest you make them do the work,' said his Head of Department. 'There comes a point where if you do not impose your personality they will take advantage of you.'

But somehow or another Mark could not impose his personality on them: they had a habit for instance of forcing him to deviate from the text he was studying with them by mentioning something that had appeared in the newspaper.

'Sir,' they would say, 'did you see in the papers that there were two babies born from two wombs in the one woman.' Mark would flush angrily and say, 'I don't see what this has to do with our work,' but before he knew where he was he was in the middle of an animated discussion which was proceeding all around him about the anatomical significance of this piece of news. The fact was that he did not know how to deal with them: if they had been boys he might have threatened them with the last sanction of the belt, or at least frightened them in some way. But girls were different, one couldn't belt girls, and certainly he couldn't frighten this particular lot. They all wanted to be hairdressers: and one wanted to be an engineer having read in a paper that this was now a possible job for girls. He couldn't find it in his heart to tell her that it was highly unlikely that she could do this without Highers. They fantasized a great deal about jobs and chose ones which were well beyond their scope. It seemed to him that his years in Training College hadn't prepared him for this varied apathy and animated gossip. Sometimes one or two of them were absent and when he asked where they were was told that they were baby sitting. He dreaded the periods he had to try and teach them in, for as the year passed and

autumn darkened into winter he knew that he had not taught
them anything and he could not bear it.

He talked to other teachers about them, and the History
man shrugged his shoulders and said that he gave them
pictures to look at, for instance one showing women at the
munitions during the First World War. It became clear to
him that their other teachers had written them off since
they would be leaving at the end of the session, anyway,
and as long as they were quiet they were allowed to talk
and now and again glance at the books with which they had
been provided.

But Mark, whose first year this was, felt weighed down
by his failure and would not admit to it. There must be
something he could do with them, the failure was his fault
and not theirs. Like a missionary he had come to them
bearing gifts, but they refused them, turning away from
them with total lack of interest. Keats, Shakespeare, even
the ballads, shrivelled in front of his eyes. It was, curiously
enough, Mr Morrison who gave him his most helpful advice.
Mr Morrison spent most of his time making sure that his
register was immaculate, first writing in the O's in pencil
and then rubbing them out and re-writing them in ink. Mark
had been told that during the Second World War while Hitler
was advancing into France, Africa and Russia he had been
insisting that his register was faultlessly kept and the names
written in carefully. Morrison understood the importance of
this though no one else did.

'What you have to do with them,' said Morrison, looking
at Mark through his round glasses which were like the twin
barrels of a gun, 'is to find out what they want to do.'

'But,' said Mark in astonishment, 'that would be abdicat-
ing responsibility.'

'That's right,' said Morrison equably.

'If that were carried to its conclusion,' said Mark, but
before he could finish the sentence Morrison said,

'In teaching nothing ought to be carried to its logical
conclusion.'

'I see,' said Mark, who didn't. But at least Morrison had
introduced a new idea into his mind which was at the time
entirely empty.

'I see,' he said again. But he was not yet ready to go as far as Morrison had implied that he should. The following day however he asked the class for the words of 'Paper Roses', one of the few pop songs that he had ever heard of. For the first time he saw a glimmer of interest in their eyes, for the first time they were actually using pens. In a short while they had given him the words from memory. Then he took out a book of Burns' poems and copied on to the board the verses of 'My Love is Like a Red Red Rose'. He asked them to compare the two poems but found that the wall of apathy had descended again and that it was as impenetrable as before. Not completely daunted, he asked them if they would bring in a record of 'Paper Roses', and himself found one of 'My Love is Like a Red Red Rose', with Kenneth Mackellar singing it. He played both songs, one after the other, on his own record player. They were happy listening to 'Paper Roses' but showed no interest in the other song. The discussion he had planned petered out, except that the following day a small girl with black hair and a pale face brought in a huge pile of records which she requested that he play and which he adamantly refused to do. It occurred to him that the girls simply did not have the ability to handle discussion, that in all cases where discussion was initiated it degenerated rapidly into gossip or vituperation or argument, that the concept of reason was alien to them, that in fact the long line of philosophers beginning with Plato was irrelevant to them. For a long time they brought in records now that they knew he had a record player but he refused to play any of them. Hadn't he gone far enough by playing 'Paper Roses'? No, he was damned if he would go the whole hog and surrender completely. And yet, he sensed that somewhere in this area of their interest was what he wanted, that from here he might find the lever which would move their world.

He noticed that their leader was a girl called Tracy, a fairly tall pleasant-looking girl to whom they all seemed to turn for response or rejection. Nor was this girl stupid: nor were any of them stupid. He knew that he must hang on to that, he must not believe that they were stupid. When they did come into the room it was as if they were searching for substance, a food which he could not provide. He began to study Tracy more and more as if she might perhaps give him the solution to his problem, but she did not appear interested enough to do so. Now and again she would hum the words of a song while engaged in combing another girl's hair, an activity which would satisfy them for hours, and indeed some of the girls had said to him, 'Tracy has a good voice, sir. She can sing any pop song you like.' And Tracy had regarded him with the sublime self-confidence of one who indeed could do this. But what use would that be to him? More and more he felt himself, as it were, sliding into their world when what he had wanted was to drag them out of the darkness into his world. That was how he himself had been taught and that was how it should be. And the weeks passed and he had taught them nothing. Their jotters were blank apart from the words of pop songs and certain secret drawings of their own. Yet they were human beings, they were not stupid. That there was no such thing as stupidity was the faith by which he lived. In many ways they were quicker than he was, they found out more swiftly than he did the dates of examinations and holidays. They were quite reconciled to the fact that they would not be able to pass any examinations. They would say,

'We're the stupid ones, sir.' And yet he would not allow them that easy option, the fault was not with them, it was with him. He had seen some of them serving in shops, in restaurants, and they were neatly dressed, good with money and polite. Indeed they seemed to like him, and that made matters worse for he felt that he did not deserve their liking. They are not fed, he quoted to himself from *Lycidas*, as he watched them at the check-out desks of supermarkets flashing a smile at him, placing the messages in bags much more expertly than he would have done. And indeed he felt that a question was being asked of him but not at all pressingly. At night he would read Shakespeare and think, 'There are some people to whom all this is closed. There are some who will never shiver as they read the lines

Absent thee from felicity awhile
and in this harsh world draw thy breath in pain
to tell my story.

If he had read those lines to them they would have thought

that it was Hamlet saying farewell to a girl called Felicity, he thought wryly. He smiled for the first time in weeks. Am I taking this too seriously, he asked himself. They are not taking it seriously. Shakespeare is not necessary for hairdressing. As they endlessly combed each other's hair he thought of the ballad of Sir Patrick Spens and the line

> wi gowd kaims in their hair.

These girls were entirely sensuous, words were closed to them. They would look after babies with tenderness but they were not interested in the alien world of language.

Or was he being a male chauvinist pig? No, he had tried everything he could think of and he had still failed. The fact was that language, the written word, was their enemy, McLuhan was right after all. The day of the record player and television had transformed the secure academic world in which he had been brought up. And yet he did not wish to surrender, to get on with correction while they sat talking quietly to each other, and dreamed of the jobs which were in fact shut against them. School was simply irrelevant to them, they did not even protest, they withdrew from it gently and without fuss. They had looked at education and turned away from it. It was their indifferent gentleness that bothered him more than anything. But they also had the maturity to distinguish between himself and education, which was a large thing to do. They recognized that he had a job to do, that he wasn't at all unlikeable and was in fact a prisoner like themselves. But they were already perming some woman's hair in a luxurious shop.

The more he pondered, the more he realized that they were the key to his failure or success in education. If he failed with them then he had failed totally, a permanent mark would be left on his psyche. In some way it was necessary for him to change, but the point was, could he change to the extent that was demanded of him, and in what direction and with what purpose should he change? School for himself had been a discipline and an order but to them this discipline and order had become meaningless.

The words on the blackboard were ghostly and distant as if they belonged to another age, another universe. He recalled what Morrison had said, 'You must find out what they want to do', but they themselves did not know what they wanted to do, it was for him to tell them that, and till he told them that they would remain indifferent and apathetic. Sometimes he sensed that they themselves were growing tired of their lives, that they wished to prove themselves but didn't know how to set about it. They were like lost children, irrelevantly stored in desks, and they only lighted up like street lamps in the evening or when they were working in the shops. He felt that they were the living dead, and he would have given anything to see their eyes become illuminated, become interested, for if he could find the magic formula he knew that they would become enthusiastic, they were *not* stupid. But how to find the magic key which would release the sleeping beauties from their sleep? He had no idea what it was and felt that in the end if he ever discovered it he would stumble over it and not be led to it by reflection or logic. And that was exactly what happened.

One morning he happened to be late coming into the room and there was Tracy swanning about in front of the class, as if she were wearing a gown, and saying some words to them he guessed in imitation of himself, while at the same time uncannily reproducing his mannerisms, leaning for instance despairingly across his desk, his chin on his hand while at the same time glaring helplessly at the class. It was like seeing himself slightly distorted in water, slightly comic, frustrated and yet angrily determined. When he opened the door there was a quick scurry and the class had arranged themselves, presenting blank dull faces as before. He pretended he had seen nothing, but knew now what he had to do. The solution had come to him as a gift from heaven, from the gods themselves, and the class sensed a new confidence and purposefulness in his voice.

'Tracy,' he said, 'and Lorna.' He paused. 'And Helen. I want you to come out here.'

They came out to the floor looking at him uneasily. O my wooden O, he said to himself, my draughty echo help me now.

'Listen,' he said, 'I've been thinking. It's quite clear to me that you don't want to do any writing, so we won't do any writing. But I'll tell you what we're going to do instead. We're going to act.'

A ripple of noise ran through the class, like the wind on an autumn day, and he saw their faces brightening. The shades of Shakespeare and Sophocles forgive me for what I am to do, he prayed.

'We are going,' he said, 'to do a serial and it's going to be called "The Rise of a Pop Star".' It was as if animation had returned to their blank dull faces, he could see life sparkling in their eyes, he could see interest in the way they turned to look at each other, he could hear it in the stir of movement that enlivened the room.

'Tracy,' he said, 'you will be the pop star. You are coming home from school to your parents' house. I'm afraid,' he added, 'that as in the reverse of the days of Shakespeare the men's parts will have to be to be acted by the girls. Tracy, you have decided to leave home. Your parents of course disapprove. But you want to be a pop star, you have always wanted to be one. They think that that is a ridiculous idea. Lorna, you will be the mother, and Helen, you will be the father.'

He was astonished by the manner in which Tracy took over, by the ingenuity with which she and the other two created the first scene in front of his eyes. The scene grew and became meaningful, all their frustrated enthusiasm was poured into it.

First of all without any prompting Tracy got her school bag and rushed into the house while Lorna, the mother, pretended to be ironing on a desk that was quickly dragged out into the middle of the floor, and Helen the father read the paper, which was his own *Manchester Guardian* snatched from the top of his desk.

'Well, that's it over,' said Tracy, the future pop star.

'And what are you thinking of doing with yourself now?' said the mother, pausing from her ironing.

'I'm going to be a pop star,' said Tracy.

'What's that you said?'—her father, laying down the paper.

'That's what I want to do,' said Tracy, 'other people have done it.'

'What nonsense,' said the father. 'I thought you were going in for hairdressing.'

'I've changed my mind,' said Tracy.

'You won't stay in this house if you're going to be a pop star,' said the father. 'I'll tell you that for free.'

'I don't care whether I do or not,' said Tracy.

'And how are you going to be a pop star?' said her mother.

'I'll go to London,' said Tracy.

'London. And where are you going to get your fare from?' said the father, mockingly, picking up the paper again.

Mark could see that Tracy was thinking this over: it was a real objection. Where was her fare going to come from? She paused, her mind grappling with the problem.

'I'll sell my records,' she said at last.

Her father burst out laughing. 'You're the first one who starts out as a pop star by selling all your records.' And then in a sudden rage in which Mark could hear echoes of reality he shouted,

'All right then. Bloody well go then.'

Helen glanced at Mark, but his expression remained benevolent and unchanged.

Tracy, turning at the door, said, 'Well then, I'm going. And I'm taking the records with me.' She suddenly seemed very thin and pale and scrawny.

'Go on then,' said her father.

'That's what I'm doing. I'm going.' Her mother glanced from daughter to father and then back again but said nothing.

'I'm going then,' said Tracy, pretending to go to another room and then taking the phantom records in her arms. The father's face was fixed and determined and then Tracy looked at the two of them for the last time and left the room. The father and mother were left alone.

'She'll come back soon enough,' said the father but the mother still remained silent. Now and again the father would look at a phantom clock on a phantom mantelpiece but still Tracy did not return. The father pretended to go and lock a door and then said to his wife,

'I think we'd better go to bed.'

And then Lorna and Helen went back to their seats while
Mark thought, this was exactly how dramas began in their
bareness and naivety, through which at the same time an
innocent genuine feeling coursed or peered as between
ragged curtains.

When the bell rang after the first scene was over he
found himself thinking about Tracy wandering the streets
of London, as if she were a real waif sheltering in transient
doss-houses or under bridges dripping with rain. The girls
became real to him in their rôles whereas they had not
been real before, nor even individualistic behind their wall
of apathy. That day in the staff-room he heard about Tracy's
saga and was proud and non-committal.

The next day the story continued. Tracy paced up and
down the bare boards of the classroom, now and again
stopping to look at ghostly billboards, advertisements. The
girls had clearly been considering the next development
during the interval they had been away from him, and had
decided on the direction of the plot. The next scene was in
fact an Attempted Seduction Scene.

Tracy was sitting disconsolately at a desk which he presumed was a table in what he presumed was a café.

'Hello, Mark,' she said to the man who came over to sit
beside her. At this point Tracy glanced wickedly at the
real Mark. The Mark in the play was the dark-haired
girl who had asked for the records and whose name was
Annie.

'Hello,' said Annie. And then, 'I could get you a spot,
you know.'

'What do you mean?'

'There's a night club where they have a singer and she's
sick. I could get you to take her place.' He put his hands on
hers and she quickly withdrew her own.

'I mean it,' he said. 'If you come to my place I can
introduce you to the man who owns the night club.'

Tracy searched his face with forlorn longing.

Was this another lie like the many she had experienced
before? Should she, shouldn't she? She looked tired, her
shoulders were slumped.

Finally she rose from the table and said, 'All right then.'

Together they walked about the room in search of his luxurious flat.

They found it. Willing hands dragged another desk out and set the two desks at a slight distance from each other.

The Mark of the play went over to the window-sill on which there was a large bottle which had once contained ink but was now empty. He poured wine into two phantom glasses and brought them over.

'Where is this man then,' said Tracy.

'He won't be long,' said Mark.

Tracy accepted the drink and Annie drank as well.

After a while Annie tried to put her hand around Tracy's waist. Mark the teacher glanced at the class: he thought that at this turn of events they would be convulsed with raucous laughter. But in fact they were staring enraptured at the two, enthralled by their performance. It occurred to him that he would never be as unselfconscious as Annie and Tracy in a million years. Such a shorn abject thing, such dialogue borrowed from television, and yet it was early drama that what he was seeing reminded him of. He had a quick vision of a flag gracing the roof of the 'theatre', as if the school now belonged to the early age of Elizabethanism. His poor wooden O was in fact echoing with real emotions and real situations, borrowed from the pages of subterraneous pop magazines.

Tracy stood up. 'I am not that kind of girl,' she said.

'What kind of girl?'

'That kind of girl.'

But Annie was insistent. 'You'll not get anything if you don't play along with me,' she said, and Mark could have sworn that there was an American tone to her voice.

'Well, I'm not playing along with you,' said Tracy. She swayed a little on her feet, almost falling against the black-board. 'I'm bloody well not playing along with you,' she said. 'And that's final.' With a shock of recognition Mark heard her father's voice behind her own as one might see behind a similar painting the first original strokes.

And then she collapsed on the floor and Annie was bending over her.

'I didn't mean it,' she was saying. 'I really didn't mean it. I'm sorry.'

But Tracy lay there motionless and pale. She was like the Lady of Shalott in her boat. The girls in the class were staring at her. Look what they have done to me, Tracy was implying. Will they not be sorry now? There was a profound silence in the room and Mark was aware of the power of drama, even here in this bare classroom with the green peeling walls, the window-pole in the corner like a disused spear. There was nothing here but the hopeless emotion of the young.

Annie raised Tracy to her feet and sat her down in a chair.

'It's true,' he said, 'it's true that I know this man.' He went over to the wall and pretended to dial on a phantom 'phone. And at that moment Tracy turned to the class and winked at them. It was a bold outrageous thing to do, thought Mark, it was as if she was saying, That faint was of course a trick, a feint, that is the sort of thing people like us have to do in order to survive: he thought he was tricking me but all the time I was tricking him. I am alive, fighting, I know exactly what I am doing. All of us are in conspiracy against this Mark. So much, thought Mark, was conveyed by that wink, so much that was essentially dramatic. It was pure instinct of genius.

The stage Mark turned away from the 'phone and said, 'He says he wants to see you. He'll give you an audition. His usual girl's sick. She's got . . .' Annie paused and tried to say 'laryngitis', but it came out as not quite right, and it was as if the word poked through the drama like a real error, and Mark thought of the Miracle plays in which ordinary people played Christ and Noah and Abraham with such unconscious style, as if there was no oddity in Abraham being a joiner or a miller.

'Look, I'll call you,' said the stage Mark and the bell rang and the finale was postponed. In the noise and chatter in which desks and chairs were replaced Mark was again aware of the movement of life, and he was happy. Absurdly he began to see them as if for the first time, their faces real and interested, and recognized the paradox that only in the drama had he begun to know them, as if only behind such a protection, a screen, were they willing to reveal themselves. And he began to wonder whether he himself had broken through the persona of the teacher and begun to 'act' in the real world. Their faces were more individual, sad or happy, private, extrovert, determined, yet vulnerable. It seemed to him that he had failed to see what Shakespeare was really about, he had taken the wrong road to find him.

'A babble of green fields,' he thought with a smile. So that was what it meant, that Wooden O, that resonator of the transient, of the real, beyond all the marble of their books, the white In Memoriams which they could not read.

How extraordinarily curious it all was.

The final part of the play was to take place on the following day.

'Please sir,' said Lorna to him, as he was about to leave.

'What is it?'

But she couldn't put into words what she wanted to say. And it took him a long time to decipher from her broken language what it was she wanted. She and the other actresses wanted an audience. Of course, why had he not thought of that before? How could he not have realized that an audience was essential? And he promised her that he would find one.

By the next day he had found an audience which was composed of a 3a class which Miss Stewart next door was taking. She grumbled a little about the Interpretation they were missing but eventually agreed. Additional seats were taken into Mark's room from her room and Miss Stewart sat at the back, her spectacles glittering.

Tracy pretended to knock on a door which was in fact the blackboard and then a voice invited her in. The manager of the night club pointed to a chair which stood on the 'stage'.

'What do you want?'

'I want to sing, sir.'

'I see. Many girls want to sing. I get girls in here every day. They all want to sing.'

Mark heard titters of laughter from some of the boys in 3a and fixed a ferocious glare on them. They settled down again.

'But I know I can sing, sir,' said Tracy. 'I know I can.'

'They all say that too.' His voice suddenly rose, 'They all bloody well say that.'

Mark saw Miss Stewart sitting straight up in her seat and then glancing at him disapprovingly. Shades of Pygmalion, he thought to himself, smiling. You would expect it from Shaw, inside inverted commas.

'Give it to them, sock it to them,' he pleaded silently. The virginal Miss Stewart looked sternly on.

'Only five minutes then,' said the night club manager, glancing at his watch. Actually there was no watch on his hand at all. 'What song do you want to sing?'

Mark saw Lorna pushing a desk out to the floor and sitting in it. This was to be the piano, then. The absence of props bothered him and he wondered whether imagination had first begun among the poor, since they had such few material possessions. Lorna waited, her hands poised above the desk. He heard more sniggerings from the boys and this time he looked so angry that he saw one of them turning a dirty white.

The hands hovered above the desk. Then Tracy began to sing. She chose the song 'Heartache'.

> My heart, dear, is aching;
>   I'm feeling so blue.
> Don't give me more heartaches,
>   I'm pleading with you.

It seemed to him that at that moment, as she stood there pale and thin, she was putting all her experience and desires into her song. It was a moment he thought such as it is given to few to experience. She was in fact auditioning before a phantom audience, she and the heroine of the play were the same, she was searching for recognition on the streets of London, in a school. She stood up in her vulnerability, in her purity, on a bare stage where there was no furniture of any value, of any price: on just such a stage had actors and actresses acted many years before, before the full flood of Shakespearean drama. Behind her on the blackboard were written notes about the Tragic Hero, a concept which he had been discussing with the Sixth Year.

'The hero has a weakness and the plot of the play attacks this specific weakness.'

'We feel a sense of waste.'

'And yet triumph.'

Tracy's voice, youthful and yearning and vulnerable, soared to the cracked ceiling. It was as if her frustrations were released in the song.

> Don't give me more heartaches,
> I'm pleading with you.

The voice soared on and then after a long silence the bell rang.

The boys from 3a began to chatter and he thought, 'You don't even try. You wouldn't have the nerve to sing like that, to be so naked.' But another voice said to him, 'You're wrong. They're the same. It is we who have made them different.' But were they in fact the same, those who had been reduced to the nakedness, and those others who were the protected ones. He stood there trembling as if visited by a revelation which was only broken when Miss Stewart said,

'Not quite Old Vic standard.' And then she was gone with her own superior brood. You stupid bitch, he muttered under his breath, you Observer-Magazine-reading bitch who never liked anything in your life till some critic made it respectable, who wouldn't recognize a good line of poetry or prose till sanctified by the voice of London, who would never have arrived at Shakespeare on your own till you were given the crutches.

And he knew as he watched her walking, so seemingly self-sufficient, in her black gown across the hall that she was as he had been and would be no longer. He had taken a journey with his class, a pilgrimage across the wooden boards, the poor abject furnitureless room which was like their vision of life, and from that journey he and they had learned in spite of everything. In spite of everything, he shouted in his mind, we have put a flag out there and it is there even during the plague, even if Miss Stewart visits it. It is there in spite of Miss Stewart, in spite of her shelter and her glasses, in spite of her very vulnerable armour, in spite of her, in spite of everything.

Survival Without Error

I DON'T OFTEN think about that period in my life. After all, when one comes down to it, it was pretty wasteful.

And, in fact, it wasn't thought that brought it back to me: it was a smell. To be exact, the smell of after-shave lotion. I was standing in front of the bathroom mirror—as I do every morning at about half past eight, for I am a creature of habit—and I don't know how it was, but that small bottle of Imperial after-shave lotion—yellowish golden stuff it is—brought it all back. Or, to be more exact, it was the scent of the lotion on my cheeks after I had shaved, not the colour. I think I once read something in a *Reader's Digest* about an author—a Frenchman or a German—who wrote a whole book after smelling or tasting something. I can't remember what it was exactly: I don't read much, especially not fiction, you can't afford to when you're a lawyer.

So there I was in the bathroom on that July morning preparing to go to the office—which is actually only about five hundred yards or so away, so that I don't even need to take the car—and instead of being in the bathroom waiting to go in to breakfast with Sheila, there I was in England fifteen years ago. Yes, fifteen years ago. Exactly. For it was July then too.

And all that day, even in court, I was thinking about it. I even missed one or two cues, though the sheriff himself does that, for he's a bit deaf. I don't often do court work: there's no money in it and I don't particularly care for it anyway. To tell the truth, I'm no orator, no Perry Mason. I prefer dealing with cases I can handle in my office, solicitor's work mainly. I have a certain head for detail but not for the big work.

I suppose if I hadn't put this shaving lotion on I wouldn't have remembered it again. I don't even know why I used that lotion today: perhaps it was because it was a beautiful summer morning and I felt rather lighthearted and gay. I don't use lotions much though I do make use of Vaseline hair tonic as I'm getting a bit bald. I blame that on the caps we had to wear all the time during those two years of National Service in the Army. Navy-blue berets they were. And that's what the shaving lotion brought back.

Now I come to think of them, those years were full of things like boots, belts and uniforms. We had two sets of boots—second best boots and (if that makes any sense) first best boots. (Strictly speaking, it seems to be wrong to use the word 'best' about two objects, but this is the first time I've located the error.) Then again we had best battle dress and second best battle dress. (Again, there were only two lots.)

We always had to be cleaning our boots. The idea was to burn your boots so that you could get a proper shine, the kind that would glitter back at you brighter than a mirror, that would remove the grain completely from the toes. Many a night I've spent with hot liquefied boot polish, burning and rubbing till the dazzling shine finally appeared, till the smoothness conquered the rough grain.

We really had to be very clean in those days. Our faces too. In those days one had to be clean-shaven, absolutely clean-shaven, and, to get the tart freshness into my cheeks, I used shaving lotion, which is what brought it all back. The rest seems entirely without scent, without taste, all except the lotion.

I went to the Army straight from university and I can still remember the hot crowded train on which I travelled all through the night and into the noon of the following day. Many of the boys played cards as we hammered our way through the English stations.

I am trying to remember what I felt when I boarded that train and saw my sister and mother waving their handkerchiefs at the station. To tell the truth, I don't think I felt anything. I didn't think of it as an adventure, still less as a patriotic duty. I felt, I think, numbed; my main idea was that I must get it over with as cleanly and as quickly as I could, survive without error.

About noon, we got off the train and walked up the road

to the camp. It was beautiful pastoral countryside with hot flowers growing by the side of the road; I think they were foxgloves. In the distance I could see a man in a red tractor ploughing. I thought to myself: This is the last time I shall see civilian life for a long time.

After we had been walking for some time, still wearing our bedraggled suits (in which we had slept the previous night) and carrying our cases, we arrived at the big gate which was the entrance to the camp. There was a young soldier standing there—no older than ourselves—and he was standing at ease with a rifle held in front of him, its butt resting on the ground. His hair was close cropped under the navy-blue cap with the yellow badge, and when we smiled at him, he stared right through us. Absolutely right through us, as if he hadn't seen us at all.

We checked in at the guardroom and were sent up to the barracks with our cases. As we were walking along—very nervous, at least I was—we passed the square where this terrible voice was shouting at recruits. There were about twenty of them and they looked very minute in the centre of that huge square, all grey and stony.

In any case—I can't remember very clearly what the preliminaries were—we ended up in this barrack room and sat down on the beds which had green coverings and one or two blankets below. There must have been twelve of these beds—about six down each side—and a fire-place in the middle of the room with a flue.

Now, I didn't know anything about the Army though some of the others did. One or two of them had been in the Cadets (I remember one small, plump-cheeked, innocent-looking youngster of eighteen who had been in the cadet corps in some English public school: he looked like an angel, and he was reading an author called Firbank) but the rest of us didn't know what to expect. Of course, I'd seen films about the Army (though not many since I was a conscientious student, not patronising the cinema much) and thought that they were exaggerated. In any case, as far as my memory went, these films made the Army out to be an amusing experience with a lot of hard work involved, and though sergeants and corporals appeared terrifying, they really had hearts of gold just the same. There used to be a glint in the sergeant's eye as he mouthed obscenities at some recruit, and he would always praise his platoon to a fellow sergeant over a pint in the mess that same night. That was the impression I got from the films.

Well, it's a funny thing: when we went into the Army it was at first like a film (it became a bit more real later on). We were sitting on our beds when this corporal came in (at least we were told by himself that he was a corporal: I was told off on my second day for calling a sergeant major 'sir' though I was only being respectful). The first we knew of this corporal was a hard click of boots along the floor and then this voice shouting, 'Get on your feet'. I can tell you we got up pretty quickly and stood trembling by our beds.

He was a small man, this corporal, with a moustache, and he looked very fit and very tense. You could almost feel that his moustache was actually growing and alive. He was wearing shiny black boots, a shiny belt buckle, a yellow belt and a navy-blue cap with a shining badge in it. And when we were all standing at a semblance of attention, he started pacing up and down in front of us, sometimes stopping in front of one man and then in front of another, and coming up and speaking to them with his face right up against theirs. And he said (as they do on the films),

'Now, you men are going to think I'm a bastard. You're going to want to go home to mother. You're going to work like slaves and you're going to curse the day you were born. You're going to hate me every day and every night, if you have enough strength left to dream. But there's one thing I'm going to say to you and it's this: if you play fair by me I'll play fair by you. Is that understood?'

There was a long silence during which I could hear a fly buzzing over at the window which was open at the top, and through which I could see the parade ground.

Then he said,

'Get out there. We're going to get you kitted out at the quartermaster's.'

And that was it. I felt as if I had been hit by a bomb. I had never met anyone like that in my life before. And it was worse when one had come from a university. Not even the worst teacher I had met had that man's controlled ferocity and energy. You felt that he hated you for existing, that you looked untidy, and that he was there to make you neater than was possible.

All this came back to me very quickly as a result of a whiff of that shaving lotion and, as I said, even during my time in the court I kept thinking about that period fifteen years before so that the sheriff had to speak to me once or twice.

The case itself was a very bad one, not the kind we usually get in this town which is small and nice, the kind of town where everyone knows everybody else and the roads are lined with trees. The background to the case was this:

Two youths were walking along the street late at night when they saw this down-and-out sitting on a bench. He had a bottle of VP and he was drinking from it. The two youths went over and asked him for a swig, but he wouldn't give them any so, according to the police, they attacked him and, when he was down, they kicked him in the face and nearly killed him. In fact, he is in hospital at this moment and close to death. The youths, of course, deny all this and say that they never saw him before in their lives, and that they don't know what the police are on about.

They are a very unprepossessing pair, I must confess, barely literate, long-haired, arrogant and contemptuous. They wear leather jackets, and one has a motor bike. They have a history of violence at dance halls, and one of them has used a knife. I don't like them. I don't like them because I don't understand them. We ourselves are childless (Sheila compensates for that by painting a lot), but that isn't the reason why I dislike them. They don't care for me either and call me 'daddy'. They are more than capable of doing what the police say they did, and there is in fact a witness, a young girl who was coming home from a dance. She says that she heard one of the youths say,

'I wish the b. . . would stop making that noise.' They are the type of youths who have never done well in school, who haven't enough money to get girls for themselves since they are always unemployed, and they take their resentment out on others. I would say they are irreclaimable, and probably in Russia they would be put up against a wall and shot. However, they have to have someone to defend them. One of them had the cheek to say to me,

'You'd better get us off, daddy.'

They made a bad impression in the court. One of them says,

'What would we need that VP crap for, anyway?' It's this language that alienates people from them, but they're too stupid or too arrogant to see that. As well as this they accuse the police of beating them up with truncheons when they were taken in. But this is a common ploy.

Anyway, I kept thinking of the Army all the time I was in court, and once I even said 'sergeant' to the judge. It was a totally inexplicable error. It's lucky for me that he's slightly deaf.

I was thinking of Lecky all the time.

Now, I suppose every platoon in the Army has to have the odd one out, the one who can never keep in step, the one who never cleans his rifle properly, the one whose trousers are never properly pressed. And our platoon like all others had one. His name was Lecky. (The platoon in the adjacent hut had one too, though I can't remember his name. He, unlike Lecky, was a scholarly type with round glasses and he was the son of a bishop. I remember he had this big history book by H. A. L. Fisher and he was always reading it, even in the Naafi, while we were buying our cakes of blanco, and buns and tea. I wonder if he ever finished it.)

Funny thing, I can't remember Lecky's features very well. I was trying to do so all day, but unsuccessfully. I think he was small and black-haired and thin-featured. I'm not even sure what he did in Civvy Street, but I believe I once heard it mentioned that he was a plumber's mate.

The crowd in our platoon were a mixed lot. There were two English ex-schoolboys and a number of Scots, at least two of them from Glasgow. There was also a boxer, who spoke with a regional, agricultural accent. One of the public schoolboys had a record player which he had brought with him. He was a jazz devotee and I can still remember him plugging it into the light and playing, on an autumn evening, a tune called 'Love, O, Love, O, Careless Love'. The second line, I think, was, 'You fly to my head like wine'. The public schoolboys were very composed people (certain officers), and the chubby-cheeked one was always reading poetry.

Lecky stood out from the first day. First of all, he couldn't keep in step. We used to march along swinging our arms practically up to our foreheads and then this voice from miles away would shout across the square, 'Squad, Halt!' Then the little corporal would march briskly across the square, and he'd come to a halt in front of Lecky and he'd say (the square was scorching with the heat in the middle of a blazing July), his face thrust up to close to him, 'What are you, Lecky?' And Lecky would say, 'I don't know, Corporal.' And the corporal would say, 'You're a bastard, aren't you, Lecky?' And Lecky would say, 'I'm a bastard, Corporal.' Then the marching would start all over again, and Lecky would still be out of step.

It is strange about these corporals, how they want everything to be so tidy, as if they couldn't stand sloppiness, as if untidiness is a personal insult to them. I suppose really that the whole business becomes so mindlessly boring after a few years of it that the only release for them is the manic anger they generate.

Of course, Lecky got jankers. What this involved was that after training was over for the day (usually at about four o'clock) he would put on his best boots, best battledress, best tie, best everything and report to the guardroom at the double. Then, after he had been inspected (if he didn't get more jankers for sloppiness) he would double up to the barrack room again, change into denims, and go off to his assigned fatigue which might involve weeding or peeling potatoes or helping to get rid of swill at the cookhouse.

Continual jankers are a dreadful strain. You have to have all your clothes pressed for inspection at the guardroom; as well as that, boots and badges must be polished and belts must be blancoed. You live in a continual daze of spit and polish and ironing, and the only time you can find to do all this is after you have come back from your assigned task which is often designed to make you as dirty as possible. There is rapid change of clothes from battledress to denims and back again. For after your fatigues are over you have to change back into battledress to be inspected at the guardroom for a second time. I must say that I used to feel sorry for him.

His bed was beside mine. I never actually spoke to him much. For one thing his only form of reading was comics, and we had very little in common. For another thing—though this is difficult to explain—I didn't want to be infected by his bad luck. And after all what could I have done for him even if I had been able to communicate with him?

The funny thing was that as far as the rest of us were concerned the corporal became more relaxed as the training progressed and treated us as human beings. He would bellow at us out on the square, but at nights he would often talk to us. He'd even listen to the jazz records though he preferred pop. All this time while the others were gathered round the record player, the corporal in the middle, Lecky would be rushing about blancoing or polishing or making his bed tidy. Sometimes the corporal would shout at him, 'Get a move on, Lecky, are you a f . . . snail or something?' And Lecky would give him a startled glance, before he would continue with whatever he was doing.

I never saw him write a letter. I have a feeling he couldn't write very well. In fact, when he was reading the comics, you could see his lips move and his finger travel along the page. Once I even saw the corporal pick up one of the comics and sit on the bed quite immersed in it for a while.

At the beginning, Lecky seemed quite bright. He even managed to make a joke out of that classic day when he was first taught to fire the bren. Instead of setting it to single rounds, he released the whole batch of bullets in one burst and nearly ripped the target to shreds. I saw the corporal bending down very gently beside him and saying to him equally slowly, 'What a stupid uneducated b . . . you are, Lecky.' He got jankers for that too.

But, as the weeks passed, a fixed look of despair pervaded his face. He acted as if his every movement was bound to be a mistake, as if he had no right to exist, and that carefree open-faced appearance of his faded to leave a miserable white mask. Sometimes you wonder if it was right.

The more I see of these two people in the court, the more I'm sure that they really are guilty of hitting that old man, though they themselves swear blind they didn't do it. They keep insisting that they are being victimised by the police and that they were beaten up at the station. They even picked on one of the policemen as the one who did it. He very gravely refuted the charges. One of them says he never drank VP in his life, that he thinks it's a drink only tramps use, and that he himself has only drunk whisky or beer. He is quite indignant about it: one could almost believe him. They also accuse the girl of framing them because one of them had a fight with her brother once on a bus. But their attitude is very defiant and it isn't doing them any good. My wife was away yesterday seeing her mother so I had to go to Armstrong's for lunch. Armstrong's is opposite the court which is in turn just beside the police station. As I was entering the restaurant I was passed by the superintendent who greeted me very coldly, I thought. He is a tall broad individual, very proud of his rank, and you can see him standing at street corners looking very official and stern, with his white gloves in his hands, staring across the traffic, one of his minions, usually a sergeant, standing beside him. I wondered why he was so distant, especially as we often play bowls together and have been known to play a game of golf.

It struck me afterwards that perhaps he thought I had put them up to their accusations against the police. After all, we mustn't undermine the authority of the police as they have a lot to put up with, and, even if they do use truncheons now and again, we must remember the kind of people they are dealing with. I believe in the use of psychology to a certain extent, but the victim must be protected too.

There was the time, too, when Lecky nearly killed off the platoon with a grenade. After a while it got so that hardly anyone in the hut spoke to him much. At the beginning they used to play tricks on him, like messing up his blankets, but that was before the corporal got to work on him (no, that's not strictly true, the Glasgow boys were doing it even after that). Most of the time we didn't see him at all, as he was so often on jankers. I don't know why we didn't speak to him. I think it was something about him that made us uneasy: I can only express it by saying that we felt him to be a born victim. It was as if he attracted trouble and we didn't want to be in the neighbourhood when it struck. We didn't want to have to do that spell of ten weeks' training all over again as Lecky was sure to do.

One morning we had an inspection. We had inspections every Saturday: the C.O. (distant, precise, immaculately uniformed) would come along, busily accompanied by the sergeant major, the sergeant, and corporal of the platoon. Oh, and the lieutenant as well (our lieutenant had been to Cambridge). We would all be standing by our beds, of course, rifles ready so that the C.O. could peer down the barrel, followed in pecking order by all the members of his entourage. If there was a single spot of grease we were for it. Our beds had all our possessions laid out on them, blanco, fork, knife and spoon, vest, pants, and much that I can't now remember. All, naturally, had to be spotlessly clean.

So there we were, standing stiff and frightened as the C.O. stalked up the room followed by the rest of his minions, the corporal with a small notebook in his hand. Unwavering and taut, we stared straight ahead of us, through the narrow window that gave out on the outside world which appeared to be composed of stone, as the only thing we could see was the parade ground.

Our hearts would be in our boots as we took the bolt out of the rifle and the C.O. would squint down the barrel to see if there was any grease. Mine was all right, but a moment later I heard a terrifying scream from the C.O. as if he had been mortally wounded. I couldn't even turn my head.

'Take this man's name. His rifle's dirty.' And the sergeant major passed it down to the corporal who put the name in the notebook. The C.O. proceeded on his tour round the room poking distastefully here and there with his stick, and staring at people's faces to see if they had shaved properly. I remember thinking it was rather like the way farmers prod cattle to see if they are fat and healthy enough. On one occasion he even got the sergeant major to tell someone to raise his feet to see if all the nails in the soles of his boots were still present and correct. Then he went on to the next hut, his retinue behind him.

And the corporal came up to Lecky, his face contorted with rage, and, punching him in the chest with his finger, said, 'You perverted motherless b . . ., you piece of camel's dung, do you know what you've done? You've gone and stopped the weekend leave for this platoon. That's what you've done. And don't any of you public school wallahs write to your M.P.s about it either. As for you, Lecky, you're up before the C.O. in the morning, and I hope he throws the book at you. I sincerely hope he gives you guard duty for eighteen years.'

Now this was the first weekend we were going to have since we had entered the camp five weeks before. We hadn't been beyond the barracks and the square all that time. Blancoing, polishing, marching, eating, sleeping, waking at half past six in the morning, often shaving in cold water—that had been the pattern of our days. We hadn't even seen the town: we hadn't been to a café or a cinema. All that time we hadn't seen a civilian except for the ones working in the Naafi. So, of course, you can guess how we felt. I wasn't myself desperate. I wasn't particularly interested in girls (though later on when I was in hospital I got in tow with a nurse). I didn't drink. All I wanted was to get that ten weeks over. But I also wanted to put on my clean uniform just for once, and walk by myself, without being shouted at, down the anonymous streets of some town and see people even if I didn't talk to them. I would have been happy just to look in the shop windows, to stroll in the cool evening air, to board a bus, anything at all to get out of that hut.

There were two Glasgow boys there, and they went up to Lecky when the corporal had left and said to him, 'You stupid c . . ., what do you think you've done?' or words to that effect. They were practically insane with rage. For the past weeks all they had talked about was this weekend and the bints they would get off with, the dance they would go to, and so on. In fact, I think that if either of them had had a knife they would have run him through with it. And all this time Lecky sat on his bed petrified as if he had been shell-shocked. He was so shell-shocked that he didn't even answer. He didn't even cry. I had heard him crying once in the middle of the night. But there was nothing I could do. What could anyone do? I must say that I felt these Glasgow boys were going too far and I turned away, feeling uncomfortable.

Lecky was trying to pull a piece of rag through his rifle in order to clean it. One of the Glasgow boys took the rag from him (Lecky surrendered it quite meekly as if he didn't know what was happening, and indeed, I don't think he did know), rubbed it on the floor and then pulled it through the rifle again. The other tumbled Lecky's bed on to the floor, upsetting everything in it. (All this time the chubby-cheeked boy was reading Firbank.)

'You'd best keep in tonight,' the Glasgow boy said. 'If I get you outside . . .' and he made a motion of cutting Lecky's throat. Lecky sat on the floor looking up at him, deadly pale, his adam's apple going up and down in his throat.

'And no help for this bastard from any of you, anymore,' said the Glasgow boy, turning on us threateningly. The boxer, I remember, grinned amiably like a big dog. I think even he was afraid of the Glasgow boys, but I don't know. He was pretty hefty too, and the corporal spoke more softly to him than to any of the rest of us.

So Lecky went up next morning and got another three weeks of jankers, and on top of that he had trouble from the Glasgow boys as well. I would have said something to them, but what would I have gained? They would just have started on me. The sergeant was a placid family man and he left everything to the corporal. The sergeant was pretty nice really: a nice stout man who was very good at handing out the parcels any of us got and making sure that he got a signature. It was funny how Lecky never wrote any letters.

So the time came for our passing-out parade, to be inspected by a brigadier, one of those officers with a monocle, and a red cap, and a shooting stick. Of course, our own C.O. would be there as well.

I remember that morning well. It was a beautiful autumn morning, almost melancholy and very still. We were up very early, at about half past five, and I can still recall going out to the door of the hut and standing there regarding the dim deserted square. I am not a fanciful person but, as I stood there, I felt almost as if it were waiting for us, for the drama that we could provide, and that without us it was without meaning. It had taken much from us—perhaps our youth—but it had given us much too. I felt both happy and sad at the same time, sad because I had come to the end of something, and happy because I would be leaving that place shortly.

I don't know if the others felt the sadness, but they certainly felt the happiness. They were skylarking about, throwing water at each other from the wash-basins and singing at the tops of their voices. The ablutions appeared on that day to be a well-known and almost beloved place though I could remember shaving there in the coldest of water, in front of the cracked mirror. Today, however, it was different. In a few hours we would be standing on the square, then we would be marching to the sound of the bagpipes.

And after that we would all leave—all, that is, except Lecky. We were even sorry to be leaving the corporal, who had become more and more genial as the weeks passed, who condescended to be human and would almost speak to us on equal terms. He had even been known to pass round his cigarettes and to offer a drink in the local pub. Perhaps after all he had to be tough; one must always remember the kind of people with whom he often had to deal. For instance, there was one recruit who was in his fourth year of National Service; every chance he got he went over the wall and the M.P.s had to chase him all over the north of England. That's just stupidity, of course. You can't beat the Army, you should resign yourself. Rebellion won't get you anywhere. I believe he had a rough time in the guardroom every time they got him back, but he was indomitable. You almost had to admire him in a way.

Anyway, I found myself standing beside Lecky at the wash basin. I could see his thin face reflected in the mirror beside my own. There was no happiness in it, and one could not call what one saw sadness: it was more like apathy, utter absence of feeling of any kind. I saw him put his hand in his shaving bag, look again, then become panicky. He turned everything out on to the ledge but he couldn't find what he was looking for. I looked straight into the mirror where my face appeared cracked and webbed. He turned to me.

'Have you a razor blade?' he said. To the other side of him I saw the two Glasgow boys grinning at me. One of them drew an imaginary razor across his throat, a gesture which in spite of his smile I interpreted as a threat.

I knew what would happen to Lecky if he turned up on parade unshaven. I looked down at my razor and remembered that I had some more in my bag. I looked at the grinning boys and knew that they had taken Lecky's blade.

I said to him, 'Sorry I've only got the one blade, the one in the razor.' After all, one must be clean. It would be a disgusting thing to lend anyone else one's razor blade: why, he might catch a disease. It is quite easy to do that. There's one thing about the Army: it teaches you to be clean. I was never so fit and clean in my life as during that period I spent in the Army.

I turned away from the grinning Glasgow boys and looked steadily into the mirror, leaning forward to see beyond the cracks as if that were possible. I shaved very carefully, because this was an important day, cutting the stubble away with ease under the rich white lather, the white towel wrapped round my neck.

I should like to describe that parade in detail, but I can't now exactly capture my feelings. I began very clumsily, not quite in tune with the music of the pipes, but, as the day warmed, and as the colours became clearer, and as the sun shone on our boots and our badges, and as I saw the brigadier standing on the saluting platform, and as my body grew to know itself apart from me, I had the extraordinary experience of becoming part of a consciousness that was greater than myself, of entering a mysterious harmony. Never before or since did I feel like that, did I experience that kinship which exists between those who have become expert at the one thing and are able to execute a precise function as one person. It was like a mystical experience: I cannot hope to describe it now. Perhaps one had to be young and fit and proud to experience it. One had perhaps to feel that life was ahead of one, with its many possibilities. Today I think of Sheila and a childless marriage and a solicitor's little office. Perhaps, for once in my life, I sensed the possible harmony of the universe. Perhaps it is only once we sense it. Not even in sex have I felt that unity. It was as if I had fallen in love with harmony and as if I was grateful to the Army for giving me that experience. And after all, at the age I was at then, it is easy to believe in music: I could have sworn that all those men were good because they marched so expertly to the bagpipes, and that anyone who was out of step was bad, and that it would be intolerable for the harmony to be spoilt. I began to understand the corporal, and to be sorry for those who had never experienced the feeling that I was then experiencing.

At that moment all was forgotten, the angry words, the barbaric barrack room, the eternal spit and polish, the heart-break of those nights when I had lain sleeplessly in bed watching the moonlight turn the floor to yellow and hearing the infinitely melancholy sound of the Last Post. All was forgiven because of the exact emotion I felt then, that pride that I had come through, that I was one with the others, that I was not a misfit.

When the parade was over, I ran into the barrack room with the others. There was no one in the room except Lecky who was lying on his bed. I went over to him, thinking he was ill. He had shot himself by putting the rifle in his mouth and pulling the trigger. The green coverlet on the bed was completely red and blood was dripping on to the scrubbed wooden floor. I ran outside and was violently sick. Looking back now I think it was the training that did it. I didn't want to be sick on that clean floor.

Of course, there was an inquiry but nothing came of it. No one wrote to his M.P. or to the press after all, not even the public schoolboys. There was even a certain sympathy for the corporal: after all, he had his career to make and there were many worse than him. The two public schoolboys became officers: one in the Infantry and the other in education. I never saw them again. Perhaps the corporal is a sergeant major now. Anyway, it was a long time ago but it was the first death I had ever seen.

The sheriff leaned down and spoke briefly to the two youths after they had been found guilty. He adjusted his hearing aid slightly though he had nothing to listen for. He said,

'If I may express a personal opinion I should like to say that I think the jury were right in finding you guilty. There are too many of you people around these days, who think you can break the law with impunity and who believe in a cult of violence. In sentencing you I should like to add something which I have often thought and I hope that people in high places will listen. In my opinion, this country made a great mistake when it abolished National Service. If it were in existence at this date perhaps you would not be here now. You would have been disciplined and taught to be clean and tidy. You would have had to cut your hair and to walk properly instead of slouching about insolently as you do. You would not have been allowed to be idle and drunk. I am glad to be able to give you the maximum sentence I can. I see no reason to be lenient.'

The two of them looked at him with insolence still. I was quite happy to see the sheriff giving them a stiff sentence. After all, the victim must be protected too: there is too much of this molly-coddling. I hate court work: I would far rather be in my little office working on land settlements or discussing the finer points of wills.

It was a fine summer's day as I left the court. There was no shadow anywhere, all fresh and new, just as I like to see this town.

The Hermit

ONE DAY A HERMIT came to live in or rather on the edge of
our village. The first we knew about it was when we saw the
smoke rising from one of the huts that the R.A.F. had left
there after the war. (There is a cluster of them just outside
the village, tin corrugated huts that had never been pulled
down, though the war was long over and their inhabitants
had returned to their ordinary lives in England and other
parts of Scotland.)

Shortly afterwards, Dougie who owns the only shop in the
village told me about the hermit. The shop of course is the
usual kind that you'll find in any village in the Highlands
and sells anything from paraffin to bread, from newspapers
to cheese. Dougie is one of the few people in the village that I
visit. He served in Italy in the last war and has strange stories
about the Italians and the time when he was riding about in
tanks. He's married but drinks quite a lot: he doesn't have a
car but goes to town every Saturday night and enjoys himself
in his own way. However, he has a cheerful nature and his
shop is always full: one might say it is the centre of gossip
in the village.

'He's an odd looking fellow,' he told me. 'He wears a
long coat which is almost black and there's a belt of rope
around him. You'd think in this warm weather that he'd be
wearing something lighter. And he rides a bicycle. He sits
very upright on his bicycle. His coat comes down practically
to his feet. He's got a very long nose and very bright blue
eyes. Well, he came into the shop and of course I was at
the counter but he didn't ask for his messages at all. He
gave me a piece of paper with the message written on it.
I thought at first he was dumb—sometimes you get dumb
people though I've never seen one in the village—but he

88

wasn't at all dumb for I heard him speaking to himself. But he didn't speak to me. He just gave me the paper with the messages written on it. Cheese, bread, jam and so on but no newspapers. And when he got the messages and paid me he took them and put them in a bag and then he put the bag over the handlebars and he went away again. Just like that. It was very funny.

'At first I was offended—why, after all, shouldn't he speak to me?—but then I thought about it and I considered, Well, as long as he can pay for the messages why shouldn't I give them to him? After all he's not a Russian spy or a German.' He laughed. 'Though for all he said he might as well be. But I don't think he is. He wasn't at all aggressive or anything like that. In fact I would say he looked a very mild gentle sort of man. The other people in the shop thought he was a bit funny. But I must say that after you have travelled you see all sorts of people and you're not surprised. Still, it was funny him giving me the paper. He wore this long coat almost down to his feet and a piece of rope for a belt. I don't know whether his coat was dirty or not. He looked a very contented sort of man. He didn't ask for a newspaper at all, or whisky. Some people who are alone are always asking for whisky but he didn't ask for any. All he wanted was the food. He had a purse too and he took the money out of the purse and he gave it to me. And all this time he didn't say anything at all. That has never happened to me before but I wasn't surprised. No, I'm telling a lie. I was surprised but I wasn't angry. They say he's living in one of the R.A.F. huts and he doesn't bother anybody. But it's strange really. No one knows where he's come from. And when he had got his messages he got on to this old bicycle and he went away again. He sits very upright on his bicycle and he rides along very slowly. I never saw anyone like him before. It's as if he doesn't want to speak. No, it's as if he's too tired or too uninterested to speak. Most people in the shop speak all the time—especially the women—but he wasn't like that at all. Still if he can pay for his messages he can be a Russian for all I care.' And he laughed again. 'There are some people in the village who don't pay for their messages but I can't say that about him. He paid on

the nail. And after all, in my opinion, people talk too much
anyway.'

TWO

That evening, a warm, fine evening, I was out at a moorland
loch with my fishing rod, pretending to fish. I do this quite
often, I mean I pretend to fish, so that I can get away from
the village which I often find claustrophobic. I don't really
like killing things, and all I do is hold the rod in my hand
and leave it lying in the water while I think of other things
and enjoy the evening. Out on the moor it is very quiet and
there is a fragrance of plants whose names I do not know.
I might mention here that I was once the local headmaster
till I retired from school a few years ago, and I live alone
since my wife died.

I was born and brought up in the village but in spite
of that I sometimes find it, as I have said, claustrophobic
and I like to get away from it and fishing is the pretext I
use. When people see you sitting down dangling a rod in
the water they think you are quite respectable and sensible
whereas if you sat there and simply thought and brooded
they would think you eccentric. It's amazing the difference
a long piece of wood makes to your reputation among your
fellow-men. After all if I never catch anything they merely
think I am a poor fisherman and this is more acceptable than
to think me silly.

So I sit there by the loch with the rod dangling from my
hand and I watch the sun go down and I smell the fragrance
of the plants and flowers and I watch the circles the fish make
in the water as they plop about the loch. Sometimes if there
are midges I am rather uncomfortable but one can't have
everything and quite a lot of the time there are no midges.
And I really do like to see the sun setting, as the mountains
ahead of me become blue and then purple and then quite
dark. The sunsets are quite spectacular and probably I am
the only person in the village who ever notices them.

So I was sitting by the lochside when I saw the hermit
at a good distance away sitting by himself. I knew it was
the hermit since there was no loch where he was and no

other person from the village would sit by himself on the moor staring at nothing as the hermit was doing. He was exactly like a statue—perhaps like Rodin's 'Thinker'—and as Dougie had said he looked quite happy. I nearly went over to talk to him but for some reason I didn't do so. If it had been anyone from the village I would have felt obliged to do so but as I didn't know the hermit I felt it would be all right if I stayed where I was. Sometimes I watched him and sometimes I didn't. But I noticed that he held the same pose all the time, that statue-like pose of which I have just spoken. I myself tend to be a little restless after a while. Sometimes I will get up from the lochside and walk about, and sometimes I will take out a cigarette and light it (especially if there are midges), but I don't have the ability to stay perfectly still for a long period as he obviously had. I envied him for that. And I wondered about him. Perhaps he was some kind of monk or religious person. Perhaps he had made a vow of silence which he was strictly adhering to. But at the same time I didn't think that that was the case.

At any rate I sat there looking at him and sometimes at the loch which bubbled with the rings made by the fish, and I felt about him a queer sense of destiny. It was as if he had always been sitting where he was sitting now, as if he was rooted to the moor like one of the Standing Stones behind him whose purpose no one knew and which had been there forever. (There are in fact Standing Stones on the moor though no one knows what they signify or where they came from. In the summer time you see tourists standing among them with cameras but it was too late in the evening to see any there now.) I thought of what Dougie had said, that the hermit was not in the habit of buying whisky, and I considered this a perceptive observation. After all, lonely people do drink a lot and the fact that he didn't drink showed that he was exceptional in his own way. It might also of course show that he didn't have much money. Perhaps he was not a monk at all, but a new kind of man who was able to live happily on his own without speaking to anyone at all. Like a god, or an animal.

All the time that I had been looking at him he hadn't moved. And behind him the sun was setting, large and

red. Soon the stars would come out and the pale moon. I
wondered how long he would stay there. The night certainly
was mild enough and he could probably stay out there all
night if he wished to. And as he obviously didn't care for
other people's opinions he might very well do that. I on the
other hand wasn't like that. Before I could leave the village
and sit out by myself I had to have a fishing rod even though
I didn't fish. And people in the village knew very well that
I didn't fish, or at least that I never brought any fish home
with me. Still, the charade between me and the villagers had
to be played out, a charade that he was clearly too inferior
or superior to care about. In any case there were no new
events happening in the village apart from his arrival there
and therefore I thought about him a lot. It was almost as if I
knew him already though I hadn't spoken to him. It was as
if he were a figment of my imagination that had taken shape
in front of me. I even felt emotions about him, a mixture of
love and hate. I felt these even though I had only seen him
once. Which was very odd as I had always thought myself
above such petty feelings.

Sometimes I thought that I would take a book out with
me and read it in the clear evening light, but that too
would have made me appear odd. Fishing didn't matter
but reading books did, so I had never done that. The
hermit wasn't reading a book but I knew that if he had
thought about it and were a book reader he would have
taken his book out with him and not cared what people
thought of him. He wasn't a prisoner of convention. I on
the other hand had been a headmaster here and I could only
do what I thought they expected of me. So I could dangle a
rod uselessly in the water—which I thought absurd—and I
couldn't read a book among that fragrance, which was what
would have suited me better. After a while—the hermit still
sitting throughout without moving—I rose, took my rod,
and made my way home across the moor which was red with
heather.

When I arrived back at the house Murdo Murray was
as usual sitting on a big stone beside the house he was
building. He has been building this house for five years
and all that he has finished is one wall. Day after day

he goes out with his barrow to the moor and gathers big solid stones which he lays down beside the partially finished house. As usual too he was wearing his yellow canvas jersey.

'Did you catch anything?' he asked and smiled fatly.

'No,' I said, 'nothing.'

He smiled again. Sometimes I dislike intensely his big red fat face and despise him for his idleness. How could a man start on a project like building a house and take such a long time to do it and not even care what people thought of him or what they were saying about him? Did he have no idea what excellence and efficiency were? But no, he lived in a dream of idleness and large stones, that was his whole life. Most of the time he sat on a stone and watched the world go by. He would say, 'One day there will be a bathroom here and a bedroom there,' and he would point lazily at spaces above the ground around him. Then he would sigh, 'My wife and daughters are always after me, but I can't do more than it is possible for me to do, isn't that right?'

After a while he would repeat, 'No man can do more than it is possible for him to do.'

As a matter of fact, we often wondered what he would do with himself if he ever finished the house. It looked as if he didn't want to finish it. The children of the village would often gather round him, and help him, and he would tell them stories as he sat on a big stone, large and fat. No, he would never finish the house, that was clear, and for some reason that bothered me. I hated to see these big useless stones lying about, as if they were the remnants of some gigantic purpose of the past.

'It's a fine evening,' he said.

'Yes,' I said, 'and there are no midges. Why don't you go out fishing yourself?' I added.

'Me?' he said and laughed. 'I've got enough to do without going fishing.' And he probably believed that too, I thought. He probably believed that he was a very busy man with not a minute to himself, living in the middle of a world of demanding stones.

'If you want any help at any time,' I would say to him,

but he would answer, 'No, I'll do fine as I am. If I don't
finish the house someone will finish it.' And he lived on in
that belief. He shifted his big buttocks about on the stone
and said, 'I used to go fishing in a boat as you know but
I never fished in the lochs. And that was a long time ago.
Myself and Donald Macleod. We used to go in the boat but
I never fished the lochs.'

I felt a tired peace creeping over me and I didn't want
to speak. Sometimes it's impossible to summon up enough
energy to talk to people, and I had been growing more and
more like that recently. I was growing impatient of those
long silences when two people would sit beside each other
and think their own thought and then finally like a fish
surfacing someone would speak, as he was doing now,
words without meaning or coherence. Why was it necessary
to speak at all?

He was clearly finished for the day, sitting there surrounded by his stones. Perhaps he didn't want to go into
the house in case his wife would nag him for not making
quicker progress. Or perhaps he was sitting there inert as
a mirror on which pictures print themselves. In the late
light I thought of him as a man sitting in a cemetery with
rough unengraved headstones around him. Perhaps that
was what our world was like, a world of rough unengraved
headstones, lacking the finished marble quality of the world
of the Greeks.

Big rough stones on a moor.

I left him there and went back to my own house.

When I entered I felt as I usually did the emptiness and
the order. The TV set, the radio and the bookcases were
in their places. The mirrors and ornaments and furniture
had their own quiet world which I sometimes had the eerie
feeling excluded me altogether. When my wife was alive the
furniture seemed less remote than it seemed to be now. Even
the pictures on the walls had withdrawn into a world of their
own. I often had the crazy feeling that while I was out my
furniture was conducting a private life of its own which froze
immediately I went in the door and that sometimes I would
half catch tables and chairs returning hastily to their usual
places in the room. It was all very odd, very disquieting.

I went to the cupboard and poured myself a whisky and then I sat down in my chair after switching on the fire and picking up a book from the bookcase. It was a copy of Browning's poems. Since I retired I had far more time to read books unconnected with my job but I didn't read as much as I thought I would have done and what I did read was mostly poetry. I would find myself falling asleep in the middle of the day and at other times I would pace about the house restlessly as if I were in a cage which I myself had built.

· In the chair opposite me my wife used to sit and she would tell me stories which I hardly ever listened to. 'Kirsty's daughter's gone away to London again. They say that she's walking the streets, did you know?' And I would raise my head and nod without speaking. And she would go on to something else. But most of the time I wouldn't say anything. It didn't occur to me that my wife's remarks required an answer and for a lot of the time I couldn't think of anything to say anyway. Her voice was like a background of flowing water, a natural phenomenon which I had grown accustomed to. Now there was no voice at all in the house except that of the radio or the TV and the only order was that which I imposed on it.

I sipped my whisky slowly and read my Browning. I drank much more now since my wife had died. Not that I actually loved her, at least I didn't think I did. It had never been a large glowing affair, much more a quieter, more continuous fire. We were companions but we weren't lovers. But in those days I didn't drink as much as I do now. I think loneliness and drink must go together, as Dougie said. Browning however is another matter. His poetry has a cheerful tone and apparently he was in love with his wife, or at least so we must believe after that dramatic elopement. I wondered what people would say of me when one day I died in this house as was inevitable. They might perhaps say, 'Well, he was a good headmaster. He was interested in the children,' and then dig a hole and leave me there. On a cold rainy day perhaps. And then they would go back to their homes. But they wouldn't say that I had done much for the village. I hadn't, of course. I had always been a stranger in the village. Just as much as the hermit was. Though I had been born and brought up in it. My thoughts had never been the villagers' thoughts, they aspired to be higher and more permanent than the business of the seasons.

It was strange how quiet I felt the house was, as if I missed that monotonous conversation, as if even yet I could see someone sitting in that chair opposite me. But of course there was no one. Mary was rotting away somewhere else, in the damp ground. In spite of Browning. In spite of the illusion of warmth which the whisky momentarily gave me.

THREE

The following day I met Kirsty who was on her way to Murdo's house with a cup in her hand. An evil Christian woman. She never misses a sermon or Communion, going about in her dark clothes, with her thin bitter face and the nose from which there is a continual drip like the drip from a tap which needs a washer and which makes an irritating sound in the sink night and day. She has a daughter who appears periodically from London and then goes away again after a stormy period at home. It is said that she works in the streets in Soho but this may be malice since anyone as bitterly Christian as Kirsty is must be brought down to the level of common humanity and given at least one cross to bear in this fallen world.

It wasn't long before she spoke about the hermit.

'It shouldn't be allowed,' she said.

'What shouldn't?' I asked.

'That man living in that hut. Why, he might be a murderer or a thief or a gangster. The police might be after him. I wonder if anyone's thought of that.'

'Oh, I shouldn't think he is any of these things,' I said. 'I'm told he looks very gentle.'

'So do lots of murderers,' she said sharply.

I didn't want to be talking to her. I was listening to the music of the sea which one can hear clearly on a fine summer's day, as this one was. Sometimes when I hear it I don't want to be talking to people at all. What would we do without this ancient unalterable music which lies below our daily concerns and which at the deepest moments of our lives we hear eternally present, with its salty echo?

'And the children,' she said, 'go to school past that hut. He might . . . why, he might . . .'

'He might what?' I asked.

'Well, you see things like that in the newspapers. People like that. Strangers, lonely people. He might give them sweets and . . .'

'I don't think you need to worry about that,' I said. In the old days I wouldn't be talking to her at all but now I would talk to anyone. That was the extent of my downfall, of my hunger. Would it not be better for me to be like the hermit if I had the strength?

After a while she said, 'Some people say that it's love that sent him here.'

'Love?' I asked.

'Yes, the women say that. That he was disappointed in love. That is why they say he won't speak to anyone.'

I nearly laughed out loud. Why should this woman be talking to anyone about love? This bitter salty woman addicted to Christianity? Why, her greatest love was to shake hands with the minister.

'It's possible,' I said. 'It's possible.'

'Well, why else would he not speak to anyone? Aren't we good enough for him? I don't suppose he even goes to church. He has never been, so far. And perhaps where he came from he never went to church either. I think the minister should go and speak to him. If he was led into the ways of God he might improve.'

The music of the sea was growing louder and louder. Why don't you drown her, I pleaded with it. Why don't you extend your salt waters as far as her skinny body and drown her? Why do you allow her to exist to spoil the harmony of your ancient world? She is the thorn in our side. Her confidence, her silly confidence, is the thorn in our side. Her invincible vanity is obscene.

'What does the minister say to that?' I asked her.

'No one has spoken to him about it,' she said.

'Well, then, perhaps you should do that,' I said. 'Perhaps that is your destiny. To bring his soul to God.'

'More than him need to be brought to God,' she said with a wicked sidelong glance. I knew she was getting at me, because I never go to church myself.

'Oh,' I said, 'I'm not a hermit. And how's your daughter?'

'What do you mean?' she asked.

'Oh, I was thinking about the hermit,' I said. I had slid the knife into her for a moment and I was pleased with myself. She had thought I was talking about her daughter haunting the streets of Soho in her hunting leathers, though I couldn't imagine that large gross body exposing itself in a nightclub or walking the yellow streets of London. I almost laughed out loud again.

'Well,' she said, 'I think something must be done about him. What does he do with himself anyway? He may be plotting something. For all we know he may be a spy. And the children should be protected.'

'From what?' I said.

'I told you already from what. But you don't care. Maybe you're a friend of his. I don't know why else you're standing up for him.'

'I'm not standing up for him,' I said. 'I'm only saying that he hasn't bothered anyone.'

'Mm, well, he may do it some day.' And she closed her bitter lips like a trap. 'It's not natural for a man to be going about not speaking to anyone. If a stranger comes to the village he should act like the other people in the village. And anyway he's dirty. Everybody says that. He wears a piece of rope for a belt. And his coat is dirty.'

I nearly said that we are all dirty but I didn't. I just wanted her to go away and leave me alone, to leave this day with its flowers growing wild around us and the sun so warm in the sky. She disfigured the day in her black clothes. And she disfigured the music of the sea. And anyway it was said that when her own daughter was home there was nothing but quarrels between them, and their own house was dirty with half empty coffee cups lying about and her daughter getting up at noon and sometimes later. And sometimes the house was not cleaned for days and weeks. Still one couldn't say these things to her. I wondered how the hermit might have handled her. Perhaps his muteness might have reduced her to an equivalent silence. The triviality of her mind confounded me. And all the time I wished to listen to the music of the sea.

She twisted the cup in her hands and said finally, 'Well, anyway, that's what I say, and remember that I said it when what will happen happens. Things that aren't natural will cause trouble, you mark my words. I'm surprised that you, a professional man, should be standing up for him.'

A few years ago she wouldn't have said that to me. She wouldn't have dared to talk to me in that way. Of course a few years ago I wouldn't have talked to her at all. But now she knew I had no power and no position and she thought she could say what she liked to me. Before my retirement she would have been bowing and scraping and speaking only when she was spoken to and she would have thought it a great honour that I spoke to her at all.

'Anyway,' she said, 'I've got to go to Murdo's house. I've got to borrow a cup of sugar.'

'And you certainly need it,' I said to myself as she walked away. 'I know of no one who needs sugar more than you do.'

Still, one couldn't live on the music of the sea. That was certain. I couldn't understand why she was going on about the hermit. She didn't truly understand as I did the spiritual threat he represented. She was only saying what she did because she had to have something to talk about and it was the same with the other women of the village who had concocted a story of disappointment in love as the reason for the hermit's appearance among us. Naturally when confronted by an inexplicable silence they had to explain that silence in their own way, and in a way flattering to themselves. It was funny that they should not have thought of him as a monk sworn to silence, they had thought of him as a man condemned to silence by love. What vanity, what enormous vanity! As if only women could be responsible for that final silence! Why, I could think of a thousand other things that might have condemned him to silence. He might for instance be a poet or physicist whose world had failed him. It seemed to me highly unlikely that his silence came from a failure in love, except perhaps from a failure of love as far as people in general were concerned, and not exclusively women. Soon, however, a myth would grow up about him that he had left the world he had lived in simply because he had been jilted and that this had perhaps driven him 'beyond the seas' and so on. What a trivial explanation! Only I, I was convinced, knew the meaning of his silence for I partially shared silence with him. Only I knew the depth of the question that he posed. Only I knew the threat his silence was to us.

FOUR

I was born and brought up in this village and there is nothing about it that I do not know. For me it is a processional play with continually changing actors. Some are playing at one time sad parts and then happy ones. There is the tragedy of the Disappearing Daughter, the comedy of the Appearing Son. The young man for some reason puts on the disguise of the middle-aged man and the middle-aged man in turn the guise of the old man. The earth flowers with corn and then becomes bare again. The sky at moments is close and then as far away as eternity. I have seen the people, as if they belonged to the Old Testament, bring water from the well, and later sit down in front of television. I have sat in a small dark desk in the school and then I have sat in the headmaster's study. I have taught the little children about the thunder and the lightning and the autumn moon.

When I was seventeen years old I left the village to go to bare beautiful Edinburgh where I attended university in the large shadow of its history. There I read many books and studied many subjects. There, I, with others of my generation, wondered what the world means and what its destiny is. I have walked down Princes Street among taxis black as hearses and been entranced by the theatrical appearance of the castle where the drama of history repeats itself nightly. That lighting told nothing: it was merely a fairy lighting. In youth one devours everything indiscriminately and ideas arrive like revelations. I have walked among the leaves of autumn tormented by desire and nostalgia as if for a world once known that would never return. I have read and debated there, but the skies had no answer to give, only the bloody answer of past history. As I listen to the sound of the sea here so I listened to the sound of the traffic there and found it senseless. I read whole libraries driven on by my merciless mind and at night I went to plays and to the cinema. One night I met a boy from our village staggering drunkenly about the street but he did not know me. The city is a terrible place of stone and mad music, of white-faced clocks and massive buildings. The city has no meaning at all, and its plays are not real plays, they are sensational potboilers.

There one day in the library I met Mary. I took her to the cinema and then back to her house where in the shadow of her garden her face shone with a greenish light, as if she had caught some demonic plague. Later she was to become my wife. In those days she used to play the violin and she told me she used to ride on horseback down the leafy avenues of Edinburgh. Together we explored the city; much later we married and I brought her to the village. She had no Gaelic and couldn't understand what people were saying unless they spoke English which some of them couldn't do very well. She did not love the seas and moors as I did. We never returned to Edinburgh, mainly because of her. At the time I did not understand that her reason for not returning there was not that she didn't love it but rather that she loved it too much and she couldn't bear having to be parted from it a second time. How self-satisfied I was! She stopped playing the violin. The two of us would sit in the evenings in our respective chairs staring at TV or at each other after I had finished my schoolwork. My schoolwork was my whole life. The little children came to me in all their freshness and were taught. Their sorrows and joys and tendernesses were my own. The secret innermost recesses of their minds were open to me. Life flooded from them to me and daily I was renewed. My life had purpose and meaning and desire. But my wife sat alone in the house in a village which she did not understand—not its secret linguistic recesses, its private clannish corners—and I did not think of her or if I did I put the thought away from me as if it were an unbearable wound. I did not wish to think of the life she led, of the life that she didn't lead. No concerts, theatre, cinemas. She did not have her orchestra as I had, she didn't understand the changing drama, closed to her because she could not speak Gaelic. She was an unwilling bored spectator all her days in this village. I condemned her to imprisonment. She was as much a prisoner as if I had passed sentence on her like a judge.

One day I arrived home unexpectedly from school and found her in the kitchen with the violin in her hand. As soon as she saw me she rushed out of the room with it and put it away again in the room from which she had taken it. I couldn't make out whether in fact she played it when I was away at school or not. She could have been a great violinist, they had said that, and I believed it. But she had given it up for me. And what had she seen in me after all? Perhaps the fatal attraction of the exotic. What is your island like, she would ask me. And I would say, The people are so pleasant and friendly. And then of course there is the sea and the moor. It is always beautiful and always changing. And she had found it boring and uncaring. What was the sea to her? Merely a meaningless mass of water. Then later she was seized by cancer, that terrible disease without music or mercy. Maybe I had condemned her to it. Some nights she would scream with pain and I could do nothing. The violin lay unused in the unused room. Bare loved Edinburgh with its resounding streets was far away. My wife's hair had become grey and hung in wisps from her head. She had nothing to say to me at all and I nothing to her. She would drink whisky and cradle the bottle absently in her arms as if it were a silent violin. And the village went on with its own concerns. What had I done to her? What did life mean after all? Was this what it meant, all it meant? All the books and philosophies, was this what they all came down to after all? All those nights of blazing discussion and debate, was this the end of them? Truly, it was. Truly it was a possible ending that had happened.

FIVE

The following day I talked to the postman. He had brought me an airmail letter from my brother in New Zealand and a catalogue from Athena. Athena is a firm which sells reproductions of paintings by post and I already had quite a lot of these, some by Van Gogh, some by Dali and some by Breughel. My favourite painters are in fact Vermeer and Breughel: I admire Vermeer for the cold mathematical clarity of his paintings and Breughel for the strange spawning fertility of his. Sometimes I myself try to paint but the paintings I have done are vicious and aggressive and inhabited by small murderous animals in an atmosphere of intense silence as of a desert.

The postman is called Hunchbacked John and he takes his time delivering the mail, sometimes stopping here and there for a cup of tea and telling everybody who he's got letters for. He knows of course when there is a letter from the Income Tax people but he is also adept at knowing all other official notifications even when there are no clues on the outside of the envelope. Season after season: spring, summer, autumn, and winter, Hunchbacked John whose gaze is not much above the level of the ground drives fiercely forward on his errands.

I accepted the thin blue letter from him and the catalogue and then asked him if he ever delivered any letters to the hermit.

'Not at all,' he said, 'he never gets any letters. None. From anywhere.'

'That's odd,' I said. Had he seen him?

'Saw him once,' he said. 'He was sitting in front of the door mending an old coat.'

'How had he looked?'

'He looked very contented. He didn't speak to me. I said, 'Hello, it's a fine day', but he didn't answer. He just carried on sewing his coat. I think he must have been mending it or putting on a button.'

'And he never got any letters?'

'No, none at all. He doesn't expect any. I can tell. I can tell the ones who get letters. Some people in this village never get any letters, others get a lot of letters. Some people don't expect any letters. The hermit doesn't. You can see by his eyes.'

'By his eyes?'

'Yes, by his eyes. He's a man who has given up expecting any letters.'

For some reason the words so baldly spoken depressed me. What must it be like to expect nothing, not even letters? I myself looked out for the mail every day. Sometimes I would stand at the window watching Hunchbacked John making his way along the road and wondering if he was going to come up the path to my house. Other times I would stand at the door of the kitchen and look down the lobby. I would wait for the letter box to click and then I would watch the white letter drifting on to the mat, like manna from heaven. I would walk down the lobby watching the letter which might after all be an agent for a complete transformation of my life, the letter innocent and packed with joy, or menace. Every day, once a day, I am like a small child waiting to see what Santa Claus has placed for him on the Christmas Tree. Maybe somewhere in the vast world a being known or unknown has decided to write to me, to me alone, with news of the greatest importance. This letter has perhaps travelled the whole world by boat or plane and then finally arrived on this mat in this particular lobby. What magic has taken place? What news lies inside that white square? How could one exist without that opening to the universe? How could one live without that possibility of renewal or resurrection?

I said to him, 'Why don't you . . .'

'Why don't I what?'

'Why don't you pretend you have a letter for him and then you could . . .'

'Why should I do that?' he interrupted bluntly before I had finished.

'Well, you could go to the door and you could see inside his house and see what he does with himself.'

'Oh, I couldn't do that, I couldn't do that.' And then for good measure, 'Oh, I couldn't do that.'

His literal mind repeated the phrases as if he were an old rusty bell.

'Of course not,' I sighed. 'But think . . .'

'No, I couldn't do that.' And he slowly raised his eyes towards me like a gun being swivelled upwards and a light of intelligence dawned in his eyes as if he were to say, 'Yes, I know you. I understand you completely.' But he didn't say anything except, 'I know the ones who will never get letters. The hermit will never get a letter. He has given up. He has given everything up.' What a desolate phrase. I wondered if Hunchbacked John himself ever got any letters, trudging on as he did through all the seasons of the year delivering other people's mail. Looking down at the ground he would see the stones and the changing seasons but he would never receive a letter of his own. It would be like a bank teller perpetually counting other people's money.

How strange the world is and how many different kinds of people there are! Before him we had a postman who rode a bicycle. He was a young boy and he was so careless that if no one was at home he would place the letter under a stone at the door. Another time, because he hadn't closed his bag properly, about twenty letters were blown away on the wind, some of them never recovered. Another time we had a very religious postman but the less said about him the better.

'Well,' he said at last, 'I must be on my way.' I hadn't offered him tea though perhaps that was what he wanted. Not that I particularly wanted to read my brother's letter which was usually nothing more than a statement that he was still alive: he never had any news of the slightest interest to me.

'Well, cheerio just now then,' I said and watched him steadily plodding away with his sturdy limited literal mind and his crooked body. No, of course he wouldn't have the imagination or the daring to do what I had suggested. And yet it would have been interesting. If I had been the postman I would have done it. Such a little white lie. But then much might have been discovered.

Perhaps for instance the hermit's house was full of books like my own. Or perhaps there was nothing at all there, not even furniture. Just the fire and perhaps one table and one chair like those in a meagre painting of Van Gogh's. He too had been a kind of hermit. That was why I liked his work so much, though not as well as I liked Breughel's or Vermeer's. The truth was that I too was like the hermit but without his extreme daring. At least I spoke a language and he didn't. Even that night on the moor I was conscious of the language of the birds which they speak among themselves. Perhaps he wasn't even conscious of that. For everything and everyone has a language except perhaps for the stones which Murdo brings home on his wheelbarrow. Even the sea has a language. Even a violin. Everything has a language but only human beings have learned to hide and not reveal their world with their language. But to have a language and choose not to use it, what a terrible decision that must be! What a terrible burden that must be, to act like a stone and be a human being! What bitter strength it must take to sustain that. What power or immense disgust. Or perhaps what holiness, as if one were talking to God and human language was seen as a slimy repulsiveness, like an old fish quivering in one's hand, like a rotten old jellyfish, phosphorescent and rotting.

SIX

There is in the village a girl called Janet. She is about eighteen years old, with long black hair, a diamond-pale face, and a marvellous bum. Every morning, cool in her morning suit, she passes my house on her way to the school where she is some sort of clerk though her spelling, according to the new headmaster, is not so good. But what does she need to be a good speller for, with that cool infuriating body, those legs, that bum?

It was a day of steady rain, drip drip, the hole appeared in the ground. The minister was speaking into the high wind, his cloak flapping about him. I could hear carried on the wind, but vaguely, as if they were the last gasps from a dying mouth, words like 'resurrection' and 'eternity'; but I was watching the coffin. We approached after a while that deep narrow hole and each took a tassel and lowered the coffin, hexagonal like a bee's hive, into the earth, into the hole. We lowered it slowly. The wreaths, few and small, were laid near the hole.

And coming home the first person I saw was Janet, her lovely alive body, eel of the day. And it was then that that sickness struck me, ridiculous object of sixty years old. The young girl was a banner, unconscious and engraved, against the stupidity of death. In bed at night I thought of her and I dreamed of that hole in the ground and above it, flourishing like a young tree with buds in its branches, Janet's young body, potent with fruit and blossom.

Every morning she passes my house in the early dew, sometimes wearing her yellow dress with its yellow collar, trim and young and cool. Who cares if she can spell or is educated? I create a picture of an Einsteinean mind being put to rout by the movement of a girl's leg or foot, by the motion of her bum. It is a plague that I suffer from, O I know it, I'm old enough to know that, but I'm not old enough to cure myself of it. Where is the remedy for it after all? Mary was never as beautiful as Janet, not even in her youth. Her face always had a serious expression as if she were concerned with some deep problem that she could never solve. Janet's face has no deep problem imprinted on it. It has grown like a blossom, it is itself, it is not concerned with the meaning of the universe, it is as natural as a leaf in the sky. Its coolness is that of the diamond, its perfection its own. I know that I am speaking words without meaning but I cannot stop myself. Language is running away with me because language cannot explain what I feel, because a young girl's perfection is beyond language, because her perfume unconscious and fertile is what language cannot embrace. There are mornings so perfect that language cannot express their perfection since the mornings are so new and our language is so corrupted by evil and distortion and double meanings and used ancient stained blasphemies. To know these mornings is to be young again. O if only I could . . . just once . . . in my youth . . . those legs, those eyes . . . that face. The sickness is delirious and intolerable. It can have no cure. It must only be endured. I have often thought of this. Life and mathematics are different from each other. Problems in mathematics are soluble since mathematics is only a game after all. Problems are insoluble in life since life is more than a game. One can often find no solution to them. The reason why we look for solutions is because we confuse mathematics with life. And that is the worst of all confusions. It is also the confusion that when a problem is spoken it is halfway to being solved. Hermit, wherever you are just now, have you solved your problems because you refuse to speak them? No, all you have done is to take all these problems on your back, since you know there is no solution. Your silence perhaps is the most honourable stance of all. You at least are not a ridiculous old man writing his silly lyrics to a young girl. At least you have saved yourself from that.

SEVEN

The day I came home unexpectedly from school and she was cradling the violin on her breast like a child . . . . That is the image I shall always keep with me. For she couldn't speak Gaelic. And people would sometimes come to the house and speak Gaelic and she couldn't understand them. And her English sounded foreign among all these people. An alien with a violin which she couldn't bring herself to play and which remained silent in that room since no one could appreciate her music. Once a man from the village came to the house and asked if she would play the violin at a local dance. He thought he was doing her a favour bringing her into the middle of things. Her violin—at a village dance. I nearly laughed out loud. The meeting of two worlds in absurdity. Naturally she wouldn't play. She was too shy to. And so the whirligig of time brings in its revenges, its mockeries, its echoes. She had no language at all to speak to them, not even the language of music. For they were used to the melodeon glittering in the moonlight in the open air at the end of the road not in fact far from the hermit's home. Their music was not the music of excellence and rigour, it was the music of abandoned gaiety, amateurish music. But she had been trained in a harder tougher more silent school, where the music was squeezed out of the soul and was not an emanation of the body. And often at night as the sun goes down I hear her voice crying with pain. Sometimes I feel that I am going out of my mind.

★   ★   ★

I opened my brother's letter from New Zealand. He wrote:

> I hope you are well. We are all well here. I hope you got the photos I sent you recently: Anne in bathing costume with myself and the kids on the beach. Colin is getting to be a great rugby player. I could send you some newspapers but I suppose you wouldn't like them. They are all full of rugby and I don't think that would interest you. Still, if it would, say the word. The weather here is as good as usual. It's not very unlike the weather in the Old Country. Anne is always asking about you. Do you remember the time we went off fishing and left her and Mary together? Ever since then she asks for you a lot. I suppose you are still reading as much as ever. I don't find much time for reading myself. We are thinking of going to Australia for our holiday later on. Why don't you come out here yourself sometime? You'd be very welcome as you know and we could show you the sights. There's plenty of room in the house. But I suppose you won't come. The plane wouldn't take long to bring you out. The children would like to see their uncle of whom we talk so much. Flora is doing well at school, you would be proud of her. I think she might end up as a teacher some day. She gets good grades in her subjects and she's also good at sport. She was chosen for her hockey team and she had a part in the school play at the end of term. She reads a lot too, like you. You would like her. Well, if you do want the newspapers let me know. But as I say they're mostly about rugby. And if you want to come out you have only to say the word.

Hermit, where are you sleeping tonight. On your stone with your rope about your middle like an ancient monk lying down in the light of the moon?

And Janet, where are you sleeping? In your murderous innocence, also in the light of the moon, not the marble moon of the Greeks but the moon of romance, a moon that transforms you into a princess in a fairy story with a knife between your thighs. Or a poisonous rose.

*   *   *

While the whole village sleeps, the only sound the barking of a dog; the village with its ills and joys, with its closed rancours and its open happinesses, with its ancient sorrows and its lethal struggles, eels everywhere squirming and writhing in that sea of moonlight.

EIGHT

I determined to do it and I did it. At three in the morning I got up from my bed and set off to the hermit's hut. Of course I didn't want anyone to see me and that was why I waited till then. The village was not like the city, it would not have people walking about it at that time. People went to bed late—about midnight—but you wouldn't see them again till the late morning. I had never been about at night in the village before, or rather so early in the day. The place was so quiet sleeping under the moonlight. I went along the road: once a cat ran from one side to the other but I saw nothing else and all I heard was the sound of the stream which flowed quietly along to the sea. I didn't know what I was going to see; surely the hermit would be asleep. And in any case his door would be locked. I didn't know why I thought this but I did. I myself have never locked the door but for some reason I was sure that he would lock his. At the place where the huts were it was said that there once used to be a ghost. Once a young man from the village was coming home from the town and he said he saw it. It was walking towards him and its face was green. He arrived at his parents' house in a state of shock. He was home on leave at the time. Shortly afterwards he went away and his ship was blown up in the Pacific and he was drowned. But I wasn't afraid of ghosts and have in fact never believed in them. I didn't even believe in the young man's story.

It was strange to be up and about at that hour in the morning. It almost gave one a feeling of power as if one held the destiny of the village in one's hands, in one's mind. People are so helpless when they are asleep, so defenceless. I felt like a burglar creeping about the night. What treasure was I seeking, what golden hoard? I kept on the grass verge of the road as if it was necessary for me to make as little noise as possible. I wondered what I would say if I met anyone. Perhaps I might say that I couldn't sleep. And that was true. I didn't sleep well. After my wife died I didn't sleep for a month though I took sleeping pills every night. Still, it was unlikely that I would meet anyone.

The village itself looked strange in the moonlight as if it had been painted in yellow. I hated yellow. It reminded me of sickness and of old faces and of autumn and of the neon lights of the city. I felt as if I myself were coloured a sickly yellow, as if I were suffering from some sickness such as jaundice.

Eventually I reached the hut and slowly went up to it. As I have said I didn't know what I was doing. I peered through the window but there was complete darkness. I put my ear to the door as if I were a doctor sounding someone's chest, someone who was dying of an incurable disease. As I did so I saw in the light of the moon that there were names and drawings on the door. The drawings were of naked women and of Cupids and hearts with arrows stuck in them. I tried to imagine those airmen going up into the sky in their planes, all rushing out from the hut and setting off into the blue sky at the time of the Battle of Britain. Of course none of them had done that at all. I was only remembering old films. And on the door too someone had carved the name of Vera Lynn. It was strange to think of the hermit lying in such a hut, as if at any moment he might take wings and set off into the sky, masked and helmeted. Into that freedom, that false freedom. *Per ardua ad astra*. Beyond that hut I could see the Standing Stones shadowy in the moonlight, ancient and undecipherable. The tinny hut looked like an accordion, yellow and black. I wondered whether the hermit was lying there asleep in a bed or on the floor in a blanket. I nearly knocked on the door as if I wanted to ask him a question though I didn't know what I should ask him. Perhaps I should ask him, What is the meaning of the world?

Perhaps in fact he was one of those airmen returned again to the huts out of nostalgia. But I knew this wasn't true. I knew that he had nothing to do with planes or the war. His war was a different one. He had perhaps been wounded in some irretrievable way and that was why he didn't speak. It would be so easy to take a plane up from that hut and set off into the illimitable blue, it would be too easy. All the time I stood there I didn't hear a sound. For all I knew there was no one there at all. For all I knew the hermit was sleeping outside and watching me at that very moment.

I turned away from the door and made my way home quickly as if someone was after me, as if I was being hunted. I actually began to run, looking behind me to see if anyone was following me, but I didn't see anyone. All there was was the moon high in the sky like a big stone and the shadows and yellowness. When I got to my room I was panting as if I had committed some terrible crime. I lay in my bed sleeplessly thinking of him lying in bed, not realising that a stranger had been looking at him through the window, listening at his door. I was ashamed of myself. I was frightened of something that was happening to me that I did not understand.

NINE

I don't think I have yet mentioned Kenneth John, though I did intend to, since he becomes important later. Kenneth John is older than me and has been married in the village for many years to a woman he met after he had given up sailing, late in life. He says himself that he has been everywhere, China, Australia, New Zealand, South America. 'In China,' he once told me, 'they leave food for the dead people. They think they will rise again and eat it.' And he looked at me with his small wrinkled face. 'That's right,' he would add, 'they do that. And they leave drink for them as well at the graves. Would you believe that?' And I would pretend that I hadn't heard any of this, since he clearly enjoyed telling an 'educated' man something new.

'Women,' he would say, 'They're no use on board ship. What use are they to any man? Wasn't it a woman who ate the apple? Doesn't it say that in the Bible? And it was because of them that sin came into the world.' At other times he would tell me that Edgar Wallace was the best writer in the world. According to him, he had read all his books.

'But there's nothing in the world like being on a ship on

a fine day with the water stretching away from you on all sides, no land to be seen anywhere. In my youth I used to climb up into the sails. Up the masts. And I would look up and the sea was miles below. And sometimes you would see porpoises playing in the water.

'Have you noticed,' he would say earnestly, looking into my face, his thin red nose almost quivering and his teeth, discoloured by tobacco, clearly visible, 'Have you noticed,' he would say, 'that women never play? They're so serious all the time. That's the thing I have against them. Women,' and he would spit on the ground, 'what use are they to man or beast?

'When I came home first I wouldn't have anything to do with the land. I would go up to the town and I would watch the ships coming in and going away. I would stand there for hours and think of all the places the ships might be going to. And it took me all my time not to go on board one of them and sail away in it. But I was married then and I couldn't do that.'

He had pictures of sailing ships in his house and he and his wife would sit by the fire and he would tell me stories and his wife would say nothing much except that at intervals she might sigh heavily and murmur, 'He could have been a captain. He could have been a captain.' They said that she was very hard on him and made sure that he kept the house clean. One day I went in and found that all the pictures of sailing ships had been taken down and new wallpaper put up. I never saw them again. In the East, he would say, the women went about with veils on their faces and they would look down at the ground. They would never look up at you at all. They were very obedient in the East. 'But when I got married first I didn't want to stay in the house at all. I would walk about the village and sometimes I would go out fishing on a boat that I had. But it was like being on a pond and I gave it up. There was no excitement at all, no excitement.

'But I'll tell you about women. They have no humour in them. The things they worry about, like whether you are wearing a good suit or not, things like that, and whether the floor is clean. And one day I broke an ornament and she went on about it for months.

'And why do we settle down? Let me ask you that. You're an educated man. You tell me that.'

'I don't know,' I said.

'Well, I'll tell you,' he said, his little rusty moustache quivering. 'It's because we're frightened. That's the reason. And don't let anyone tell you different. That's the reason and the only one. There was a boy once who went up to the top of the mast and he started screaming. He was frightened, you see, looking down into the water. That's the way we are. But I was never frightened up in the mast. Never.

'We're frightened, that's why we take up with women. I used to go into port and enjoy myself and get drunk. There was a lot of fighting and drinking in those days. But I would have ended up as a drunkard, you see. But in those days I didn't care. And so, I thought to myself, do I want my freedom so that I'll be a drunkard? And what do you think is the best thing?' he asked.

'To have your freedom and not be a drunkard,' I said.

'You can't have the two of them,' he said. 'Not at all. You can't have the two of them. Women. They've caused all the trouble in the world. We're frightened and we don't know what the world is about. That's the truth. No one knows what's right and what's wrong. You read books and you find that out. When I came home first I didn't want to have anything to do with the land. I was like a man in a cage. I used to go up and down the village as if I was on the deck of the ship. Why can't we have a house on water, on the sea? They have that in some countries. That's what I would like, a house on the sea. They have that in China and some places.' And he would spit in the fire. And then he would say, for his stories were always the same, 'Do you know the strangest thing that ever happened to me? One night I went into this bar in Australia. Myself and some of the boys from the ship. And do you know who I saw there sitting in the bar? It was Squinty. You remember Squinty, he had a squint eye. Well, he saw me and I was going over to speak to him but he turned away from me. He wouldn't even recognise me. He was playing dominoes with some people and he was wearing an old ragged coat. And he came from the same village as me. He didn't want the people at home to know what he had become. He had gone to the dogs, you see. To the dogs. He must have been drinking hard. A lot of these boys never write home, you know. No one hears of them, they go to the dogs and they drink. Well, he didn't speak to me and he had been brought up with me. And he was drinking wine. Imagine. He was like a Frenchman, drinking wine. And he just turned away from me. It was a queer thing.

'Well, that night, I went into the lavatory in that pub and I looked in the mirror that was there. I had been drinking, you see, and my face was red and my eyes were red. And I said to myself, "Where are you heading for, boy? Where are you sailing your ship?" That was what I said, "Where are you heading for, boy?" And that was why I got married. My wife is older than me and she had been looking after her parents, that was why she didn't marry before. She was very sweet to me at first, she wouldn't say anything about my suit then. Nothing but, "You do what you like, Kenneth John, you always do that anyway." That's what she used to say. But then she began to buy things for me, handkerchiefs and things like that. Then she would buy shirts and at last she bought me a suit. And ever since then I've been in a cage. Women. What can you say about them? They brought sin into the world. The Bible teaches you that. But you've never seen a woman on board ship, have you? They would be no good. They would be putting on their lipstick while water was coming in in a storm. You have to have some give and take on board a ship if you don't want a fight. That's what I say.'

And his wife would murmur, as she sat by the fire, 'He could have been a captain, you know. He could have been a captain.'

TEN

On a fine day our village looks very peaceful and lovely. The blue sea is in the distance, with perhaps a ship passing by, smoke coming out of its funnel, and behind us there is the moor which is wine-red with heather. In the early morning you can hear cockerels crowing from here and there, their red claws sunk in the earth, their coloured brassy heads extended. Sometimes too you hear a dog barking. The Clamhan, in front of the house, may be hammering a post into the ground or mending a net in front of his door. Or at this time of year you may see people going down to the corn which is yellow in the sunlight. As the sun comes up, small boys start running about. As the day passes and it gets hotter, you may see them building tents. I don't know why they do it, but on the very hottest days you will find them sitting inside these tents and trying to make fires just like Red Indians.

And beside me Murdo sits regarding his unfinished house.

Practically every morning I go over and talk to him after I have got up and have had my breakfast (which usually consists of a cup of tea and a slice of bread). I don't eat much for breakfast. I offer as usual to help him but he says as usual that he doesn't need any help. His two daughters who have now left school are usually going about the outside of the house with pails and pans. They are not pretty, are in fact spotty with very thin legs.

Today he tells me about a big stone that he has taken home on his barrow the day before.

'There were hundreds of worms below it,' he tells me. 'Hundreds of them. All so red. I could have killed them all but I left them for the birds.'

I thought: the birds will make songs from them. There are in fact few animals to be found around here. No foxes, rabbits, weasels. Hardly any wild life at all. And no trees. I miss the trees. That is why I often think of Edinburgh. For some reason I specially associate trees with university days. But this is a bare bleak island especially in winter when it's wet and misty.

'What are you doing today?' Murdo asks.

'Oh, I've got a few letters to answer,' I say. I have no croft and this means that time passes very slowly for me. I am driven to reading and writing, since I don't visit many houses in the village apart from Dougie's. As I'm talking to Murdo the idea comes to me that I could buy milk from Janet's parents. They sell milk and are one of the few families in the village that have a cow. It strikes me as a good idea. In the distance I see a cow eating some clothes on a clothes line at the far end of the village: that was what brought the idea into my mind. I can't make out whether it is Stork's house or that of the two sisters Maclean, one of whom has been lame all her life, practically, from polio. Sometimes I find the mornings here exhilarating and most beautiful; other times I find them boring. There is a rhythm about the place, a slow deep sometimes exasperating rhythm. People talk slowly, chewing every word and releasing it as if it were a precious possession whose extinction in air is to be mourned. Language almost becomes like tobacco which is as much chewed as smoked.

'Ah, well,' says Murdo, 'it's going to be another fine day.' And I say that in my opinion it probably almost certainly will be. And I know that all we are doing is making sounds, that silence embarrasses us after a while, and we are not using language at all but making comforting motions. I look down at Murdo as he sits on his stone: there are red hairs in his nostrils. He looks like a large plump red animal. He is, as I have said before, like a man surrounded by tombstones. And I try to penetrate his mind but I often feel that he has no mind to penetrate. He has never thought about the world, about its meaning. He is, it seems to me, perfectly suited to his environment in a way that I shall never be. His environment makes on him the few demands that he can easily cope with. Day after day he rises from his bed and day after day he takes out his barrow and brings his stones home. It is almost as if he has forgotten what the stones are for, as if the house itself which is his ultimate aim has receded into the distance and it is only now and again that he recalls that the purpose of gathering the stones is for building the house. A slight breeze ruffles his canvas jersey which moves slightly about his big belly.

After a while he says, 'Isn't that Kirsty there setting off to the shop?' It is indeed. Then he says, 'I hear that her daughter is in London.' He looks at me slyly. 'I hear she's on the streets there. Someone from the village saw her.'

I was in London myself once. I remember it as a vast place glittering with cinemas and theatres and people with braziers selling nuts late at night on the streets. That was a long time ago when I was at a Conference.

A long time ago too Murdo was in the War, in the Fusiliers as he says himself. He says that he didn't like the French, that they were tricky and lazy, not like the Germans. I can't imagine him ever having done anything that required rapid movement but I suppose that he must have been young once as we all were.

'Well,' he says at last, 'this won't do,' and he levers himself slowly to his feet and goes to his barrow. His hands must now be cracked and broken with the weight of the vast stones that he brings home.

'And I'd better be going too,' I say. At least he has something definite to do every day: I don't even have that. He spits on his hands and then takes the handles of the barrow and sets off to the moor again. I watch him as he plods steadily along. Then I turn back into the house.

After a while I take out my writing pad and my pen and write to my brother. The phrases flow easily. They are always the same phrases. My brother is a salesman in New Zealand and I really don't know him very well. Even when we were young I didn't know him: he was much more active than me and though younger he always beat me in fights. I was amazed at times by his aggressiveness and frightened by his mad possessiveness for property. We used to play sometimes in the attic of my parents' house and he would turn somersaults over the rafters which I couldn't do.

Now I have little to say to him but I feel a certain obligation to write. 'Everything here is as usual,' I write, feeling at the same time that the phrase is perhaps slightly too literary, too stilted. I have no gossip to give him. I merely tell him that all is well, that I hope his children and wife are well, that I am sure he is busy and so on. We don't communicate more than I communicate with Murdo and his work appears to me to be precisely as useful as Murdo's.

The only event that has happened is the arrival of the hermit but for some reason I don't tell him about it. I don't tell him how much I hate that mirror image of myself, which is yet stronger than me, at the end of the road. I don't tell him of my obsession with that being, because I have so little to do. I don't tell him that the reason I hate the hermit is because I am frightened I will become like him, for at the moment at least I still hold on to language, though it is possible that that too may go. I don't however want the New Zealand papers, I tell him. Rugby is the very least of my interests in life, it is certainly far on the periphery.

My brother was always far better at sport than me. I was never any good at any sport, neither football nor shinty, nor any other game that the boys used to play. I was never any good at rock climbing or jumping across streams. Perhaps that is why I became a schoolmaster in the end. I can't at any rate imagine myself as ever having been a salesman. That would be the final indignity of all.

I seal the letter slowly and after I have done that I turn to one of my paintings. The painting shows a thin Van Gogh-like figure sitting on a thin gaunt chair while above it as if about to jump on it a picture of a wild cat. On the wall which is red there is a framed picture of a violin.

ELEVEN

I went to see Janet's parents to ask them about the milk. When I went in, the mother and father stood up from the table where they had been eating but Janet remained where she was. She continued eating, her head downcast, concentrated on her plate. O, my dear, chewing your bacon and eggs, so shy and sweet. Her father said, 'Come in, come in. What a stranger you are!' And he held out his hand. His wife, flurried and red-cheeked, was wiping her hands in her apron.

It wasn't often that they saw the ex-headmaster of the school in their house. I didn't know them very well—they lived at the far end of the village—all I knew was a story about her husband who used to go about selling fish that they found him one night drunk in a ditch, his horse and cart at the side of the road, the horse patiently cropping the grass. Now of course he had a van.

'Would you like something to eat?' he asked me.

'Yes, something to eat,' said the mother, as if she had just thought of it.

'No, thanks,' I said. 'As a matter of fact I came to ask a favour.'

All this time Janet was eating her bacon and eggs and drinking her tea. They had put a chair out for me and I sat down and they sat down but of course they wouldn't continue with their food. I shouldn't have come at that time, I thought, they took their meal later than me.

'And what favour is that?' said her father. 'I'm sure if we can help you we will.'

'Surely, surely,' said his wife, mumbling downwards at the table.

'Well,' I said, 'it occurred to me the other night that you sell milk. And I would like to buy some. I'm getting tired of the milk I have. I would like really fresh milk.'

They both smiled now that they knew that the favour didn't make a great demand on them. Janet looked up at me for the first time, her fork and knife still in her hand. I suppose I thought even Juliet had to eat sometimes, while the tragedy raged around her. There was a spot of yellow egg on her lip.

'Oh, I think that could be arranged,' said her father. 'I'm sure we could do that. Couldn't we do that?' he asked his wife.

'Oh, surely, surely,' she said. 'Surely,' she repeated. She was about the same size as her daughter but her jowls had begun to grow fat and gross and there were lines round her eyes.

'I was thinking,' I said, 'that Janet could leave the milk at the foot of the path when she was on her way to school.'

Janet gave me another piercing glance and then looked down at her plate again.

'I'm sure Janet would do that,' said her father. 'I don't see why she shouldn't do that. She's passing the house every day anyway. You'll do that, Janet, won't you?'

'Yes, that will be all right,' said Janet speaking for the first time.

'Well, that's fine then,' said her father. 'That's fine.'

'Well then . . .' I prepared to get to my feet and leave.

'You can't go without a wee one, eh?' he said looking at his wife and then away from her. She pursed her lips but said nothing. He poured me out a large dram and one for himself.

'Since you won't take anything to eat,' he explained. 'Your good health then. It's better than milk anyway.' His wife glanced at him for a moment and then glanced away again.

'Your health,' I said and drank.

Janet was still eating, her small composed head with the black hair bent over the plate.

Her father said laughingly, 'She'll bring the milk all right if she can stop thinking of Dolly.'

'Dolly?' I said.

'Oh, he works on the fishing boats,' said her father. 'They're thinking of getting married. He's a nice boy.'

'But the young ones nowadays,' said her mother in a sudden rush of nervous words, 'look for a house and washing machine and TV straight away.' It sounded as if she spoke that short speech often.

Dolly, dark and threatening, on the fishing boat.

'That's right enough,' said the father as if placating his wife for having taken the whisky. 'It's not like in our day. They want everything at once nowadays. And they marry so young. Still, maybe it keeps them out of mischief.'

'Oh, I'm sure she'll remember the milk all right,' I said. Janet looked at me again quickly and directly as if she had discovered some hidden meaning in my words.

'Yes,' said her mother, 'that's what they all do. They marry without thinking. And then they find themselves without a house or furniture. But Dolly is a nice enough boy.'

'I'm sure he is,' I said.

I put down the glass and got to my feet. 'Well,' I said, 'thank you for the dram. I didn't expect it and as you say it's better than the milk. Janet will bring the milk then?'

'Oh, you can be sure of that,' said her father. 'You can be sure of that.'

I went out of the house wishing in a way that I hadn't visited them. But as I had sat there in their kitchen while they ate their food a thought had hovered around the depths of my mind, a vague shape, a fish from the shadows, and it had something to do with Janet and her approaching marriage. But I couldn't think exactly what it was. It was a phantom thought without substance. But I felt that I knew Janet. I felt I knew her utterly and completely. And the thought had something to do with that feeling.

But I had been shaken by the news of her approaching marriage, if it were true, though after all it was natural enough that a girl like her in the ripeness of her youth, a fruit on the tree, would soon marry. And Dolly, this boy without a shape or a face, this enemy from the sea, would enjoy her. Well, youth must go its own way though it was bitter to think of it. How bitter it was to think of it.

And her parents looked so ordinary too, so ordinary and covetous. For even I could not miss the fact that they had jumped at the chance of selling the milk to me. And all her mother could think about was washing machines, houses and TV sets. Perhaps Janet was like that too. I was sure she was. In the mornings when she got up she probably switched on Radio Luxembourg, listening to the disc jockey with his false voice introducing songs about Love to people who lived in streets that he didn't know but pretended that he cared for. Ah, I thought, the whole world is a cemetery and among the gravestones there walk the young ones with their Japanese transistors, small as diamonds, while a voice which could be the voice of anyone tells them that love is a song, that it consists of flowers and furs, that disease and cancer are for the old, that the young lovers walk armoured in crystal and carrying boxes of chocolates to the world's end. And that always waiting for the young girls are boys like Dolly, ordinary and loveable and uncomplicated and faithful, thinking only about fish and TV sets, huge dark oceans and washing machines.

TWELVE

Shortly after this a strange thing happened. Kenneth John, whom I have already mentioned, left home. It was just before five o'clock in the evening, about the time that the bus passes through our part of the village on its way to town that I saw him walking down the path from his house, carrying what I was sure was a kitbag and wearing a dark well-pressed suit and a jaunty dark hat. He seemed for the moment much younger and spryer than I had ever seen him. As he walked down the path his wife shouted after him, 'Come back, Kenneth, come back.' It must have been her voice penetrating my room through the open window that brought me in turn to my own door to find other villagers at their own doors watching. It was an almost Victorian scene, for by this time there were two women against whom Kenneth's wife was leaning in a state of collapse while at the same time she was shouting and crying. I had never seen anything like it in the village in my whole life. But the crying and shouting seemed to have no effect upon Kenneth John who proceeded on his way with a youthful jauntiness, without looking back, presenting an adamantine back to those behind him involved in the Victorian scene.

For some reason that I didn't understand till afterwards I took it on myself to run down to the road to try and reason with him. Perhaps deep in the back of my mind was the envious thought that he should not be allowed to leave behind him all that made life precious and poisonous to him, especially at an age when all confidence in himself should have long ago been burned out in the ashes of defeat. So I half ran along beside him as he made his way to the bus-stop, trying to keep up with him as in the past I had tried to keep up with bigger boys when we were on our way to school. The large red sun was shining dead ahead of us as we walked along, Kenneth John silent, his hat tipped back slightly on his head as in the days of his youth when he had set off for Hong Kong, San Francisco and Valparaiso. He didn't speak to me at all. And behind me his wife was shouting and crying while the two women, one on each side of her, sustained her.

'Where are you going?' I asked him. 'What do you think you're doing?' But he didn't answer.

'Have you any idea where you're going?'

Still he didn't answer.

A white handkerchief flowered from the pocket of his jacket and he looked very spruce and composed as if he had come to a definite conclusion about his life.

'You can't leave your wife like this,' I insisted. 'She has always done her best, hasn't she? She has done what every wife in the village does. She has looked after you all these years.' My voice sounded hollow and false as if I were creating for the moment opportunist reasons for him to return to his world.

'You don't have anywhere to go,' I said. 'You'll regret it.' But he remained silent as if he knew he was listening to lies or as if he did not recognise my right to speak at all. In a short time the bus would be coming and it would be too late.

'You're too old,' I said, 'you can't go away now.' And all the time I was talking to him I was thinking perhaps of myself, that what he was doing was what I should have done, and I was afraid that he would succeed in doing what I myself had failed to do. We walked on steadily side by side till finally we reached the bus stop, where we halted. He turned away from me and looked back to see if the bus was coming.

'Think what will happen to your wife,' I continued unashamedly. 'Think what her life will be like without you. She has always done her best. You can't deny that. It's an illusion,' I said, 'you're not young any more. San Francisco and Hong Kong are in the past. You can't go back there. They won't take you.'

And as I spoke I heard the bus coming. His wife was now rushing towards us, large and fat. She was standing beside us, tears streaming down her fat decaying face, while she looked at him, spruce and jaunty, with longing and amazement. As the bus stopped and the driver leaned down, Kenneth John, still in silence, climbed the steps and walked to the back of the bus and sat down. The driver gazed from me to his wife and back again in astonishment and seemed to be about to say something but then he put his foot on the accelerator and drove off leaving the two of us standing in the middle of the road watching the bus, red and lumbering, make its way to town. Kenneth John didn't even look back to wave.

I helped his wife up the path to her house and left her there with the two women who had been helping her before.

Then I returned to my own house as empty-hearted as if I had suffered a defeat. For a long time I seemed to hear Kenneth John's wife crying. She didn't really understand what had happened. I knew it was the hermit's fault. I knew that it was his apparently free life, brooded upon by Kenneth John, which had caused this dash for an illusory freedom. She didn't know this because she lived in the flesh but I who lived in the spirit knew what was happening. I knew what illusory flag he was following on his way to his youth and Hong Kong. I knew what danger the hermit represented to the village. That poor penniless man would find himself haunting the shops and streets of the town as well as the quays and the ships, and would discover to his cost that he was now not a figure of the future but rather a figure of comedy and pathos in a world which had left him behind.

And the poor woman he had abandoned didn't even know what had happened to her. She didn't know the true significance of the event. Soon she would waken up and find herself alone by the fireside and as if stunned would mope and moan, comforted by women who were secretly laughing at her. In fact the whole village would turn on her a face of apparently comprehending sorrow while there would be another face beneath that one, of revengeful laughter. A Janus Hallowe'en mask.

And yet I couldn't help admiring Kenneth John, if he was in his right mind and not sleepwalking into the past. But perhaps he hadn't been in his right mind. Perhaps his apparent composure, his hat set at a cocky angle, his spotless suit, were all disguises for a final desperation which was almost suicidal in its deeper meaning. He had stepped out of the village into nothingness. He was hanging over the water, high in the swaying mast.

THIRTEEN

After some time the Clamhan who stays opposite me came up to the house. Most of the time he sits at the door wearing spectacles and mending a green net so that he looks like a spider intently weaving, his spectacles glittering.

'What did you think of that, eh? Eh?' he said.

'I don't know what to think of it,' I said.

'No,' he said, 'no.' And then, 'He was never interested in the land, you know. Never. Or in the peats. He didn't care for them. Imagine him going away like that though. He had some spunk, eh? Some spunk.' As if pleased with the word, like a girl with a new necklace, he repeated it. As if he had found a new shining word. And this was not my imagination, for the Clamhan was the local bard who composed songs about any event, unusual or comic, that happened in the village. Such as, for instance, his song about the cart that had fallen down, loaded with peats, while the horse broke one of its legs. Perhaps he was thinking of composing a song now. Perhaps this was what he did, immersed in his green net all day.

His small eyes peered at me.

'Nothing's gone right since that hermit came,' he said. 'I wonder what he does with himself all day. Do you know anything about him?'

'No,' I said.

'I wonder what he eats. Do you think he's got the Pension? They say that he goes to the well for water since there is no water in the house. And there's Murdo. He'll never finish his house.' And he glanced over at the pile of chaotic stones. 'He was in the Army with me, you know. Always idle. He never finished anything. And what do you think of Kenneth John, eh? Who would have believed it?' His little eyes darted about all the time, as if he were a bird perched on an invisible twig.

'What is happening to the village at all?' he said. No one was coming out of Kenneth John's house. Already it had taken on the appearance of a grave.

'I'll tell you something,' he said. 'She had him on a tether. Maybe I would have left her as well.' His own wife was large and heavy and submissive. 'Maybe,' he repeated, 'I would have left her years ago. But I don't know. I don't know if I would have the courage. The strength. I don't know.' And he gazed down at the ground and following his eyes I too gazed down at the ground to see his large shapeless boots with the dust of the road on them.

'He mentioned the hermit to me, you know,' he said.

'He mentioned him to me once. He said that he would like to stay in the house by himself just like that. He never settled down, you know. He always wanted to be sailing. He had no time for the land. I don't understand that. I don't understand that at all. Still,' he said, 'I was never away from the island like him. The ones who were away from the island never settled down. Think of Kirsty's daughter. She never settles down.' And he looked at me askance with his small glittering eyes.

And I was thinking, I never ran away. In spite of everything I never ran away: that must count for something surely. In our mortal accounts that must count for something. Perhaps what lay between us was love after all, in spite of the cancer, in spite of the pain.

'Did he say anything to you while you were talking to him?' he asked.

I looked up startled, as if I had forgotten that he was still there. 'No,' I said, 'he didn't say anything. Nothing at all.'

'That's funny,' he said, 'that he shouldn't have said anything. It's funny, that. You would think he would have said something.'

'What should he have said?' I asked.

'I don't know,' he repeated. 'You would think he would have said something.'

'Well,' I said decisively and almost angrily, 'you can take it from me that he didn't say anything.'

What are you angling for, I was thinking. Are you trying to get hold of some saying that you can use for your poem when you can get round to composing it? His small bald head glittered in the light, like a small round stone.

'I just thought,' he said, 'that he might have said something.' I was too tired to repeat what I had already said and anyway we both stopped talking as we saw Kenneth John's wife making her way to the peatstack. Her body was bent as if under a great weight. She stood for a moment at the peatstack as if wondering why she was there. Then she put out her hand slowly as if in a dream, and withdrew two peats. She stared down at them for a while and then still very slowly and with bent back she made her way back to the house. His gluttonous quick eyes followed her movements.

'Well,' he said, 'well . . .'

'I'm sorry,' I said, 'I have to leave you now. I have things to do.'

'Of course, of course,' he said. 'Of course.' I went into the house without looking at him and I poured out a very large whisky and drank it in one gulp. It was very bitter and raw. When I was finished I could have smashed the glass against the wall. For a long time I stood there thinking of many things. Then I went up to the room where the violin was and I got it down. I played a little, with joy and sorrow. I drew the bow rapidly across the strings and it was as if new confident feelings sprang up in me. I played as I watched the Clamhan make his way down to his house and his eternal green net. Then I laid the violin down on the table—heart-shaped, coffin-shaped violin—and I almost wept for us all, for our strange hectic appalling lives. For poor Kenneth John's wife who at that very moment was probably sitting next door staring into the fire which she had composed from her black peats.

FOURTEEN

The following morning as usual I went down to the foot of the path to collect the milk from Janet. She was as usual cool and lovely, wearing yellow, her black hair contrasting strongly with her dress. I held the bottle of milk in my hand as I said, 'Another fine morning.' She said it was.

I continued, 'I've been thinking about what your mother said when I was at your house.'

She looked at me without speaking.

'About marriage and so on,' I said. 'It's true that people need money before they marry nowadays.' I just wanted to talk to her and didn't really know what I was talking about. Cool mornings, how I love you before the sun rises demanding decisions. 'One needs a house,' I went on. 'It must be even worse now, more expensive. Furniture and so on. When are you thinking of getting married?'

'I don't know yet,' she said. 'We aren't even engaged.'

'Oh,' I said, 'I thought . . . But still, it won't be long, a girl like you.' I thought I could see the cool wheels of her mind turning in the still early morning. After what seemed a long while she suddenly said in a hard cold voice, 'There's a suite I saw in the town. It's a red suite. Two chairs and a sofa. I've never seen one like it anywhere. That's what I would like to get.'

'A suite,' I said.

'I saw it in the window of a shop in the town,' she said. Dead ahead of her the sun was red and strong in the sky. A suite of clouds overhead.

'How much does it cost?' I asked.

'Two hundred pounds,' she said. And then she added, 'I must be going or I'll be late.' And she set off at her brisk pace, her lovely cool body moving so freely. In the early cool morning. Towards the red sun. A suite at two hundred pounds. Why had she mentioned that? I considered it and as I was considering it the hermit rode past on his bicycle on his way to the shop for his messages. At least that was what I assumed. It was the first time I had seen him close to. He rode past me, his eyes fixed straight ahead, looking neither to right nor to left. Janet had turned her head to look at him but he hadn't looked at her. He was sitting upright on his bicycle, the belt of rope around him. Coming out of the red sun he looked like Death in his dark dirty clothes. His face looked tanned and unlined. Was the brown complexion from the sun or was it that he was naturally dark-skinned? He was like a man I had once seen who cleaned chimneys and had a small black dog running after him as he rode along on his bicycle. And he looked so contented, so silent, so harmonious. As if he was happy enough to rest in his silence. His coat was very long, almost touching his shoes. 'How do you live?' I spoke to him in a whisper. He never bought whisky or beer, just bread and cheese and butter and so on. Maybe he was a monk or a holy man. He hadn't looked at Janet at all. He was much stronger than me.

I returned slowly to my house, the bottle of milk in my hand, thinking about the red suite which Janet had seen in the shop window and whose like was not to be found anywhere. Her voice had sounded hard and greedy as she spoke. Even in the dew of the early morning which hung on flowers with its silver bells wobbling there was greed and hardness.

The hermit passed out of my sight on his way to the shop with his piece of paper in his pocket.

FIFTEEN

On the Friday night I went to visit Dougie as I often did. Sometimes we played chess and sometimes we just sat and talked. I had forgotten that his brother and wife were home on their annual summer holiday from Edinburgh but when I did go in, there they both were.

'Come in, come in,' said Dougie. His house is the largest in the village and with its large windows gives a wide panoramic view of the sea. His brother Edward and his sister-in-law Lorna got to their feet from the sofa on which they had been sitting as I entered. Edward is a commander of some sort in the Navy and is a silent perceptive tall darkish man who bears about with him the easy manner that is common to successful people. His wife on the other hand looks a bit neurotic and stringy and restless. She drinks vodka. After the usual greetings, I was given a drink.

'And how are you enjoying your holiday?' I asked them.

'Oh, fine,' said Lorna. 'We were out fishing in a boat today.'

'We didn't catch anything,' said Edward.

'Like me,' I said. 'I fish in the loch but I never catch anything either.'

I like sitting in the evening with professional people, preferably ones who have come from outside the village and are there only for a short time. I should have preferred to talk about books, art, music and even philosophy but one can't have everything. Lorna pretends she's cultured but she isn't, though she goes to the theatre quite a bit as her husband is often away from home. She told me that Edinburgh is as beautiful as ever and just as cold.

Dougie said to her, 'Of course you know that Charles's wife came from Edinburgh, but she settled here quite happily.' I was surprised that his own wife wasn't in the room till I remembered that there was an evening service on in church. He looked flushed as if he had been drinking rather heavily before I had come in. We talked about Edinburgh for a while, Edward silent as usual.

'I go to quite a lot of things at the Festival,' said Lorna. 'But there's so much. It's impossible to see it all.'

I envied her for that. To be able to see all the drama that one wanted to watch, to hear all the music that one wished to hear, and to see films and read books, that would have been my ideal life. But of course it was impossible.

'It's quite often the case,' she said, 'that people who come from the city settle down happily in the country.' She was referring to my wife.

'Yes,' said Dougie, 'she settled down happily here. I don't know whether she missed Edinburgh at all.'

'A little,' I said. 'She missed it a little. Especially in the spring.'

'I should like to stay here all the time,' said Lorna sipping her vodka.

I discounted what she said. They all spoke like this when they came home for their annual holiday but they would have been driven out of their minds by boredom if they stayed for more than a month and especially if they remained during the winter.

So much of language is lying, polite lying but still lying. The difference between men and animals is that men lie, animals don't. This thought came to me quite clearly as I listened to her bubbling on.

There were so many definitions about the difference between men and animals but this one came to me quite effortlessly. Man is the animal who lies. I sipped my whisky meditatively till Dougie suddenly said, 'The hermit was in today. He was getting his provisions.'

'Hermit?' said Lorna looking up.

'Oh yes,' said Dougie, 'didn't I tell you we have a hermit? No one speaks of anything else here these days.'

He went over and refilled our glasses, all except Edward's, who said that he was quite happy. One could never tell what he was thinking. He let his wife do all the talking and sat quietly listening. One couldn't imagine him saying or doing anything rash. One could however quite easily imagine him in a coldly computerised ship absorbed in instruments.

'Isn't that interesting?' Lorna said to him. 'A hermit. Imagine that. And, tell me, does he stay entirely by himself?'

'He does,' said Dougie, 'in one of those huts the R.A.F. used to have. And he doesn't speak to anyone. He had the same routine today,' he said, turning to me. 'He took a piece of paper out of his pocket with the messages written on it but he didn't speak. Funny thing, the people are turning against him. The children were shouting after him after he got on his bicycle.' As he was speaking Dougie's voice was becoming slurred and lazy.

'I can imagine it,' I said.

'And another odd thing. Stork's wife went in front of him in the queue, though she had no right to. But you know her. And he just accepted it. I wondered what he would do. He just smiled but didn't say anything.'

'Is he dumb or something that he doesn't speak?' Lorna asked.

'Not at all,' said Dougie. 'He's not at all dumb. He just doesn't want to speak at all.'

'That's really odd, isn't it, Edward,' said Lorna. One couldn't imagine her not speaking.

'It is,' said Edward.

'Still,' said Dougie, 'if he's got the money I'm not going to refuse him his provisions.'

'Well,' I said, 'I suppose you're right.'

'How do you mean?' said Dougie, as if he had detected some hint of argumentativeness in my voice.

'It's just,' I said, 'that he doesn't seem to care for the village. He belongs to it and he doesn't belong to it. He's a villager and he isn't.'

'Well,' Dougie answered, 'he's a man anyway. He's a human being.'

'I suppose,' I said, 'it depends on how you define a man.'

'I don't understand,' said Dougie again.

'Well,' I persisted, as if driven by an inner compulsion, 'a man is someone who lives in society. He can't be said to live in society.'

'That's true in a way,' said Lorna as if thinking deeply and trying to follow what we were saying. Her husband was taking it all in, his hand round his glass which had still quite a lot of whisky in it.

'Yes,' said Dougie, 'but you're not going to say that because he doesn't bother with the village I shouldn't sell him provisions.'

'And there's another thing,' I said. And I told them about Kenneth John and what the Clamhan had told me.

Lorna looked at me in astonishment or pretended astonishment. 'Well, there seems to be goings on without doubt. And where is he now?'

'I don't know,' I said and then speaking to Edward, 'He used to be in the Merchant Navy, you know, in his youth. He was all over the world. Hong Kong, Valparaiso, the lot. He's well over seventy now and he just went and left his wife like that. He took the bus and he wouldn't speak to anyone and he went off to town and no one's heard of him since.'

'Isn't that extraordinary?' said Lorna, finishing her vodka. 'Isn't that quite extraordinary?' Her husband agreed that it was.

'You say he was over seventy?' he said.

'Yes,' I said, 'and he left his wife. He had apparently been saying that he should be like the hermit, fancy free. Of course he never really settled down.'

'More of us should do that,' said Dougie jokingly as he refilled the glasses again, including mine. 'More of us should do that. Leave our wives, I mean. A lot of people want to do that.'

'Do you want to do that?' said Lorna to her husband.

'No, I'm quite happy. In any case, I'm in the Navy already.'

'I'll tell you something though,' said Dougie whose voice was becoming even more slurred and his face redder. 'It's a question of principle, isn't it? I mean if the hermit—whoever he is—wants provisions from me I'm bound to sell them to him. Else why was I fighting the Germans, tell me that.'

'That's a point,' said Lorna brightly, looking from me to him as if she were watching a tennis match.

Dougie repeated what he had said.

'After all, we're living in a democracy, aren't we? At least, that's what they call it.'

Democracy, I thought. Is cancer a democracy? Cancer is what destroys the unity of the cells, the Greek polis. Maybe the hermit was a cancer. Was that what he was?

'Still,' I said, 'if a lot of people start to leave their wives because of him that will be something else again. You won't find the women talking about democracy.'

Dougie was about to say something, I felt sure, about women not being democratic anyway but then looking at Lorna he stopped himself in time and merely remarked, 'Well, all I can say is what did I fight the Germans for? I'll tell you,' he went on forcefully, 'I fought the Germans so that hermits can buy their groceries at my shop even if they don't want to speak to me. That's why I fought the Germans.'

'And quite right too,' said Lorna as if to a child. 'Quite right too. Though on the other hand Charles has some right on his side as well. Still it was odd about that old man.'

'It was,' I agreed. 'It was very odd.'

I was looking out of the window at the moon which was rising bright and stunningly clear above the sea. Pure lovely moon, pure merciless moon. There was a long pause in the conversation which no one seemed to wish to break. I felt comfortable and yet at the same time I was restless. Soon I would have to leave. That is what is so odd about lonely people, they want to be alone and yet they do not want to be alone. There were times when I needed solitude like food and drink and other times when I couldn't bear it.

The fact was I didn't particularly care for Lorna or Edward. They seemed to me to be artificial superficial people who could not see and did not wish to see anything profound. They were made uncomfortable by deep discussion. I was much more interested in Dougie than I was in them, though he was being rather incoherent about the Germans.

Suddenly he said, looking at me in what he imagined must be an affectionate roguish manner, 'I hear that you're getting your milk every morning.'

'Oh,' I said, 'that's true. I thought I'd buy fresh milk every morning.'

'And very nice too,' said Dougie as if he were back in his wartime barracks again and using the sort of language he might have spoken then. 'I wouldn't mind getting her in the corn,' he said. 'Still, every man to his own taste.'

'And who is this?' said Lorna, looking at me almost roguishly. 'I detect something.'

'Oh, you can detect something all right,' said Dougie. 'She's a stunner. Mind you, she's pretty young.' And he laughed. I was angry but remained smooth on the surface.

'There is nothing in it,' I said, 'but a pure business transaction.'

'Ah, you old rogue,' said Dougie again. 'There's depths to Charles that you wouldn't believe,' he told the others, going over to pour himself another whisky. 'She's a stunner. A real hum dinger.'

This went on for some time till finally around eleven o'clock I said I would have to go.

'You don't have to go yet,' said Dougie. 'The night's still young.' In the old days I would have left even earlier when my wife was alive and in fact there was really no reason why I should be leaving at eleven o'clock as I could stay in bed as long as I wished. Nevertheless I wanted to leave. The pressure of words without meaning was beginning to tire me. And also I was wondering if other people were saying or hinting what Dougie was saying and hinting. With him it was just words and not for a moment did he believe that there was any truth in what he was saying but other people in the village might be less charitable. The trouble was that though as far as I was concerned nothing had happened, the desire was there, and this was what prevented me from being angrier.

The moon above the sea which I could see so clearly through the large window reminded me of her, the circles of light on the water. Great white breast of the moon, lovely unattainable Diana, stunningly lovely.

I insisted on leaving. At the door Dougie said that I must not be offended by his chatter as it was all a joke. He seemed

suddenly drunk and pathetic while behind him stood his
brother so cool and remote and collected.

Perhaps, I thought, the village does this to us. It doesn't
present us with enough challenges, it allows us to run
to seed.

Astoundingly, Lorna put her face up to be kissed and as
my eyes approached it, it looked grained and rutted like a
close-up picture of the moon. There was a smell of stale
perfume from her and altogether she reminded me of a
string' bag such as one might carry home from a shop.
Edward's clasp was cool and faint. They were still standing
at the door when I left. I wondered what they would say
about me in my absence. Poor Charles, Dougie might say,
he's getting old and narrow-minded. Imagine saying all that
about the hermit! But I knew that Dougie was serious about
democracy and the Germans, he was fair and straight and
kind. Maybe, I thought vaguely, I shall come up against
him. Perhaps he too is my enemy. Or rather perhaps I am
his enemy. I waved and then they went into the house and
the square of light closed.

And I began my walk home.

As I walked along I thought of myself as a tramp without
destiny, without purpose. I had worn my best suit to visit
Dougie as I always did on a Friday but nevertheless I thought
of myself as a tramp. The fact was that since my wife died
I had had trouble even with maintaining my clothes in a
reasonable condition, quite apart from my trouble with
cooking. I couldn't be bothered with darning my socks
and often I just threw them away when they were holed and
bought new ones. A lot of my jackets had buttons missing
and I couldn't be bothered sewing new ones on. And this
was really absurd since I had all the time in the world but
at the same time I couldn't spare the time to sew buttons on
jackets or darn my socks. I could hardly be bothered making
food for myself.

As I walked along I could see the hermit's hut in the
distance. Perhaps he was now sleeping quietly and peacefully
while I was walking along the road to my lonely house,
restless, yet not wishing to go back to it. The sky above
was bright with moonlight. Even the Greeks, it occurred

to me, must have had trouble with their cooking and their clothes. But of course nothing of that was mentioned in their philosophy. They seemed so wholly concerned with the merciless mind, like the moon that raced between the clouds, remote and hard, and so goldenly unlike the stones which Murdo took home for his house. Imagine what it must be like to compose a house of moons.

And as I walked along thinking of the hermit and his hut and the planes rising from it into the night sky on their unimaginable missions, black planes headed for their destiny of dumbness and silence, I heard above the noise of the running stream another sound. It was the sound of dancing. I halted and listened. Every Friday night the young people would dance to the music of the accordion at the end of the road. They had been doing this for generation after generation—at first it had been the melodeon—and they were doing it tonight. The wheel circled, night was an affair of whiteness and perfume, the ring of erotic flesh. And I myself in the past had sometimes joined in the dance. And many of the girls with whom I had danced had now become old and flabby and fat and had varicose veins. But now if I were to enter that circle they would all withdraw from me as if I were a ghost and the accordion player would stop playing and there would be a dead silence. But in the old days it hadn't been like that. In the light of the autumn moon the world appeared brave and brilliant, the future lay before us all, our feet derived strength from the earth as we danced and we were young. There was no disease in the world, no sorrow, nothing but certainty. The dance was the symbol of eternity which repeated itself endlessly. Now it was merely a nostalgic charm. But perhaps that was the image I should have been seeking for, the image of the dance, not the image of silence and dumbness. If only one could live forever in the world of the dance, if only we had the luck. But, no, I didn't even dance very well and now I wouldn't be able to dance at all. Time had slowed me down, made my body stiff. I would find it undignified to dance. I would be too aware of those forces which were like a high wind trying to break up the dance. How could one be so innocent again? How could one have the

fierce animal eye that gazed at the moon and tried to stare
it down?

And as I walked along I thought that if I had a bomb
I would destroy this village where my idealism had died.
Here my heart which had burned with fervour had turned
to ashes. It was all the fault of the village and its people. They
too easily had lost their vision of the dance and because of
that I had lost it too. The dance to them was frivolous, it
was a stage in their lives which had to be transcended so
that they could settle down and raise families and cultivate
their land. But what, I thought, if the dance itself is the
centre of the world? For in the dance we do not consider
what other people may be thinking about us, we are not
looking for hidden meanings in their conversations. In the
dance we put out our hand and we grasp another hand and
the two hands are mortal and warm. We are all together in
the dance creating together whatever our souls and minds are
like, an image of harmony. In the centre of the dance there
is no fear, no horror. There are no skulls staring at us from
the centre of the dance and no cries of pain are heard.

And these thoughts and wishes brought me to the house
and to my own door. I have to say at this point, if I have
not said it already, that when I go out I always leave the
door unlocked: there is no history of stealing in the village.
I switched on the light and there sitting in my chair was
my wife. She had always sat there and for a moment in
my slightly drunk state I didn't find it wholly odd that she
should be there. She always used to sit by the fire knitting
or sewing in that very chair with the blue cover on it.

Then the whole world turned over again and it wasn't my
wife, it was Janet.

I looked at her in amazement, almost buckling at the
knees. She had clearly been waiting there patiently for me
in the chair by the unlit fire, her legs crossed perhaps as
they were now.

'My parents think I'm at the dance,' she said.

I looked from her to the window and then I walked over
and drew the curtains. What would happen to me if anyone
saw her there. She was wearing a white dress and her long
black hair flowed down behind her back.

'I haven't much time,' she said.

I went over to the cupboard and poured myself a whisky.

'Would you like one?' I asked.

'No thanks,' she said.

I now knew why she had come. With my whisky in my hand I walked over to the bureau in the corner of the room and took out my money. I didn't care how much I was giving her and I poured the notes in her lap. It was the two hundred pounds for the red suite, that was what she wanted. She counted the money carefully and put it in her handbag which lay on the floor beside the chair.

I drank the whisky quickly and she said: 'Where do we go?'

I put the glass down on the table, my lips dry. It was impossible that she should be there and yet she was there in her white dress with the pure glow of youth on her face.

I went into the bedroom and she followed me, shining palely in the darkness. I drew the curtains in this room too, shutting out the light of the moon, though I could still hear the dancing.

I undressed and climbed into bed. My legs seemed scrawnier than usual, my skin unhealthy looking. She stood over at the dressing table looking briefly in the mirror in front of which my wife had used to sit in the mornings and at night. This was the bed the two of us had shared for so many years.

She climbed into bed and her flesh felt cool and marbly. I put my arms around her in the darkness. The desert had blossomed with water.

'I haven't got much time,' she whispered again.

She had come out of the darkness for two hundred pounds for a red suite, for its cheap rays. I had plenty of money. I didn't grudge that. I grudged the torment of my soul that had led to this.

It took only fifteen minutes, that was all. When it was over she got up and dressed again in front of the mirror. There was a comb there which she used: in it were still a few grey hairs. I looked at her while she was dressing. She was like a fish, lively and cool. She seemed to have forgotten about me. After a while she was completely dressed again, this child, this cool child.

'Shall I close the door after me?' she asked as I lay there.

'Yes,' I said.

She pulled the door behind her and then I heard the main door close.

I felt corrupted and yet light as if some great weight had been lifted from me. Forgive us our sins . . . I imagined her making her way home like a thief through the night while the dance continued. I nearly got up to take some more whisky but after the door had closed I stayed where I was. I knew that would be the last time, the only time, that she would never come again, but my heart was humming with joy. After a while I fell asleep still hearing, before I dropped off, the music of the accordion and the sound of the dancers' feet.

SIXTEEN

The following evening Kenneth John came back to the village on the bus.

I didn't talk to him that night but the following day I was able to. He was sitting in front of his house on a chair which his wife had set out for him and he looked diminished and shorn as if some vital part had been removed from him. As I came over his wife looked at me and for the first time I realised that she didn't like me very much. There was a hard hostile gleam in her eye which however she masked immediately. She brought me out a chair as well and I sat beside Kenneth John: she had given him a pillow to lean against but hadn't brought one for me. After a long while he began to talk, at first almost to himself and then later to me.

'I tried to get a job on a ship but I couldn't get one. I went down to the quay and there were some men there but when I told them what I wanted they just laughed. I told them I had been to Hong Kong and Valparaiso and that I had been on the big sailing ships up in the rigging. They said that they didn't have sails on ships nowadays. They called

me "old man" and told me that I should go home. And
I'm sure none of them had ever been to Australia or New
Zealand or any of those places. "You can't go to Valparaiso,
old man," they said, "you're too old." They didn't realise,'
he said, turning to me at last, 'the thirst I felt. The day we
went to San Francisco, years ago, I saw the bridge shining
in the sun and I couldn't believe that the world could be so
beautiful. There was a slight haze too, a slight blue haze. But
the bridge was shining. They didn't understand the thirst I
had to see that place again. And every day I saw them and
they said the same thing. They used to call me Valparaiso
Jim. And I used to see them loading and unloading the ship
and in the evening I would see it setting out. It was so big
and white. But they just laughed at me.

'At first I walked about the town but I didn't see
anybody I knew. Nobody at all. It was like being in a
new country. People just going to the shops and walking
along the pavements and their eyes looking into themselves
and they were all so gloomy.

'And I stayed in this house run by a Mrs Malloy, a small
greedy woman. She wouldn't even let me watch the TV. And
the house inside was all dark and there was a smell of polish
and cabbage. And there were pots with shiny plants in them
and big leaves. I used to sit in my room every night and
watch the walls, there was nothing else to do. And I'm sure
she didn't clean the dishes properly. I'm sure the dishes were
dirty. She wouldn't even wash my clothes unless I gave her
extra money. I just had forty pounds altogether, I didn't
have much money. It was funny, wasn't it, after leaving
here, I ended up in a room watching the walls. On the wall
there was a painting showing three deer on a mountain side
and it looked like a painting I had seen on a train a long
time ago. I think she must have stolen it from the train,
that's what I thought. She was a small sour-looking woman
and I didn't like her at all. The furniture was very dark and
the house was dark. She didn't seem to draw the curtains
aside and there was a smell of cooking. She wouldn't even
darn my socks for me. I didn't like her at all. Not at all.
And there was no one in the town I knew. I was used to a
hot water bottle every night and she wouldn't even let me

put the fire on. She said I could go to the lounge but there was no one in the lounge and it was full of old furniture.

'And, in the mornings, I would go down to the quay. The weather was so beautiful, there's never been a summer like it, and there were boats in the bay and I would ask these people if I could get a job. In the early morning I was full of hope. But they still laughed at me. And they told others about me and they laughed at me as well. Valparaiso Jim they called me. They had no pity for me at all. I said I didn't want any pay while I was on the ship. All I wanted was bed and board but they had no pity on me at all. I thought that everybody had been at San Francisco at some time or another. But no, they hadn't, not one of them had been, and it didn't worry them. They were happy where they were and all they thought about was making their money for the day and then going home at night. They said I should go home and put my feet up at the fire. You're too old, they said. You're too old for San Francisco. But one of them seemed to understand and he took me in for coffee one day and he said that he had a family and three children. You should go home, he told me. Look at me, he said, I've never been to San Francisco, not even once. And you're better off than me. You've been at least once. And that was true too. I hadn't thought of that before. What he said was right enough. But I still had this thirst. That's what they don't understand, the thirst. I didn't want to lie down and die and that's what they wanted me to do. But they didn't have any pity.

'And when I went back to the house at night there was no TV and there was no fire and this woman wouldn't even wash my clothes. And sometimes in the morning there would be a queue at the bathroom. And there was a man who never spoke to me, he read the paper all the time, even at his breakfast. And there was a smell from the house, a smell of polish and cabbages and some other smell that I have never smelt before. It was an old smell, it almost made me sick.

'And at night I used to look at the picture with the three deer on it. They were green deer and they were on this brown mountain and there was an old gold frame to the picture. And in the lounge there was an old piano and no one ever played it. You had to be at your breakfast at a certain time and if you weren't there you didn't get any. I didn't like the place at all and I didn't like the woman. She also asked me for my money in advance. I couldn't help thinking of the old days when you had somewhere to go. When you're young there's always somewhere to go. I didn't have anywhere to go there, I couldn't even walk the street because I didn't know anybody. I never met anybody all the time I was in town, nobody at all. They were all strangers and they were looking ahead of them and they looked so worried and so old. It wasn't like that in San Francisco.

'You know, I always thought that everybody had been in San Francisco at some time or another and there were these people and they hadn't been and they didn't want to go.

'So one morning I got up and I looked out the window at the bay where the ships were and I knew that I would never get to San Francisco again. I would never be on board a ship again. So I put all my clothes in my case and I told the woman I was leaving and I left the house and I went down to the bus. I didn't even go to the quay in case I changed my mind when I saw the ships.

'So I came back home and I knew all the time as I was sitting in the bus that I would never leave the village again. But I'll tell you something, I can get a hot water bottle now and I can watch the TV and I don't have to sit in a lounge. It's funny how those things mean so much to you. I knew that I was old and that all my youth had gone. Sometimes you don't realise that till it's very late in life. I've realised it now.'

He turned and looked me full in the face. 'I'm home now,' he said, 'for the last time.' A wisp of sand blew about us and I thought of the little girl who had come from school and said that she had gone to the window of the hermit's hut and she had heard him singing.

He was altering things because he was there, his existence was an affront.

'I'm sure you did the right thing,' I told Kenneth John. 'I'm sure you did the right thing.' But my heart felt empty as I said it. How could the knowledge of the right thing make one feel so shorn and diminished, so totally void?

SEVENTEEN

When the minister, the Rev. Murdo Mackenzie, came to
see me I thought at first that he was looking for money.
I never of course go to church and haven't done so for
many years now. The minister is a very thin man with a
cadaverous face, one of those faces that Highland ministers
have, grained and deeply trenched so that they look like
portraits of Dante in his old age. When he came in I asked
him to sit down but he gazed vacantly at the chair and didn't
sit on it. He paced about the room nervously, sometimes
passing his hand across his eyes as if he were dazzled by an
enormous problem.

'I suppose you are wondering why I came to see you,' he
said at last. For one frightening moment I thought it might
have something to do with Janet and that he was going to
warn me about the terrible moral consequences my sin might
involve me in. But it wasn't about that at all. As a matter of
fact I had nothing against this particular minister. He had
never pestered me to come to church as some of them do and
as far as I knew he was a very competent minister, visiting
the sick regularly and making no distinction between the
rich and the poor.

'As a matter of fact,' he said, 'I came to you simply because
you do not attend church. I couldn't tell my congregation or
my elders because they wouldn't understand.' He paused for
a long moment staring into vacancy then sat down in a chair
and almost immediately got up again.

'It's difficult to tell you this,' he said. 'Very difficult. I
don't know where to begin. It's so strange. So strange.
Nothing like it has ever happened to me before.'

I waited patiently. I knew now that whatever it was it
had nothing to do with Janet or me. I wondered, if he had
known about that, whether he would have come to consult
me. Almost certainly not.

'Well,' he said at last, as if preparing to take the brunt
of a large cold wave, 'I suppose I'd better tell you. You'll
probably think I'm mad, utterly mad, and perhaps I am.
You see, I always prepare my sermons in advance of the
Sunday. I like writing them out, I get a great amount of
pleasure out of my little efforts. I feel that I am creating

something, you understand.' I nodded. I was sure he must feel like that about his trivial orations.

'I spend quite a lot of time preparing them,' he continued. 'I write them down in longhand and sometimes after that if I have time I type them. I don't just use headings for my sermons. No, I write the whole sermon out. The sermon I was preparing this week was on God and His gift of His son to us and how, sinful though we are, God has thought it expedient to save us out of His great mercy. There is nothing unusual about the sermon. In fact I have often used a similar kind of sermon before. O I believe in God and in Christ. When I was in the pulpit the words would pour out of me like a fountain. For what after all is a minister unless he has the gift of words? I don't mean the gift of language, for few have that, but the gift of eloquence, the gift of words. It would certainly be odd if you had a minister who couldn't speak, who couldn't use words. A minister needs words and he needs hope. What would his congregation think of him if he had no hope and he couldn't preach? He would be like a thorn without sap, he would be a useless plant in the desert. He would be nothing.' He looked at me keenly and I thought I knew what had happened. He had lost his faith. I had often wondered what would happen to a minister if he lost his faith. Most of us at some time or another lose our faith in what we do, we find our work absurd, we feel that our motions and operations in the world are meaningless and dispensable. But what if this happened to a minister whose business after all is faith, and who must rest in it or be without function?

'I know what you're thinking,' he said. 'You're thinking that I've lost my faith. It's not as simple as that. For, as I said, what is a minister without a voice, without words? If silence descended on a minister what would he be? Nothing. Nothing at all. Do you understand?'

'I'm not sure,' I said.

'Well, I'll tell you what happened,' he said. 'I wrote my sermon and then I tried to speak it. Aloud in my room, standing up, as if I were talking to the congregation. I was talking about God and Christ and the fact that the Son of Man was born in a stable. Well,' he said looking at me with horror, 'I tried to speak the words and no words would come out of my mouth. It was as if I had gone dumb. I thought at first that I was suffering from some sickness, some disease, but no, for I am speaking to you now, am I not? And I could speak to my wife and children. But whenever I tried to speak the words of that sermon it was as if I had gone dumb.'

'This sermon about God and Christ?' I said.

'Yes,' he said, 'about the blessings of God.'

'And did you mention in it,' I asked ironically, 'the blessing of pain which has been granted to us?'

'No,' he said, 'I didn't mention that.'

I was silent for a long time. The stable and the hut. The dumbness and the hermit.

The wings ascending to the sky.

The words written on paper.

Was I going out of my mind? The minister paced about my house like an animal in a cage. Understanding nothing.

First there was Kenneth John and now there was the minister.

It was like a plague, a language dying.

The big stones in the mouth.

'Well,' I said, 'you should tell the congregation that you've got a cold, that you're hoarse, and maybe the words will come back to you later.'

'But it might happen to me again,' he said.

'It won't,' I said. 'It won't. You just tell them that you're hoarse.'

The soul of the village dying. Not that I cared about the minister but it was as if I owed a debt to the village. Truth moving restlessly about my room, dumb.

The white Greek moon in the sky like a stone screaming. And its dumbness lying on the earth. The veins and tentacles dead and finished.

'Everything will be all right,' I said. 'It's just a momentary crisis. It happens to all of us at some time or another. Sometimes when I was teaching I felt the same, as if I didn't want to say anything, as if for that time I had nothing to say.'

His eyes pleaded with me.

'Is that true?' he asked.

'Of course it's true,' I said. 'It happens to all of us at some time or another. The dark night of the soul.'

'Well,' he said, 'I feel much better. I'm glad I came.'

'That's because you talked about it,' I said. From the closed grave the soul rose fluttering. When the stone moved.

After some time he left looking much happier. But he left me thinking hard.

The hermit would have to leave the village, that was certain. I would have to save the village. And no one else could save it except me. No one else knew the extent of the threat, the potential damage. It wasn't that I was concerned with the minister. Much of what he said seemed to me false and irrelevant. But what if this happened to others? If the silence of the dead descended on the village? If people grew too tired even to speak to each other, if language, that necessity of the human being, failed? No village, no society, could survive that. I didn't need the minister but others did. His words for them were significant and important. And what if they failed? It was as if the influence of the hermit extended outwards like a cold ray without his knowing it. Or perhaps he did know it.

Truth lay perhaps in silence but it was not a human truth. Human truth lay in lying speech. And who in the village knew this except me? Who would be able to deal with this but me? Only I saw what was happening because it was what I mistakenly wished to happen. Dougie didn't understand it with his talk about democracy. This had nothing to do with democracy, this was a fight to the death. The silence of death. Snow falling over the village dulling its traffic. The roads that joined us together slowly being throttled.

After the minister had gone I sat for a long time thinking. I couldn't think what to do but I knew that something must be done. And I would have to do it myself. Even if I passed the limits of morality, even if I struck deep at my own image. The monster of silence would have to be driven out of the village, even by corrupt means. Later perhaps someone might understand why it had been necessary but more probably no one would: there would be no biographer to tell of my achievement since the people for whom I was acting as benefactor didn't themselves understand the problem. This was a metaphysical question, and they lived in the physical world of stone and corn and hay and houses.

But no solution came to me. The hermit had apparently harmed no one. I couldn't hire the policeman to drive out a metaphysical criminal. I thought of that opening chapter in Frazer's book where one prince hunts another one in the dark wood, the new god taking over from the old, while the moon poured down its equal rays.

But I felt so tired. And there was no one I could talk to. Not to Murdo, not to Kenneth John, not to Dougie. Not even to Kirsty. Her narrow brutal mind would be of no use here. This needed much greater fineness, much deeper cunning.

And I thought too, Why shouldn't I leave him where he was? After all when he left what would I have to think of? That black silence of his, so attractive to me, would perish with his disappearance and I would be alone. The moon was now rising in the sky. O my Greek volumes, why don't you bring me an answer to this unanswerable question, with your brimming knowledge, your endless fertility? Why don't you bring me your manifold gifts? But this question went beyond those texts. There was a deep loch and there was a thought which needed to take the bait but the thought wasn't rising to the surface clear and strong. Still, it might come to the surface eventually.

It would have to. I stared directly into the face of the moon which was as pure and direct and strong as Janet's face and that was the last vision I had before I fell asleep, still searching for that thought, that solution which would permit me to rid the village of the hermit who was to a great extent myself, and yet more dangerous and much stronger than me.

EIGHTEEN

And as I slept I dreamed of my childhood. It returned to me in all its clarity and fullness. I saw again my father and my mother, my father so silent and large and my mother so quick and busy and demanding. She seemed always to be running about the house with a duster, or washing, or drying dishes, or sweeping the floor. A vivid insect presence in her blue gown with the white flowers printed on it. And always saying to me, Keep at your books. You have to get on in the world. What is there here for you? Look at all those other boys. What are they doing but wasting their lives fishing and crofting? You keep at your books.

While my father, slow and silent, said nothing and did nothing to protect me from this quick demanding presence which wouldn't leave me alone, which would not let me ripen in my own darkness but was always shining its sharp little torch on me. Always without cease. And my father was so slow and heavy and perhaps lazy and silent. It seemed to be an effort for him to speak, as if he had allowed my mother to speak for both of them. It was she who was proud and small and quick, who was alert to insults, even imagined ones, from the villagers who didn't like her because of her ambition. He on the other hand seemed to have no sense of honour but he got on better with them than she did. In a way he was like Murdo Murray but deeper, more vulnerable. He wasn't at ease in his environment but perhaps more so than she was. She saw her environment as something hostile, she confronted it with her quick agile mind and her quick body: she was always improving it, cleaning it up, tidying it. And my father would sit by the fireside reading the paper and he didn't protect me at all. He would hardly touch me except that now and again he might lay his hand on my head absently in passing, but he would say nothing.

Eventually he withdrew to a shed where he kept his loom and there he would play his ancient dark music among a smell of oil, his feet on the treadles, his hands busy. He was like a big composer in the half darkness, a sort of Beethoven, heavy and silent and dull. I would go there and watch him and marvel at his quick skill as he made the cloth, but in the house he was so quiet.

And my mother would say, Keep at your books. And I wasn't allowed out at night hardly at all in those years. All the other boys of the village including my brother whom she had given up as far as education was concerned would play football and shinty and go bird nesting but I stayed in the house reading and writing. She didn't understand what I was studying but had a superstitious reverence for it all and made sure that I kept at it. And all the time my father would sit by the fireside sometimes sleeping, sometimes looking at a newspaper, or at other times he would be down at the shed or sometimes he would stand at the door gazing outwards perhaps at the sky, perhaps at some imagined land of his own. And this quick insect hummed about me and would not let me alone. It cleaned everything up and tidied my life and kept it on course. And I brought home all the prizes from school and she would place the cups on the sideboard and show them to visitors till I grew tired of her as they did too. They disliked her for her ambition, they much preferred my father, he was much more like themselves than she was. She was like a sliver of wood in a fingernail, never resting. And my father would play the music of his loom, dark and silent and dull, till one day he had a heart attack while he was in the shed. His body toppled off his seat and he lay under it, his eyes sightless and gazing upwards and it was I who found him. And I remember the humming of the large black flies about the shed on that summer day with the door open to the fragrance of flowers outside.

He was buried, and I was left to the mercies of my mother who became very religious. She would even look in the Bible for texts which would prove to me that study was important. It was as if my father had never been, as if that dark music was buried forever in the dark earth.

And the world passed me by with its perfume for others but for me nothing but books. My mother's small sharp beak was always probing at me. Till one day she also died. Before she died I used to sit at her bedside listening to the business of her breath which was like an accelerating train. She was very brave. Even then she told me to keep at my books lest, I suppose, she should feel betrayed in eternity. She told me that death dues were in a drawer in a dressing table and that there was money there for her coffin as well. She wasn't afraid to die, she thought that she had done her work in the world by bringing me up to study books which she did not understand, though her faith was great. 'I am going to that place where there is rest and calm,' she said.

And I thought that perhaps there too she would be going about dusting heavenly tables and making sure that the saints kept at their theology.

I was then twenty years old and in university. While home one Christmas I had taken a girl to the house but after she had left my mother said, 'She won't do for you. She smokes.' And after that I never brought anyone home. I cried when she died. I cried more than I had cried for my father. I hadn't really known my father, that dark musician of the flesh. My mother's quick agile spirit had however sustained me, she had taught me the way to go though at times I hated it. And after all but for her would I ever have read the Greek authors? Would I ever have listened to great music, would I ever have seen great works of art? And that, in spite of the pain, is something. And also in spite of the fact that she herself had never looked at a painting in her life nor ever listened to Mozart or any other composer. Her favourite magazine was the *People's Friend* where after a great struggle the nurse eventually married the surgeon who had never noticed her till finally she had helped him in that Great Operation. But her will was indomitable and her ambition without end.

So I wept for her more than my brother did, for he knew that she had found him wanting and therefore he resented her.

And my mother is always clearer in my mind than my father is, he who had never shielded me from her remorseless light, who sat in his dumbness and his hopelessness. At least she had been optimistic. She had looked into the future and made me a school-master. But at least she had been conscious of a future. My father had only been conscious of a past.

Once in Edinburgh I went to the Zoo and in it I saw in a corner of a cage a great hulking bear lying down in its dark stink. In another cage I saw a leopard or perhaps a panther pacing restlessly up and down. And I wished to say to the bear, Why don't you get up from there? Why do you accept the darkness and the stink and the servitude? And I far preferred the leopard with its restless proud pacing. And also I liked the birds with their quick movements and their

colourful plumage and their beaks that seemed to question
the world around them. All that perhaps was dreams. But
I did not like the dark bear. I wished to be like the leopard,
optimistic and angry and agile.

For the bear had never used its strength but the leopard
used all its energy without surrender to the end.

When I woke up I knew perfectly well what I must do. The
idea came to me in my sleep.

NINETEEN

'I don't believe it,' said Dougie.

'You heard what she said, that she was . . .'

'Attacked. I heard her and I don't believe it. The man is,
was, quite harmless.'

'We have to believe her,' I said, 'and anyway after that
the villagers wouldn't have allowed him to stay.'

'I can see *that*,' said Dougie. His eyes were cold and hard
and hostile. 'Did you see his eyes?'

'His eyes?'

'Yes. When he set off on that bicycle of his again. It was
like watching a refugee that I'd once seen in Europe. The
same expression on his face.'

I didn't tell Dougie, but I did remember his expression
when he set off again, upright on his bicycle in his dark
clothes with the belt of rope around his waist. And the
villagers standing watching him, hostile and threatening.
The hermit's eyes had turned for a moment to look at me
as if by strange magic the hermit had recognised his true
enemy. After all, really, he had done nothing to me. And
that perhaps accounted for his expression.

'I must say again,' said Dougie, 'that I don't believe
it, that she was attacked. That man would never attack
anyone. He has no possessions at all, did you notice? That
was the hellish thing. He had nothing. He set off again.
With nothing. And where was he going? And if he goes
somewhere else will the people there also put him out? And
we never,' he said, 'found out anything about him. He spoke
to no one and no one spoke to him. He could be a fool or a

genius—he could be anybody.' And he looked at me with
horror.

Well, I had used the corrupted to get rid of the corrupted, I thought. Sometimes such things are necessary,
sometimes ethics themselves have to be poisoned in order
to create health.

'There didn't seem to be anything wrong with Janet
that I could see,' Dougie repeated. 'She seemed to me
self-possessed enough.'

'Why should she say she had been attacked unless she
had been?' I asked innocently.

'I don't know but I have an idea,' he said. And there was
the glitter of hate in his eyes.

The village would now be silent. It would now return
to its ancient ways, it would not be disturbed. The mirror
image of myself would have left it, expelled forever.

'What the hell is he going to do?' said Dougie again. 'I
can't stand thinking about it. Wandering about forever on
that bicycle.' I thought for a moment that he would weep.

But what in fact he did was to turn away.

'I don't think it would be a good idea if you came to the
house again,' he said.

I didn't say anything but watched him go. Now I myself
was truly alone, but then loneliness was something to be
suffered in the service of one's kind. I knew that Dougie
would be relentless and that his sense of fairness might not
let him rest. But Janet wasn't going to talk. After all she
had plenty of money now.

I looked at Murdo's unfinished house, I heard the music
of the sea. I turned back into the house, feeling as if I didn't
wish to talk to anyone. I thought of my wife, then of Janet,
sitting in the chair by the fire, as I poured myself a whisky.
No one understood what had happened. Not even Dougie
understood that. It was true that like him I saw the figure
of the hermit setting off into nothingness on his old bicycle.
But it was true that it was necessary to make a refugee. I had
saved them from silence at the expense of my own silence. I
laughed bitterly as I sat down by the fireside. Even Kirsty
would congratulate me. Even the minister. And yet I had
a frightening feeling of emptiness as if I were suffering

from a strange disease. What else could I think about now, now that that hut had no inhabitant, now that questions of metaphysics had been removed from me?

As I sat there for what seemed to be hours the day became dusk and then slowly the moon rose in the sky. I looked at it. It was dazzlingly white and clear, a brilliant stone, it was the eye of a Greek god or goddess. It was the stunning beauty of the mind, it had no physical beauty. It no longer reminded me of Janet, it was pure intellect. For Janet had been only an evanescent being, a sparkle of moonlight on the water. It was the cold stony mind that illuminated its own dead world remorselessly, its own extinct craters. I imagined the hermit cycling along in its light forever.

The house was extraordinarily peaceful as if by an act of will I had banished all the fertile ghosts. It had an unearthly calm as if I were floating on a dumb sea of solitude. I found myself humming to myself as if I had come to the silence of myself. I went to the bookcase and took out a book and began to read. Strangely enough I didn't realise at first what book it was. Then I saw that it was the Bible. I turned to the New Testament and began to read,

'In the beginning was the Word . . .'

Listen to the Voice

FOR THE PAST year he has been writing a book and for
the past year he has been dying. In fact the disease, cancer
of course, seems to have blossomed in harmony with the
progression of the book. He will not show it to me till it is
finished. It is a book about existentialism: Sartre, Camus,
and the rest. He has been reading them thoroughly for
many years in his spare time as a French teacher in the
school where I myself taught. I have retired, in the natural
order of things, and he has retired because of his illness
though he has been keeping up a gay battle to the end. I
have not been surprised by this. He has always been a man
of immense intelligence and courage, a rare combination. I
have known for years that his marriage was not a happy one
(his wife did not understand his passion for research). She
is a very ordinary common woman from England and he
should never have married her. They met, I think, when he
was at Oxford in the first dew of his youth. (At that time I
believe that he was a dedicated left winger, anti-Franco, and
the rest of it. The transition from left wing politics towards
absurdity must show something about his life.) He has had
to put up with a lot from her, not simply indifference but
active malevolence and petty spitefulness. I have seen him
humiliated by her in company though he smiled all the time.
The humiliations were constant and searching, and might
take the form of suggesting that he had not done as well
as he should have done financially, or even of questioning
his intelligence (he was not very practical), or of perfectly
placed stab wounds with regard to money. When I have
visited him I have treated her strictly as an enemy in whose
custody a prisoner happens to be. She hates me as much
as she hates him and for the same reasons, that I am like

155

her husband in that I genuinely do not care for material things, I cannot understand why people should need more than one simple meal at a time. In fact the two of us have been unpopular with the staff of the school because at a certain meeting called to discuss possible strike action we spoke up against the greed of the society in which we live. Naturally we failed to persuade our colleagues to adopt our principles (they genuinely seemed to think we were cranks since we talked of money as being a superficial gloss), but our stand didn't make us popular. Simmons in particular was our bitter foe. He is a devious though apparently bluff fellow who is not only his own worst enemy but everyone else's as well. I cannot tolerate his hyprocrisy, and he has the scorned woman's ability to strike neatly at the underbelly.

Anyway we were both interested in our hobbies, he in his Existentialism and I in my literature. I mean in the novel and in poetry. He has always respected my mind and I have respected his. I have never written anything creative of course. How could one have the temerity to add to what is already there, unless what one writes is necessary? And I have never felt the pressure of the necessary. I listen to a great deal of music. I hear the note of necessity even in the flawed opulence of Wagner and over-whelmingly in the apparent simplicity of Mozart. But never within myself. I even wonder why he has decided to write his book. It is in a way unlike him to commit his dreamed perfection to paper. I know that he has taken a certain pleasure in the composition of examination papers and the preparation of notes on French writers but I never thought that he would actually write a book. Certainly not on anything as complicated as Existentialism.

More recently he has been moved to hospital where he has been getting intensive radiation treatment. I hate hospitals but I have been going to see him every Sunday afternoon. His bed is at the far end of the hospital, in a very distant ward, and I pass old people staring into space with dull eyes. His table beside the bed has the usual assemblage of grapes and oranges: no one ever dreams of bringing him a book to read. But in spite of the heavy atmosphere, relieved only by the sparkling presence of the nurses who know he is doomed, he has managed to finish his own book. We talk about various things. Once we had a long discussion on Keats and wondered how far tuberculosis animates the creative soul. He seems to think it does, though I feel it almost blasphemous to think that without the presence of tuberculosis Keats would never have been a great poet. Still, he lies there in all that white. He knows he is going to die. I suppose being an existentialist—for he holds the beliefs that they hold—he will die in a different way from those who do not hold such beliefs. He sees neither priest nor minister. I sit in my rather shabby coat—for the ward is sometimes rather cold—beside his bed. I do not think about justice or mercy. What use would there be in that?

His long haggard face, like one of those windows that one sees in churches, is becoming more and more refined each time that I visit him. The book, it seems, will be his last justification. It may be that he thinks he will posthumously justify his life to his wife, if the book turns out to be a good one. I know that she couldn't care less, as far as the content goes, but in his strange way he loves her. What could she know of the literature of France? It is only people like himself who have shed the world who can know about literature. In fact he is beginning to look more and more like a saint as the weeks pass. The pure bone is appearing through the flesh. One day I almost said to him, 'What is it like to die?' but I caught myself in time. In any case the nurses are often hovering about. Some of them are pupils whom he has taught. He told me that one of them (one of the dimmer ones in fact) had gone to the trouble of speaking to him one day in halting French. He felt that this was a compassionate gesture and so indeed it was. His eyes filled with tears as he told me about it. 'And yet,' he said wonderingly, 'she couldn't do French at all.' I don't think he told his wife about the incident.

He was of course a perfectionist when he was teaching. 'No, no, no,' he would shout, 'that is not how you say it. Not at all.' I could hear him two rooms away. 'Listen again. Listen. You must always listen. Listen to the voice.' And he would say the word over and over. The inflexion must be exactly right, the idiom must be perfect. Perhaps it was that lust for perfection that brought on his cancer. His own daughter had been one who had not flourished under his teaching (she was intelligent but rebellious), and his wife had never forgiven him for that. 'But,' he would say to her, as he told me, 'she isn't as good as the others.' However it happened that one of the others had been the daughter of one of her bitterest enemies and how could one expect that she could reconcile herself to his honesty? 'Women,' he would say to me, 'can't be impersonal. You cannot ask that of them.' How much futile quarrelling was concealed under that statement. For his daughter was now working in a shop, Frenchless, resentful, single.

How and why had he taken up Existentialism? I don't know. Was it perhaps that he was driven towards it by the absurdity of his own life? How can one tell why some writers and systems of thought attract us and others don't? (The other night I had a visitor from the chess club and there were two tarts on a plate, one yellow and one pink. I asked him which one he wanted and he said the yellow one. I myself had preferred the pink one. How can one explain that?) He hadn't of course been in the war either. And neither had I. (Yet I suppose the system of Existentialism, if one can talk of it in terms of a system, emerged out of the last war.) We had that in common. But there are differences too. For instance he has a good head for figures. I remember the marking system he once worked out in order to be fairer to candidates. The headmaster couldn't understand it and so it was left in oblivion. I couldn't understand it either.

And so he is dying in this ward with the walls whose paint is coming off in flakes. And quite a lot of his former pupils visit him. It is surprising how many of them have done well for themselves. I do not mean that they have done well materially (though many have done that as well). What I was thinking of more precisely was that they have kept their minds true to themselves. One of them is now a Logic Professor in America and a leader of thought in his own field. I can't say that all of them have done as well as that but at least they have kept their integrity. What is even more striking is that they bring their wives along with them, however briefly they may be in town. He lies there like a medieval effigy, hammered out of some eternal stuff, and he listens to them and they listen to him. He has a great flair for listening and they tell him a great deal. In his youth he used to take them on expeditions, sometimes to France, and he and his pupils would talk into the early hours of the morning under other skies. Naturally, I wonder whether he did this because he wished to get away from his wife. I think this is partly true though perhaps he did not realise it himself. He did far more of this extramural activity than I ever did. I have never liked people as much as he has done. I have never had any warmth of nature. It has always struck me as strange that such perfectionism could be combined with such a liking for people.

He hasn't really had much in his life, an embittered wife and daughter, and that is all, apart from his schoolwork. And his book. That is not really very much to bear with one into the darkness of the absurd. Yet what else could he have done? How could he have known in those early days that his wife would turn out as she did? How could he have done other than take the side of his inflexible perfectionism against his daughter? Some men are lucky and some are not. I think one may say that he was not. Though naturally he doesn't believe in luck. I remember one revealing incident. There was a boy who wasn't able to get into university because his French was weak. He spent all his spare hours with him after school for weeks and months and managed to get him a pass in the examination. A year afterwards, the boy was working in a bar, he had simply gone to pieces after he had reached university. He had done no work at all. That was bad luck. Or was it bad judgement?

He is lying there and his book is finished. He has spent all his time on that book since his enforced retirement. He spent many years on it before that. He will take it with him into the final darkness. It may perhaps be a present for his wife, his last cold laurel. He may hold it out to her with a final absurd gesture, his lips half twisted in a final smile. To leave such as her the last product of his mind, the one least capable of understanding it! That would certainly be irony. Even now she may be thinking that she can make a little money from it. How else could one think of a book, of anything, but in terms of money?

I have been reading it. In fact I have read it all.

Last night I did not sleep. I read and reread the book. I searched page after page for illumination, for a new insight. The electric light blazed into my tired eyes, the bulb was like one of his sleepless eyes. Was it like a conscience? I revolved everything so slowly. O so slowly. After all we are human beings, condemned to servitude and despair. We are rags of flesh and bone though now and again pierced by flashes of light. I looked round my own monkish room. After all what had I done with my life? I didn't even have a wife or daughter. I thought of the world around me and how people might condemn me if they knew. They would condemn me out of their own shallowness, precisely because they were committed to no ideal and walked swathed in the superficial flesh. In fact at one time during the night while I was studying a page for the third or fourth time I heard on the street below the music of a transistor, though I could not make out the words of the song that was being sung. I supposed it was something to do with love and had travelled here from Luxembourg.

But not merciless love. No, love with all the mercy in the world. Love that would forgive anything because there was in the end nothing to forgive. Love that had no knowledge of the knife. But only of the tears. The light blazed on page after naive page. He had been too long in teaching. His mind had adjusted itself to immature minds. It was as if the book had been written for a Lower Fifth Form. All had been explained but all had been explained away. Sartre and Camus had lost the spring of their minds, the tension, they had been laid out flat on the page as his own body had been laid on its white bed. All was white without shadow. There was no battle. The battle had been fought elsewhere. The battle had been fought against his wife and daughter in the real world of money and teaching and jobs. The energy had gone into that. I stared for a long time at the book. After all, were we not poor human beings? After all, what was our flesh against the absurdity of the skies?

I walked to the hospital carrying the book. It was a June day and the birds were singing and the air was warm. The windows of the hospital were all open and the air was rushing in, scented and heavy. The whole world was in blossom. On the lawn there were some old people in chairs being sunned and tanned before being replaced in their beds. The sky was a mercilessly clear blue without cloud. I walked along the whole length of the ward and he was waiting for me. He would want to know what I thought immediately.

I handed him the book. I said to him quite clearly, aware of everything, 'It's no good, James. It's just no good.' The book lay between us on the bed. 'It's too naive,' I said. 'There are no new insights. None at all.'

Without a word he held out his hand towards me. And then he said equally clearly, 'Thank you, Charles.' I felt as if we were two members of a comic team as I heard our names spoken, two comedians dancing on a marble floor somewhere far from there.

He didn't say anything else. We started talking about other things. Three days afterwards he was dead. When I heard this I stared for a long time out of the window of my flat as the tears slowly welled in my eyes. No one can ever know whether he has done right or wrong. I stared around me at the books and they stood there tall and cold in their bookcases. I went and picked up a Yeats but I could find nothing that I wanted and I replaced it among the other books.

At the funeral the wife ignored me. Perhaps he had told her not to publish the book and she had guessed what had happened. Simmons was with her and he also ignored me. Later I heard that he had been advising her to get it published. I thought that if James had been alive this would have served as a true example of the absurd, his wife and Simmons in such an alliance. The two of them stood gazing down into the grave at the precious despised body and mind disappearing from view, she rigid and black, Simmons large and stout. As I turned away my shoes made a dreadful rustling noise on the gravel.

The Black and The Red

I ARRIVED HERE last night at 9 p.m. and I am writing this in my room at the lodgings.

The journey was pleasant. I was in my bunk on the boat—the bunk you ordered for me—but in the early morning—about six—I had an impulse to go on deck. I passed a steward in white as I walked, rather unsteadily, down the corridor in that sort of sick smell one gets on board ship. The morning was chill, with much sea stretching freely away. I felt my hair lifting gently in the breeze, and then saw it—the sun—very red, like a banner rising over Skye. There was no one on the deck except myself. I have never seen anything so beautiful—that sun rising through the mist, very red, very raw.

When we landed at Kyle there was a great screaming of gulls, porters hurrying past with barrows, smell of rolls and butter from the restaurant. My mouth felt foggy somehow. And then I saw my first train. It was long and brown, the colour of mahogany or that kind of reddish-brown shoe polish I sometimes get. I sat down in one of the rather dirty carriages which at the time was empty but later three boys entered. They were of my own age, perhaps, if anything, slightly older.

I discovered that they were students at the University too. They were reading brand-new Penguin crime stories while I had a copy of Homer, which surprised them. They were rather amused at the newness of my case which was on the rack above me. I think they were also amused at my scarf and tie and blazer. They do not seem to appreciate what is being done for them. However they are friendly. One of them—the most interesting—is called George. He is stocky and redhaired and quite irreverent. He studies medicine and

calls one of his lecturers The Spinal Cord. It turns out that
he is in the same lodgings as me. I like him.

The countryside through which we passed is divided into
geometrical sections—for farms—some squares, some rec-
tangles. Sometimes it's straw-coloured, sometimes lemony
yellow, and sometimes green, but very orderly and beautiful,
comparing very favourably with the untidy patches at home.
It looks very rich and fertile. Nothing of interest happened
on the journey except that my companions tried to buy my
dinner for me but I refused. They had all been working
during the holidays and had plenty of money. One was at
the Hydro-Electric, George at the fishing. His father comes
from Kyle and is skipper of a fishing boat.

A train seems to move much more slowly than one thinks.
I could hear the pounding of the wheels but I was still seeing
the same fields. After a while the others curled up and went
to sleep. But I didn't sleep. Sometimes I read Homer to the
thunder of the wheels. It's strange how unprotected people
look when they are asleep.

At ten o'clock we entered the station, but before that I
could see the lights of a great city. George and I went out
together into the confusion. I was going to order a taxi but
George would not hear of it. We climbed the steps into the
glare of the light and went in search of a bus. After dashing
across the street—or rather after I had dashed across the
street—we found ourselves at a big cinema—much bigger
than the one in T—with winking lights of different colours,
some violet, some purple.

Sitting on the stone pavement with his back against the
wall was a beggar, his cap—containing a few pennies—beside him, and he himself staring blankly into space. At that
moment I was terrified. I put my hands into my pockets
as if to steady myself and would have given him a pound
if George hadn't said:

'Don't be a fool. He's better off than you are. He's not
blind at all.' But George put a two-shilling piece in his cap:
I didn't give him anything—I don't like people who lie.

When we arrived at the house the landlady came to the
door. She is smallish, plump, with a Roman nose. She is
said to be greedy for money but perhaps that is scandal.

She looks very inquisitive and it is said that her favourite
words are: 'Youse students with all the money.' She has a
husband who works on the taxis and two children. I saw
one of them. He was plump and dressed in white shorts,
white socks and a white blouse. He looked at me without
speaking, his thumb in his mouth.

Last night, as I was lying in bed watching the lights of
cars traverse the walls and the ceiling and listening to the
patter of footsteps on the street, I thought I heard someone
whistling a Gaelic tune. But it wasn't a Gaelic tune at all.

Your loving son,
Kenneth

Yesterday was my first day at the University. I travel by
bus leaving at 8.30 a.m. The distance is about three miles.

The University—a place of bells and ivy—fronts a rough
road, curiously enough in one of the ugliest parts of the city,
so that it appears like an oasis. There are many notice boards
with green baize and notices all of which I have read. Some of
them are announcements of prizes, others of the formation of
societies (I doubt whether I shall have time to take part in
any of these). There is of course a large library with ladders,
and a librarian so tall that she doesn't need a ladder.

My first lecture was Greek. I climbed the wide stairs,
my nostrils quivering to a strange smell. It was in fact the
smell of varnish, and I later saw the typical watery waxy
yellow. I sat at the back during the lecture—we are studying
Sophocles—feeling the sun warm on my neck and watching
the shadows of the leaves dancing on my desk. However, I
didn't have time to do that for long.

Our lecturer is a rather small man with a half-open mouth
like that of a fish and he seemed to me to be in some vague
way untidy. (I don't know quite what I expected—perhaps
a flourish of trumpets and a great man in red robes, but
that wasn't what came.) He kept saying: 'Now this may be
Greek to you, gentlemen . . .' Sometimes after saying this
he would look out of the window and stand thus as if he
had forgotten us. I noticed a curious smile on his face, like
water round a stone. He speaks rather slowly—his hands
behind his back—and I found it quite easy to write down

everything he said. In the shops there is quite a large variety of notebooks and I have bought half-a-dozen, as I foresee much writing. There are thirty students in the class, more men than girls as one would expect. Many of them spend much time taking coffee in the Union and talking intensely. I go to the library. Most of them are far ahead of me at the moment.

There is one thing. For some reason I feel freer here. At home somehow or other I felt constricted. Do you remember how old Angus used to ask me those pointless riddles?

I am sorry to hear about the squabbles in the church. This money-grabbing is distasteful, and black. I think you should go out more.

Please don't talk about me to people so much. One doesn't know what might happen.

My second lecture was Latin—here we are doing Catullus and my lecturer is called Ormond. He is different altogether from Mulgrew—the Greek one—Ormond is more like a businessman, with bright fresh cheeks, a successful-looking man who sways back and forward on his heels when he is talking. He looks kind and self-possessed. Curiously enough, he wears a waistcoat, but on him it doesn't look old-fashioned. He talks quite fast and it takes me all my time to keep up with him.

I haven't been out at night since I came. Apart from George there are three other lodgers, a lady lecturer at the training college, a young girl who works in a shop, and a man of about 28 who's very keen on motor-cycles. The landlady doesn't like him much as his hands are very oily most of the time. However he has the most cheerful face imaginable and he talks in a very quaint slow way except when he's speaking about motorcycles.

As for me I work at night sitting by the electric fire. Sometimes the landlady comes in, rather unnecessarily I think, and looks at me as if she were going to say something about working too hard but she doesn't actually say anything. Once however she did say that I ought to go out more. George says this work and close-sitting by the fire are not good for me, and not profitable for my landlady! He is a very pleasant person, George.

The landlady can't be so bad after all. She took us in to see TV night before last. It was the first time I had seen TV and she was very surprised by this as also by my answers to her questions on life at home. George however looked more serious.

It is now 10.30 p.m. and I have to translate some Sophocles.

By the way I don't know whether George drinks or not. I have never seen him drunk if that's what you mean.

Your loving son,
Kenneth

This afternoon George and I went for a long walk and this in fact is probably the first time that I've been out since I came. After leaving the house we turned left down the street with its silvery tram rails. It was a fine warm afternoon and we saw many people strolling, some with dogs. After a while we turned left again towards Hutton Park. At the entrance to this park are great wrought iron gates and flowers of many colours arranged very cleverly to read WELCOME. I wondered how this was done but George wouldn't tell me, and didn't appear to be interested. He was telling me a story of a visit to the mortuary recently. The body of a young boy of 19 had been found drowned in the River Lee. In his cigarette case they found a note which read: 'I am tired of being drained of my blood.' That was all. Yet he apparently had adoring parents.

This park is near a cemetery which is orderly and has some green glass urns containing paper flowers. It is almost too orderly, like streets.

When we entered the park I saw that it had swings on which children were playing. In other parts of the park fathers were playing football with their sons, teaching them. One of them was showing his little son how to kick a ball, and though he appeared amiable seemed to me to be exasperated. Many of the balls were rainbow-coloured. We also passed a great startling peacock with purplish plumage like a bride's train. He was superb and alone and, I thought, completely out of place, unable even to fly.

We lay down on the grass (having removed our jackets)

in the warm day. For the first time in three weeks I was completely relaxed. I had taken a book with me—about Catullus—but I didn't read it. I watched small white clouds passing over me and heard birds singing in the trees (for there are many trees in the park). Our white shirts were dazzling in the light. George went for some ice-cream and we ate it and talked.

He doesn't write home much. 'After all,' he says, 'they know I am here.' He often gets letters but hardly ever answers them. He told me of his father who seems a good man, not able to spell well, for example 'colledge' for 'college'. I would have been ashamed to admit this: George isn't. He invited me to their house for part of the holidays. What do you think? He is going with a girl called Fiona. I gather that she is very intelligent, and sometimes he talks as if he were her (at least that's what I think) about the nuclear bomb. I think we need it. What else have we got? To defend our religion with. He smiled when I said this, clapped me on the knee, and told me to get up. We walked along the bank of the river (it was here that that boy was drowned) and saw a fisherman wearing thigh-length leathers, patiently casting in the middle. I thought for one horrible moment that we might find a body. Later we saw swans. They have a curious blunt blindness when seen close up. After a while I found I had forgotten my book and we went back to the park to collect it. We talked to two little boys. They were both very grave and very polite and told us all about themselves. They were dressed exactly alike in blue tunics and shorts, white shirts and blue ties. They were like echoes of each other. Eventually their nurse or whatever she was came to collect them. She frowned a little and I think they were very sorry to go, for George at any rate has the gift of friendliness. He makes fun of me sometimes—says I'm too serious. And I argue, he says, too self-righteously, especially with that college lecturer. My views on education are absolutely incomprehensible to him. Sometimes he asks me questions about home and confesses himself utterly perplexed. That people should be talked about for being out on a Sunday!

I hope this confusion of the church accounts will be sorted

out. I've seen it reported even in the newspapers here. That's what comes of living in a small village.

Don't think I'm wasting my time. I'm working very hard and I know what has been done for me. I study for about seven hours a day. There is so much to be done. Recently my eye was caught by a book in the library by a man called Camus. It's very strange but interesting.

I go to church here, but the minister Mr Wood isn't very impressive. He is a small stout man who seems to me to have nothing to say. The church itself is small and quite pretty and fresh. But it's his voice that I find peculiar . . . as if he could be thinking of something else when he's preaching. He is not in his voice. It's difficult to explain this. The flowers are beautiful, there are fine texts, fresh varnished tables, but he himself—he doesn't bring these things together. All is forced somehow. I sometimes think we should have more sense of humour. George is very humorous. He kept us in stitches last night composing a romance between the shopgirl and our cyclist friend—the third in the eternal triangle was the motor bike. Actually however Joan and Jake quite liked it, I think, and apart from their being lodgers (whom I suppose she can easily replace) the landlady's romantic soul appears to be touched. She seats them together at meals! And one day Jake took Joan to the shop on his motor bike. The trouble is he blushes too easily.

I've been invited to Mr Mulgrew's house and I think I might go on Wednesday. George's girl friend is coming for dinner soon.

It's very late—11.30—and I must finish—I shall post this at 8.30: there's a pillar box quite near.

I think I shall sleep better tonight: I feel much fresher.

Please remember that as I say again I know all that you have done for me.

> Your loving son,
> Kenneth

Last night I called on Mr Mulgrew our Greek lecturer. It was 7.30 when I arrived at the door of his house which lies in a quiet area about five hundred yards past a busy blue crossroads.

There were two bells, one a white one set in the stone at

the side of the door, and the other a black one set in the middle of the door itself. First, I pressed the white one but sensed by the lack of pressure that it wasn't working. Then I pressed the black one which also did not appear to be working. Finally I knocked on the door. There was no light in the hall. Then I knocked again more loudly.

I saw a light flash on—rather a dim one—and Mr Mulgrew himself came to the door wearing no jacket, but a blackish pullover and reddish slippers. Eventually he recognised me, his mouth closing as he did so and a light being switched on in his eyes. I have heard that he is very lonely and that he goes to the cinema regularly once a week no matter what the film is and that he prefers to sit in the same seat each time.

He seemed glad to see me and shepherded me into a room on the right which contained a lot of books, an electric fire (with the two bars on) two easy-chairs (both green) an electric lamp (lit) one table (heavy mahogany) and a smaller, flimsier one. He sat me down in the armchair opposite his own. Beside him on the floor was an open book.

We sat for some moments in silence, he with his legs crossed, dangling one red slipper uneasily, then he took out a packet of cigarettes which he offered me. He seemed surprised when I did not take a cigarette and returned the packet to his pocket. I have the impression that he bought that packet just for me! At the same time he said:

'Very few young people don't smoke nowadays, isn't that right? You're not afraid of cancer, are you ?' He looked at me steadily as if he himself was. I said No I wasn't.

'That's a mistake,' he continued. 'We should be. I am. Very much. I find the thought unbearable. Of course it's psychological.' I didn't say anything.

'The reason I asked you here is that your work is good, you know, good. Honest. Yes I think honest is the word. Not slick. So little honesty now, don't you agree. I mean real honesty.'

His eyes seemed to look at me then flicker away again so that I was uneasy.

'Do you know that Wittgenstein used to read Black Mask?' he asked suddenly.

I said I didn't know anything about Wittgenstein (though I've found out a little since).

'He was a great philosopher you know and he used to go to the cinema regularly—gangster films mainly he liked. Imagine that! You should read him, he was very honest.'

Then without transition he began to talk about Sophocles. 'You know the thing I find extraordinary about him,'—for some reason he stood up and began to walk about the room—'the thing I find extraordinary about him is that he did so much and especially—do you know what I find most extraordinary of all?—that he served in the army!

'Nowadays people serve in the army and then they write a book about it. That's putting it in reverse you know. It shouldn't be like that at all. No, you don't find anything about his experiences in the army in Sophocles. He doesn't exploit them. He just lived.'

Abruptly he sat down again and leaning forward said, 'He just lived. Isn't that fine? To be able to do what Sophocles did.'

Of course I understood what he was saying but I couldn't become enthusiastic—yet in a way he seemed to be enthusiastic—sometimes stabbing forward with his finger—but he didn't make me enthusiastic. It was as if—like Wood—he could be thinking of something else while he was talking.

'Nowadays they talk of their military experience and of women and of drink—but do we find these in Sophocles? No, we don't. That's what we must understand—what did make the Greeks great? He lived till he was 90—he took part in his civic duties, he served in the army and he wrote all these plays. That's greatness. Especially serving in the army.'

At that moment I heard a tram rocking past into the blue lights and he himself stopped as if he had heard a gun exploding.

Then suddenly he began to talk about Gilbert Murray. 'I once met him,' he said, 'an Australian. But I don't like his translations. You know, he served on the League of Nations. He should have concentrated on his translations. Would you care to see . . .' Suddenly he got up saying, 'I think I have somewhere here a review I wrote for the Classical Studies on his . . .' And he went straight to a magazine, took it out and it opened at the correct page. I read the review. It was I thought indecisive and rather mean at the same time. 'One is not sure that . . .' However I said it was quite good.

'About your own work, that's reasonable. It's got the classical . . . spirit, you know,' said he, pleased with my praise. He was flattering me for some reason.

'Excuse me a moment.' He almost pranced out leaving me alone in the room. I felt desolate and an emptiness throbbed through me. I looked at the clock: it said 8.15. I looked at the books but had no inclination to read them. I noticed that the lamp-shade was red.

In a minute or two he returned. 'I was ordering tea,' he said.

Then for some reason or other I heard myself saying that I couldn't stay for tea. I listened to my own voice with astonishment: it was creating a number of the most plausible lies, the main one being that the landlady had invited me to see TV and he himself knew as a student what these landladies were like. He was listening with his mouth open and agreeing now and then. Then I noticed a certain pride being drawn up over his face like a drawbridge.

'Of course if you can't stay,' he began. I said I wished to but I couldn't and then with an attempt at humour—there was that essay he had set us! He half laughed. I found myself walking to the door as if across a great space. He said he had been going to show me some of his translations, but of course . . .

I repeated I was sorry. At the door he began with a sudden curious depth to his voice but at the same time jocularly:

'And what do you think of us?'

I stared.

'Of the lecturers.'

'Oh,' I mumbled, 'different from school . . . mature . . . more interesting . . . very different . . .'

'Yes,' he said, 'isn't it? I remember when I went to university first . . .' Then he stopped. 'But I'm keeping you.'

He opened the outer door and we looked out into the night which had a chill dryness and a lot of stars.

'The strange thing about Sophocles, you know,' he said,

'was that he served in the army. A man of action.' He seemed to stand more upright. 'Nowadays . . . he would have written his memoirs.'

I walked down the path to the gate, half-running. I turned to wave but the door had been shut.

Not very far from the crossroads I was approached by a big fat red-faced drunken woman who asked me for a shilling. I seem always to be approached by these people. I gave her the money and strangely enough I looked after her with pleasure as she rolled on huge and healthy and happy to wherever she was going. She called me 'dear'.

So that was the visit. Peculiar. I doubt if I shall go again. I worked again after coming home but somehow . . . No, I won't let you down. Still there was something odd . . .

George comes in now and again. His girl friend is coming up on Saturday and he wants me to meet her. I don't know. He too is uneasy these days. Of course he goes out oftener than me—to dances, etc.—but there's a hectic quality about him. Perhaps he's seeing too many bodies and going to hospitals too much.

Once he brought some records in and played me some jazz. It's really powerful music, blasting. We have nothing like it in Gaelic.

'What do you think of that, eh?' he said, his red hair falling over his face. 'Isn't it tre*men*dous?' He's got a trick of emphasising the middle syllable—tre*men*dously! Sometimes he plays on his trumpet in an almost religious manner—and I think he's quite good—very serious. He bought a small trumpet for little Bertie and it's funny to see them playing together. He's very fond of children. But I'm afraid he doesn't like the college woman. 'Too prim,' he said. And even me he considers prim but he says there's hope for me.

One night at 11 o'clock he was sitting on my bed looking down at the floor and listening to a record. Then he suddenly switched it off and said to me: 'You know you may not know it—clever as you are—but you are on the side of life. I can tell. It's the way you listen—and that wistfulness of yours as if you were listening for . . . a different music.' I don't even know what he means.

I'm sorry you don't think I should go to visit him. It's true enough that we only have a fortnight but it doesn't matter really. I think you would like him, however. I think I told you before he doesn't drink. Why are you asking me again? Something's disturbing him though I don't know what it is. Last night he talked about the hydrogen bomb and about his parents and about the fishing. 'It's so far away, somehow,' he said. 'All that. Don't you find that?' I said nothing. Then he made one of his sudden changes of mood and said: 'Never mind, we'll hear what Mr Bryden (our landlord) has seen in the pictures this week. *The Son of Hippocrates* or *Hippocrates Rides again.*'

I'm sorry to hear this squabble continues. It's indecent. Now I must work. And I am working. Harder than ever since I was up at the lecturer's.

Did you say Alasdair was dying? I hope not. He was a good man. There's too much dying in our island.

Goodnight,
Your loving son,
Kenneth

P.S. By the way it *was* Sunday George and I went for that walk.

I have nothing much to write about tonight except that I was thinking how in the city at night the lamp-posts are so separate from each other like professors studying the road. At home it isn't like this. At home there is moonlight connecting ditches and so on. Here it isn't like that. In the city you are freer, yet . . .

The romance between Jake and Joan goes on. Joan is what one would say fleshily pretty with a prettiness that will run to fat. Her smile goes outward in a curiously candid manner. And Jake still blushes! George insists that they call him in for their first child and hands her a plate full of vegetables. I couldn't do that. He is so natural and never offensive. Why aren't we like that? He was telling us of the fishing, how the boats used to go out in the evening in the sunset and how they'd come back again in the cold sunrise. He spent most of his trips cooking. Once according to himself he filled the soup with sugar instead of salt and imitated the crew's expressions as they drank it. Even the landlady was in hysterics. I think Jake and Joan will get married eventually. She's only 19 but girls get married earlier here. I often wonder why at home marriages are so late. I have ideas about it, and I've been reading some of the works of a man called Freud lately. He's very interesting. Why aren't we taught about him in school? I seem to know very little really.

I often wonder too why I used to be ill so often when I was young. All that bronchitis and asthma every summer. It was very strange. And those mustard baths. And the sun on the partition. I am never ill here at all. I have never felt so well, even though I work hard.

Sometimes in the evenings after supper we sit in the dining room by the fire, George and I and Miss Burgess the lecturer (she is small and plump and sews a great deal). We argue—rippingly—I never realised how splendid it is simply to argue. George talks about the hydrogen bomb, but as I said before he seems to be an echo of someone else. He's not really interested, except that he once said something which set me thinking: 'Is the image of hell connected with the hydrogen bomb?' That's interesting, you know. And he's mischievous too. He asks the landlord what pictures he's seen and the landlord who's very slow (with a moustache and white teeth) explains all about the picture at great length. He is not really a good narrator and is soon tangled up. For example he was telling us about *The Goat Woman Strikes Back*, and George was questioning him freely as if it had been an argument by Russell.

'And why did she put a spell on him? I want to know. We must be reasonable.'

I thought this was funny since he seemed to take a pleasure in discomfiting the landlord (no, that's not true, the landlord didn't realise his leg was being pulled). We sometimes listen to the songs on the radio and sometimes he asks me about home. It's incredible to him that they don't like dancing, that we daren't walk outside on Sundays, that we don't have cinemas . . . However, I defend us. Mind you, there's something in what he says.

I don't go to dances, because I *enjoy* reading and studying. I *enjoy* books. They are like food to me. Or at least have been . . . Though sometimes I grow tired. I don't read Latin and Greek all the time. I've been reading Eliot and Camus and . . . but there are so many.

I sometimes go to the cafe in the morning for coffee. It's a small cafe run by an intelligent man of 35 who speaks and acts like a student himself and has a sort of crackling wit. Behind the cafe there is a lawn and on fine days—most of the days have been fine—we sit out at the back under the trees in the speckled sunshine on yellow deckchairs. Will we ever be as happy as this again? The bells, the ivy, the conversation, the books, the sun.

Coming home yesterday I saw two men fighting at a street corner. Neither of them was drunk so far as I could see. I watched their faces. They were terrible with hatred, not blind, because they were looking at each other as if they could kill each other. One of them brought his knee up at the other's stomach. And yet was the expression on their faces not hatred at all but fear? Two ragged boys were watching them at the edge of the lot, but all the others like me hurried past. I had soon forgotten them.

I'm sorry to hear about Alasdair but he was quite old, wasn't he? I suppose we have to accept that. Once I didn't accept it so much but was terrified. Now, I see that one must learn to take it as it is.

The thought has just occurred to me. I wonder what Mr Mulgrew would have said if he had seen that fight. Sophocles must have seen worse and yet it's not there, not really. Strange! 'What has Sophocles to do with us?' George asked me. What indeed! And the library with its sculptured busts of alabaster? What have they? That has to be answered.

Yes, I go to church every Sunday but Mr Wood has very little to say. In fact he has nothing to say. He has invited me to his home but I shan't go. I would only be hypocritical.

I am working as hard as ever. I hope to do well. I drive myself to work every night. There are more distractions here than at home but so far I've maintained my hard work.

George often asks me about you. He seems very interested

in my early childhood illnesses. Last week he sounded me but said I was as clear as a bell. He says that sometimes he envies me for my background but at other times . . . I don't see what you have against George. I like him very much.

I think you should be going out more. I really do. It's not good to depend on one person so much.

George's girl friend is coming here tomorrow. I shall be interested to see what she is like.

Anyone would think from your letter that I was leading a dissipated life. I can assure you I'm not. And after all, you were at Lowestoft yourself when you were only 16. I know it was cold and miserable and the fishing was dreadful but it was a way of life.

> Your loving son,
> Kenneth

Well, Fiona was up visiting George this afternoon and I'm not sure that I like her very much. She is quite unlike anyone I've met before not I mean physically but mentally and in her style. I don't know, but the girls at home seem vague somehow, they're not keenly interested in *anything*. But this girl thinks like a man: she has a cutting edge to her. After we had dinner and all the others except George, Fiona and I had gone to their work we went out to the lawn in front of the house and sat down on deckchairs. No, that's not true, George sat on a deckchair: Fiona and I sat on the ground. George, I thought, was looking rather unsure of her. He lay back in his striped deckchair with his hands clasped behind his red hair, listening. Another thing by the way is that Fiona wears slacks. She *cross-examines* one and I don't like that. In fact I dislike it immensely.

'Well,' said George lazily, 'why don't you argue?'

'Shut up,' Fiona snapped.

There was a long silence inside the green shadows. One could almost hear the grass grow.

Without thinking I said: 'This is much less bleak than home.'

'Oh?' said Fiona. 'Of course you come from Raws.' Then after a while she added thoughtfully: 'I suppose it must really be pretty bleak there.'

For some reason I became angry: 'It's not as bleak as all that.'

She looked at me in surprise, 'Well, it was you who said so.' Her face is very intense and pale. I don't think she wears lipstick. The pallor however is of the kind which is rich, almost creamy, and not a wasted whiteness.

'Don't believe him,' said George mischievously, 'they live like prisoners up there—and they believe in hell! They can't even go for a walk on Sunday.'

'Is that right?' asked Fiona wonderingly.

'No.'

'Do you believe in hell then?'

'Yes.'

'But what kind? You mean fire, brimstone, the little devils, etc?'

'No, but I believe in . . .'

George was looking at me quizzically, half-swivelled round in his chair.

'You're abandoning your people,' he said at least laughingly.

'I'm abandoning nothing,' I retorted. 'I believe in hell but not that sort of hell. There are other hells.'

'Yes,' she said thoughtfully, 'there are indeed,' coolly picking a thin green blade of grass and chewing it.

I don't know exactly what's going on but George told me that two years ago she left her parents' home (which is apparently in the city here) and went to live in digs with another girl.

I didn't like the turn the conversation was taking. I had noticed this in George before—that sometimes without meaning to he's inclined to take advantage of people. It's as if he were testing them. It's as if he's looking for someone who will ring true.

'And what of death?' I said to George, 'what of that?'

'Death?' he said blinking into the sunlight. 'Death? What has death got to do with us?' Infront of us a small bird, possibly a wren—I think wrens are brown and this bird was brown—was hopping across the grass, stopping sometimes and staring up at us almost questioningly.

'Do you think he's frightened?' asked Fiona stretching her finger out. But the bird hopped away again, sideways.

'I once did that,' I heard myself saying, 'it was a snail: it was on a road, a pathway, dusty, with little stones. I shifted a very small stone in front of the snail but for some strange reason before it reached the stone it turned away as if it sensed that the stone was there, without even touching it. I did it a few times and each time it seemed to know.'

Fiona looked at me, I thought, with some respect.

'That's very interesting,' she remarked, but immediately turned away again chewing her grass like a straw in lemonade. Her gaze is almost impersonal as if she were studying a brief.

'It's true just the same,' said George leaning forward from his deckchair and looking animated for the first time. 'Death has nothing to do with us. Fiona here—she's always on about the hydrogen bomb and the rest of it' (Fiona was regarding him very quietly) 'but after all if it comes—pouf.' Though he was fervent in his speech I saw the despair in his eyes. 'We won't know. It'll just come. Like bashing a fish with a stone. That's the point. You die anyway.'

'You talk very queerly—for a prospective doctor,' said Fiona, her eyes following the bird which was now perched bright-eyed on a branch. I had the impression that she had heard this often before.

'But that's why,' George almost shouted, leaning further forward, his elbows on his knees. 'Can't you see? You people make such a lot out of death. It's death, that's all, it's a fact! It's a fact! It comes one way or another. I'd try to save them of course, of course I would. But what can I do about politics? What would we ever do? My father now—it's like the sea—sometimes he gets a good catch sometimes not. If he doesn't who is he to appeal to? We've had all this out before. I can't help it. I'm going to be a doctor but I'm not a blazing enthusiast. I love children, yes, all right but what can I do? What can we do?'

I had never heard him speak like this before and I didn't understand it. What had become of the jazz enthusiast? What had become of the joker?

'It's when you see death you begin to accept it. Oh I know

one fights it—one does. But when you see and hear some stories, well, that's different. Of old people living on and that boy, who was drowned. I tell you, sometimes I hate that.' He stood up and aimlessly kicked a stone into the trees. The little bird flew away.

'Now see what you've done,' Fiona protested, 'you've scared him away.'

He looked at her in astonishment as if about to say 'The bird' but instead shut his mouth again. At the same time a wasp swooped on her—striped rather like a deckchair—and she swept it away with her hand almost absent-mindedly.

With one of his sudden changes of mood George slumped back into the deckchair saying: 'I'm not going to speak another word. That's me finished.' However he was speaking very good-humouredly.

Fiona stood up removing some of the grass from her slacks and began:

'But *I'm* not. You think like Kenneth here,' (he started) 'you think you don't but you do. You accept hell too. That's what you do, you accept it. You say you can't do anything about it. Why can't you? You can't because you don't care. You think you're on the side of life because you play your jazz tunes and go to dances, but you aren't. You don't care because you don't see. What's your father got to do with this? It's not your father. It's you. And what has the fishing to do with it?'

George looked at me half-laughingly but didn't speak. Instead he took out two cigarettes and tossed one to her. She caught it while still speaking.

We don't have girls like this at home, not with this passion. I was listening but not speaking. When eventually she turned to me I said:

'I'm sorry. I'm not on your side. I think we need the bomb. I know you go to meetings and I honour you for it but I can't see it. We need it to defend ourselves. That's all. I doubt if it will ever be used anyway.'

That was all I said. I was honest when I said I honoured her for attending these meetings but I—there was something too ruthless about her, too dominating. I didn't want to be dominated. I was afraid of her in some queer way. It was like these riddles old Angus used to ask me. I dreaded them as if I would make a mistake and I don't like making mistakes. And I'm sure I'm right too and she's wrong. Where will this tenderness get us? These birds? Then she said a strange thing:

'You're different from George, though. You'll see.' And she added: 'You'll see.'

But what am I to see? The afternoon sun was waning slightly and I felt a slight chill. I wanted to stay here and argue but at the same time I wanted to leave. She reminded me of someone but I could not think of whom.

In fact I've been thinking that these letters are sometimes difficult for me to write. You want to know about everything but writing in English I can't communicate somehow. It's so formal. I begin to feel that we have never really communicated. However . . .

So we left it there and the three of us relaxed in the chilling air for a while, George with his eyes closed, I feeling rather out of things as if I had caused a quarrel between George and Fiona and wondering what he had told her about me before she came, and Fiona in her red slacks curled up on the ground tightly like a spring. How had they ever come into contact? Well, George told me. They met at a dance and I suppose hearing that he was a prospective doctor she thought he would be a natural for her ideas and she might discover interesting information as well. Not that she was as calculating as this: no one as passionate as she is could be as calculating as that, but it must have crossed her mind.

Anyway they're not suited to each other. George is too pedestrian for her. I can see that. I think medicine is getting him down.

As for me I have a greater capacity for suffering than either of them. These long summer days in bed—the blackness—the eternal fire—these things have hardened me. I'll not be broken, I know that, not by her arguments. And after all it may be we shall never meet again.

For some reason the thought came into my mind just now. Do you remember Mrs Armstrong? You remember that the day her husband died she stopped the clock and never wound it again. Why did I think of that just now?

And when we went into her house—the silence there was, the silence you could hear.

When I saw the two of them going out together, George clowning again and she walking briskly to keep up with him, I thought they looked so young. And yet both of them are older than me! By one year. It's the heart of man. Will that ever change? Will it ever change?

I'm still working hard—in fact harder than ever—and doing reasonably well.

Why did you send me that money? Don't martyr yourself. It makes me feel guilty.

Your loving son,
Kenneth

P.S. The thing that fascinates me most about university is the way one argues as if the mind matters. At home it wasn't like that. Nothing we could do seemed to matter. Like that bird hopping about, that's how it is now. Of course it wasn't free. But in a way it was. Perhaps that was why Fiona was watching it all the time, the diminutive wren hopping about. I'm sure that phrase diminutive wren is from some book or other, probably Shakespeare but I can't remember where.

Last night sitting in the dining room after supper I listened to a monologue from George. We were in our armchairs in a sort of restful near-midnight silence with the radio playing nostalgic music. Perhaps that's what started him off.

'After we left you today,' he began, 'we didn't talk much. And yet what I said this afternoon was true. They say it all goes back to your childhood. I don't know. My father is a fisherman. You have to know about fishing. It's not like a profession. It's more—precarious. All fishermen drink, you know, well, most of them. You see, they're living under strain. My father doesn't drink all that much but he drinks, a little. Living in a small place does that too. He's a big man, very friendly, very slaphappy. My mother's different—good worker, you know the sort, very industrious. No, I didn't have an unhappy childhood, not at all. I spent a lot of time at the motor boats tinkering about and watching them at the harbour, most of them painted yellow with their names

and the yellow buoys on the deck and the green nets . . .
But sometimes we were hungry, very hungry. I could have
savaged a piece of meat in my childhood. You can't eat fish
all of the time.

'Once my father told me a story. He used to tell me a
lot of stories. It was when he was younger—when he was
sailing—he ended up in New Zealand. A few of them
jumped ship and stayed behind. One holiday they went
out in a small boat—two of them, the day was warm. Very
lazy they were, very lazy, drifting along. Then they began
to take off their clothes—it was so hot—first the jackets,
then the shirts. The sea was—you know—glassy with that
tremendous eye-shattering heat. They decided they'd have
a plunge—smell of tar from the boat too. So they lowered
themselves over the side. No, his friend went first while he
kept the boat steady. It was very warm, very calm. Then the
shark came. It sheared right through his friend. The boat
toppled slightly then he steadied it, sort of. There was some
threshing through which he rowed, then nothing. Later they
found his friend's stocking—one stocking.

'He often used to tell me stories. You know he didn't
drink at all then. Later of course he didn't drink much, but
some. There was some—precariousness, but I was happy.
I don't write to them, not because I don't like them but
because I'm lazy—I'm quite lazy really. I suppose I became
a doctor to enter a profession. I didn't want to be poor, you
see, again.

'And sometimes, you know, you see certain things, like
that drowned boy. They don't get you down all that
much, but Fiona, she's romantic, she thinks that life is
so tremendously important, and death too. I . . . Well,
she's pretty you know. Sometimes you don't think so, but
there's bone there. Intensity. So few people have it. Like
. . . It's precious. Oh, I'll be a doctor all right and a good
one. Remember I told you once you were on the side of life?
You are. I laugh more than you, and I joke, but perhaps
it's defensive. Since I came here I saw an old woman. She's
hanging on to life like a leech in the hospital. Why? And
her daughter comes in, weary, weary. It would be better
if the old woman died. But she doesn't. She hates life too.

She's always complaining. She's 80—and I once heard her call on her mother. What do you think of that?

'Oh well. Up. Bed, boy. End of Reminiscences of George Morton.

'But I'll tell you this. I've never met anyone like Fiona. I've been out with a lot of girls but . . . she's alive you know. At the dance I met her, you couldn't help being attracted, it was as if she was gulping up life. If you take her to the pictures she's leaning forward, she takes part in the film. You can feel her throwing the pies—and cracking nuts between her teeth. There's a quality of carelessness about her—a divine carelessness.

'Hey! That's great. I ought to be a poet. "Divine carelessness." That's good, that's good. Come on, let's go upstairs and pull the chain and wake Mrs Bryden from her dreams of filthy lucre.'

So that's George since you wanted to know about him.

As he was talking, for some reason this came into my head. Do you remember Mrs Murray who died about five years ago, you know at 10a. You remember Donald her son—he died of tuberculosis—he was 16. I used to visit him. It was in the black house. I remember listening to her once. She was telling me the minister had been in—in fact he used to come in often. 'Donald,' she said, 'he talks about these practical jokes of yours, you know when you let Norman's horse loose and when you took that dead rat into school. He laughs at all these things remembering them and yourself. These are the things he's always talking about and the jam jar you ran away with. And he doesn't know what's waiting for him. The doctor says he'll die but Donald doesn't know it. He's gay—but he coughs a lot. And all he talks about is these nonsensical things! The minister tells him to read the Bible but he hardly ever does. And he doesn't pray. He says he doesn't know how to. He sometimes can't stop himself laughing when the minister is praying. What am I going to do with him?'

I don't know why I thought of that but it came back to me very clearly, and especially the last thing she told me. They told him he was going to die and the minister was always there. Strangely enough he wanted the minister to be with him and he was already reading the Bible. She said however that he was always following her about with his eyes as if he were asking her something and she couldn't think what it was. The moment he died she was sitting in a chair knitting. The Bible fell out of his hand and she went to give it back to him but he was dead. She told me that when she bent down she remembered that the Bible itself was cold but the sun on the floor below was warm. For some reason she remembered this.

I hate the deaths of our island. There are too many. There are far too many deaths.

Your loving son,
Kenneth

I do not understand your letter. Why this attack on Fiona? No, I haven't seen her since that day but that is no reason for your letter. I don't understand it. I begin to think you are not trying to understand me, though I am trying to understand you. You are not even trying. I know what you have done for me, believe me. I appreciate it. But at the same time it is clear that you are not trying to understand me. That is terrifying. I hadn't realised it before. Fiona is not like that at all. You say she has no right to meddle with these things, that it's not woman's work. What do you expect her to do? Go to the well for pails of water? You say that the government know best. I don't agree. What have they done for us? I'm beginning to see a lot of things. Hell paralyses the will. I don't agree with her, but I don't see why she shouldn't go to meetings if she wishes to. I am not under bad influence. I work hard. I drive myself far into the night. But sometimes I wonder why I do it. At home one doesn't question these things, but I can't prevent my mind from developing.

I will tell you something. I have a picture of an island. It is bleak but the people are gentle. Oh they are gentle enough and polite and well mannered . . . But it may be the gentility of the dead. I see them sitting by their TV sets as here and not walking casually into each other's houses as before without knocking. There is nothing we can do against that, but prepare ourselves. Gentility is not enough in the world we're born into. It is a weakness. To break the will of the children is wrong.

What have I seen in the city since I came? I have seen beggars and lonely men, I have seen the yellow lights of the mind, and the crooked shadows. Yet we must learn to live with it. I know we must. You should not have written that letter. Children should be able to respect their parents. You must try to learn to understand. I know it is difficult but you must learn to try. There is nothing else for you to do, *nothing else*.

Sometimes I get terrified. In this house there are seven or eight people. The landlady—what does she live for, but the making of money? And what will she do with it? She will leave it to her children. And her husband who smokes his pipe and watches films twice or thrice a week? Were the two of them always like that? Or were they once like Jake and Joan? How have they been cheated? And this lady lecturer, who spends her evenings sewing or visiting her friend, the other lady lecturer, what has she to look forward to? These things *have to be answered*. I sometimes wonder: Might they not as well be dead? Perhaps that's what happened to man: he was unfortunate enough to be able to prolong his life. For most people might as well be dead at thirty. And yet . . . I feel that's wrong. There is some meaning if one can find it—a precarious balance somewhere. One looks out and sees, like the Lady of Shalott. But one day the mirror breaks. One should not think like this. Or is it that others don't see it, the abyss?

Jake and Joan are happy. They will be married. They follow each other with their eyes and to others appear silly: but they are precious to each other. And perhaps that is enough: even for a short while. I don't know. Today I got a wedding invitation from Norman, Norman Morrison. He knows I can't go to the wedding but he sent me the invitation and a flattering letter calling me his dearest friend. And it's true I suppose. We went to school together. We used to be sent out gardening together by the head-master. We ate the stolen strawberries with their almost unbearable tartness together. We studied for our bursaries and read the crates of books from the library, surreptitiously checking over our answers to arithmetic problems. And I am glad he is to be married, but I know that we will never speak to each other again in the same way.

I am sick of our melancholy, sick of it. I want to see things as they are. It is necessary. I am sick and tired of people saying No. It is necessary to stop saying No.

I am sorry about your letter. I am very sorry and shocked. I do not think you should have written it. I think it's time you went out amongst people more. I think it is time you depended less on me, although I shall never abandon you. It is time you looked at the facts. I do not want this burden of guilt. It is time we laughed more—high time.

> Your loving son,
> Kenneth

TWO

Yesterday quite by chance I ran into Fiona. I went into the cafe in front of the reading room—where I sometimes study—and there she was. After my ten days at home I had completely forgotten about her. She was sitting by herself in a corner seat drinking coffee. At first she didn't see me, and I watched her. She was idly stirring the coffee with a spoon—her brown and white leather bag was slung over a chair: and she was staring into the cup as if it was—well, perhaps something nuclear! Then she saw me, her face brightened and we began to talk.

I have this bad Highland manner of wanting to know about people—all about them. I pointed to her CND badge and asked her about it. She also showed me the card they are given with its peculiar biblical message. I think she intends going to Aldermarston for the march.

'I'm tired of studying,' she said, 'I feel suffocated. Honestly I do. Suffocated. As if I can't get enough air. Sometimes I walk down to the quay and watch the ships. That helps a little but not much.'

I found it strange listening to her because that was how I felt when I was home—as if I were being strangled to death by invisible hands. However I don't feel so bad now.

She talked fairly freely about her parents after a while:

'My mother's dead,' she said, 'my father's alive. He's a lawyer. He's a fairly successful lawyer—here. Once he had a chance to try for a bigger job in England: but my mother was ill at the time, with her nerves, and he couldn't go.'

She twisted her fingers on the table and I'm sure she didn't notice.

'They used to have the most terrible rows at first. He used to blame her for holding him back. He drinks a lot. Families are like that,' she said, looking out into the street where the large statue of Sir Walter Scott confronted us. 'They fight each other and kill each other and feed off each other.'

I told her a little about George.

'That's different,' she maintained, 'that's honest. My father wasn't like that. His hatred at the end was a cold hatred. Eventually he wouldn't speak to my mother at all. It's strange that. Sometimes I saw him actually grit his teeth. She was one of these defenceless people who invited bullying. But he didn't bully her. He would simply get drunk and ignore her. Once I saw her pouring tea into his cup. It was late, I remember, and he had just come in. The hot tea spilt over her hand. She didn't scream and I saw the red coming up on her hand. But he did nothing. He carried on drinking his tea, as if he hadn't noticed. But I saw that he had noticed, and yet he pretended that he hadn't.

'When my mother died two years ago I left him. That was all. One afternoon when he was at the office I simply packed a bag and left the house. I left a note. I remember I had difficulty with the key. First of all I locked the door and then I had the key in my hand. So I threw it in through the window and walked away. He didn't ask for me back. It was as if he was tired of the lot of us. He tried to give me money (it's very easy to give people money) but I didn't take it. I had some from my mother. She was saving up in a bank for me. She was all I had you see. Anyway he didn't really bother about me much. I can imagine him in the morning shaving and sitting down to have his breakfast and getting the car out, but it's as if I was thinking of a stranger. I have no sympathy for him. I don't hate him, I have no feeling for him. That's all.'

She added, 'I think that was why I joined the CND.'

'How do you mean?'

'I don't know. It's something to do with that pressure. Do you think about it like that?' I didn't understand. Sometimes I'm quite stupid.

'Well, the pressure builds up and you get a nuclear bomb, that's all. But I don't want it to be like that—that would be like my father you see. Something went wrong in his ambitions and the pressure built up. It would have been more honest if he had left my mother. But in his position, you know, that would never do. Like a lawyer I heard of recently. His girl friend wanted to be married in a registry office. But no—not him. He wanted a church wedding: and he's an atheist too.' Looking out of the window she suddenly burst out laughing, a pure bell-like laugh. It's difficult to describe it. It's not the laugh of innocence. It's the laugh which has gone beyond pretensions, it's the pure laugh of comedy which almost for a moment accepts the universe as it is.

Yet I didn't laugh like that. I believe these lies and hypocrisies are evil. They are the greatest evil. And they are within the church too. I dream of another church, a more precarious one, and that laughter will be its bell . . .

I didn't know what else to say except:

'It's the same everywhere. Because people refuse to look. They've got to protect themselves.'

'I suppose so,' she said. 'Can I get you a coffee?'

Instinctively I said 'No' (By the way that's a very funny thing about me which I thought of recently. If anyone asks me a question and I haven't been listening but I pretend that I have I always say 'No': I never say 'Yes') because I don't like women buying anything for men, and because she can't have much money. Then I changed my mind for some reason and said 'Yes'.

For a long time we said nothing and then we went out and walked along the street in the cool of the evening. We said nothing at all. When we parted I simply said 'Goodnight Fiona' and she said 'Goodnight Kenneth'—she had asked me no questions about myself or my home—and I walked home. That was all. The sky was green above the tram rails.

When I got home George was not yet in. At ten o'clock he came in slightly drunk. I had never seen him drunk before. I think it's a bad sign. I managed to keep him from stumbling over anything and from getting himself entangled with one of the stair rails which is slightly loose and got him to bed. He slept almost as soon as his head hit the pillow. His red hair was sweating and his face was white. I don't know what's wrong with him.

This is quite a long letter. I shall write again soon. I hope you are well.

> Goodnight,
> Your loving son,
> Kenneth

Tonight at seven I put down my books and I thought I'd write to you. I kept finding there was something I ought to explain but I couldn't think what it was. Then George came in and we played some records. He lay on the bed with his hands behind his head looking up at the ceiling and saying nothing. Sometimes I caught him looking at me as if he wished to say something but he didn't. (By the way Jean and Jake have announced their engagement. When Jake told us about it he was grinning and there was oil on his face: I thought that was very endearing.) I nearly asked George what was the matter with him but I didn't. I just sat and listened, or rather at first I wasn't listening at all. Then it came into my consciousness that this was a woman singing and there was a kind of catch in her voice. It was the Blues—a sort of jazz—and a spiritual. For some strange reason this made me think of our church. I think it must have been the black disc spinning. (All this time George was lying on the bed looking up at the ceiling, perfectly motionless.) Then it struck me. This was the sort of church I wanted. This woman had more faith and more depth and more sheer melody of life than our Minister.

I remembered an incident which took place at home. You know Mrs McInnes the widow, the one with a son in Australia. I was in her house one night and Mrs MacLeod was there. They were talking about how her son had sent money home by a local sailor and they had never seen it. He must have spent it. This Mrs MacLeod—she's got a sort of moustache and I remember she was wearing a sort of rabbit collar—she suddenly said:

'He will pay for his sins. There's one thing I always believe in. People must be made to pay for their sins.'

I looked at her and there was hate in her face. Her lips were tight. And yet really it had nothing to do with her. She wasn't even concerned. Listening to that record I thought of that and I realised something which I suppose I must have known for a long time.

WE ARE A NEW GENERATION.

WE ARE DIFFERENT FROM YOU.

I remember too when you were reminiscing with some of your friends. I didn't understand you. You told each other your jokes but they had no meaning for me. They were past. They were finished.

And I think I know why George started drinking. The reason is he is supposed to cure people, but he doesn't know WHAT FOR. That is why he listens to the music. He wants to find out why he should cure people. That's all. I watched him. His eyes were open at first and I could see him studying the light bulb. Then slowly they shut but he wasn't sleeping. It was as if he were really listening. I heard a trumpet, one clear note—a single pure note like water—no, George said it was like a drink of cool milk during fever or after a hangover, the very cold milk you get in cartons from these machines—this single note held perfectly steady—like a guarantee of something—rising out of the wrestlings of the music, out of the sweat of billiard rooms and men with green eyeshades—this single pure note, and then George opened his eyes, and that was all. The record ended then.

I wanted to tell you that because it's the thing that's been troubling me. The pressures are so tremendous. You must try to understand, please. It will be terrible if you don't try.

I haven't had an answer to my last letter yet so this is an extra.

Your loving son,
Kenneth

I am sorry I'm late in answering your letter. The truth is, I've been ill but not at all seriously. Strangely enough, it is a recurrence of my asthma which I haven't felt since I was 12. I was sitting down to my books the other night when it began. I went to bed and felt like a fool.

I lay in my room in absolute silence for most of the day. It was a strange experience listening to the silence, and watching the leaves swaying slightly against the window. My room is high up and I don't hear the traffic. In the evening George would come in and sit at my bedside (for company) studying. He has exams soon and he's working hard. He looks more cheerful now. Jake also came to see me, and appears more responsible. I think Joan must be making him wash the oil from his face. He doesn't spend so much time with his motor cycle now.

The landlady left me alone during the daytime. In a way it was a luxurious illness. I felt, not quite alone, but rather at ease for the first time during an illness. I read nothing and would lie there for hours not even thinking but allowing thoughts to flit across my mind like leaves across the window pane. I can't understand why I should have this asthma now.

The landlord sometimes came in after he'd been to the pictures. He is fairly tall with a moustache and very white teeth. He told me all about the pictures he had seen. At first I used to laugh at him quietly inside myself but I don't any more. My new humility almost frightens me. He talked to me about the taxis. Apparently he prefers to drive by night. That's surprising isn't it? When he has no film to speak about he says nothing but sits there with his hands between his legs as if he were a guest in my house. Funny, isn't it? George listens to his stories very seriously which is a new development.

One morning I was awake watching the dawn come up. Usually in the past I have felt nervous in the early morning, with a hollow in the pit of my stomach. This morning however I felt at ease as if in tune with the day which was coming into being like a poem into a poet's mind. And I thought: what a miracle light is. What would happen to us if one night we suddenly realised that the thick darkness would last forever, the thick furry darkness. Fiona wrote me a note but did not come to see me.

I spent four days in bed and when I got up I decided I would not be sick again. I went into the bathroom. The sun was shining on the white bath, and its rays were on the mirror. The diamonds on the floor were very bright and real. After I had shaved and washed my face I felt new. Then I went downstairs for my breakfast: it was like a royal entrance. I loved everybody. Rising from the sick bed is like being reborn. I knew that this love of mine would not last but it did not matter. For that moment it was precious—the stumpy landlady with her vulpine face appeared angelic, her tray silver and her tea wine: her two children could even have sprouted wings: red-haired George was my dearest friend: Jake and Joan were Adam and Eve in the Garden: and there was no evil in the world. (Strangely enough I happened that same evening to overhear the landlady complain about her tiredness caused by her climbing stairs with my food but that did not matter either.)

No, I believe that people are essentially good. If it is possible to see them like that at all, then that is the way we must see them. (Do I sermonise too much?)

In the evening George and I went to the cinema. It is an old cinema. Once upon a time one could get in with empty jam jars (presumably lemon curd for the balcony) and during the performance, believe it or not, a man sprayed us all over with disinfectant. It was a western film and I enjoyed it very much. After sickness, how much one enjoys the world, like a dewdrop on a thorn! We had no need to talk to each other.

Tomorrow I'm going to one of the CND parades with Fiona. It should be interesting.

I hope you are well. Here the weather is good and I suppose it will be the same at home.

I mean that: I'm not going to be sick again.

> Your loving son,
> Kenneth

An extraordinary thing has happened which I must think about. Today Fiona and I went to the CND sit down demonstration. We sat down on the pavement opposite the City Chambers which are next to the Art Gallery. It was all very quiet and companionable somehow, people sitting down in the sunshine eating sandwiches as if they were on holiday. The pavement was quite warm (unusually warm—mind you, I don't make a practice of sitting on pavements). There were no speeches. The speeches had already been made at Hutton Park. We sat there surrounded by a crowd of people most of whom we had never seen before and would never see again. It is interesting to watch people passing. After a while you only see their legs, some dumpy, some thin, some active, some slow, some old, some young. There were one or two mounted policemen. They look tall on their gleaming horses, and in their leather leggings.

What does one talk about? We talked about examinations mainly. It was almost weird. I wondered what many of them were doing there. I wondered what I was doing there. Everyone was very orderly and placed sandwich papers in bags or in those wire bins one sees attached to posts. There was one woman beside me: she was dressed entirely in red and reading *Woman's Own*. Extraordinary! Then something happened. We were such an orderly crowd with this hum of conversation going on, like a gala, girls in light summery dresses, men in open-neck shirts. There were babies, milk bottles and lemonade bottles.

Then it happened. One of our group—a student I think—had been pushed towards the middle of the road. It wasn't his fault. It was simply the pressure of the crowd. A policeman came up to him—one of the ones who had been directing the traffic.

It's a funny thing about policemen. Usually you don't notice them at all. You don't somehow think of them as people with emotions. They are there to look calm and controlled and placid and that is what they do. That is what they are paid for. They walk in such a deliberate manner as if they have an understanding with time.

Anyway this policeman came up to him and began to tell him to move back. Now I can understand that some of the policemen must have been harassed. The day was

warm—even hot—and there were a lot of people and
perhaps they didn't quite know what to do. Furthermore
it can't be very comfortable for a policeman to walk about
in cloth of such thick texture on a hot day. This was quite
a young policeman. I looked at his face and in a surprised
flash I realised something. This policeman wasn't being
merely tired and harassed, he actually appeared to hate
this student. It was in his eyes and also in his teeth which
I saw for a moment bared as he hissed out a command.
It startled me coming out of that fine day. He pushed the
student ahead of him roughly: the student pushed him back,
(I saw his blue untidy scarf). Then the policeman twisted
the student's arm behind his back, and shouted, upon which
another policeman came running up: it was like the natural
order being over-turned. The student's face was white with
pain: whistles were being sounded: the crowd was milling
aimlessly around. I saw some milk spilled on the pavement
beside me and bits of glass. Then I saw Fiona pushing her
way through the crowd. I could hardly recognise her. Her
face was pale and set. I tried to follow her but I lost her.
I climbed up on the top steps to see. She went up to the
policeman and hit him on the back of the head with her
handbag. Then she was seized by another policeman. By
this time a black van had driven up. She and the student
were bundled inside. The door was locked. The van was
driven away.

I stood there watching. The young policeman faced the
crowd. He was almost grinning. I heard him shouting but
I couldn't hear what he was saying. It was as if he hated us.
The crowd began to move away until I stood on the steps
alone. It wasn't the steps of the Municipal Chambers at all:
it was the steps of the Art Gallery. There are ten: I counted.
The young policeman was at the bottom looking up, his legs
wide apart, while the crowd drifted away. I looked down at
him. There was a book in my hand. My flannel trousers
swayed slightly in the breeze. I felt thin, even though I was
angry. I nearly threw the book at him but he looked and
was stronger than me. He did not seem to be standing on
the soles of his feet but rather on his toes. I could see his
face under the diced cap. It was of a high red complexion:

his shoulders were wide and he had the free composure of the fit. His lips appeared petulant and cruel. He stood as if grinning at me for a while—I had the strangest sensation as if he was daring me to attack him—then with an arrogance which was entirely unlike that of a policeman he turned and began as if in parody to pace up and down with a slow deliberate tread.

I left that place and began to walk, not knowing where I was headed for. Eventually I found myself at the iron gates of the university. I walked past the sacrist in his navy-blue uniform with the yellow facings, up the flagged road and into the library. The ivy was very green and grassy, the library very cool. I sat down at a table to rest my feet. In an alcove the logic professor was leaning down close over a book so that his face almost seemed to touch it. I watched him for a while, then suddenly realised that he was asleep. I looked at the dead-white cool busts scattered round the library. I laid my sweating hands on the cool table. I was surrounded by rows and rows of books, but I had no desire to read them. After I had sufficiently rested I got up and went out, carefully closing the door after me. Then I walked down the flagged path. The sacrist was no longer to be seen and the sliding window at the enquiry office was shut. I walked back into town over the rough tarry stones and went home. Then I sat down at the window and thought. Eventually I dipped my pen into the ink and began to write. That is what I could do.

But I shall have to think.

Your loving son,
Kenneth

Today I went to the courtroom. It was 11 in the morning and I was allowed to enter among the few spectators. I sat down on one of the varnished benches, feeling the hot sun warm on my shoulder. There was a big clock which I could see through the window. The atmosphere in the courtroom was very cool and quiet, as in a church, but on the seat at the front of the adjoining benches sat that policeman, his cap beside him on the seat, his hair brilliant and black and cropped, the back of his neck scrubbed and red. Sometimes he looked round as if he were waiting to arrest one of us but none of us was making a noise. He didn't seem to recognise me. Why should he?

At 11 o'clock the clerk—or whoever he is—came in and we all stood up. Then the judge, a small old man, walked rather unsteadily to his raised seat. He wore a hearing-aid. Imagine it! It was like something out of Dickens. It's perfectly true! Then Fiona and the student were led in. She did not look at me, though she was looking towards me. It was strange how that was: yet she appeared calm, though pale. The student was thin, dark-haired, with dark rings under his eyes. He didn't look as if he had slept and he answered questions in a low voice. I noticed that one of his turn-ups was turned down: I found this endearing and pitiful. His tie was also slightly askew. He kept feeling in his pocket as if he were hunting for something—perhaps his cigarette case—but all these things are taken away from prisoners.

The first witness called was the policeman. (I now noticed that there was another policeman beside him: I hadn't noticed before.) My policeman walked up to the witness box and stood there for a moment before reading his statement in a heavy placid self-satisfied tone. But before he began to read, the judge suddenly turned to Fiona and said:

'I hear your father is a lawyer and that you refused his services. Is that true?'

'Yes.'

He looked at her for a moment as if there was something he didn't understand, then said to the policeman:

'Carry on, constable.'

I thought that was a very old-world word. The policeman had hardly begun when the judge said: 'Could you please speak a little louder?'

The policeman glanced at him, I thought, with a curious masked contempt, but raised his voice as he had been ordered, the judge meanwhile cupping his hand over his right ear, and leaning towards him. Fiona was staring right through me and through the window asking nothing of me but existing in a world of her own which was also a real world for she did not look like a statue or a coin:

she looked what she was, pale and weak. I wondered
what sort of night she had spent and sensed that she
was frightened. I thought of how my own stomach turns
over when I am frightened and how the sweat prickles
my hands.

'. . . then the accused'—looking briefly at the student
—'began to rain blows on me.'

'That is not true.' I had stood up. It was my voice. I had
said, 'That is not true' because it was not true but I had not
said it as one interrupts a lecturer who is demonstrating a
theorem and who has made an error. I had said it as if I
were throwing a stone. It was curious how the policeman
continued as if he had not heard me: it was the judge who
stopped him. The judge was old, but he had heard me.
Fiona was looking at me, as if she was seeing me for the
first time. Beyond the hearing-aid, the judge's mind was
feeling towards me.

I said, 'It is not true. He was not raining blows at him.'
I was appealing to the judge but at the same time I had the
strangest feeling as if I was happy though I was frightened.
It was like having the sweetness and terrible coldness of ice
cream on your teeth at the same time. The policeman had
stopped speaking, and was standing as if he didn't know
what to do.

The old judge's eyes moved slightly. It was as if he
was puzzled by something for a shadow passed across the
redness—as you can see a crow at sunset—I have seen that
look often in the eyes of the old, the shock of the unexpected
and the strange. I thought he was going to fine or imprison
me, and I began:

'It is untrue because I was there. The witness was doing no
harm. I was watching him. He was pushed into the middle
of the road.'

I now knew what had happened. I had spoken these
words not because of the bomb but because of Fiona. I
knew now what she meant by being on the side of life. She
had asked nothing of me. She had stood there in her pallor
and her weakness and had made no demands. Therefore
I had offered her myself. It was like the amethyst at her
breast exploding into a new bomb, which in turn exploded

within me, the bomb of truth. It is not preaching I want, but vision!

Therefore, there was the old judge leaning between us with his hearing aid and the policeman with his neat diced evil cap laid beside him. There was the smell of varnish and the court which was like a church. The sun exploded through the window, drunkenly. It flashed on the judge's head, leaped through the glass of water, and shone on Fiona's face which was smiling and dizzy. It swayed the wall diagonally towards the policeman, scything him in two, it made the varnish into a stifling musk, and punched me between the eyes exploding light in my head. The prison fell in like a pack of cards. I looked up. The floor swayed like a deck beneath me. The sun was rising over the sea. There was the noise of a train and coloured flowers. Above me was George's face. And Fiona was standing beside him. The floor steadied. I was calm, so calm. I had never been so calm. Now I write out of this calmness, Fiona and I. George has gone and we are alone. We send you this letter, Fiona and I.

Your loving son,
Kenneth

The Old Woman, the Baby and Terry

THE FACT WAS that the old woman wanted to live. All her faculties, her energies, were shrunken down to that desire. She drew everything into herself so that she could live, survive. It was obscene, it was a naked obscenity.

'Do you know what she's doing now?' said Harry to his wife Eileen. 'She keeps every cent. She hoards her pension, she's taken to hiding her money in the pillow slips, under blankets. She reminds me of someone, I can't think who.'

'But what can we do?' said Eileen, who was expecting a baby.

Harry worked with a Youth Organization. He earned £7,000 a year. There was one member of the organization called Terry MacCallum who, he thought, was insane. Terry had tried to rape one of the girls on the snooker table one night. He was a psychopath. Yet Harry wanted to save him. He hated it when he felt that a case was hopeless.

'She won't even pay for a newspaper,' said Harry.

'I know,' said Eileen. 'This morning I found her taking the cigarette stubs from the bucket.'

The child jumped in her womb. She loved Harry more than ever: he was patient and kind. But he grew paler every day: his work was so demanding and Terry MacCallum was so mad and selfish.

'I've never met anyone like him,' said Harry. 'His self-ishness is a talent, a genius. It's diamond hard, it shines. I should get rid of him, I know that. Also he's drunk a lot of the time. He said to me yesterday, I don't care for anyone. I'm a bastard, you know that. I'm a scrounger, I hate everyone.'

Harry couldn't understand Terry. Everything that was

done for him he accepted and then kicked you in the teeth. He was a monster. He haunted his dreams.

The child kicked in Eileen's womb. She wanted it badly. She had a hunger for it. She wanted it to suck her breasts, she wanted it to crawl about the room, she wanted it to make her alive again.

And all the time the old lady hoarded her banknotes. One day Eileen mentioned to her that they needed bread but she ignored hints of any kind. She even hoarded the bread down the sides of her chair. She tried to borrow money from Eileen. She sang to herself. She gathered her arms around herself, she was like a plant that wouldn't die. Eileen shuddered when she looked at her. She thought that she was sucking her life from her but not like the baby. The baby throve, it milked her, it grew and grew. She was like a balloon, she thrust herself forward like a ship. Her body was like a ship's prow.

'I tried talking to him,' said Harry. 'I can't talk to him at all. He doesn't understand. I can't communicate. He admits everything, he thinks that the world should look after him. He wants everything, he has never grown up. I have never in my life met such selfishness. If he feels sexy he thinks that a woman should put out for him immediately. If he feels hungry he thinks that other people should feed him. I am kind to him but he hates me. What can you do with those who don't see? Is there a penance for people like that? What do you do with those who can't understand?'

The baby moved blindly in her womb, instinctively, strategically. She said to Harry, 'I'm frightened. Today I thought that the ferns were gathering round the house, that they wanted to eat me. I think we should cut the ferns down.'

'Not in your condition,' said Harry. He looked thin, besieged.

The old lady said, 'I don't know why you married him. He doesn't make much money, does he? Why doesn't he move to the city? He could make more money there.' She hid a tea bag in her purse. And a biscuit.

The child moved in the womb. It was a single mouth that

sucked. Blood, milk, it sucked. It grew to be like its mother. It sang a song of pure selfishness. It had stalks like fern. The stars at night sucked dew from the earth. The sun dried the soil. Harry had the beak of a seagull.

'Last night he wouldn't get off the snooker table,' said Harry. 'There are others who want to play, I said to him. This is my snooker table, he said. It isn't, I said. It is, he said. You try and take it off me. And then he said, Lend me five pounds. No, I said. Why, he said. Because you're selfish, I said. I'm not, he said. I'm a nice fellow, everyone says so. I've got a great sense of humour. What do you do with someone like that? I can't get through to him at all. And yet I must.'

'What for?' said Eileen.

'I just have to.'

'You never will,' said Eileen.

'Why not?'

'Just because. Nature is like that. I don't want the child.'

'What?'

'I know what I mean. Nature is like that. I don't want the child.'

Harry had nightmares. He was on an operating table. A doctor was introducing leeches into his veins. The operating table was actually for playing snooker on. It had a green velvet surface. He played with a baby's small head for a ball.

The ferns closed in. In the ferns she might find pound notes. She began to eat bits of coal, stones, crusts. She gnawed at them hungrily. The old lady wouldn't sleep at night. She took to locking her door. What if something happened? They would have to break the door down.

The baby sucked and sucked. Its strategies were imperative. It was like a bee sucking at a flower with frantic hairy legs, its head buried in the blossom, its legs working.

Terry stole some money after the disco. He insisted it was his.

'You lied to me,' said Harry.

'I didn't lie.'

'You said you were at home. I phoned your parents. They said you were out. You lied to me.'

'I didn't lie.'

'But can't you see you said one thing and it wasn't the truth. Can you not see that you lied?'

'I didn't lie.'

'For Christ's sake are you mad. You did lie. What do you think a lie is? Can't you see it?'

'I didn't lie.'

'You'll have to go.'

The old lady had a pile of tea-bags, quarter pounds of butter, cheese, in a bag under the bed.

'You owe me,' she said to Eileen. 'For all those years you owe me. I saw in the paper today that it takes ten thousand pounds to rear a child. You owe me ten thousand pounds. It said that in the paper.'

'You haven't paid for that paper,' said Eileen. 'I've tried my best, don't you understand? How can you be so thick?'

'You owe me ten thousand pounds,' said the old lady in the same monotonous grudging voice. 'It said in the paper. I read it.'

'You are taking my beauty away from me,' said Eileen to the baby. 'You are sucking me dry. You are a leech. You are Dracula. You have blood on your lips. And you don't care.'

She carried the globe in front of her. It had teeth painted all over it.

Harry became thinner and thinner. I must make Terry understand, he kept saying. He must be made to understand, he has never in his whole life given anything to anyone. I won't let him go till I have made him understand. It would be too easy to get rid of him.

Put him out, said Eileen, abort him.

What did you say?

Abort him.

You said abort. I'm frightened.

*   *   *

'Can't you see,' said Eileen. 'That's what it is. People feed and feed. Cows feed on grass, grass feeds on bones, bones feed on other bones. It's a system. The whole world is like a mouth. Blake was wrong. It's not a green and pleasant land at all. The rivers are mouths. The sun is the biggest mouth of all.'

'Are you all right, Eileen?'

'Oh hold me,' said Harry.

And they clung together in the night. But Eileen said, 'Look at the ceiling. Do you see it? It's a spider.' It hung like a black pendant. A moth swam towards the light from the darkness outside. The spider was a patient engineer. Suddenly Eileen stood on top of the bed and ripped the web apart. Bastard, she said. Go and find something else to do. The spider had chubby fists. It was a motheaten pendant.

Terry the psychopath smiled and smiled. He bubbled with laughter.

'Give me,' he said to his mother, 'ten pounds of my birthday money in advance.'

'No.'

'Why not? You were going to give it to me anyway.'

'And what are you going to give me for my birthday?'

'I'll think of something.'

'You won't give me anything, will you? Not a thing will you give me!'

The old woman stole sausages from the fridge, matches from the cupboard. She borrowed cigarettes from Eileen. The latter gazed at her in wonderment, testing how far she would go. The old woman began to wear three coats all at the one time. She tried to go to the bathroom as little as possible: she was hoarding her pee.

'The old woman will live forever,' Eileen screamed. 'She will never die. She will take me with her to the grave. She will hoard me. She will tie string round me, and take me with her to the grave. And the innocent selfish ferns will spring from me. And the baby will feed head down in it, its legs working.'

*   *   *

'No,' she said to Harry, 'I don't want to.'

'Why not? What's wrong with you?'

'I don't want to. It's like the bee.'

'What bee?'

'The bee, I tell you.'

'For Christ's sake,' he said. The bee sucked at her body. It sucked her breasts in a huge wandering fragrance.

'I don't know you,' said her mother. 'Who are you? Are you the insurance lady? I'm not giving you any more money. You're after all my money. Are you the coalman? Eileen should pay for that. She owes me ten thousand pounds. I saw that in the paper.'

'It will cost ten thousand pounds,' Eileen said to Harry.

'What will?'

'The baby. To bring it up. It was in the paper. I don't want to have it. It will want its own snooker table. It will smile and smile and be a villain.'

'You will have to go,' Harry told Terry.

'What for?'

'Because I can't do anything with you.'

'What do you mean? You'll be sorry.'

'Are you threatening me?'

'No, I'm not threatening you. But you'll be sorry. You'll wake up one day and say to yourself: Did I destroy that boy?' And Terry began to cry.

'You won't get anything out of me that way,' said Harry. 'I can see through your tricks. You will have to go.'

'All right. But you'll be sorry. You'll hate yourself.'

'I failed but he went,' said Harry to Eileen. 'And he started to cry before he went. Oh he's so cunning. But there comes a time.'

'A time?'

'Yes, a time to save oneself. It's a duty. I see that now. She will have to go.'

'She?'

'Yes. She'll have to go. There comes a time. I made a mistake. I shall have to act.'

'Act?'

'That's it. Act. She will simply have to go. We can't afford her.'

'What do you mean?'

'What I say. You've done enough. This is not asked of us. I can see that now. Tell her she will have to go.'

'You tell her.'

'Right. I'll tell her.'

The two of them were alone. The house seemed to close in on them.

'What's that?' she said.

'What?'

'The phone,' she said.

'It isn't the phone. You're imagining things. The phone isn't ringing.'

'Yes it is.'

'No, it isn't.'

The ferns shut off the light. The floor was a huge beach of sand. She saw the child crossing it towards her. It smiled.

'I love you,' she said.

'I love you,' she repeated.

'The Club is quieter now,' he said. 'Ever since he left. We know where we are. I'm putting on weight.'

'Yes, I see that.'

'It's much quieter. He kept us on our toes. Everyone is obedient.'

'Yes.'

The child cried.

'I love you,' she said. The circle closed again. The baby smiled and smiled and laughed and laughed. It wobbled on unsteady legs among the ferns.

'I'm wounded,' she said, 'between the legs. Between the legs.' And its hairy head blossomed there. 'Between the legs. I'm wounded,' she said.

*   *   *

In the operating theatre on the snooker table its wild cry came towards her. She cradled the globe of its wet head, which had streamed out of the earth. Her hands closed, opened.

'I love you,' she said. 'There's nothing else for it.'

The phone rang. There was heavy breathing. 'You'll be sorry,' said a voice.

'He never gives up,' said Harry. 'But I don't care.'

'He has become remorseless,' she thought. 'We have been infected.' And she clutched the baby's head to her breast. 'We inherit the disease,' she thought. The baby warbled in its own kingdom. 'Isn't he beautiful?' she said.

'Yes.'

And the baby burbled like an unintelligible phone.

Murdo

WITH HIS PEN in his hand Murdo looked out at the tall white snow-covered mountain that he could see ahead of him through the window.

He was trying to write a story.

He looked down at the green pen in his hand. The day was cold and white, and now and again he could see a black bird flying across the intensely blue sky.

His wife was working in the kitchen. After she had finished cooking she would polish the table and chairs and the rest of the furniture. Now and again she would come to the door and say,

'Are you finished yet?'

And Murdo would say, 'I haven't even started,' and he would look out at the mountain again, he would resume his enchanted scrutiny of it. The white stainless mountain that was so cold and high.

Murdo had left his work as a bank clerk and was trying to write. When he had arrived home and told his wife that he would not be going back to the bank any more, she had begun to weep and scream but Murdo had simply walked past her to his room and had taken out a pen and a sheet of paper. He had left his work in the bank on an autumn day when the brown leaves were lying on the ground, and now it was winter.

He would sit at his desk at a little past nine o'clock every morning.

The white paper lay on the wood in front of him, as white as the mountain that he could see through the window which itself was entirely clean since his wife was always polishing it. He had not written a single page so far.

'Your tea's ready,' said his wife at eleven o'clock.

'Right,' said Murdo.

He went into the kitchen where she was. The room was as neat as a pin, as it always was. He couldn't understand how she could spend her time so remorselessly cleaning rooms, as if it had never occurred to her that a particular table or a particular set of chairs could be elsewhere rather than where they were: that they could be in another house, in another country, on another planet even.

From the time of the dinosaurs, Murdo said to himself, was it predestined that this table should be standing by this window, that these chairs should be settled in the centre of this room? This was the sort of question that perplexed him and made his head sore.

He didn't say any of this to his wife, for he knew that she wouldn't understand it.

They sat at the table opposite each other, and between them the pot of tea. His wife, Janet, was as neat and tidy as the room.

'When are you going back to your work?' she asked him as she did so often.

'I don't know,' said Murdo, putting a spoonful of sugar in his tea. His wife didn't take sugar, but kept saccharins for occasions like these. The saccharins were kept in a tiny blue box.

'Oh?' said his wife. 'You know of course that people are talking about you.'

'I don't care,' said Murdo, drinking his tea.

'But I care,' said his wife. 'They're always asking me if you're ill. You aren't ill, are you?'

'Apart from a touch of the Black Death there's nothing wrong with me,' said Murdo.

'And my mother and father are always asking me when you intend to go back to the office.'

'Are they?' said Murdo, thinking of the red cross on the door. There was green paint on the wall. Why had he in those early days of happiness put green paint on the wall? Why not blue paint or yellow? Ah, the soul of man cannot be plumbed, Murdo sighed to himself. A clock, colour of gold, was ticking between two clay horses that he had once won in a fair.

Her father was a large red angry man who would sometimes become bloated with rage. He had been on the fishing boats in his youth.

Janet had left school at fifteen. When she married Murdo she expected that her life would be as limpid as a stream, that there would be money coming into the house regularly, that Munro would at weekends be working stolidly in the garden reclaiming it from the wilderness, that they would have a daughter and a son, and that she would sit knitting by the fire when she wasn't talking to the neighbours.

She was a very capable housewife, small and alert. A good woman.

Murdo was trying to write a story about a bank clerk who had one day left his work and had begun to try and write. But one morning he had been enchanted by the white tall mountain with the snow on it and he had written nothing.

'This tea is very good,' he told Janet.

'Huh,' said Janet.

She would now begin to cook the dinner, and that was her life, and that life perplexed and astonished Murdo.

Why were the two horses set exactly like that, one on each side of the silently ticking clock?

'I'm going out tonight,' said Janet.

'Where?' said Murdo.

'Out,' she said. 'You can carry on with your writing.' She spoke simply, without irony.

'Where are you going?'

'I'm going to call on Mother,' said Janet.

'Oh,' said Murdo. 'I thought you had called on her on Monday.'

'I did,' said Janet. 'But I'm going to call on her again tonight.'

Your eyes are blue and cunning, said Murdo to himself. She was still pretty with her blue eyes, her dark hair, her red healthy cheeks.

'That's all right,' he said.

He rose and went back to his room.

He sat at his desk and gazed at the white mountain.

I should really, he thought, leave the house this minute

and climb the mountain. I should leave my prints in the snow.

It occurred to him that his wife might have been lying, that she wasn't going to see her mother at all. But he said nothing about his suspicion to her at lunch or at tea. She left the house at five o'clock and he went back to his room again.

The red sun was lying across the snow like blood.

What am I going to do? Murdo asked himself. Am I going to stay here staring at this mountain without writing anything?

The house felt empty after his wife had left it. He wandered about in it, looking at the made bed, the still ornaments, the mirrors, the dishes, the books.

The whole machinery of her world was impeccably in its place, his wife had built a clean orderly world around them.

But this world wasn't as clean as the mountain.

At half-past five he left the house and went to his mother-in-law's house and rang the bell at the side of the door. There were actually two bells but only one of them worked. His father-in-law came to the door and his face was as red as the sun that shone on the white mountain.

'Is Janet there?' Murdo asked timidly.

'No, she isn't,' said his father-in-law and didn't ask Murdo to come in. Murdo could see through the window that the TV was on.

'Oh,' he said. 'I only thought . . .'

'You thought wrong,' said his father-in-law. The houses around them were quiet and grey. Murdo saw a man going past with a large brown dog. 'Oh,' he said again, shivering in the cold since he wasn't wearing a coat. He turned away and walked down the street. Where was Janet? He felt his breast empty and he had a sudden terrible premonition that she had run away with another man, a man who never tried to write, but who was happy with the world as it was and his own position in it, and he felt shame and fear as if the event had happened in reality. He went into a bar but she wasn't there either. When he came out he looked round him in the raw cold but he couldn't see the white mountain from where he was since there were houses between him and it.

He stood on the pavement and he didn't know where to go next. Why had she lied to him?

Well, he said to himself, I shall have to find her or I shall have to climb the mountain. What shall I do?

I'll see if she is in this bar.

He went in and there she was sitting in a dark corner and there were some people with her.

He recognised John, who was a teacher in the only large school on the island, and his wife, Margaret. And another teacher (he thought) with a red beard, but he didn't know his name. And his wife as well. And a man who worked as a reporter on the local paper, a small pale-faced fellow who smoked endless cigarettes and whose name was Robert.

'Do you want a pint?' asked John, half rising from his seat.

'No thanks,' said Murdo. There was a glass of vodka or water in front of his wife. Murdo sat down on the edge of the company.

The bar was warm and dark with reddish lights and black leather seats.

'Where have you been?' Janet asked him.

'Oh, just walking around,' said Murdo.

'He's trying to write,' said Janet to the others.

'Write?' said Robert, his eyes lighting up. 'What are you writing?'

'Nothing,' said Murdo. 'I'm only trying to write.'

'Oh,' said Robert, the light almost visibly leaving his eyes as the light at the tip of a cigarette might cease to glow.

John and the red-bearded man began to talk about the school and Murdo listened to them.

At last he asked John why he taught.

'Why?' said John. 'Why am I teaching?' as if he had never asked himself such a question before.

'For the money,' said his wife, laughing.

'That wasn't what I meant,' said Murdo and in a whisper to himself, 'What the hell am I doing here anyway?' He was grinding his teeth against each other to prevent himself from howling like a wolf.

'This is a philosopher we have here,' said Janet in a sharp bitter voice, her lips almost shut.

'You must answer his questions.'

'Oh,' said John, 'I'm teaching History. What can people do without History? They would be like animals.'

'Right,' said Murdo, 'Right. Right.' And then,

'Are you an animal?'

John looked at him for a moment with such ferocity that Murdo thought he was going to leap at him like a wildcat but at last he said quietly: 'Animals don't teach each other History.'

'Very good,' said the red-bearded man. 'And now do you want a pint?' he asked Murdo.

'No thanks,' said Murdo and then quite untruthfully, 'My doctor has told me not to drink.' (He used the phrase 'my doctor' with an air of elegant possession though he had hardly ever been to a doctor in his life. He would also sometimes talk about 'my lawyer' in the same aristocratic tone.)

'It would be very funny,' said Robert, 'if animals taught History to each other.'

'It would indeed,' said Murdo.

They were silent for a while till at last Murdo said: 'Once I was sitting opposite a man in a café and there were cakes on the table, some yellow and some white. I took a yellow cake and he took a white one. What's the reason for that?'

'My coat is yellow,' said Margaret. 'That's because I like yellow.'

Janet looked at her own coat which wasn't as rich-looking as Margaret's and a ray of envy passed momently across her face.

'That's a question,' said John to Murdo. 'That's really a difficult question.'

'What café did this happen in?' said Robert as if he was about to take the story down for his newspaper.

'I can't remember,' said Murdo.

'Didn't I tell you he's a philosopher?' said Janet, sipping some vodka or perhaps water or perhaps gin.

Murdo was gazing at the bearded man's wife, a beautiful girl with long blond hair who was very silent. Beauty, O beauty, he said to himself. Yeats said something about that. My head is so heavy.

Margaret said, 'I just went into the shop and I bought

this yellow coat. I don't know why I bought it. I just liked it.'

'Exactly,' said Robert. 'What more can one say about it?'

'What are you writing?' he asked Murdo again.

'Nothing,' said Murdo.

'Uh huh,' said John.

Murdo knew that his wife was angry because he had come into the bar disturbing people with his strange questions, and he was glad in a way that she was angry.

At the same time he was afraid that she would get drunk.

John said, 'Well, it's time I was going.' And he and his wife rose from their seats.

'You're sure I can't buy you a pint before I go,' said John again to Murdo.

'I'm sure,' said Murdo.

The bearded man and his wife also rose.

They all went away muttering their goodbyes and Janet, Murdo and Robert were left sitting in their dark corner by a table which was wet with beer.

'What are you writing yourself?' Murdo asked Robert.

Robert looked at him with small bitter eyes. What did he write but pieces about whist drives, local football matches, things without importance?

He didn't answer.

'Did you ever see' Murdo asked him, 'the white mountain?'

'White mountain,' said Robert. 'What's that?'

'Don't listen to him,' said Janet. 'He doesn't know what he's talking about?'

'Sometimes you're right,' said Murdo.

Robert had been working as a journalist on the local newspaper since leaving school and he had never been out of the island.

'I read in your paper yesterday,' said Murdo, 'that a car was hit by another one on Bruce Street. Do you think that was predestined since the beginning of the world?'

'I don't know,' said Robert curtly, thinking that he was

being got at. Murdo felt his head sore again, as often happened to him nowadays.

'It doesn't matter,' he said.

And again,

'But it does matter. Once I was looking at a triangle which was drawn on a piece of paper and it looked so clean and beautiful. And I saw a fly walking across it, across the paper on which the triangle was drawn, and I didn't know where the fly was going. But the triangle was motionless in its own world, in its own space. That was on a summer's day when I was in school. But I forget the year,' he said to Robert.

'I have to go,' said Robert. 'I have something to do.'

'Have you?' said Murdo.

The only people left at the table now were himself and his wife.

'Well,' she said, 'it didn't take you long to send them away with all your questions. What are you trying to do?'

'Why did you lie to me?' said Murdo. 'Why didn't you tell me you were coming to this pub?'

'I don't know,' said Janet.

'You knew I would find out,' said Murdo. 'That's why you did it.'

'Maybe you're right,' said Janet.

We are like animals right enough, said Murdo to himself. We don't know why we do the things we do.

And he saw his wife like a fox walking across the white mountain.

'Come on home,' he said.

She rose and put on her coat.

'Where's your own coat?' she asked Murdo.

'I left it at home,' said Murdo.

They left the bar and walked home down the street and Murdo put his arm round her.

He felt the warmth of her body on that cold winter's night and his bones trembled.

Then he began to laugh.

'Whist drives,' he said looking up at the sky with its millions of stars. And he made little leaps shouting 'Whist drives' at intervals.

'Are you out of your mind?' said Janet.

He pulled her towards him.

'Do you see that mountain?' he asked her. 'That white mountain. Do you see it?' She was like a ghost glimmering out of the darkness.

'Ben Dorain,' he said laughing.

'I see it,' said Janet. 'What about it?'

'Nothing about it,' said Murdo, looking at the mountain, his warm head beside hers.

The white mountain was shining out of the darkness.

The tears came to his eyes and he felt them on his cheeks.

'You're crying,' she accused him.

'No I'm not,' he said.

She turned towards him and gazed into his eyes.

'Everything will be all right,' she said.

'Yes,' he said. 'I'm sure of it.' And he looked into her eyes. 'Yes,' he repeated.

She tightened her arm round him as if she was frightened that he was going to melt like the snow.

'Come on home,' she said to him in a frightened voice.

'I won't leave you,' he said, 'though your coat is green.'

They walked home quietly together except that now and again Murdo would make another of his leaps shouting 'Whist drives' at the moon that was so bare and bright in the sky above the white mountain.

One morning Murdo put on a red rubber nose such as clowns wear or small children at Hallowe'en and went downtown to get the morning papers. Norman Macleod's wife met him at the door of the shop and he said to her:

'It's a fine morning.'

'Yes,' said she, looking at him slightly askance, since he was wearing a red rubber nose.

'But it is not as beautiful a morning as it was yesterday,' Murdo said seriously. 'Not at all as good as yesterday morning. No indeed.'

'You're right there,' said Norman Macleod's wife, looking at his nose. Murdo pretended that he didn't notice her amazed stare.

'You're right there indeed,' said Murdo. 'I myself am of

the opinion that it is not so warm this morning as it was yesterday morning,' glancing at the snow which glittered back at him from the roadside.

'Without doubt, without doubt,' said the wife of Norman Macleod.

'For,' Murdo pursued relentlessly, 'the clouds were whiter yesterday than they are today,' drawing nearer to Mrs Macleod and putting his red rubber nose quite close to her face.

'For,' said Murdo, 'when I got up from my bed this morning I nearly went back into it again, a thing that I did not think of doing yesterday. But in spite of that I put one leg before the other as we all have to do in this life at some time or other, indeed at all times, and I decided that I would come for the newspapers, for what can we do without them? What indeed?'

'You're right,' said Mrs Macleod, shifting slightly away from him.

'Yes,' said Murdo, 'in these days especially one must put one leg in front of the other. When the light comes out of the darkness we go in search of the *Daily Record*, those sublime pages that tell us about the murders that have been committed in caravans in the south.'

'Yes,' said Mrs Macleod in a voice that was becoming more and more inaudible as she moved further and further away from the red rubber nose.

'I myself often think,' said Murdo, 'how uninteresting my life would be without the *Daily Record*. That occurs to me often. Often. And often I think what would we do without neighbours? Their warmth, their love . . . These thoughts often occur to me, I may tell you.'

'I suppose . . .' muttered Mrs Macleod, her grip tightening on the newspaper she had in her hand as if she was thinking of using it as a weapon.

'For,' said Murdo intently, 'do you yourself not think that the warmth of the morning is like the warmth we derive from our neighbours. The sun shines on everything and so does the warmth of neighbours. There is a lot wrong with each one of us, we are all flawed in some way but our neighbours forgive us for they say to themselves, "Not one of us is perfect, not one of us is without flaw, so how therefore can we say that others are flawed." These are the thoughts that often occur to me anyway,' said Murdo. 'And I don't think I'm wrong.'

'I'm sure you're . . .' said Mrs Macleod trying to back steadily away while Murdo fixed her closely with his red rubber nose as if he were a demented seagull standing among the snow.

'Give me,' said Murdo, 'one neighbour and I will move the world.' He considered this for a long time, turning his nose this way and that, the only bright colour that was to be seen on the street. Mrs Macleod wanted desperately to leave but she couldn't move her feet and she didn't know what to say.

Murdo went closer to her.

'I am of the opinion,' he said, 'to tell the truth and without concealing anything from any man or woman, white or black, whoever they are and whatever their colour of skin, I am of the opinion without regard to anyone's politics or religion, for no one can accuse me of being biased, that yesterday morning was as beautiful a morning as we have had for many years. I'm not saying that there don't exist people who would deny that, and who would come to me if they liked with armfuls of records going back to the seventeenth century and before, that would prove that I was wrong, and even naive in that statement, but in spite of that I still hold to my opinion as I am sure you would under the same circumstances, for I have never thought of you as a coward. Oh I know that there are people who will maintain that neither the summers nor the winters that we endure now are as beautiful and unspotted as the summers and winters of their various childhoods but I would say humbly to these people that they are wrong. THEY ARE WRONG,' he shouted, pushing his nose as close to Mrs Macleod's nose as it could go.

'THEY ARE WRONG,' he repeated in a loud vehement voice. 'As wrong as people can be. I know in my bones that they are wrong. Totally wrong. Totally.' He sighed heavily and then continued:

'As well as that I know that there are professors who would

oppose me on this matter. But I know that they are wrong as well. Though I have nothing against professors. Not at all, not at all.

'But I'm keeping you back. I shouldn't have done that. I know that you're busy, that you work without cease, without cease. Lack of consideration, that's what I suffer from, I admit it freely. But I wished to tell you how much more beautiful than this morning yesterday morning was. And I'm glad that you agree with me in my opinion. I am so glad. So glad. It is not often that I feel such gladness. But I know that you wish to go home. I am so glad to have met you.'

Mrs Macleod half walked, half ran, away, looking behind her now and then as if trying to verify that he did indeed have a red rubber nose. Murdo raised his hand to her in royal salute and then went into the shop, having first removed his rubber nose, and bought a newspaper. On his way home he would kick a lump of ice now and again with his boot.

'Drama,' he said to himself. 'Nothing but drama and catharsis. One must look for it even when there is snow on the ground.'

He arrived at a wall and opened out the paper and began to read it, glancing now and again at the white mountain.

He read one page and then threw the paper away from him, but after a while he picked it up and laid it flat on a large piece of ice.

The headlines of the paper said in large black type:

I STILL LOVE HIM THOUGH HE KILLED FOR ME

Murdo found an old boot in the ditch and laid it on top of this headline so that passers-by could read it and then went on his way whistling.

One night Murdo was on his way home with a half-bottle of whisky in his hand. He looked up at the sky that was trembling with stars and he began to shout to a group of them that were brighter than the rest:

'Lewis,'
and then
'Skye'
and finally

'Betelgeuse.'

He looked down at his shoes that were yellow in the light of the moon and he said,

'I'm drunk. Murdo is drunk. There is whisky on his shoes. On his shoes there is whisky.'

He then sat down on the road and took off his shoes and raised them towards the moon:

'Here is Murdo. There are Murdo's shoes. They are yellow. Murdo's shoes are yellow.'

'O world,' he said, 'how yellow Murdo's shoes are. Ah, Lewis, ah, Skye, ah, Betelgeuse.'

He thought of small yellow men with small yellow shoes drinking on Betelgeuse and he had compassion for them as they sat on the road with a half-bottle of whisky in the hand of each one.

'Ah,' said he, 'do you see the white mountain even on Betelgeuse? Do you have in your hands yellow pencils and are you writing on yellow paper a story about a clerk who left his work in an office on Betelgeuse?'

And the tears came to his eyes.

'Is there a split,' he said, 'between the soul and the body even on Betelgeuse? Is there on that illustrious star a woman like Mrs Macleod, of that ilk?'

And he began to laugh in harmony with the trembling of the stars which also seemed to laugh.

He looked at the sky and he shouted,

'Conscience.'

'Soul.'

'MacBrayne's boats.'

He looked down at his shoes again.

'Leather,' he said.

'Nails,' he said.

'Shoemaker,' he said.

'A shoemaker was born just for me,' he said and he felt pity for the shoes and the shoemaker, a little yellow man with little yellow nails in his mouth.

'Why,' he shouted to Betelgeuse, 'did you put skin on my bones, a worm in my head?'

And he felt the yellow worm in his head like a thin stream of whisky the colour of the moon.

'Existentialism,' he shouted to the moon.

'A lavatory of diamonds.'

'Plato in a thatched house.'

'Mist.'

He stood up and began to sing under the millions of stars a verse of a song he had composed.

'The Isle of Mull
has no grief or sorrow,
It is so green,
and will be here tomorrow.'

And he thought of his father and mother and they were like a pair of people who moved in and out of a Dutch clock, yellow and fat with fat red cheeks.

'And,' he said, in a mimicking voice, 'is it from Betelgeuse that you are yourself? When did you come home and when are you going away again?'—the age-old Highland questions.

'I was reared,' he said, 'when I was young and soft. When I grew a little older I thought that I myself was creating the morning and the evening. And at that moment I grew old. The mountains were like fangs in my mind.'

The stars winked at him and he winked back at them and he thought that there was a yellow crown on his head, a sharp yellow crown.

'Without me,' he said, 'sick as I am from *angst* and diarrhoea, you would not be there at all. Are you listening to me? Without me there would be darkness among all the planets.'

He lifted the half-bottle of whisky and he began to drink.

'Your health,' he said. 'Your good health.'

He reached his own house and he saw a ray of yellow light coming out from under the door.

'Like an arrow,' he said.

'Like a knife,' he said.

'Like a pen,' he said.

and

'Like a spade,' he said.

and finally,

'16 Murchison Street,' he said, 'with the green walls.'

'We are all,' he said, 'of a mortal company. Of a proud company,' said he swaying from side to side, the key in his hand.

'Drunkards of the universe,' he said.

'Glory be to the yellow universe,' he said in the yellow light.

He tried to fit his key in the door but couldn't.

'It is not fated,' he said, 'it is not fated that I shall open the door of 16 Murchison Street. The universe is against it.'

He thought of the key as a soul that could not enter its proper body.

'Lewis,' he said to Betelgeuse.

'Skye,' he said.

And finally as if he had climbed a high mountain,

'Tiree.'

And he fell asleep, the key in his hand and the yellow closed door in front of him and a heavy snore coming from him in that cold calm yellow night.

Murdo's Letter to the Poet Dante

Dear Friend,

Can you please tell me when and how you began to write first, and what magazines you sent your first poems to? And what was the animal you saw in the middle of the wood?

For myself, I see this white mountain all the time, day and night. With snow on it.

And in the room next to me there is a table and chairs as like each other as pictures in a mirror. Anyway I hope you will answer my letter for I am trying to write a story about a clerk.

And I don't know how to start.

With much respect and a stamp so that you can answer my letter.

Yours sincerely,
MURDO MACRAE

PS. You did very well, my friend, with that poem the *Inferno*. But what would you have done without Virgil? I think we all need a friend.

Murdo was (as they say) good with children and this is one
of the stories he told to his nephew Colin who was six years
old at the time:

There was a lad once (said Murdo), and he was seventeen
years old. Well, one day he thought that he would leave
home where he lived with his father and mother. It was a
beautiful autumn day and he saw many strange sights on
his way. In the place where he was, there were many trees
and the yellow leaves were falling to the ground and they
were all so beautiful and sad. But the most wonderful thing
of all was that wherever he went—and the day very calm
and now and again a fox running through the wood and red
berries still on some of the trees—he would see his father's
face and his mother's face. Wasn't that strange? Just as if
he was in a land of mirrors. In the leaves, in the ground,
he would see these faces. This amazed and astonished him.
And he didn't know what to do about it. Once in a leaf he
saw his house with the door and the windows and his mother
standing in the doorway in a blue gown. And once in another
leaf he saw his father bending down with a spade, digging.

Well this went on for a long time but at last he didn't
see the pictures of his father and mother at all. And then
he came to a small village and every man in the village was
hitting big stones with hammers, every one of them. When
he asked them the name of the village no one would tell him.
In fact they wouldn't speak to him at all. But they just kept
hammering away at the stones with their hammers. This was
the only sound that could be heard in the village. Think of
it, this was all they did all day and every day. And they never
spoke to anyone. And he didn't know why they were doing
this. He asked them a lot of times why they were hammering
the stones but they wouldn't answer him. This astonished
him and he himself sat on a stone in his blue dusty suit but
they pretended not to see him.

At last he grew tired of sitting down and he went
over and looked at one of the men and what he was
doing. And he saw that this man was cutting names of
people in the stone on which he was working. Murdo
didn't recognise any of the names and he was just going
to go away when he looked very sharply indeed and

he saw that the man was cutting his own name in the stone.

Well, this made Murdo very puzzled and frightened him too, and before he knew what he was doing he was running away from that place till he reached a wood which was very quiet. Not even the voice of a bird was to be heard, and it was very dark there. However, there were some nuts on the trees and he began to eat them. He wandered through this wood for a long time till at last he saw ahead of him a high mountain white with snow though it was still autumn. He stood and stared at this mountain for some time.

Well, just as he was standing there who should he see but a beautiful girl in a green dress just beside him. She had long yellow hair like gold and she said to Murdo in a quiet voice:

'If you will climb that mountain and if you bring me a blue flower that you will find on its slope I will reward you well. My house is quite near here, a small house made of diamonds, and when you get the flower you will come to it and knock on the door and I shall answer.'

Murdo looked around him and sure enough there, not very far away, was a small house made of diamonds.

Well, Murdo made his way towards the mountain and in a short while he found a blue flower and he ran back to the small house with it and knocked on the door, but no one came to answer his knock. He knocked a few times but still no one came and he didn't know what to do, for he wanted the reward. At last he thought it might be a good idea to return to the mountain and find an even more beautiful flower and bring it back with him. And with that he left the small house made of diamonds and he went back to the mountain. And he climbed with difficulty further up the slope and found a larger even more beautiful blue flower but he was feeling slightly tired by this time, and he walked much more slowly to the house. Anyway he reached it at last, and he knocked on the door again. The house was shining in the light of the snow and the windows were sending out flashes of light. He knocked and knocked but still no one came to the door. And Murdo returned to the mountain for the third time and this time he decided that he would climb to the very top and he would find a flower so lovely that the beautiful girl would be forced to open the door for him. And he did this. He climbed and climbed and his breath grew shorter and shorter and his legs grew weaker and weaker and sometimes he felt dizzy because of the great height. For four hours he climbed and the air was getting thinner and thinner and Murdo was shivering with the cold and his teeth were chattering in his head, but he was determined that he would reach the top of the mountain.

At last, tired and cold, he reached the top and he saw in front of him the most beautiful flower he had ever seen in his life but this flower was not blue like the other ones. It was white. Anyway Murdo pulled the beautiful white flower out of the ground and he looked at it for a long time as it lay in his hand. But a strange thing happened then. As he looked, the beautiful white flower began to melt and soon there was nothing left of it but a little water. And all around him was the cold white mountain.

Slowly Murdo went down the mountainside, feeling very tired and cold, and he looked for the small house made of diamonds but he couldn't find it anywhere. There was only a small hut without windows or doors. And Murdo looked at it for a long time and said to himself, 'But it may be that I shall meet that beautiful girl again somewhere.' And he continued on his way through the wood. But I don't think he ever met that beautiful girl again, though he travelled through many countries, except perhaps for one moment when he was lying on the ground, very tired, and he was staring at an old boot and he saw a flash of what might have been her. But perhaps it was his imagination for the moon was shining on the old boot at the time.

Murdo looked down at Colin who had fallen asleep.

'Well,' he said to himself, 'maybe he didn't like the story after all.'

This is an advertisement which Murdo sent to the editor of the local paper but which was never printed:

Wanted: a man of between a hundred and two hundred years of age who knows the works of Kant and the poetry of William Ross, and who can drive a tractor and a car, for work on the roads for three weeks in the year. Such a man will get—particularly if he's healthy—two pounds a year. It would be an advantage if he knew a little Greek.

The reader must now be told something about Murdo. He was born in a small village where there were twenty houses and which stood beside the sea. When he was growing up he spent a lot of his time drawing drifters on scraps of paper: and the most wonderful day of his life was the day that he jumped across the river Caras.

When he was on his way to school he would think of himself as walking through the forests of Africa, but the schoolmistress told him that he must learn the alphabet.

One day she asked him to write an essay with the title, 'My Home'. Murdo wrote twenty pages about a place where there were large green forests, men with wings, aeroplanes made of diamond, and rainbow-coloured stairs.

She said to him, 'What does all this stuff mean? Are you laughing at me or what?' She gave him two strokes of the belt.

After that Murdo grew very good at counting, and he could compute in his head in seconds $1,005 \times 19$. This pleased the schoolmistress and when the inspector visited the school she showed him Murdo with great pride. 'This boy will make a perfect clerk,' said the inspector, and he gave him a hard white sweet.

Murdo went home and told his father and mother what the inspector had said. But he didn't tell them that in the loft he kept an effigy of the schoolmistress which was made of straw and that every evening he pierced it with the sharp point of his pencil.

Nor did he tell them that he painted the walls of the loft with pictures of strange animals that he could see in his dreams.

One day when Murdo was fifteen years old the headmaster sent for him.

'Sit down,' he said.

Murdo sat down.

'And what do you intend to do now that you are leaving school?' said the headmaster who had a small black moustache.

'27 × 67 = 1,809,' said Murdo.

The headmaster looked at him with astonishment and his spectacles nearly fell off his nose.

'Have you any idea at all what you're going to do?' he asked again.

'259 × 43 = 11,137,' said Murdo.

The headmaster then told him that he could leave, that he had much work to do. Murdo saw two girls going into his study with a tray on which there was a cup of tea and two biscuits.

When he came out the other boys asked him what the headmaster had wanted with him and Murdo said that he didn't know.

Anyway he left the school on a beautiful summer's day while the birds were singing in the sky. He was wearing a white shirt with short sleeves and it was also open at the neck.

When he was going out the gate he turned and said,

'45 × 25 = 1,125.'

And after that he walked home.

His mother was hanging clothes on the line when he arrived and taking the pegs out of her mouth she said:

'Your schooldays are now over. You will have to get work.'

Murdo admitted that this was true and then went into the house to make tea for himself.

He saw his father working in the field, bent like a shepherd's crook over a spade. Murdo sat at the table and wrote a little verse:

> He he said the horse
> ho ho said the goat
> Ha ha, O alas,
> said the brown cow in the byre.

He was greatly pleased with this and copied it into a little book. Then he drank his tea.

*   *   *

One day Murdo said to his wife, 'Shall we climb that white mountain?'

'No,' she said with astonishment. 'It's too cold.'

Murdo looked around him. The chairs were shining in the light like precious stones. The curtains were shimmering with light as if they were water. The table was standing on its four precious legs. His wife in her blue dress was also precious and precious also was the hum of the pan on the cooker. 'I remember,' he told his wife, 'when I was young I used to listen every Sunday to the sound of the pot boiling on the fire. We had herring all during the week.'

'We too,' said his wife, 'but we had meat on Sunday.' She was thinking that Murdo wasn't looking too well and this frightened her. But she didn't say anything to him.

'Herring,' said Murdo, 'what would we do without it? The salt herring, the roasted herring. The herring that swims through the sea among the more royal fish. So calm. So sure of itself.'

'One day my father killed a rabbit with his gun,' said his wife.

'I'm sure,' said Murdo.

'I'm telling the truth,' Janet insisted.

'I'm not denying it,' said Murdo as he watched the shimmering curtains. And the table shone in front of him, solid and precious and fixed, and the sun glittered all over the room.

O my happiness, he said to himself. O my happiness. How happy the world is without me. How the world doesn't need me. If only I could remember that. The table is so calm and fixed, without soul, single and without turmoil, the chairs compose a company of their own.

'Come on, let's dance,' he said to Janet.

'What now?' she said.

'Yes,' said Murdo, 'now.'

'Let's dance now.'

'All right, then,' said Janet.

And they began to dance among the chairs, and the pan shone red in a corner of its own.

And Murdo recalled how they had used to dance in their youth on the autumn nights with the moon above them and his heart so full that it was like a bucket full of water, almost spilling over.

At last Janet sat down, as she was breathless.

And Murdo sat on a chair beside her.

'Well, well,' said he, 'we must do that oftener.'

'Oh the pan,' said his wife and she ran over to the cooker where the pan was boiling over.

The pan, said Murdo to himself, the old scarred pan. It also is dancing.

On its own fire.

Everything is dancing, said Murdo, if we only knew it. The whole world is dancing. The lion is dancing and the lamb is dancing. Good is dancing with Evil in an eternal reel in an invisible light. And he thought of them for a moment, Good and Evil, with their arms around each other on a fine autumn evening with the dew falling steadily and invisibly on the grass.

Sometimes Janet thought that Murdo was out of his mind. Once when they were in Glasgow they went into a café where there was a juke box which was playing 'Bridge over Troubled Water' and Murdo sat at the green, scarred, imitation marble-topped table. He was wearing a thick heavy black coat such as church elders wear and a hard black hat on his head.

When the music stopped he went over to the juke box, put money in the slot and the music started again, whereupon sitting at the table in his black coat and stiff black hat he swayed to the music, moving his head from side to side as if he were in a trance of happiness. A number of girls gazed at him with astonishment.

Also in Glasgow he went up to a policeman and asked him, 'Could you please direct me to Parnassus Street, officer? I think it's quite near Helicon Avenue, or so I was told.'

He bent his head as if he were listening carefully to what the policeman might say.

'Parnassus Street,' said the policeman, a large heavy man with a slow voice. 'What part of the city did you say it was in again?'

'I think, or so I was told, I don't know whether it's right

or wrong, I'm a stranger in the city myself,' said Murdo, 'I'm sure someone said to me that it's very near Helicon Avenue.'

'Helicon Avenue?' said the policeman, gazing at Murdo and then at Murdo's wife and then down at his boots.

'It may be in one of the new schemes,' said Murdo helpfully, his head on one side like a bird's on a branch.

'That may be,' said the policeman. 'I'm very sorry but I can't inform you where the places you mention happen to be.'

'Oh that's all right,' said Murdo looking at a radiant clock which had stopped at three o'clock. 'There are so many places, aren't there?' (Muttering under his breath, 'Indonesia, Hong Kong, Kilimanjaro.')

'You're right,' said the policeman, and then turned away to direct the traffic, raising a white glove.

'I think that policeman is from the Highlands,' said Murdo. 'He's got a red neck. And red fists. Big red fists.'

But at other times Murdo would sit in the house completely silent like a spider putting out an invisible web. And Janet wasn't used to such silence. She came from a family that always had something to say, always had morsels of news to feed to each other.

And for a lot of the time she felt lonely even when Murdo was with her. Sometimes when they were sitting in the kitchen Murdo would come over to her with a piece of paper on which he had written some such word as BLOWDY.

'What do you think that word means?' Murdo would say to her.

'Blowdy?' Janet would say. 'I never heard that word before.'

'Didn't you?' Murdo would say. Blowdy, he would say to himself again.

Blowdy, blowdy, among the chairs, the green walls.

Once when his mother-in-law was in drinking tea Murdo said to her quietly:

'It's a fine blowdy day today.'

'What did you say?' said his mother-in-law, the cup of tea in her lap and a crumb of bread on her lip.

'A fine blowdy day,' Murdo said, 'a fine windy bright blowdy day.'

'It's a windy day right enough,' said his mother-in-law, looking meaningfully at Janet.

'That's an Irish word,' said Murdo. 'The Irish people used it to give an idea of the kind of marbly clouds that you sometimes see in the sky on a windy day, and also when the wind is from the east.'

'Oh?' said his mother-in-law looking at him carefully.

When Murdo had gone back to his room she said to Janet:

'I don't think Murdo is all there. Do you think he is?'

'Well,' said Janet, 'he acts very funny at times.'

'He's worse than funny,' said her mother. 'Do you remember at the wedding when he took a paper ring from his pocket and he was wearing a piece of cabbage instead of a flower like everybody else?''

'I remember it well enough,' said her daughter. 'But he's very good at figures.'

'That's right enough,' said her mother, 'but a man should be more settled than he is. He should be indeed.'

After her mother had left Janet sat in her chair and began to laugh and she could hardly stop, but at the same time she felt frightened as if there was some strange unnatural being in the house with her.

For about the seventh or the eighth time Murdo tried to write a story.

'There was a clerk once and he was working in a bank . . .'

When Murdo was working he used to go into the bank at nine in the morning and he would finish at five in the afternoon. And he had an hour for his lunch. There were another ten people working in the bank with him and Murdo would sit at a desk and add figures all day, at the back of the bank, in the half-dark.

Beside him there sat a small bald man who had been in the bank for thirty years and who was always wiping his nose as if there was something there that he wished continually to clean off. At last Murdo said to him, 'Why do you do that?'

'What?' said the man.

'Why do you wipe your nose all the time?' said Murdo.

'It's none of your business,' said the bald man and after that he wouldn't speak to Murdo. They would sit beside each other all day and they wouldn't speak to each other. They wouldn't even say Good morning to each other.

Murdo would begin to think about money. When he was in the bank he would see thousands and thousands of banknotes and it would occur to him:

What if I stole some money and went away to the Bahamas or some place like that? But actually the place he really wanted to go to was Rome and he imagined himself standing among these stony ruins wearing a red cloak while the sun was setting and he was gazing down at the city like a conqueror.

After a time, he would, in his imagination, enter a café and eat spaghetti and he would meet a girl in a mini-skirt and he would say to her:

'Is your name Beatrice?'

And they would stand in the sunset where red fires were burning and there would be a church behind her, a church with gigantic carvings by Michelangelo.

'Have you ever heard of Leonardo da Vinci?' he would say to her and she would look at him with dull pebbly eyes in which no soul was visible.

And in the morning Murdo would rise from his bed and he would see a new world in front of him, a bright clean world, a new morning, and he'd say:

'Where will we go today?'

And she would be asleep and he would leave her there like a corrupted angel with arms as white as those of Venus and a small discontented mouth, and he would go out and he would talk to the women with their long Italian noses and after that he would leave Rome and travel to Venice and sail on a gondola, his red cloak streaming from his shoulders.

And all around him there would be colours such as he had never seen before and his nose would twitch like a rabbit's.

And in an art gallery he would stand in front of a painting and the painting would show a man walking down a narrow

road while ahead of him the sun was setting in a green light
like the light of the sea.

And he would meet a priest and he would say to him,
'What is keeping you alive?'

And the priest would say to him, 'Come with me and I'll
show you.'

And they would go into a small room in a small dirty
house and there would be a child lying in bed there with
a red feverish face, and beside the bed there would be a
woman wearing a black snood. And she would be sitting
there motionless while the child stirred restlessly in the bed.
And the priest would say to Murdo:

'She has been sitting by that bed for nearly a week
now.'

'Do you think,' Murdo would ask, 'that Leonardo had
as much care for the Mona Lisa as this woman has for
her child?'

And he would look around him, at the picture of the
Virgin Mary and the candle that was burning in a corner
of the room.

'I understand what you're saying,' the priest would say.

'I hope the child will recover,' Murdo would say.

'Exactly like that,' the priest would say, 'God keeps a
watch over the world till the sun rises.'

Murdo would leave the priest and the woman and the
child and walk down a street where he would be met by
the two men who would attack him, beating him on the
head and chest, and steal all the money he had except for
the six thousand pounds that were tied round his pants.

'Well, well,' he'd say to the blank Italian sky, 'there is
nothing here but troubles.'

He would then see a group of people standing beside a
house that had fallen to the ground.

One of the women would say, 'My mother and father are
in there dead. And what I want to know is, what is the
government going to do about it?'

'I am from the government myself,' Murdo would say.
'And here are two hundred pounds for you.'

'Two hundred pounds isn't enough,' the woman would
say, 'to compensate for all the love I felt for my father and

mother. I would require five hundred pounds at least. But I'll take the two hundred pounds just now.'

'Right,' Murdo would say and he would run away, his red cloak streaming down his back and from his shoulders as if they were the wings of an angel or a devil.

He would hear sweet voices floating from the gondolas and his heart would be at peace.

When he would wake from his Italian dream the man beside him would be wiping his nose.

'I'm sorry,' Murdo would say to him, 'for what I said to you before.'

But the man wouldn't answer him.

After Murdo had resigned from the bank he sent the man a letter saying,

> I had nothing against your nose. But I'm certain that if you hope to get on in the world you must stop wiping your nose. Napoleon didn't wipe his nose continually. Or William Wallace. I'm sorry to tell you this but I'm only doing it for your own good.
>
> Yours sincerely,
MURDO MACRAE

What was Murdo like? Well, he was about five feet ten inches in height, thin, pale-faced (like the clerk he once had been) and blue-eyed. He shaved himself every morning at half-past eight, sometimes listening to the radio and sometimes whistling in a monotonous melancholy manner. He often cut himself with his razor blade and for this reason he bought sticks of styptic which he could never find and which, after being dipped in water, became soggy. He ate very little food and this worried Janet. He had a theory that too much food made his brain feel heavy, and that this was particularly the case with meat and soup, though not with fish. At nine o'clock he would go and sit at his desk, open the notebook in which he had been trying to write and look at it. He would then take out of his pocket the green pen which he had once found on the road near the house and chew it for a long while, still looking down at the paper. Now and again he would get up from his chair and walk about the room, stopping to study a purple bucket in the corner. He had a strong affection for this bucket: he thought that some day it would yield him some extraordinary vision.

Then he would go back to his chair and sit down again.

He would sometimes think that there was a crown on his head and that he was king of a country which did not yet exist but which would some day emerge with its own constitution. In this country poets and novelists, painters and ballet dancers, musicians and singers would be the most respected citizens. He would think to himself:

How did other writers work? It is said that Schiller (was it Schiller?) would keep a rotten apple in his desk and that he would take it out every morning, and its corrupt smell would arouse his imagination.

For this reason Murdo got an apple, and kept it in his desk till it was rotten, but one day Janet found it and threw it out. And some bird or other ate it.

After some time he might leave the house altogether and go for a walk.

No matter how cold the day was he never wore a coat.

One morning he was walking down the main street when he met the manager of the bank, a man called Maxwell. Maxwell always carried a rolled umbrella even if the day was perfectly fine with no sign of rain. He also wore thick black glasses.

'Imphm,' he said to Murdo.

'Good morning,' Murdo said.

'Imphm,' said Maxwell.

At last he recognised Murdo and he said to him, looking at him sideways all the time in a furtive manner:

'I'm sorry you felt you had to leave the bank. We needed you.'

'Imphm,' said Murdo.

'It's not easy to get work nowadays,' said Maxwell. 'What are you doing?'

'Imphm,' said Murdo.

He was afraid that if he told Maxwell that he didn't do anything, was in fact totally idle though committed to a blank sheet of paper, that Maxwell would fall dead in the road.

At last he said, 'I'm looking after my grandfather. There

is no one in the house but myself and him and his old dog
which he had in the Great War.'

'An old dog?'

'Yes,' said Murdo. 'An old dog. He's very fond of
my grandfather. He saved his life at Passchendaele. He
picked him up between his teeth and took him back to
the British lines after he had been very badly nay almost
fatally wounded. Nay. He laid him down at the feet of a
first lieutenant called Griffiths. From Ilfracombe.'

'Well, well,' said Maxwell, 'well, well.' Murdo was gazing
directly at a point between Woolworths and the Italian café
and Maxwell was gazing at a point between Lows and
Templetons, and they stood like that for a long while in
the cold morning. At last Maxwell said, 'I must go to the
office. I'm glad I met you. Imphm.'

And he went away. Murdo looked after him in a vague
negligent manner and then went into Woolworths.

He weighed himself and found that he was ten stone two
pounds.

He walked from counter to counter. He picked up a book
about vampires, glanced at it and then went up to a girl in
a yellow dress who was paring her nails. On her breast the
name *Lily* was written.

'Lily,' said he, 'have you any tins of Arragum? Lily. It's
a kind of paint,' he added trying to be helpful.

'Arragum?'

'Yes,' said Murdo. 'It's for windows and doors and tables.
It's used a lot in places where there is great cold and
sometimes much rain. The Eskimos use it a great deal.'

'Arragum?' she said. 'I don't think that . . .'

'Well,' said Murdo, 'maybe it's called Arragul, I'm
not sure. I saw it advertised in the *Observer* Colour Sup-
plement.'

'Wait a minute,' she said, and she went and got another
girl in the same yellow uniform as her own, except that
instead of *Lily* the name *Mary* was written on the breast.

'Arragum?' said Mary. 'I never heard of that.'

'Well,' said Murdo, 'it doesn't matter. You can't have
everything in the shop. But it just occurred to me that as
I was passing anyway . . .'

'What was that name again?' said Mary, taking a pencil from her breast pocket.

'Arragum,' said Murdo. 'A-R-R-A-G-U-M. I think the Queen uses it.

'Well, we can try and get it,' said Mary.

'All right,' said Murdo. 'I think there'll be a big demand for it after that article.'

And with that he left.

He was thinking of his grandfather and the dog that looked after him, and this imagined world became real to him. The dog was large and had gentle brown eyes and he would lie there on the rug in front of the fire gazing at his slightly damaged grandfather, who was thinking of Passchendaele and the Somme and the early sun glittering on the early bayonets. O those early days, those days of untarnished youth.

I could have gone to Vietnam myself, said Murdo, but I was too lazy. I didn't do anything about it, I stayed where I was in the bank reading about it in the papers. I did not set my breast against battle, no indeed. And why didn't I? Who knows the answer to that question? Because I believe in nothing, said Murdo to himself.

He saw a Pakistani a little ahead of him but did not go to speak to him.

For what could I say to him? He has come from another world, he belongs to another civilisation. I myself come from the civilisation of TV. He walked up the road and sat on a bench. After a while the town fool called Donnie came and sat beside him. He was carrying a brown paper parcel from which there came the smell of salt herring.

'Fine day,' said Donnie, his eyes blinking rapidly. 'Fine day.'

He was wearing a long brown dirty coat which trailed to his ankles. The smell of salt herring was in Murdo's nostrils.

'A fine day,' said Donnie again.

After a while he said, 'I don't suppose you could give me a penny. A penny so I can buy sweets.'

'No understand,' said Murdo. 'No understand. Me German. Tourist.'

The fool turned his head away slowly and gazed towards the farther shore, his large head like a cannon ball, his body like a dull rusty gun. His dirty brown hair streamed down the collar of his coat.

At last he turned to Murdo and said, 'I was wondering if you could spare a shilling for a man in poor circumstances.'

Murdo rose rapidly from his seat, and said, 'Me German. Me no understand your money. Me without pity. Have done enough for shrinking pound already. What fought war for, what sent Panzer divisions into civilised treasuries of the West for, if required to prop up currency now? Regard this as paradox of our time.' And he went away thinking of the fool.

He stood for a long time watching the children play in an adjacent park and then went slowly home.

A Letter to the Prime Minister

I am of the opinion that there is a strong conspiracy afoot to undermine this country of ours.

Why do people sit watching TV all the time? I am convinced that there are certain rays which come out of the TV set and that these rays are causing people to lose their commitment to the pure things of life.

Did you ever consider the possibility that John Logie Baird was a Communist?

Do you really believe that there is no connection between the rise of TV and the rise of Communism in the Western world?

Who controls TV? Let me ask you that. Let me put that question to you in all sincerity.

And if the Russians attacked this country what would our people be doing? I think they would continue to sit and watch the TV.

AND THEY WOULD NOT BELIEVE IT WAS AN ATTACK BY THE RUSSIANS AT ALL. THEY WOULD THINK IT WAS A TV DOCUMENTARY.

Did this ever occur to you?

And as well as that there are many people who do not believe that you yourself exist at all. They believe that you have been assembled on TV.

If this is false please answer this letter at once and establish your identity.

With great respect.
Murdo Macrae

I nearly signed my letter PRO PUBLICO BONO but there has been such a decline in the use of the Latin language that I could not do so. And what is the cause of that? Is it not the TV.

Now and again Murdo would go and visit his father whose health was rather poor and who lived by himself since the death of his wife. His father would be sitting by the fire on the cold winter's day and Murdo would think of the days when his father had been fit and strong and how when he himself was young his father would take him out fishing.

And now all he had was his pension and a moderately warm hearth. He wouldn't go and live with Murdo and Janet not because he didn't like them but because he didn't want to leave his own house.

Sometimes he would speak of Libya where he had fought in the war.

'There was this fellow from Newcastle beside me,' he would say, 'when we were in the trenches, and he was always saying that he wanted a quick death. Well, that happened right enough. One evening I looked down at him (he was beside me, you see) and he had no head. A shell had taken his head off. It was like a football.'

'Well, well, imagine that,' his visitors would say. 'Isn't that funny. Well well. Think of that, no head on him.'

'Ay, ay, that's the way it was,' Murdo's father would say. 'He had no head. The head was beside me in the sand there like a football.' And Murdo would see the naked head on the sand, the head without thought or imagination.

'And how are you today?' Murdo would say as he went into the house.

'Oh, no complaints, no complaints,' his father would answer. There would often be an open tin of Spam on the table.

'Is there anything to be done?'

'No, nothing, nothing at all.'

When Murdo was young, his father would carry him on his shoulders and show him off to people and he would buy for him chocolate sweets in the shape of cats or dogs.

And he would teach him how to fish on red sunset evenings.

Murdo would sweep the floor or dry the dishes of which the sink was full. And his father would say to him, 'You don't need to do that. I'll do that myself.'

And at last Murdo would sit in front of the fire and his father would tell him a story.

'One time,' he said, 'we were in Libya and there was a man there from the islands and he was always reading the Bible. I don't know whether he was frightened or what. Anyway he was always reading the Bible any chance that he had. He knew it from end to end, I would think.

'Well, he once told me this story. One night, he told me, there was a great sandstorm and the sand was thick about the desert, so thick he said that he couldn't see hardly a yard in front of him, and he was afraid that the Germans would suddenly come out of the middle of it with their guns. Well, he said he was waiting there ready with his own gun and he was looking into the middle of the sandstorm with a handkerchief over his mouth. "Well," he said, "I don't know whether you'll believe this or not but about three in the morning out of the middle of the sandstorm there came this man with a beard and in a long white gown. He was like an Arab and some were saying that many of the Arabs were on the side of the Germans. Anyway," he said, "I raised my gun and I fired at this fellow in the long white gown. But he came straight on and there were no marks at all in his breast where I had hit him at point-blank range and he came right on in his long white gown and he went straight through me. He was smiling all the time and he went straight through me. Isn't that funny?"

'Think of that now,' said his father to Murdo. 'Eh? But he was a bit queer that same fellow right enough.'

These were the kinds of stories that Murdo's father would tell Murdo as they sat in front of the fire on a cold winter's day while now and again Murdo's father would light and relight his pipe. Nearly all his stories were about the war.

And Murdo would look out of the window and he would
see the movements of the grass under the cold wind, and
the world outside so dark and dull and sometimes stormy.

And he would think of his mother in her long blue apron
with the red flowers on it as she walked about the house
while his father would be quietly reading the paper. And
he himself would be playing on the floor with a train which
his father had bought for him.

What had his father been doing in Libya anyway dis-
guised as a soldier? What good had his soldiership done for
him, now as he sat by the fire and the wind blew coldly and
endlessly round his house.

His father didn't know that Murdo was unemployed: he
thought of him with pride as a clerk in a well-known and
well-trusted bank.

Once his father had said to him, 'Do you know something? Your mother always said that you should have been
a minister. Did you know that?'

'No, I didn't know that,' said Murdo, astonished by the
absurdity of the statement.

'Ay,' said his father, 'she used to say that. She used to
say that often to me. "Murdo should be a minister," she
would say. "One day Murdo will be a minister. You mark
my words. He's got the face of a minister." '

'Well, well,' said Murdo, 'well, well.'

And he would look into the red glowing fire as if he was
seeing a pulpit there and he would hear himself saying, 'In
the immortal words of our theologian De Sade . . .'

After a time he would get to his feet and he would say,
'I'll come again next week. Look after yourself.'

And his father would say, 'Don't worry about me. I'll do
that all right.'

And Murdo would leave the house and look at the snow
and test the thin roof of ice over the pools with the toe
of his shoe delicately and elegantly as if he were thinking
of some new ballet, and he would think of his father
in Libya and his dead mother and Maxwell walking up
and down the winter landscape with a rolled umbrella in
his hand.

*   *   *

Here is another story that Murdo told little Colin:

In a country far away (he said), there once lived a little mouse and this mouse used to go to her work every day. She would sit at a desk and write in a big book. She even wore glasses. When her work in the office was over she would take the bus home and then she would make her tea and look at the TV and put her feet up on the sofa.

At eight o'clock at night she would make her supper, wash the dishes and watch the TV again. And after that she would go to bed.

At eight o'clock in the morning she would get up, listen to the radio for a little while, wash herself, eat her breakfast and then she would go to the office again. And she did this every day from Monday to Friday.

Sometimes on Friday night after the week's work was over she would have a party for the other mice in the neighbourhood, and they would eat a lot of cheese.

Well, one day, about twelve o'clock, she came out of the office and she took a walk down to a big quiet river that was quite near the place where she worked and she was eating her dinner on the bank of the river—a piece of bread and cheese—when she saw a large white swan swimming in the water. The swan was very beautiful and as white as snow and it had a large red beak which now and again it dipped into the water as if it was drinking. Now and again it would glance towards the bank of the river and stare as if it was seeing the mouse, but of course it couldn't have, as the mouse was so small.

That swan seems to have a very easy life of it, said the mouse to herself. All it does all day is swim about in the water and look at its own reflection and eat and drink. No wonder it looks so beautiful and clean. It doesn't have to cook its dinner or its supper or its breakfast; it doesn't have to wash and dry dishes; it doesn't have to sweep the floor; and it doesn't have to get up in the morning. That swan must be very happy.

And the swan looked so queenly, so calm, swimming in the river like a great white picture. And the mouse said to herself, wouldn't it be wonderful if I could lead the same sort of life? I too would be like a queen.

Well, one day the mouse's manager in the office was very angry with her because of a mistake she had made in her books, and he told her that she must come back and work late at five o'clock at night. When the mouse left the office she began to cry.

Look, she said to herself, at the life I lead. I try to do my best and look what happens to me. Tonight I was going to wash my clothes and now I have to go back to the office though I don't want to do that. Some of the other mice in the office laugh at me and some of them steal my food.

And so she looked out at the swan that was swimming so calmly in the water.

'I'm just as good as you,' she said to the swan. 'I do more work than you. You never did any work in your life. What use are you to the country? You never do anything but admire yourself in the water. Well, it's high time I got some rest as well. I need it more than you do. Anyway in my own way I'm just as beautiful as you. And there were kings and queens in my family as well, I'm sure, in the past, though now I'm working in an office.'

She was so upset that she couldn't eat her food and later a crow came down from the sky and ate it.

Anyway the mouse jumped into the river thinking that she would swim just as well as the swan was doing.

But she slowly began to sink because she wasn't used to swimming and she was drowned in the river and the swan continued to swim round and round, dipping her throat now and again in the water, and then raising it and looking around her with her long neck and her blunt red beak.

Murdo sent the following to the local newspaper, but it was never printed.

Is Calvin Still Alive?

Many people think that Hitler is still alive and that he is living in South America with money that he stole from the Jews.

But there is a rumour going about this island that Calvin is still alive. He is supposed to have been seen in a small house a little out of town on the road to Holm.

He is a small hunchbacked man with spectacles, who speaks to no one, or if he does speak he speaks in very sloppy not to say ungrammatical Gaelic.

He has a face like iron and he is said to sit at a table night and day studying a Bible almost as big as himself.

He can't stand a candle in the same house.

If he sees anyone drinking or smoking he rushes out of the house and shouts insults at him and dances up and down on the road, shaking his fist.

He also has a strong aversion to cars.

If he sees a woman approaching he shuts the door at once and sits at the window shaking his fist at her and mouthing inaudible words. If she looks at him he shuts his eyes and keeps them shut till she has gone past. After that he washes his face.

He wears black gloves on his hands. He hardly ever leaves the house in the summer but in the winter he goes on long walks.

Now a number of people in the village wonder if you can find a picture of Calvin so that they can establish his identity. It may be that this is a man who is impersonating Calvin for some reason of his own.

If anyone were to say that it would certainly be odd to find Calvin still alive, I would answer that stranger things have happened down the centuries.

What about for instance the man in the Bible who rose to heaven in a chariot?

And what about Nebuchadnezzar who lived on grass for many years?

It is also odd that this man won't go to any of our churches but that now and again on a Sunday he will be seen hanging about one of them though he won't actually go in.

I await your answer with much interest. I enclose a stamp.

Yours etc.,
Murdo Macrae

One day Murdo visited the local library and he said to the thin bespectacled woman who was standing at the counter:

'I want the novel *War and Peace* written by Hugh Macleod.'

'Hugh Macleod?' she said.

'Yes,' he said, 'but if you don't happen to have *War and Peace* I'll take any other book by the same author, such as *The Brothers Karamazov*.'

'I thought,' she said doubtfully, 'I mean are you sure that . . .'

'I'm quite sure that the book is by Hugh Macleod,' said Murdo, 'and I often wonder why there aren't more of his books in the libraries.'

'Well,' she said, 'I think we have *War and Peace* but surely it was written by Tolstoy.'

'What's it about?' said Murdo. 'Is it about a family growing up in Harris at the time of Napoleon?'

'I thought,' she said, 'that the story is set in Russia,' looking at him keenly through her glasses.

'Bloody hell,' said Murdo under his breath and then aloud,

'Oh well I don't think we can be talking about the same Hugh Macleod. This man was never in Russia as far as I know. Is it a long book, about a thousand pages?'

'I think that's right,' said the woman, who was beginning to look rather wary.

'Uh huh,' said Murdo. 'This is a long book as well. It's about Napoleon in Harris in the eighteenth century. Hugh Macleod was an extraordinary man, you know. He had a long beard and he used to make his own shoes. A strange man. I don't really know much about his life except that he became a bit religious in his old age. But it doesn't matter. If you haven't got *War and Peace* maybe you could give me his other book *The Brothers Karamazov*. It's about three brothers and their struggle for a croft.'

'I don't think,' said the woman, 'that we have that one.'

'Well, isn't that damnable,' said Murdo. 'Here you have an author as distinguished as any that has ever come out of the Highlands and you don't have his books. And I can't get them in any other library. I think it's shameful. But I bet you if he was a Russian you would have all his books.

I'm pretty sure that you'll have *Tramping through Siberia* by Gogol. Anyway it doesn't matter.

'But I was forgetting another reason for my call,' and he took a can out of his pocket. 'I'm collecting money for authors who can't write. A penny or two will do.'

'Authors who can't write?' said the woman looking suspiciously at the can as if it might explode in her face.

'That's right,' said Murdo. 'Poor people who sit at their desks every morning and find that they can't put a word to paper. Have you ever spared a thought for them? Those people who can write don't of course need help. But think,' he said, leaning forward, 'of those people who sit at their desks day after day while the sun rises and the sun sets and when they look at their paper they find that there isn't a word written on it. Do you not feel compassion for them? Aren't your bowels moved with pity? Doesn't it surprise you that in our modern society not enough is done for such people?'

'Well,' she said, 'to tell the truth . . .'

'Oh, I know what you're going to say,' said Murdo. 'Why should you give money for non-existent books? And that point of view is natural enough. There is a great deal in it. But has it ever occurred to you that the books that have never been written may be as good as, nay even better than, the ones that have? That there is in some heaven or other books as spotless as the angels themselves without a stain of ink on them? For myself, I can believe this quite easily as I put a lot of credence in the soul as I am sure you do also. Think,' he said, 'if this room were full of non-existent unwritten books how much easier your job would be.'

He saw her hand creeping steadily towards the phone that lay on her desk and said hurriedly,

'Perhaps that day will come though it hasn't come yet.'

He took the can in his hand and half-ran half-walked out of the library down the corridor with the white marble busts of Romans on each side of him.

Still half running he passed a woman laden with books and said, 'I'm sorry. Bubonic plague. Please excuse me. I'll be all right in a few minutes. Brucellosis,' and half crouching he ran down the brae among the bare trees and the snow.

Ahead of him he saw the white mountain and he shook his fist at it shouting

'Neil Munro. Neil Munro.'

After a while he took a black hat out of his bag and he went home limping, now and again removing his hat when he saw a child walking past him on the street.

'The potato,' said Murdo to his wife one night, 'what is like the potato? What would we do without the potato especially in the islands? The potato is sometimes wet and sometimes dry. It is even said that the dry potato is "laughing" at you. Now that is a very odd thing, a laughing potato. But it could happen. And there are many people whose faces are like potatoes. If we had no potatoes we would have to eat the herring with our tea and that wouldn't be very tasty. In the spring we plant the potatoes and we pick them in the autumn. Now in spite of that no poet has made a poem for the humble potato. It didn't occur to William Ross or Alexander Macdonald—great poets though they were—to do so, and I am sure that they must have eaten a lot of potatoes in their poetic careers.

'There is a very big difference, when you think of it, between the potato and the herring. The herring moves, it travels from place to place in the ocean, and they say that there aren't many fish in the sea faster than the herring. But the potato lies in the dark till someone digs it up with a graip. We should therefore ask ourselves, Which is the happier of the two, the potato or the herring? That is a big philosophical question and it astonishes me that it hasn't been studied in greater depth. It is a very profound question. For the potato lies there in the dark, and it doesn't hear or see anything. But in spite of that we have no evidence that it is less happy than the herring. No indeed. And as well as that we have no evidence that the herring is either happy or unhappy. The herring journeys through the ocean meeting many other kinds of fish on its way, such as seals and mackerel.

'But the potato stays in the one place in the dark in its brown skin, without, we imagine, desire or hope. For what could a potato hope for? Or what could it desire? Now at a certain time, the potato and the herring come together on the one plate, say on a summer day or on an autumn day. It greatly puzzles me how they come together in that fashion. Was it predestined that that particular herring and that particular potato should meet—the herring that was roving the sea in its grey dress and the potato that was lying in the earth in its brown dress. That is a very deep question. And the herring cannot do without the potato, nor for that matter can the potato do without the herring. For they need each other.

'They are as closely related as the soul and the body. But is the herring the body or the soul?

'That is another profound question.

'And also you can roast a potato and you can roast a herring but I don't think they are as good when they are roasted. I myself think that the herring is better when it is salted and I may say the same about the potato.

'But no one has ever conjectured about the feelings of the potato or the feelings of the herring. The herring leaves its house and travels all over the world and it sees strange sights in the sea, but the potato sees nothing, it is lying in the darkness while the days and the weeks and the years pass. The potato doesn't move from the place in which it was planted.

'I must make a poem about this sometime,' said Murdo to his wife. 'I am very surprised that up till now no one has made a poem about it.'

And he stopped speaking and his wife looked at him and then got up and made some tea.

One night Murdo woke from sleep, his wife beside him in the bed, and he was sweating and trembling.

'Put on the light at once,' he shouted. His wife jumped out of bed and did as he had told her to do.

'What's wrong?' she said. 'What's wrong?' Murdo's face was as white as the sheet on the bed. He was sitting up in bed as if he was listening to some odd sound that only he was hearing: in the calmness they could hear the gurgling of the water from the stream that ran past their house among the undergrowth.

'A dream I had,' said Murdo. 'It was a dream I dreamed. In the dream I saw a witch and she was coming after me and she had a cup of blood in her hand as if it was a cup of tea. And her face . . . There's something wrong with this house.'

'There's nothing wrong with the house,' she said, and when he looked at her he began to tremble as if she herself might indeed be the witch.

'Her face was sharp and long,' he said, 'and she had a cup of blood in her hand and I was making the sign of the cross. The devil was in that dream, there was real evil in that dream. I never dreamed a dream like that before.' And his face was dead white, his teeth were chattering, and he was looking around him wildly.

He thought that the room was full of evil, of devils, that his wife's face was like the face of a witch among the evil.

'I never thought that evil existed till now,' he said. 'Leave the light on. Don't put it off.'

He was afraid to leave his bed or to walk about the house and he felt that there was some evil moving about the outside of the house in the darkness. He thought that there were devils clawing at the walls, trying to get in through the windows, perhaps even breaking the glass or tapping on it.

'Her face,' he said, 'was so sharp and so long, and her back was crooked and she had black wings.'

'You're all right now, aren't you?' said his wife and her blue eyes were gazing at him with what he thought was compassion. But he couldn't be sure. He thought again, What if she is a witch? What if I am a devil myself? What world have we come from, what evil world? What dark woods?

Sitting upright in bed it was as if he was a ghost rising from the grave.

'You're all right, you're all right,' said Janet again.

'Who lived in this house before us?' he asked. 'It was an old woman, wasn't it?'

'Not at all,' said Janet. 'You remember very well who lived here. It was a young family. Surely you remember.'

'You're right,' he said, 'you're right enough.'

Masks, he said to himself. Masks on all the faces, as happens on Hallowe'en. Masks that don't move. Stiff cardboard masks. A wolf's face, a bear's face.

And he felt as if the house were shaking in a storm of evil and the evil hitting it like a strong wind and light pouring out of the house.

'I'm sorry,' he said to Janet. 'I'm sorry I wakened you.'

'Do you want some tea?' she asked him.

'No,' he said. 'But leave the light on for a while.' He listened to the sound of the river flowing through the darkness. Directly underneath the window there was grass where he had buried the black dog when it had been killed on a summer's day by a motor car.

The bones rotting.

'I'm all right now,' he said. 'I'm all right. You can put the light off.'

And she rose and did that and he sat awake for a long time listening to his wife's breathing and he heard above her tranquil breathing the sound of the river flowing past.

At last he fell asleep and this time he had no frightening dreams.

But just before he fell asleep he had a vision of the house as a lighted shell moving through the darkness, and animals around it with red beaks and claws and red teeth, leaping and jumping venomously at the windows and walls to get at him.

'What's wrong with that man of yours if he can be called a man at all?' said Janet's father to her one day. He was sitting in an easy chair, his face red with the light of the fire, like a cockerel about to crow.

'When I was young,' he said, 'I used to be at the fishing no matter what kind of weather it was.'

'You've told me,' said Janet. She was more familiar with her father's world than she was with Murdo's. She didn't understand what attraction the white mountain, of which he was continually speaking, had for him.

She herself was of the opinion that the mountain though beautiful was very cold. She much preferred the spring to winter or autumn. She liked to hang billowing clothes on a line in breezy spring and to watch the birds flying about the moorland.

'You don't even have any children,' her father said to her. They were alone together for her mother was at the midweek evening service in the church hall. Her father never went to church.

He was always wandering about in the open air with a hammer or a piece of wood or standing at the door studying the weather.

'It's easy enough to work in an office,' he said. 'Anyone can do that. Why did he leave his work?' In the days before Murdo left the office he used to write letters for his father-in-law about matters connected with the croft, which he couldn't understand but which he could transform into reasonably official English.

'Is he going to stay in that house forever?' said her father again. 'What does he do all day?'

In a way Janet was on her father's side for she couldn't really understand Murdo any more than he did. When she married him she had thought she understood him and that he was normal enough but now she wasn't so sure. He did such odd not to say abnormal things. Her father was not at all odd, he was the quintessence of normality: he was like stone on a moor. Murdo would sometimes come home from the office and he would say, 'I don't understand why I am in that office at all. Why do people work anyway? A sort of fog comes over my eyes when I look at Maxwell and the rest of them. They actually believe that what they are doing is important to the human race. They actually believe that by gathering in money and counting, and by adding figures in columns, they are contributing to the salvation of the world. It's really quite incredible. I mean, the absurdity of what they do has never occurred to them at all. They haven't even thought about it. They are so glad and so pleased that they can actually do the work they're doing, and they make a great mystery of it, as if it were of some immense secret importance. They don't realise at all the futility of what they're doing, and sometimes it takes me all my time to keep from bursting out laughing. If they all dropped dead with pens in their hands it wouldn't make the slightest difference to the world. They would be replaced by other people equally absorbed in the same absurd work.'

'What are you talking about?' she would say to him. 'What do you mean?' She didn't understand clearly what he was saying.

'Well, the world would carry on in the same way as before, wouldn't it,' said Murdo. 'I only hope that Maxwell's umbrella is struck by lightning one of these days. It might teach him a lesson.'

Her father was saying, 'Many people would be happy with the work he's got. There are people I know who clean the roads, clever people too. And look at the warm dry job he had.'

He lifted a newspaper and laid it down again. He bought the paper every day but he never read it right through. He would glance at it now and again and then he would put it down.

'You would be as well to leave him,' said her father.

She had actually thought of leaving him but she knew that she would never go through with it. It wasn't that she was frightened to leave him but she really hoped that one morning he would suddenly leap out of bed and say, 'I'm going back to my work today.' She was hoping that this would happen. And also she thought that she should be loyal to him so long as he was being attacked by his strange sickness.

'No I won't leave him,' she said looking into the fire.

'Well, I hope you know what you're doing,' said her father.

Janet sometimes thought that everything would be all right if Murdo would find himself able to write something instead of staring at that white mountain which obsessed him so much.

Her father was so large and definite and red in his opinions: she actually thought of his opinions as red and bristly.

'I never thought much of him,' he said. 'There was a foolishness in his people. His grandfather was a daft bard. He used to write silly songs.'

And sometimes her father would pace about the room like a prisoner, his great red hands at his sides.

He raised his fist and said, 'What he needs is a good thump. That's what he needs.' And his face became a deep red with anger.

'You can make tea for yourself if you like,' he told Janet and he went to the door and looked out. 'The weather looks as if it's going to take a turn for the worse.' His round red head was like a tomato on top of his stocky body.

Poor Murdo, she said to herself. What are you going to do? Poor Murdo. And she felt a deep pity for him, in her very womb.

'No I don't want any tea,' she said. 'I have to go home.'

On the way home, she looked at the white mountain for a long time, but all she saw was the mountain itself. At last she turned her eyes away, for the glitter of the snow was dazzling her.

What am I going to do? she thought. There's no money coming into the house and the neighbours are laughing at me.

But in spite of that there was no one she knew as witty and lively as her own husband.

If only we had children, she thought. If only there was some money coming into the house I'd be happy enough.

But a small persistent voice was saying, 'Would you really? Would you really?' like a small winter bird with a small black beak.

'Would you? Would you?' twittered the small bird.

For every day now as she looked in the mirror she saw herself growing older all the time.

And Murdo also growing older.

And the chairs and tables closing in on her.

Last Will and Testament by Murdo Macrae

1. To my beloved wife I leave my shoes and clothes, my pencil and my pen and papers (All my love such as it is).
2. To my mother-in-law I leave the newspapers that I've been collecting for many years. And my rubber nose.
3. To my father-in-law I leave a stone.
4. To tell the truth I haven't much else except for my

bicycle and I leave that also to my mother-in-law. And I leave my watch to Maxwell.

I wish my wife to send the following letter through the post:

To Whomsoever it may Concern

If anyone can tell me why we are alive, I will give him TWO POUNDS, all my money.

For in the first place we are created of flesh and lightning.

And in the fullness of time the flesh and the lightning grow old.

And also we are working in a world without meaning. Yesterday I looked at an egg and I couldn't understand why it was in the place where it was.

Now I should know the reason for its position in space. For that surely is not a mysterious thing. And I could say the same about butter. And salt. And Bovril. Now we have come out of the lightning, in our ragged clothes. And at last we arrived at Maxwell with his umbrella.

This is the problem that Newton never unravelled.

We kill each other.

For no reason at all.

These thoughts climb my head as if it were a staircase.

And that is why I am an idiot.

WE CANNOT LIVE WITHOUT SOME BELIEF.

I believe in my mother-in-law. She will live forever. She will be knitting in a country unknown to the Greeks. I believe in my mother-in-law and in my father-in-law and also in Mrs Macleod.

They will all live forever.

For in their condition they are close to that of the animal.

They survive on dressers and sideboards.

Those who approach most closely to the conditions of the animal are the ones most likely to survive.

And Woolworths.

Woolworths will live forever.

Too much intelligence is not good for one.

Too much of the spirit is not good for the body, but
the following are good for the body:

Bovril.

Sanatogen.

Butter.

Crowdie.

Eggs.

Water.

Bread.

Meat.

And the sun on a warm day.

And a girl's breast,

and

a spoonful of honey.

I am sending you this letter, nameless one, with
much happiness and without a stamp.

Murdo Macrae

Murdo's father was dying and Murdo and Janet were watching him. Now and again his father would ask for water so
that he could wet his lips and his breath was going faster
and faster. Janet was sitting on a chair beside the bed but
Murdo was walking up and down restlessly, unceasingly.
On a small table beside the bed he saw a letter that had come
to his father and had not been opened: it was in a brown
envelope and looked official. And the tears came unbidden
to his eyes.

Why didn't I do more? he was saying to himself all
the time. He couldn't sit down. Outside the window the
darkness was falling quickly, and he felt cold. He was
shaking as if he had a fever, and his teeth were chattering.
Now and again he would look at his father's thin grey face
as the head turned ceaselessly on the pillow.

Murdo nearly knelt and prayed. He nearly said, 'Save my
father, save my father, and I will do anything You want me
to do.' He thought of earlier days when his father used to
tease him or carry him about on his shoulders. He thought
of his father as a soldier in the war.

What did he get out of life? he asked himself. What did he get? Janet amazed him sitting there so serenely on her chair as if she were used to deaths, as if this room were her true element though in fact as far as he knew she had never seen anyone die before.

A voice was screaming in his head, 'I'm sorry. I'm sorry.' He knew that his father was dying, but he didn't know why he should feel so sorry.

The smell of death was in the room: death was an inevitability of the air.

In a strange way he had never thought that his father would die though he was old and frail.

He saw his father's pipe on the table and the tears again welled to his eyes. He was grinding his teeth together. 'I'm sorry, I'm sorry,' the voice was screaming silently like a voice that might be coming down from the sky, from some bleak planet without light.

His father's breath was accelerating all the time as if he were preparing himself: for a journey, as if he were in a hurry to go somewhere.

And Murdo paced restlessly up and down the room. Pictures flashed in front of his eyes.

His father with a spade, his father at the peat bank, his father reading the paper. And below each picture like an image in a dark pool was the thin grey face.

The stars, they are so far away, Murdo thought.

He was thinking of the other houses in the town with their lights, and they did not know what was going on in this room.

And all the time his body was shaking and shivering as if with the coldness of death itself.

He put his hand on his father's brow and it had the chillness of death on it. Like marble.

Janet rose and went for some more water. Once his father opened his eyes and looked around him but Murdo knew that he wasn't seeing either of them.

And his breath was going like an engine, fast, fast.

Murdo turned away and went to the window. He looked out but he could see nothing in the darkness.

Is this what we were born for? he was saying to himself

over and over. He turned back to his father who was melting away before his eyes like snow.

He looked out of the window again.

When he turned round next time he felt a deep silence in the room.

The breath had ceased its frantic running.

His father's head had fallen on one side and the mouth was twisted. Murdo began to cry and he couldn't stop. He knew that his father was dead. He himself was crying and shivering at the same time.

He couldn't stop crying. Janet put her hand on his shoulder and he in turn put his face on her breast like a child, crying.

There was no sound in the room except his own weeping.

He rose abruptly and went outside. Through the darkness he could see the white mountain. Like a ghost.

It frightened him.

It looked so cold and distant and white.

Like a ghost staring at him.

He stayed there for a long time looking at it. He expected no help from it.

There was no happiness nor warning nor comfort nor sadness in that terrible cold whiteness.

It was just a mountain that rose in front of him out of the darkness.

I must climb it, he thought. I must do that now.

He went into the room again and said to Janet, 'I'll be all right now.' She looked at him with love in her eyes and her face was streaming with tears as if the snow had begun to melt in spring, for her face was so pale and tired and white.

'There are no angels,' said Murdo. 'There is only the white mountain.'

Janet looked at him with wonder.

'I'll be all right now,' said Murdo. He knew what he was going to write on white leaves.

A story about his father. At least one story, while he fought with the white mountain, wrestled with it, and after that if he couldn't defeat the white mountain he knew also what he would do.

He picked up his father's pipe and put it in his pocket.

Janet was looking from Murdo's face to his father's. Something was happening to Murdo but she didn't know what it was. His face was becoming more settled, white as snow, but at the same time the trembling life and vibrancy were leaving it.

He was like a tombstone above his father's body.

And she felt fear and happiness together.

For Murdo was growing more and more, minute by minute, like his father and her own father.

It was as if he was settling down into a huge heaviness.

But at the same time there was a terrible question in his face, a question without end, without boundary, a question without laughter.

Murdo took her by the hand and led her out of the house and he showed her the mountain.

'Soon,' he said, 'we shall have to climb it.'

And his face was set as stone.

And her father-in-law's face was in front of her as well.

It glared gauntly out of the middle of the chairs and the table and the dresser.

That grey question.

That grey thin shrunken question.

The Wedding

IT WAS A FINE blowy sunshiny day as I stood outside the church on the fringe of the small groups who were waiting for the bride to arrive. I didn't know anybody there, I was just a very distant relative, and I didn't feel very comfortable in my dark suit, the trousers of which were rather short. There were a lot of young girls from the Highlands (though the wedding was taking place in the city) all dressed in bright summery clothes and many of them wearing corsages of red flowers. Some wore white hats which cast intricate shadows on their faces. They all looked very much at ease in the city and perhaps most of them were working there, in hotels and offices. I heard one of them saying something about a Cortina and another one saying it had been a Ford. They all seemed to know each other and one of them said in her slow soft Highland voice, 'Do you think Murdina will be wearing her beads today?' They all laughed. I wondered if some of them were university students.

The minister who was wearing dark clothes but no gown stood in the doorway chatting to the photographer who was carrying an old-fashioned black camera. They seemed to be savouring the sun as if neither of them was used to it. The doors had been open for some time as I well knew since I had turned up rather early. A number of sightseers were standing outside the railings taking photographs and admiring the young girls who looked fresh and gay in their creamy dresses.

I looked at the big clock which I could see beyond the church. The bride was late though the groom had already arrived and was talking to his brother. He didn't look at all nervous. I had an idea that he was an electrician somewhere and his suit didn't seem to fit him very well. He was a small person with a happy rather uninteresting face, his black hair combed back sleekly and plastered with what was, I imagined, fairly cheap oil.

After a while the minister told us we could go in if we wanted to, and we entered. There were two young men, one in a lightish suit and another in a dark suit, waiting to direct us to our seats. We were asked which of the two we were related to, the bride or the groom, and seated accordingly, either on the left or the right of the aisle facing the minister. There seemed to be more of the groom's relatives than there were of the bride's and I wondered idly whether the whole thing was an exercise in psychological warfare, a primitive pre-marital battle. I sat in my seat and picked up a copy of a church magazine which I leafed through while I waited: it included an attack on Prince Philip for encouraging Sunday sport. In front of me a young girl who appeared to be a foreigner was talking to an older companion in broken English.

The groom and the best man stood beside each other at the front facing the minister. After a while the bride came in with her bridesmaids, all dressed in blue, and they took their positions to the left of the groom. The bride was wearing a long white dress and looked pale and nervous and almost somnambulant under the white headdress. We all stood up and sang a psalm. Then the minister said that if there was anyone in the church who knew of any impediment to the marriage they should speak out now or forever hold their peace. No one said anything (one wondered if anyone ever stood up and accused either the bride or groom of some terrible crime): and he then spoke the marriage vows, asking the usual questions which were answered inaudibly. He told them to clasp each other by the right hand and murmured something about one flesh. The groom slipped the ring onto the bride's finger and there was silence in the church for a long time because the event seemed to last interminably. At last the ring was safely fixed and we sang another hymn and the minister read passages appropriate to the occasion, mostly from St Paul. When it was all over we went outside and watched the photographs being taken.

Now and again the bride's dress would sway in the breeze

and a woman dressed in red would run forward to arrange it properly, or at least to her own satisfaction. The bride stood gazing at the camera with a fixed smile. A little boy in a grey suit was pushed forward to hand the bride a horseshoe after which he ran back to his mother, looking as if he was about to cry. The bride and groom stood beside each other facing into the sun. One couldn't tell what they were thinking of or if they were thinking of anything. I suddenly thought that this must be the greatest day in the bride's life and that never again would a thing so public, so marvellous, so hallowed, happen to her. She smiled all the time but didn't speak. Perhaps she was lost in a pure joy of her own. Her mother took her side, and her father. Her mother was a calm, stout, smiling woman who looked at the ground most of the time. Her father twisted his neck about as if he were being chafed by his collar and shifted his feet now and again. His strawy dry hair receded from his lined forehead and his large reddish hands stuck out of his white cuffs.

Eventually the whole affair was over and people piled into the taxis which would take them to the reception. I didn't know what to make of it all. It had not quite had that solemnity which I had expected and I felt that I was missing or had missed something important considering that a woman to the right of me in church had been dabbing her eyes with a small flowered handkerchief all through the ceremony. Both bride and groom seemed very ordinary and had not been transfigured in any way. It was like any other wedding one might see in the city, there didn't seem to be anything Highland about it at all. And the bits of conversation that I had overhead might have been spoken by city people. I heard no Gaelic.

For some reason I kept thinking of the father, perhaps because he had seemed to be the most uncomfortable of the lot. Everyone else looked so assured as if they had always been doing this or something like this and none of it came as a surprise to them. I got into a taxi with some people and without being spoken to arrived at the hotel which was a very good one, large and roomy, and charging, as I could see from a ticket at the desk, very high prices.

We picked up either a sherry or whisky as we went in the door and I stood about again. A girl in a white blouse was saying to her friend dressed in creamy jacket and suit, 'It was in Luigi's you see and this chap said to me out of the blue, "I like you but I don't know if I could afford you".' She giggled and repeated the story a few times. Her friend said: 'You meet queer people in Italian restaurants. I was in an Indian restaurant last week with Colin. It doesn't shut till midnight you know . . .' I moved away to where another group of girls was talking and one of them saying: 'Did you hear the story about the aspirin?' They gathered closely together and when the story was finished there was much laughter.

After a while we sat down at the table and watched the wedding party coming in and sitting down. We ate our food and the girl on my left spoke to another girl on her left and to a boy sitting opposite her. She said: 'This chap came into the hotel one night very angry. He had been walking down the street and there was this girl in a blue cap dishing out Barclay cards or something. Well, she never approached him at all though she picked out other people younger than him. He was furious about it, absolutely furious. Couldn't she see that he was a business man, he kept saying. He was actually working in insurance and when we offered him a room with a shower he wouldn't take it because it was too expensive.'

The other girl, younger and round-faced, said: 'There was an old woman caught in the lift the other day. You should have heard the screaming . . .' I turned away and watched the bride who was sitting at the table with a fixed smile on her face. Her father, twisting his neck about, was drinking whisky rapidly as if he was running out of time. Her mother smiled complacently but wasn't speaking to anyone. The minister sat at the head of the table eating his chicken with grave deliberation.

'Did you hear that Lindy has a girl?' said the boy in front of me to the girls. 'And she's thinking of going back home.'

They all laughed. 'I wouldn't go back home now. They'll be at the peats,' said the girl on my left.

'Well,' said the boy, 'I don't know about that. There was a student from America up there and he wanted to work at the peats to see what it was like. He's learned to speak Gaelic too.'

'How did he like it?' said the girl at my left.

'He enjoyed it,' said the boy. 'He said he'd never enjoyed anything so much. He said they'd nothing like that in America.'

'I'm sure,' said the small girl and they laughed again.

'Wouldn't go back for anything anyway,' said the girl to my left. 'They're all so square up there.'

When we had all finished eating, the Master of Ceremonies said that the groom would make a speech which he did very rapidly and incoherently. He was followed by the best man who also spoke very briefly and with incomprehensible references to one of the bridesmaids who blushed deeply as he spoke. There were cheers whenever an opportunity arose such as, for instance, when the groom referred for the first time to his wife and when there was a reference to someone called Tommy.

After that the telegrams were read out. Most of them were quite short and almost formal, 'Congratulations and much happiness' and so on. A number, however, were rather bawdy, such as, for instance, one which mentioned a chimney and a fire and another which suggested that both the bride and groom should watch the honey on their honeymoon. While the telegrams were being read some of the audience whispered to each other, 'That will be Lachy,' and 'That will be Mary Anne'. I thought of those telegrams coming from the Highlands to this hotel where waitresses went round the tables with drinks and there were modernistic pictures, swirls of blue and red paint, on the walls. One or two of the telegrams were in Gaelic and in some strange way they made the wedding both more authentic and false. I didn't know what the bride thought as she sat there, as if entranced and distant. Everything seemed so formal, so fixed and monotonous, as if the participants were trying to avoid errors, which the sharpwitted city-bred waitresses might pick up.

Eventually the telegrams had all been read and the father

got up to speak about the bride. I didn't know what I
expected but he certainly began with an air of business-like
trepidation. 'Ladies and gentlemen,' he said, 'I am here
today to make a speech which as you will know is not my
speciality.' He twisted his neck about inside the imprisoning
collar and continued. 'I can tell you that the crossing was
good and the skipper told me that the *Corona* is a good boat
though a bit topheavy.' He beamed nervously and then said,
'But to my daughter. I can tell you that she has been a good
daughter to me. I am not going to say that she is good at the
peats for she is never at home for the peats and she never
went to the fishing as girls of her age used to do in the past.'
By this time people were beginning to look at each other or
down at their plates and even the waitresses were smiling.
'I'll tell you something about the old days. We turned out
good men and women in those days, good sailors who fought
for their country. Nowadays I don't know about that. I was
never in the city myself and I never wore a collar except to
the church. Anyway I was too busy. There were the calves
to be looked after and the land as you all know. But I can
tell you that my daughter here has never been a burden to
us. She has always been working on the mainland. Ever
since she was a child she has been a good girl with no
nonsense and a help to her mother, and many's the time
I've seen her working at the hay and in the byre. But things
is changed now. Nowadays, it's the tractors and not the
horses. In the old days too we had the gig but now it's
the train and the plane.' The bride was turning a deadly
white and staring down at the table. The girls on my left
were transfixed. Someone dropped a fork or a spoon or a
knife and the sound it made could be heard quite clearly.
But the father continued remorselessly: 'In my own place I
would have spoken in the Gaelic but even the Gaelic is dying
out now as anyone can read in the papers every week. In the
old days too we would have a wedding which would last for
three days. When Johnny Murdo married, I can remember
it very well, the wedding went on for four days. And he
married when he was quite old. But as for my daughter
here I am very happy that she is getting married though
the city is not the place for me and I can tell you I'll be

very glad to get back to the dear old home again. And that is all I have to say. Good luck to them both.'

When he sat down there was a murmur of conversation which rose in volume as if to drown the memory of the speech. The girls beside me talked in a more hectic way than ever about their hotels and made disparaging remarks about the islands and how they would never go back. Everyone avoided the bride who sat fixed and miserable at the table as if her wedding dress had been turned into a shroud.

I don't know exactly what I felt. It might have been shame that the waitresses had been laughing. Or it might have been gladness that someone had spoken naturally and authentically about his own life. I remember I picked up my whisky and laid it down again without drinking it and felt that this was in some way a meaningful action.

Shortly afterwards the dancing began in an adjoining room. During the course of it (at the beginning they played the latest pop tunes) I went over and stood beside the father who was standing by himself in a corner looking miserable as the couples expressed themselves (rather than danced) in tune to the music, twisting their bodies, thrusting out their bellies and swaying hypnotically with their eyes half shut.

'It's not like the eightsome reel,' I said.

'I don't know what it is like,' he said. 'I have never seen anything like it.'

'It is rather noisy,' I agreed. 'And how are the crops this year?' I said to him in Gaelic.

He took his dazed eyes off a couple who were snapping their fingers at each other just in front of him, and said: 'Well, it's been very dry so far and we don't know what we're going to do.' He had to shout the words against the music and the general noise. 'I have a good few acres you know though a good many years ago I didn't have any and I worked for another man. I have four cows and I sell the milk. To tell you the honest truth I didn't want to come here at all but I felt I couldn't let her down. It wasn't an easy thing for me. I haven't left the island before. Do you think this is a posh hotel?'

I said that I thought it was. He said, 'I tell you I've never been in a hotel before now. They've got a lot of carpets, haven't they? And mirrors, I've never seen so many mirrors.'

'Come on,' I shouted, 'let's go into the bar.' We did so and I ordered two beers.

'The people in there aren't like human beings at all,' he said. 'They're like Africans.'

After a while he said, 'It was the truth I said about her, she's never at home. She's always been working in hotels. I'll tell you something, she's never carried a creel on her back though that's not a good thing either. She was always eating buns and she would never eat any porridge. What do you think of her husband, eh? He was talking away about cars. And he's got a good suit, I'll give him that. He gave the waiter a pound, I saw it with my own eyes. Oh, he knows his way around hotels, I'll be bound. But where does he come from? I don't know. He's never ploughed any ground, I think.'

I thought at that moment that he wouldn't see his daughter very often in the future. Perhaps he really was without knowing it giving her away to a stranger in a hired cutprice suit.

After a while we thought it politic to go back. By this time there was a lull in the dancing and the boy in the lightish suit had started a Gaelic song but he didn't know all the words of it, only the chorus. People looked round for assistance while red-faced and embarrassed he kept asking if anyone knew the words because he himself had lost them. Suddenly the father pushed forward with authority and standing with his glass in his hand began to sing—verse after verse in the traditional manner. They all gathered round him and even the waitresses listened, there was so much depth and intensity in his singing. After he had finished there was much applause and requests for other songs for he seemed to know the words of all of them. The young girls and the boys gathered round him and sat on the floor in a circle looking up at him. He blossomed in the company and I thought that I could now leave, for he seemed to be wholly at home and more so than his audience were.

An American Sky

HE STOOD ON the deck of the ship looking towards the approaching island. He was a tall man who wore brownish clothes: and beside him were two matching brown cases. As he stood on the deck he could hear Gaelic singing coming from the saloon which wasn't all that crowded but had a few people in it, mostly coming home for a holiday from Glasgow. The large ship moved steadily through the water and when he looked over the side he could see thin spitlike foam travelling alongside. The island presented itself as long and green and bare with villages scattered along the coast. Ahead of him was the westering sun which cast long red rays across the water.

He felt both excited and nervous as if he were returning to a wife or sweetheart whom he had not seen for a long time and was wondering whether she had changed much in the interval, whether she had left him for someone else or whether she had remained obstinately true. It was strange, he thought, that though he was sixty years old he should feel like this. The journey from America had been a nostalgic one, first the plane, then the train, then the ship. It was almost a perfect circle, a return to the womb. A womb with a view, he thought and smiled.

He hadn't spoken to many people on the ship. Most of the time he had been on deck watching the large areas of sea streaming past, now and again passing large islands with mountain peaks, at other times out in the middle of an empty sea where the restless gulls scavenged, turning their yellow gaunt beaks towards the ship.

The harbour was now approaching and people were beginning to come up on deck with their cases. A woman beside him was buttoning up her small son's coat. Already he could see red buses and a knot of people waiting at the pier. It had always been like that, people meeting the ship when it arrived at about eight, some not even welcoming anyone in particular but just standing there watching. He noticed a squat man in fisherman's clothes doing something to a rope. Behind him there was a boat under green canvas.

The ship swung in towards the harbour. Now he could see the people more clearly and behind them the harbour buildings. When he looked over the side he noticed that the water was dirty with bits of wooden boxes floating about in an oily rainbowed scum.

After some manœuvring the gangway was eventually laid. He picked up his cases and walked down it behind a girl in yellow slacks whose transistor was playing in her left hand. Ahead of her was a man in glasses who had a BEA case with, stamped on it, the names of various foreign cities. There were some oldish women in dark clothes among the crowd and also some girls and boys in brightly coloured clothes. A large fat slow man stood to the side of the gangway where it touched the quay, legs spread apart, as if he had something to do with the ship, though he wasn't actually doing anything. Now and again he scratched a red nose.

He reached the shore and felt as if the contact with land was an emotionally charged moment. He didn't quite know how he felt, slightly empty, slightly excited. He walked away from the ship with his two cases and made his way along the main street. It had changed, no doubt about it. There seemed to be a lot of cafés, from one of which he heard the blare of a jukebox. In a bookseller's window he saw *From Russia with Love* side by side with a book about the Highlands called *The Misty Hebrides*. Nevertheless the place appeared smaller, though it was much more modern than he could remember, with large windows of plate glass, a jeweller's with Iona stone, a very fashionable-looking ladies' hairdressers. He also passed a supermarket and another bookseller's. Red lights from one of the cafés streamed into the bay. At the back of the jeweller's shop he saw a church spire rising into the sky. He came to a cinema which advertised Bingo on Tuesdays, Thursdays and Saturdays. Dispirited trailers for a Western filled the panels.

He came to a Chinese restaurant and climbed the steps, carrying his two cases. The place was nearly empty and seemed mostly purplish with, near the ceiling, a frieze showing red dragons. Vague music—he thought it might be Chinese—leaked from the walls. He sat down and, drawing the huge menu towards him, began to read it. In one corner of the large room an unsmiling Chinaman with a moustache was standing by an old-fashioned black telephone and at another table a young Chinese girl was reading what might have been a Chinese newspaper. A little bare-bottomed Chinese boy ran out of the kitchen, was briefly chased back with much giggling, and the silence descended again.

For a moment he thought that the music was Gaelic, and was lost in his dreams. The Chinese girl seemed to turn into Mary who was doing her homework in the small thatched house years and years before. She was asking their father about some arithmetic but he, stroking his beard, was not able to answer. At another table an old couple were solidly munching rice, their heads bowed.

The music swirled about him. The Chinese girl read on. Why was it that these people never laughed? He had noticed that. Also that Chinese restaurants were hushed like churches. A crowd of young people came in laughing and talking, their Highland accents quite distinct though they were speaking English. He felt suddenly afraid and alone and slightly disorientated as if he had come to the wrong place at the wrong time. The telephone rang harshly and the Chinaman answered it in guttural English. Perhaps he was the only one who could speak English. Perhaps that was his job, just to answer the phone. He had another look at the menu, suddenly put it down and walked out just as a Chinese waitress came across with a notebook and pencil in her hand. He hurried downstairs and walked along the street.

Eventually he found a hotel and stood at the reception desk. A young blonde girl was painting her nails and reading a book. She said to the girl behind her, 'What does "impunity" mean?' The other girl stopped chewing and said, 'Where does it say that?' The first girl looked at him coolly and said, 'Yes, Sir?'

Her voice also was Highland.

'I should like a room,' he said. 'A single room.'

She leafed rapidly through a book and said at last, 'We can give you 101, Sir. Shall I get the porter to carry your bags?'

'It's not necessary.'

'That will be all right then, Sir.'

He waited for a moment and then remembered what he was waiting for. 'Could I please have my key?' he asked.

She looked at him in amazement and said, 'You don't need a key here, Sir. Nobody steals anything. Room 101 is on the first floor. You can't miss it.' He took his cases and walked up the stairs. He heard them discussing a dance as he left.

He opened the door and put the cases down and went to the window. In front of him he could see the ship and the bay with the red lights on it and the fishing boats and the large clock with the greenish face.

As he turned away from the window he saw the Gideon Bible, picked it up, half smiling, and then put it down again. He took off his clothes slowly, feeling very tired, and went to bed. He fell asleep very quickly while in front of his eyes he could see Bingo signs, advertisements for Russian watches, and seagulls flying about with open gluttonous beaks. The last thought he had was that he had forgotten to ask when breakfast was in the morning.

TWO

The following day at two o'clock in the afternoon he took the bus to the village that he had left so many years before. There were few people on the bus which had a conductress as well as a driver, both dressed in uniform. He thought wryly of the gig in which he had been driven to the town the night he had left; the horse was dead long ago and so was his own father, the driver.

On the seat opposite him there was sitting a large fat tourist who had a camera and field-glasses slung over his shoulder and was wearing dark glasses and a light greyish hat.

The driver was a sturdy young man of about twenty or so. He whistled a good deal of the time and for the rest exchanged badinage with the conductress who, it emerged, wanted to become an air stewardess. She wore a black uniform, was pretty in a thin, sallow way, and had a turned-up nose and black hair.

After a while he offered a cigarette to the driver who took it. 'Fine day, Sir,' he said and then, 'Are you home on holiday?'

'Yes. From America.'

'Lots of tourists here just now. I was in America myself once. I was in the Merchant Navy. Saw a baseball team last night on TV.'

The bus was passing along the sparkling sea and the cemetery which stood on one side of the road behind a grey wall. The marble of the gravestones glittered in the sun. Now and again he could see caravans parked just off the road and on the beach men and children in striped clothing playing with large coloured balls or throwing sticks for dogs to retrieve. Once they passed a large block of what appeared to be council houses, all yellow.

'You'll see many changes,' said the driver. 'Hey, bring us some of that orangeade,' he shouted to the conductress.

'I suppose so.'

But there didn't seem all that many in the wide glittering day. The sea, of course, hadn't changed, the cemetery looked brighter in the sun perhaps, and there were more houses. But people waved at them from the fields, shielding their eyes with their hands. The road certainly was better.

At one point the tourist asked to be allowed out with his camera so that he could take a photograph of a cow which was staring vaguely over a fence.

If the weather was always like this, he thought, there wouldn't be any problem . . . but of course the weather did change . . . The familiar feeling of excitement and apprehension flooded him again.

After a while they stopped at the road end and he got off with his two cases. The driver wished him good luck. He stood staring at the bus as it diminished into the distance and then taking his cases began to walk along the road. He came to the ruins of a thatched house, stopped and went inside. As he did so he disturbed a swarm of birds which flew out of the space all round him and fluttered out towards the sky which he could see quite clearly as there was no roof. The ruined house was full of stones and bits of wood and in the middle of it an old-fashioned iron range which he stroked absently, making his fingers black and dusty. For a moment the picture returned to him of his mother in a white apron cooking at such a stove, in a smell of flour. He turned away and saw carved in the wooden door the words MARY LOVES NORMAN. The hinges creaked in the quiet day.

He walked along till he came to a large white house at which he stopped. He opened the gate and there, waiting about ten yards in front of him, were his brother, his brother's daughter-in-law, and her two children, one a boy of about seventeen and the other a girl of about fifteen. They all seemed to be dressed in their best clothes and stood there as if in a picture. His brother somehow seemed dimmer than he remembered, as if he were being seen in a bad light. An observer would have noticed that though the two brothers looked alike the visitor seemed a more vivid version of the other. The family waited for him as if he were a photographer and he moved forward. As he did so his brother walked quickly towards him, holding out his hand.

'John,' he said. They looked at each other as they shook hands. His niece came forward and introduced herself and the children. They all appeared well dressed and prosperous.

The boy took his cases and they walked towards the house. It was of course a new house, not the thatched one he had left. It had a porch and a small garden and large windows which looked out towards the road.

He suddenly said to this brother, 'Let's stay out here for a while.' They stood together at the fence gazing at the corn which swayed slightly in the breeze. His brother did not seem to know what to say and neither did he. They stood there in silence.

After a while John said, 'Come on, Murdo, let's look at the barn.' They went into it together. John stood for a while inhaling the smell of hay mixed with the smell of manure. He picked up a book which had fallen to the floor and looked inside it. On the fly-leaf was written:

Prize for English
John Macleod

The book itself in an antique and slightly stained greenish cover was called *Robin Hood and His Merry Men*. His brother looked embarrassed and said, 'Malcolm must have taken it off the shelf in the house and left it here.' John didn't say anything. He looked idly at the pictures. Some had been torn and many of the pages were brown with age. His eye was caught by a passage which read, 'Honour is the greatest virtue of all. Without it a man is nothing.' He let the book drop to the floor.

'We used to fight in that hayloft,' he said at last with a smile, 'and I think you used to win,' he added, punching his brother slightly in the chest. His brother smiled with pleasure. 'I'm not sure about that,' he answered.

'How many cows have you got?' said John looking out through the dusty window.

'Only one, I'm afraid,' said his brother. 'Since James died . . .' Of course. James was his son and the husband of the woman he had met. She had looked placid and mild, the kind of wife who would have been suited to him. James had been killed in an accident on a ship: no-one knew very much about it. Perhaps he had been drunk, perhaps not.

He was reluctant for some reason to leave the barn. It seemed to remind him of horses and bridles and bits, and in fact fragments of corroded leather still hung here and there on the walls. He had seen no horses anywhere: there would be no need for them now. Near the door he noticed a washing machine which looked quite new.

His brother said, 'The dinner will be ready, if it's your pleasure.' John looked at him in surprise, the invitation sounded so feudal and respectful. His brother talked as if he were John's servant.

'Thank you.' And again for a moment he heard his mother's voice as she called them in to dinner when they were out playing.

They went into the house, the brother lagging a little behind. John felt uncomfortable as if he were being treated like royalty when he wanted everything to be simple and natural. He knew that they would have cooked the best food whether they could afford it or not. They wouldn't, of course, have allowed him to stay at a hotel in the town during his stay. That would have been an insult. They went in. He found the house much cooler after the heat of the sun.

THREE

In the course of the meal which was a large one with lots of meat, cabbages and turnip and a pudding, Murdo suddenly said to his grandson:

'And don't you forget that Grandfather John was very good at English. He was the best in the school at English. I remember in those days we used to write on slates and Mr Gordon sent his composition round the classes. John is very clever or he wouldn't have been an editor.'

John said to Malcolm, who seemed quietly unimpressed: 'And what are you going to do yourself when you leave school?'

'You see,' said Murdo, 'Grandfather John will teach you . . .'

'I want to be a pilot,' said Malcolm, 'or something in science, or technical. I'm quite good at science.'

'We do projects most of the time,' said his sister. 'We're doing a project on fishing.'

'Projects!' said her grandfather contemptuously. 'When I was your age I was on a fishing boat.'

'There you are,' said his grandson triumphantly. 'That's what I tell Grandfather Murdo I should do, but I have to stay in school.'

'It was different in our days,' said his grandfather. 'We had to work for our living. You can't get a good job now without education. You have to have education.'

Straight in front of him on the wall, John could see a photograph of his brother dressed in army uniform. That was when he was a corporal in the Militia. He had also served in Egypt and in the First World War.

'They don't do anything these days,' said Murdo. 'Nothing. Every night it's football or dancing. He watches the TV all the time.'

'Did you ever see Elvis Presley?' said the girl who was eating her food very rapidly, and looking at a large red watch on her wrist.

'No, I'm sorry, I didn't,' said John. 'I once saw Lyndon Johnson though.'

She turned back to her plate uninterested.

The children were not at all as he had expected them. He thought they would have been shyer, more rustic, less talkative. In fact they seemed somehow remote and slightly bored and this saddened him. It was as if he were already seeing miniature Americans in the making.

'Take some more meat,' said his brother, piling it on his plate without waiting for an answer.

'All we get at English,' said Malcolm, 'is interpretations and literature. Mostly Shakespeare. I can't do any of it. I find it boring.'

'I see,' said John.

'He needs three Highers to get anywhere, don't you, Malcolm,' said his mother, 'and he doesn't do any work at night. He's always repairing his motor bike or watching TV.'

'When we got the TV first,' said the girl giggling, 'Grandfather Murdo thought . . .'

'Hist,' said her mother fiercely, leaning across the table, 'eat your food.'

Suddenly the girl looked at the clock and said, 'Can I go now, Mother? I've got to catch the bus.'

'What's this?' said her grandfather and at that moment as he raised his head, slightly bristling, John was reminded of their father.

'She wants to go to a dance,' said her mother.

'All the other girls are going,' said the girl in a pleading, slightly hysterical voice.

'Eat your food,' said her grandfather, 'and we'll see.' She ate the remainder of her food rapidly and then said, 'Can I go now?'

'All right,' said her mother, 'but mind you're back early or you'll find the door shut.'

The girl hurriedly rose from the table and went into the living room. She came back after a while with a handbag slung over her shoulder and carrying a transistor.

'Goodbye, Grandfather John,' she said. 'I'll see you tomorrow.' She went out and they could hear her brisk steps crackling on the gravel outside.

When they had finished eating Malcolm stood up and said, 'I promised Hugh I would help him repair his bike.'

'Back here early then,' said his mother again. He stood hesitating at the door for a moment and then went out, without saying anything.

'That's manners for you,' said Murdo. 'Mind you, he's very good with his hands. He repaired the tractor once.'

'I'm sure,' said John.

They ate in silence. When they were finished he and his brother went to sit in the living room which had the sun on it. They sat opposite each other in easy chairs. Murdo took out a pipe and began to light it. John suddenly felt that the room and the house were both very empty. He could hear quite clearly the ticking of the clock which stood on the mantelpiece between two cheap ornaments which looked as if they had been won at a fair.

Above the mantelpiece was a picture of his father, sitting very upright in a tall narrow chair, his long beard trailing in front of him. For some reason he remembered the night his brother, home from the war on leave, had come in late at night, drunk. His father had waited up for him and there had been a quarrel during which his brother had thrown the Bible at his father calling him a German bastard.

The clock ticked on. His brother during a pause in the conversation took up a *Farmers' Weekly* and put on a pair of glasses. In a short while he had fallen asleep behind the paper, his mouth opening like that of a stranded fish. Presumably that was all he read. His weekly letters were short and repetitive and apologetic.

John sat in the chair listening to the ticking of the clock which seemed to grow louder and louder. He felt strange again as if he were in the wrong house. The room itself was so clean and modern with the electric fire and the TV set in the corner. There was no air of history or antiquity about it. In a corner of the room he noticed a guitar which presumably belonged to the grandson. He remembered the nights he and his companions would dance to the music of the melodeon at the end of the road. He also remembered the playing of the bagpipes by his brother.

Nothing seemed right. He felt as if at an angle to the world he had once known. He wondered why he had come back after all those years. Was he after all like those people who believed in the innocence and unchangeability of the heart and vibrated to the music of nostalgia? Did he expect a Garden of Eden where the apple had not been eaten? Should he stay or go back? But then there was little where he had come from. Mary was dead. He was retired from his editorship of the newspaper. What did it all mean? He remembered the night he had left home many years before. What had he been expecting then? What cargo was he bearing with him? And what did his return signify? He didn't know. But he would have to find out. It was necessary to find out. For some reason just before he closed his eyes he saw in the front of him again the cloud of midges he had seen not an hour before, rising and falling above the fence, moving on their unpredictable ways. Then he fell asleep.

FOUR

The following day which was again fine he left the house and went down to a headland which overlooked the sea. He sat there for a long time on the grass, feeling calm and relaxed. The waves came in and went out, and he was reminded of the Gaelic song *The Eternal Sound of the Sea* which he used to sing when he was young. The water seemed to stretch westward into eternity and he could see nothing on it except the light of the sun. Clamped against the rocks below were the miniature helmets of the mussels and the whelks. He remembered how he used to boil the whelks in a pot and fish the meat out of them with a pin. He realised as he sat there that one of the things he had been missing for years was the sound of the sea. It was part of his consciousness. He should always live near the sea.

On the way back he saw the skull of a sheep, and he

looked at it for a long time before he began his visits. Whenever anyone came home he had to visit every house, or people would be offended. And he would have to remember everybody, though many people in those houses were now dead.

He walked slowly along the street, feeling as if he were being watched from behind curtained windows. He saw a woman standing at a gate. She was a stout large woman and she was looking at him curiously. She said, 'It's a fine day.' He said, 'Yes.'

She came towards him and he saw her red beefy face. 'Aren't you John Macleod?' she asked. 'Don't you remember me?'

'Of course I do,' he replied. 'You're Sarah.'

She shouted jovially as if into a high wind, 'You'll have to speak more loudly. I'm a little deaf.' He shouted back, 'Yes, I'm John Macleod,' and it seemed to him as if at that moment he were trying to prove his identity. He shouted louder still, 'And you're Sarah.' His face broke into a large smile.

'Come in, come in,' she shouted. 'Come in and have a cup of milk.'

He followed her into the house and they entered the living room after passing through the scullery which had rows of cups and saucers and plates on top of a huge dresser. In a corner of the room sat a man who was probably her son trapped like a fly inside a net which he was repairing with a bone needle. He was wearing a fisherman's jersey and his hands worked with great speed.

'This is George,' she shouted. 'My son. This is John Macleod,' she said to George. George looked up briefly from his work but said nothing. He was quite old, perhaps fifty or so, and there was an unmarried look about him.

'He's always fishing,' she said, 'always fishing. That's all he does. And he's very quiet. Just like his father. We're going to give John a cup of milk,' she said to her son. She went into the scullery for the milk and though he was alone with George the latter didn't speak. He simply went on repairing his net. This room too was cool and there was no fire. The chairs looked old and cracked and there was an old brown radio in a corner. After a while she came back and gave him the milk. 'Drink it up,' she instructed him as if she were talking to a boy. It was very cold. He couldn't remember when he had last drunk such fine milk.

'You were twenty-four when you went away,' she said, 'and I had just married. Jock is dead. George is very like him.' She shouted all this at the top of her voice and he himself didn't reply as he didn't want to shout.

'And how's that brother of yours?' she shouted remorselessly. 'He's a cheat, that one. Two years ago I sold him a cow. He said that there was something wrong with her and he got her cheap. But there was nothing wrong with her. He's a devil,' she said approvingly. 'But he was the same when he was young. After the penny. Always asking if he could run messages. You weren't like that. You were more like a scholar. You'd be reading books sitting on the peat banks. I remember you very well. You had fair hair, very fair hair. Your father said that you looked like an angel. But your brother was the cunning one. He knew a thing or two. And how are you?'

'I'm fine,' he shouted back.

'I hope you've come to stay,' she shouted again. He didn't answer.

'You would be sorry to hear about your mother,' she shouted again. 'We were all fond of her. She was a good woman.' By 'good' she meant that she attended church regularly. 'That brother of yours is a devil. I wonder if your mother liked him.' George looked at her quickly and then away again.

He himself shouted, 'Why do you ask that?' She pretended not to hear him and he had to shout the words again.

'It was nothing,' she said. 'I suppose you have a big job in America.'

He was wondering what she had meant and felt uneasy, but he knew that he wouldn't get anything more out of her.

'They've all changed here,' she shouted. 'Everything's changed. The girls go about showing their bottoms, not like in my day. The boys are off to the dances every night.

George here should get married but I wouldn't let him marry one of these trollops. And you can't visit your neighbours any more. You have to wait for an invitation. Imagine that. In the old days the door would be always open. But not any more. Drink up your milk.'

He drank it obediently as if he were a child.

'Jock died, you know. A stroke it was. It lasted for three years. But he never complained. You remember Jock.'

He didn't remember him very well. Was he the one who used to play football or the one who played tricks on the villagers? He couldn't summon up a picture of him at all. What had she meant by his mother and his brother? He had a strange feeling as if he were walking inside an illusion, as if things had happened here that he hadn't known of, though he should have. But who would tell him? They would all keep their secrets. He even had the feeling that this large apparently frank woman was in fact treacherous and secretive and that behind her huge façade there was lurking a venomous thin woman whose head nodded up and down like a snake's.

She laughed again. 'That brother of yours is a business-man. He is the one who should have gone to America. He would have got round them all. There are no flies on him. Did you not think of coming home when your mother died?'

'I was . . . I couldn't at the time,' he shouted.

George, entrapped in his corner, the net around his feet, plied his bone needle.

'It'll be good to come home again,' she shouted. 'Many of them come back. Donny Macdonald came back seven years ago and they hadn't heard from him for twenty years. He used to drink but he goes to church regularly now. He's a man of God. He's much quieter than he used to be. He used to sing a lot when he was young and they made him the precentor. He's got a beautiful voice but not as good as it was. Nobody knew he was coming home till he walked into the house one night off the bus. Can you imagine that? At first he couldn't find it because they had built a new house. But someone showed it to him.'

He got up and laid the cup on the table.

'Is Mr Gordon still alive?' he shouted. Mr Gordon was his old English teacher.

'Speak up, I can't hear you,' she said, her large bulging face thrust towards him like a crab.

'Mr Gordon?' he shouted. 'Is he still alive?'

'Mr Gordon,' she said. 'Yes, he's alive. He's about ninety now. He lives over there.' She took him over to the window and pointed out a house to him. 'Oh, there's the lad,' she said. 'He's always sitting on the wall. He's there every day. His sister died, you know. She was a bit wrong in the head.'

He said goodbye and she followed him to the door. He walked out the gate and made his way to where she had pointed. The day seemed heavy and sleepy and he felt slightly drugged as if he were moving through water. In the distance a man was hammering a post into the ground. The cornfields swayed slightly in the breeze and he could see flashes of red among them. He remembered the days when he would go with a bucket to the well, and smelt again the familiar smell of flowers and grass. He expected at any moment to see the ghosts of the dead stopping him by the roadway, interrogating him and asking him, 'When did you come home? When are you going away?' The whole visit, he realised now, was an implicit interrogation. What it was really about was: What had he done with his life? That was the question that people, without realising it, were putting to him, simply because he had chosen to return. It was also the question that he himself wanted answered.

Ahead of him stretched the moors and in the far distance he could see the Standing Stones which could look so eerie in the rain and which had perhaps been used in the sacrifice of children in Druid times. Someone had to be knifed to make the sun appear, he thought wryly. Before there could be light there must be blood.

He made his way to see Mr Gordon.

FIVE

Gordon recognised him immediately: it was almost as if he had been waiting for him. He came forward from behind a table on which were piled some books and a chessboard on which some pieces were standing, as if he had been playing a game.

'John,' he said, 'John Macleod.'

John noticed that standing beside the chair was a small glass in which there were the remains of whisky.

'Sit down, sit down,' said Gordon as if he hadn't had company for a long time. He was still spry, grey-haired of course, but thin in the body. He was wearing an old sports jacket and a shirt open at the neck. There was a slightly unshaven look about him.

'I play chess against myself,' he said. 'I don't know which of us wins.' His laugh was a short bark. John remembered himself running to school while Gordon stood outside the gate with a whistle in his hand looking at his watch impatiently.

'I suppose coming from America,' he said, 'you'll know about Fischer. He's about to do the impossible, beat the Russian World Champion at chess. It's like the Russians beating the Americans at baseball—or us at shinty,' he added with the same self-delighting barking laugh. 'He is of course a genius and geniuses make their own rules. How are you?'

'Very well. And how are you?' He nearly said 'Sir' but stopped himself in time.

'Oh, not too bad. Time passes slowly. Have you ever thought about time?' Beside his chair was a pile of books scattered indiscriminately. 'I belong to dozens of book clubs. This is a book on Time. Very interesting. From the point of view of physics, psychiatry and so on.' He pointed to a huge tome which looked both formidable and new. 'Did you know, for instance, that time passes slowly for some people and rapidly for others? It's a matter of personality, and the time of year you're born. Or that temperature can affect your idea of time? Very interesting.' He gave the impression of a man who devoured knowledge in a sterile way.

John looked out of the window. Certainly time seemed to pass slowly here. Everything seemed to be done in slow motion as if people were walking through water, divers with lead weights attached to them.

'Are you thinking of staying?' said Gordon, pouring out a glass of whisky for his guest.

'I don't know that yet.'

'I suppose you could buy a house somewhere. And settle down. Perhaps do some fishing. I don't do any myself. I read and play chess. But I suppose you could fish and do some crofting. Though I don't remember that you were particularly interested in either of these.'

'I was just thinking,' said John, 'of what you used to tell us when we were in your English class. You always told us to observe. Observation, you used to say, is the secret of good writing. Do you remember the time you took us out to the tree and told us to smell and touch it and study it and write a poem about it? It was a cherry tree, I recall. We wrote the poem in the open air.'

'I was in advance of my time,' said Gordon. 'That's what they all do now. They call it Creative Writing. But of course they can't spell nowadays.'

'And you always told us that exactitude was important. Be observant and exact, you said, above all be true to yourselves.'

'Drink your whisky,' said Gordon. 'Yes, I remember it all. I've kept some of your essays. You were gifted. In all the years I taught I only met two pupils who were really gifted. How does one know talent when one sees it? I don't know. Anyway, I recognised your talent. It was natural, like being a tiger.'

'Yes, you kept telling us about exactitude and observation. You used to send us out of the room and change objects in the room while we were out. You made Sherlock Holmeses out of us.'

'Why do you speak about that now? It was all so long ago.'

'I have a reason.'

'What is your reason?' said Gordon sharply.

'Oh, something that happened to me. Some years ago.'

'And what was that? Or don't you want to talk about it?'

'I don't see why not. Not that it's very complimentary to me.'

'I have reached the age now,' said Gordon, 'when I am not concerned with honour, only with people.'

'I see,' said John, 'but suppose you can't separate them. Well, I'll tell you anyway.' He walked over to the window, standing with his back to the room and looking out at the empty road. It was as if he didn't want to be facing Gordon.

'I was an editor for some time as you know,' he said. 'Your training stood me in good stead. It was not a big paper but it was a reasonable paper. It had influence in the largish town in which I stayed. It wasn't Washington, it wasn't New York, but it was a largish town. I made friends in this town. One was a lecturer in a university. At least that is what we would call it here. As a matter of fact, he wasn't a lecturer in English. He was a lecturer in History. It was at the time of the McCarthy trials when nobody was safe, nobody. Another of my friends went off his head at that time. He believed that everyone was persecuting him and opening his mail. He believed that planes were pursuing him. In any case this friend of mine, his name was Mason, told me that files had been dug up on him referring to the time when he was a student and had belonged to a Left Wing university club. Now there were complaints that he was indoctrinating his students with Communism and, of course, being a History lecturer, he was in a precarious position. I told him that I would defend him in my paper, that I would write a hard-hitting editorial. I told him that I would stand up for principles, humane principles.' He stretched out his hand for the whisky and decided against drinking it. 'I left him on the doorstep at eleven o'clock on a Monday night. He was very disturbed because of course he was innocent, he wasn't a Communist and anyway he had great integrity as a teacher and lectured on Communism only theoretically as one ideology among others. But the McCarthy people of course were animals. You have no conception. Not here. Of the fog of lies. Of the quagmire. No conception.' He paused. A cow outside had bent its head to the grass and was eating.

'Anyway this was what happened. I walked home because I needed the exercise. The street was deserted. There were lampposts shining and it was raining. A thin drizzle. I could hear the echo of my feet on the road. This was the kind of thing you taught us, to remember and listen and observe, to be aware of our surroundings sensuously. By then it had become a habit with me.

'As I was walking along two youths came towards me out of the shadow, from under the trees. I thought they were coming home from the cinema or from a dance. They wore leather jackets and were walking towards me along the sidewalk. They stayed on the sidewalk and I made as if to go round them since they were coming straight for me without deviating. One of them said, "Daddy." I stopped. I thought he was going to ask me for a light. He said, "Your wallet, daddy." I looked at him in amazement. I looked at the two of them. I couldn't understand what was going on. And something happened to me. I could feel everything very intensely, you see. At that moment I could have written a poem, everything was so clear. They were laughing, you see, and they were very casual. They walked like those cowboys you see on the films, physically at ease in their world. And their eyes sparkled. Their eyes sparkled with pure evil. I knew that if I protested they would beat me up. I knew that there was no appeal. None at all. One of them had a belt, and a buckle on it sparkled in the light. My eyes were at the level of the buckle. I took out my wallet and gave them the money. I had fifty dollars. I observed everything as you had trained us to do. Their boots which were shining except for the drizzle: their neckties: their leather jackets. Their legs which were narrow in the narrow trousers. And their faces which were looking slightly upwards and shining. Clear and fine almost, but almost innocent though evil. A rare sort of energy. Pure and bright. They took the wallet, counted the money and gave me back the wallet. They then walked on. The whole incident took perhaps three minutes.

'I went into the house and locked the door. The walls seemed very fragile all of a sudden. My wife had gone to bed and I stood downstairs thinking, now and again removing a book from the shelves and replacing it. I felt the house as thin as the shell of an egg: I could hear, I thought, as far away as San Francisco. There was a tap dripping and I turned it off. And I didn't write the editorial, I didn't write anything. Two weeks after that my friend killed himself, with pills and whisky.'

The whisky which Gordon had given him was still untouched.

'Observation and exactitude,' he said, 'and elegance of language.' There was a long silence. Gordon picked up a chess piece and weighed it in his hand.

'Yes,' he said, 'and that's why you came home.'

'Perhaps. I don't know why I came home. One day I was walking along a street and I smelt the smell of fish coming from a fish shop. And it reminded me of home. So I came home. My wife, of course, is dead.'

'Many years ago,' said Gordon, still holding the chess piece in his hand, 'I was asked to give a talk to an educational society in the town. In those days I used to write poetry though of course I never told anyone. I was working on a particular poem at the time: it was very difficult and I couldn't get it to come out right. Well, I gave this talk. It was, if I may say so myself, a brilliant talk for in those days I was full of ideas. It was also very witty. People came and congratulated me afterwards as people do. I arrived home at one o'clock in the morning. When I got home I took out the poem and tried to do some work on it. But I was restless and excited and I couldn't get into the right mood. I sat and stared at the clock and I knew quite clearly that I would never write again. Odd, isn't it?'

'What are you trying to say?'

'Say? Nothing. Nothing at all. I don't think you'd better stay here. I don't think this place is a refuge. People may say so but it's not true. After a while the green wears away and you are left with the black. In any case I don't think you'd better settle here: that would be my advice. However, it's not my business. I have no business now.'

'Why did you stay here?' said John slowly.

'I don't know. Laziness, I suppose. I remember when I was in Glasgow University many years ago we used to take the train home at six in the morning after the holiday started. At first we were all very quiet, naturally, since we were half-asleep, most of us. But then as the carriages warmed and the sun came up and we came in sight of the hills and the lochs we began to sing Gaelic songs. Odd, and Glasgow isn't that far away. What does it all mean, John? What are you looking at?'

'The broken fences.'

'Yes, of course. There's a man here and he's been building his own house for ten years. He carries stone after stone to the house and then he forgets and sits down and talks to people. Time is different here, no doubt about it.'

'I had noticed.'

'If you're looking for help from me, John, I can't give you any. In the winter time I sit and look out the window. You can see the sea from here and it can look very stormy. The rain pours down the window and you can make out the waves hitting the islands out there. What advice could I give you? I have tried to do my best as far as my work was concerned. But you say it isn't enough.'

'Perhaps it wasn't your fault.'

John made his way to the door.

'Where are you going?'

'I shall have to call on other people as well. They all expect one to do that, don't they?'

'Yes, they still feel like that. That hasn't changed.'

'I'll be seeing you then,' said John as he left.

'Yes, yes, of course.'

He walked towards the sea cliffs to a house which he had visited many times when he was a boy, where he had been given many tumblers of milk, where later in the evening he would sit with others talking into the night.

The sea was large and sparkling in front of him like a shield. No, he said automatically to himself, it isn't like a shield, otherwise how could the cormorants dive in and out of it? What was it like then? It was like the sea, nothing else. It was like the sea in one of its moods, in one of its sunny gentle moods. As he walked pictures flashed in front of his eyes. He saw a small boy running; then a policeman's arm raised, the baton falling in a vicious arc, the neon light flashing from his shield. The boy stopped in midflight, the picture frozen.

SIX

He knocked at the door of the house and a woman of about forty, thin and with straggly greying hair, came to the door.

She looked at him enquiringly.

'John, John Macleod,' he said. 'I came to see your mother.' Her face lighted up with recognition and she said, 'Come in, come in.' And then inexplicably, 'I thought you were from the BBC.'

'The BBC?'

'Yes, they're always sending people to take recordings of my mother singing and telling stories, though she's very old now.'

He followed her into a bedroom where an old white-faced white-haired woman was lying, her head against white pillows. She stretched out her prominently veined hand across the blankets and said, 'John, I heard Anne talking to you. There's nothing wrong with my hearing.'

They were left alone and he sat down beside the bed. There was a small table with medicine bottles and pills on it.

'It's true,' she said, 'the BBC are always sending people to hear me sing songs before I die.'

'And how are you?'

'Fine, fine.'

'Good, that's good.' Her keen wise eyes studied his face carefully. The room had bright white wallpaper and the windows faced the sea.

'I don't sleep so well now,' said the old woman. 'I waken at five every morning and I can hear the birds twittering just outside the window.'

'You look quite well,' he said.

'Of course I'm not well. Everybody says that to me. But after all I'm ninety years old. I can't expect to live forever. And you're over sixty but I can still see you as a boy.' She prattled on but he felt that all the time she was studying him without being obvious.

'Have you seen the BBC people? They all have long hair and they wear red ties. But they're nice and considerate. Of course everybody wears long hair now, even my daughter's

son. Would you like to hear my recording? My grandson
took it down on a tape.'

'I would,' he said.

She tapped on the head of the bed as loudly as she could
and her daughter came in.

'Where's Hugh?' she asked.

'He's outside.'

'Tell him to bring in the machine. John wants to hear my
recording.' She turned to John and said, 'Hugh is very good
with his hands, you know. All the young people nowadays
know all about electricity and cars.'

After a while a tall quiet long-haired boy came in with a
tape recorder. He plugged it into a socket beside the bed,
his motions cool and competent and unflurried. He had
the same neutral quizzical look that John had noticed in
his brother's two grandchildren. They don't want to be
deceived again, he thought. This generation is not interested
in words, only in actions. Observation, exactitude, elegance.
The universe of the poem or the story is not theirs, their
universe is electronic. And when he thought of the phrase
'the music of the spheres' he seemed to see a shining
bicycle moving through the heavens, or the wheels of some
inexplicable machine.

Hugh switched on the tape recorder and John listened.

'Tonight,' the announcer began, 'we are going to hear the
voice of a lady of ninety years old. She will be telling us about
her life on this far Hebridean island untouched by pollution
and comparatively unchanged when it is compared with our
own hectic cities. This lady has never in all her life left the
island on which she grew up. She has never seen a train.
She has never seen a city. She has been brought up in a
completely pastoral society. But we may well ask, what will
happen to this society? Will it be squeezed out of existence?
How can it survive the pollution of our time, and here I
am speaking not simply of physical but of moral pollution?
What was it like to live on this island for so many years? I
shall try to elicit some answers to that question in the course
of this programme. But first I should like you to hear this
lady singing a Gaelic traditional song. I may interpolate
at this point that many Gaelic songs have apparently been

anglicised musically, thus losing their traditional flavour. But Mrs Macdonald will sing this song in the way in which she was taught to, the way in which she picked it up from previous singers.'

There followed a rendering of *Thig Tri Nithean Gun Iarraidh* ('Three things will come without seeking . . .') John listened to the frail voice: it seemed strange to hear it, ghostly and yet powerful in its own belief, real and yet unreal at the same time.

When the singing was over the interviewer questioned her:

I: And now, Mrs Macdonald, could you please tell me how old you are?

Mrs M: I am ninety years old.

I: You will have seen a lot of changes on this island, in this village even.

Mrs M: O yes, lots of changes. I don't know much about the island. I know more about the village.

I: You mean that you hardly ever left the village itself?

Mrs M: I don't know much about the rest of the island.

I: What are your memories then of your youth in the village?

Mrs M: Oh, people were closer together. People used to help each other at the peat gathering. They would go out with a cart and they would put the peats on the cart. And they would make tea and sing. It was very happy times especially if it was a good day.

I: Do they not do that any more? I mean, coal and electricity . . .

Mrs M: No, they don't do that so much, no. Nowadays. And there was more fishing then too. People would come to the door and give you a fish if they had caught one.

I: You mean herring?

Mrs M: No, things like cod. Not herring. They would catch them in boats or off the rocks. Not herring. The herring were caught by the drifters. And the mackerel. We used to eat herring and potatoes every day. Except Sunday of course.

I: And what did you eat on Sunday?

Mrs M: We would always have meat on Sunday. That was always the fashion. Meat on Sundays. And soup.

I: I see. And tell me, when did you leave school, Mrs Macdonald?

Mrs M: I left school when I was fourteen years old. I was in Secondary Two.

I: It was a small village school, I take it.

Mrs M: Oh, yes, it was small. Perhaps about fifty pupils. Perhaps about fifty. We used to write on slates in those days and the children would bring in a peat for a fire in the winter. Every child would bring in a peat. And we had people called pupil-teachers.

I: Pupil-teachers? What were pupil-teachers?

Mrs M: They were young people who helped the teacher. Pupils. They were pupils themselves.

I: Then what happened?

Mrs M: I looked after my father and mother. We had a croft too. And then I got married.

I: What did your husband do?

Mrs M: He was a crofter. In those days we used to go to a dance at the end of the road. But the young people go to the town now. In those days we had a dance at the end of the road.

I: Did you not know him before, your husband I mean?

Mrs M: Yes but that was where I met him, at the dance.

I: What did they use for the dance?

Mrs M: What do you mean?

I: What music did they use?

Mrs M: Oh, you mean the instrument. It was a melodeon.

I: Can you remember the tunes, any of the tunes, any of the songs?

Mrs M: Oh yes, I can remember *A Ribhinn Oig bheil cuimhn' agad*?

I: Could you tell our listeners what that means, Mrs Macdonald?

Mrs M: It's a love song. That's what it is, a sailors' song. A love song.

I: I see. And do you think you could sing it?

And she proceeded to sing it in that frail voice. John listened to the evocation of nights on ships, moonlight, masts, exile, and he was strangely moved as if he were hearing a voice speaking to him from the past.

'I think that will be enough,' she said to the boy. He switched off the tape recorder without saying anything, put it in its case and took it away, closing the door behind him.

John said, 'You make it all sound very romantic.'

'Well, it was true about the peats.'

'But don't you remember the fights people used to have about land and things like that?'

'Yes but I remember the money they collected when Shodan was drowned.'

'But what about the tricks they used to play on old Maggie?'

'That was just young boys. And they had nothing else to do. That was the reason for it.'

There was a silence. A large blue fly buzzed in the window. John followed it with his eyes. It was restless, never settling, humming loudly with an angry sound. For a moment he nearly got up in order to kill it, he was so irritated by the booming sound and its restlessness.

'Would you like to tell me about my mother?' said John.

'What about your mother?'

'Sarah said something when I was speaking to her.'

'What did she say?'

'I felt there was something wrong, the way she talked. It was about my brother.'

'Well you know your brother was fond of the land. What did you want to know?'

'What happened. That was all.'

'Your mother went a bit odd at the end. It's quite common with old people. Perhaps that's what she was talking about. My own brother wouldn't let the doctor into the house. He thought he was poisoning him.'

'You say odd. How odd?'

'She accused your brother of wanting to put her out of the house. But I wouldn't pay any attention to that. Old people get like that.'

'I see.'

'You know your brother.'

'Yes. He is fond of land. He always was. He's fond of property.'

'Most people are,' she said. 'And what did you think of my singing?'

'You sang well. It's funny how one can tell a real Gaelic singer. It's not even the way they pronounce their words. It's something else.'

'You haven't forgotten your Gaelic.'

'No. We had societies. We had a Gaelic society. People who had been on holiday used to come and talk to us and show us slides.' The successful and the failed. From the lone sheiling of the misty island. Smoking their cigars but unable to go back and live there. Since after all they had made their homes in America. Leading their half lives, like mine. Watching cowboys on TV, the cheapness and the vulgarity of it, the largeness, the spaciousness, the crowdedness. They never really belonged to the city, these Highlanders. Not really. The skyscrapers were too tall, they were surrounded by the works of man, not the works of God. In the beginning was the neon lighting . . . And the fake religions, the cheap multitudinous sprouting so-called faiths. And they cried, some of them, at these meetings, in their large jackets of fine light cloth, behind their rimless glasses.

He got up to go.

'It's the blood, I suppose,' she said.

'Pardon.'

'That makes you able to tell. The blood. You could have seen it on my pillow three months ago.'

'I'm sorry.'

'Oh, don't be sorry. One grows used to lying here. The blood is always there. It won't allow people to change.'

'No, I suppose not.'

He said goodbye awkwardly and went outside. As he stood at the door for a moment, he heard music coming from the side of the house. It sounded American. He went over and looked. The boy was sitting against the side of the house patiently strumming his guitar, his head bent over it. He sang the words in a consciously American way, drawling them affectedly. John moved quietly away. The sun was still on the water where some ducks flew low. He thought of the headland where he was standing as if it were Marathon. There they had combed each other's long hair, the effeminate courageous ones about to die.

As he walked back he couldn't get out of his mind an article about Billy Graham he had read in an American magazine not long before. It was all about the crewcut saint, the electric blue eyed boy perched in his mountain eyrie. The Victorian respect shown by the interviewers had been, even for him with a long knowledge of American papers, nauseating. Would you like these remarks off the record, and so on. And then that bit about his personal appearances at such shows as *Laugh-in* where the conversation somehow got round to Jesus Christ every time! In Africa a corps of black policemen, appointed to control the crowd, had abandoned their posts and come forward to make a stand for Jesus!

Mad crude America, Victorian and twentieth century at the one time. Manic country of the random and the destined. What would his father or his mother have thought of Billy Graham? The fundamentalist with the stereophonic backing. For the first time since he came home he laughed out loud.

SEVEN

It was evening when he got back to his brother's house and the light was beginning to thicken. As he turned in at the gate his brother, who must have seen him coming, walked towards it and then stopped: he was carrying a hammer in his right hand as if he had been working with posts. They stood looking at each other in the half-light.

'Have you seen everybody then,' said his brother. 'Have you visited them all?' In the dusk and carrying the hammer he looked somehow more authoritative, more solid than his brother.

'Most of them. Sarah was telling me about the cow.'

'Oh, that. There was something wrong with the cow.

But it's all right now. She talks too much,' he added contemptuously.

'And also,' said John carefully, 'I heard something about our mother.'

'What about her? By God, if that bitch Sarah has been spreading scandal I'll . . .' His hands tightened on the hammer and his whole body seemed to bulge out and bristle like a fighting cock. For a moment John had a vision of a policeman with a baton in his hand. John glimpsed the power and energy that had made his brother the dominant person in the village.

After a while he said, 'I didn't want to worry you.'

'About what?' said John coldly.

'About our mother. She went a bit queer at the end. She hated Susan, you see. She would say that she was no good at the housework and that she couldn't do any of the outside work. She accused her of smoking and drinking. She even said she was trying to poison her.'

'And?'

'She used to say to people that I was trying to put her out of the house. Which of course was nonsense. She said that I had plotted to get the croft, and you should have it. She liked you better, you see.'

'Why didn't you tell me any of this?'

'I didn't want to worry you. Anyway I'm not good at writing. I can dash off a few lines but I'm not used to the pen.' For that moment again he looked slightly helpless and awkward as if he were talking about a gift that he half envied, half despised.

John remembered the letters he would get—'Just a scribble to let you know that we are well and here's hoping you are the same . . . I hope you are in the pink as this leaves me.' Clichés cut out of a half world of crumbling stone. Certainly this crisis would be beyond his ability to state in writing.

'She was always very strong for the church. She would read bits of the Bible to annoy Susan, the bits about Ruth and so on. You know where it says, 'Whither thou goest I will go . . .' She would read a lot. Do you know it?'

'I know it.'

John said, 'I couldn't come back at the time.'

'I know that. I didn't expect you to come back.'

As he stood there John had the same feeling he had had with Sarah, only stronger, that he didn't know anything about people at all, that his brother, like Sarah, was wearing a mask, that by choosing to remain where he was his brother had been the stronger of the two, that the one who had gone to America and immersed himself in his time was really the weaker of the two, the less self-sufficient. He had never thought about this before, he had felt his return as a regression to a more primitive place, a more pastoral, less exciting position, lower on the scale of a huge complex ladder. Now he wasn't so sure. Perhaps those who went away were the weaker ones, the ones who were unable to suffer the slowness of time, its inexorable yet ceremonious passing. He was shaken as by a vision: but perhaps the visions of artists and writers were merely ideas which people like his brother saw and dismissed as of no importance.

'Are you coming in?' said his brother, looking at him strangely.

'Not yet. I won't be long.'

His brother went into the house and John remained at the gate. He looked around him at the darkening evening. For a moment he expected to see his mother coming towards him out of the twilight holding a pail of warm milk in her hand. The hills in the distance were darkening. The place was quiet and heavy.

As he stood there he heard someone whistling and when he turned round saw that it was Malcolm.

'Did you repair the bike?' said John.

'Yes, it wasn't anything. It'll be all right now. We finished that last night.'

'And where were you today, then?'

'Down at the shore.'

'I see.'

They stood awkwardly in each other's presence. Suddenly John said, 'Why are you so interested in science and maths?'

'It's what I can do best,' said Malcolm in surprise.

'You don't read Gaelic, do you?'

'Oh, that's finished,' said Malcolm matter-of-factly.

John was wondering whether the reason Malcolm was so interested in maths and science was that he might have decided, perhaps unconsciously, that his own culture, old and deeply rotted and weakening, was inhibiting and that for that reason he preferred the apparent cleanness and economy of equations without ideology.

'Do you want to go to America?' he asked.

'I should like to travel,' said Malcolm carelessly. 'Perhaps America. But it might be Europe somewhere.'

John was about to say something about violence till it suddenly occurred to him that this village which he had left also had its violence, its buried hatreds, its bruises which festered for years and decades.

'I want to leave because it's so boring here,' said Malcolm. 'It's so boring I could scream sometimes.'

'It can seem like that,' said John. 'I shall be leaving tomorrow but you don't need to tell them that just now.'

He hadn't realised that he was going to say what he did till he had actually said it.

Malcolm tried to be conventionally regretful but John sensed a relief just the same.

They hadn't really said anything to each other.

After a while Malcolm went into the house, and he himself stood in the darkening light thinking. He knew that he would never see the place again after that night and the following morning. He summoned it up in all its images, observing, being exact. There was the house itself with its porch and the flowers in front of it. There was the road winding palely away from him past the other houses of the village. There was the thatched roofless house not far away from him. There were the fields and the fences and the barn. All these things he would take away with him, his childhood, his pain, into the shifting world of neon, the flashing broken signals of the city.

One cannot run away, he thought to himself as he walked towards the house. Or if one runs away one cannot be happy anywhere any more. If one left in the first place one could never go back. Or if one came back one also brought a virus, an infection of time and place. One always brings back a judgment to one's home.

He stood there for a long time before going into the house. He leaned over the fence looking out towards the fields. He could imagine his father coming towards him, in long beard and wearing wellingtons, solid, purposeful, fixed. And hadn't his father been an observer too, an observer of the seasons and the sea?

As he stood thinking he saw the cloud of midges again. They were rising and falling in the slight breeze. They formed a cloud but inside the cloud each insect was going on its own way or drifting with the breeze. Each alive and perhaps with its own weight, its own inheritance. Apparently free yet fixed, apparently spontaneous yet destined.

His eyes followed their frail yet beautiful movements. He smiled wryly as he felt them nipping him. He'd have to get into the house. He would have to find out when the bus left in the morning. That would be the first stage of the journey: after that he could find out about boats and trains and planes.

The Professor and the Comics

HIS MOON GLASSES shining on his round red-cheeked face Professor MacDuff cycled happily along through the March day which made the streets as white as bone. On days like these the city looked freshly coloured and new, the butchers in their striped smocks standing at shop doors, knives clutched absent-mindedly in their hands, young boys racing each other on bicycles, older boys hanging about with yellow crash helmets, women pushing prams and groceries along, window panes flashing, church spires climbing into a blue sky, cinemas advertising (he noticed sadly) Bingo instead of Wild Westerns.

Professor MacDuff waited placidly at the red traffic lights, in his tweed suit, his white shirt and large green tie. He felt fine as if newly resurrected from the grave of winter. What a fine month March was, bringing with it scents as from a rich soil, memories of boyish escapades, ladders, paint, whooping dogs, hosepipes. He cycled on past the Art Gallery (where they were holding an exhibition of Magritte's paintings), past streets lined with flaring green trees, past small shops which said things like 'M NS CL T ES' (the brood which flourished and so quickly died) till he arrived at last at the open steel gates of the university from which rose green sweeping lawns towards the mellow-bricked building itself.

Students (boys hardly distinguishable from girls wearing long hair like Charles I's doomed followers or the Marlborough he hugely admired) strolled about, books under their arms, talking. They waved to him. He waved back, by now wheeling his bicycle. The clock in the tower boomed. Ah, the forest of Arden where all was green, where Rosalind and Celia and Orlando and Oliver (indistinguishable from each other in their virginal green) wandered happily forever. He waved to the Professor of Logic who on dusty days sometimes wore a gas mask. Logic could of course be carried too far.

He parked his bicycle and walked along the corridor where the notices proliferated, so many of them that one didn't have the time or the inclination to read them: a Violin Concerto cheek by jowl with a performance of *Uncle Vanya*, a teach-in on Communism next to a notice about Nationalism, a Wine and Cheese Social next to a poster which showed a lynx-eyed Chinaman with a machine gun.

He said 'Hello' to young Hilton who looked, as usual, aloof and saturnine. He wondered if he was wearing his red socks again and looking back saw that he was. The Moral Philosophy Professor of course never wore socks at all.

He stood outside the door of his lecture room looking at the wooden seats which arose in tiers towards the back, smelling as he so often did the smell of varnish, a reminiscence of his first day in university as a student. 'Ah,' said the History Professor, 'narcissising again?' The History Professor was called Black, wore a black gown and was a very precise Civil Service type of man who read out his lectures with great deliberation in a very even unexcited voice. His students liked him because he arranged and tabulated everything so neatly that it really seemed as if the precise year 1485 was a new departure in English History and the Renaissance did begin in a particular year and perhaps even on a particular day.

'The lecture rooms look different in spring,' said Professor MacDuff.

'Everything is different in spring,' said Professor Black, 'except History.'

'It is as if the people in there were plants,' said Professor MacDuff, turning moon glasses benevolently towards Black who had however moved on. Having not a single jot of imagination himself he was uneasy in the presence of anyone who had.

'Uptight, that's what you are,' said Professor MacDuff grinning.

He went into his room, and put on his gown. Soon his

students would be appearing for the lecture. He smiled with satisfaction, and for a moment he appeared different, as if he were about to embark on a difficult adventure.

It seemed at first to be as it had always been before, the lecture room filling slowly then more rapidly with chattering students who quoted at each other the possibly more obscene bits of Anglo-Saxon or opened notebooks on which were drawn in bold imaginative detail anatomical sections of the human (feminine) form with words like SEX and CRAP prominently displayed. Some lounged, some sat up attentively, some shifted about, some half closed their eyes (after late night hangovers), some dreamed. And here and there of course were the pale intense bespectacled ones who had really come to drink at the fount of Helicon, to whom for instance Donne's poetry was not merely an academic abstraction but a possible experience. The students wore all sorts and styles of clothing: the only constant was difference. Some of the girls wore long sweeping red Lady Macbethish coats which swung open to frame like Renaissance pictures voluptuous legs below brief skirts. Boys wore dungaree trousers, leather jackets, silken scarves, polo-necked jerseys, a proliferation of costumes.

When he arrived at the dais the noise as usual died down. Professor MacDuff had been at the university for some time, was an institution and was expected to provide not only information but some urbane and even vaguely comic jokes or at least some entertainment. Bred on the unrelated stories of TV the students did not so much want a lecture as a performance, not however insincere but at least with the sincerity of the actor who has his own truth. They expected the medium and the message to coincide and were quickly bored if the medium (in this case the lecturer) should provide a message which had no relation to his own life style. As a Professor at the university had recently remarked with some bewilderment, 'They not only want us to lecture on Che Guevara but in some measure to be Che Guevara.' They did not like dissection of the dead and were therefore impatient with literary criticism.

It need not be said that what the Professor was about to do was remarkable and in some ways revolutionary.

He had his own reasons for doing it and they were perhaps not mean reasons. What the students were looking for was excitement. They were young volatile energetic (fed on the milk of the Welfare State), already, many of them, veterans of demonstrations, obscurely irritated by restlessnesses whose source they could not focus. It was, Professor MacDuff often thought, a hunger for drama. There was something theatrical about their clothes even. They were pseudo-Elizabethans without any world (except dead planets) to conquer. They seemed to be continually dressing up for a stage which had been shifted while they were preparing or which, though still there, had no audience waiting. For no one wanted to be a member of an audience, everyone wanted to be an actor. Everyone wanted colour, the brighter the better, and drama, the more exciting the better. Perhaps many of them thought they could do the Professor's job better than he could himself.

Nevertheless it was a big thing he was about to do . . . 'Today,' said Professor MacDuff drawing himself up to his full height, 'and for the next few weeks of this term I shall talk about comics.'

The reaction of the students to this was at first complete stunned silence and then after a moment a spontaneous roar of applause in the middle of which he stood benevolent and fresh-faced as if he were a kind of happy personification of a vernal rural god.

Some however refrained from cheering as if they sensed that they were being got at in some way, as if they felt a daring breathtaking irony, a parody so piercing that it was a kind of hatred.

One or two among the pale and the bespectacled looked at him as if he had gone mad.

But he continued unperturbed referring duly to his lecture notes, a rotund slightly untidy figure with moon glasses.

'Today,' he said, 'I shall begin since it is spring with a short lecture on the World of the Comics with special reference to Desperate Dan. Later I shall mention other such heroes of the Comics as Korky the Cat. My sources are the *Dandy* and the *Beano* and to a lesser extent the *Rover*, the

Wizard, the *Hotspur*, etc. I shall sometimes refer to comics that are now extinct though at one time they flourished in the imaginations of many who for instance set out to found the British Empire. It is partly with this buried imaginative world, so like Atlantis, that I shall be concerned.

'Now you will all be familiar I take it with the red and yellow pages of the *Dandy* which I place I may say at this point much higher than the rather belligerent papers such as the *Victor*, the *Wizard* and the *Hotspur* in accordance with the one law which I shall enunciate, that distinguishing the truly creative from the uncreative. This law states that no truly creative work of any kind can omit the vulgar.

'For it is clear,' the Professor continued, 'that whereas the *Wizard* for instance is a merely inferior version of such overrated books as *Treasure Island*, the *Dandy* on the other hand represents pure creativity and belongs to the same world as the silent films and the inimitable Charlie Chaplin, the *Dandy* oscillating as it does between the human world of Desperate Dan and the animal world of Korky the Cat.

'It would however be invidious for me to draw comparisons between these two characters since in fact in such a world comparisons are not possible and would in fact be odious nor would it be meaningful for me to point out that an animal and a man are not essentially different in this world before good and evil (notice that I do not say beyond good and evil) theological terms which cannot be applied to material of this kind. It is a world rather of errors and inexactitudes. There is a difference one might interpose between an error and a sin. A sin is not an aesthetic term, whereas an error may be so classified.

'Now should comparisons be made on the grounds of vocabulary. I myself would not wish to use neo-Bradleyan techniques in this matter since to do so would be to exile these characters from their own separate world. In the short time that I shall spend today on an introduction to this theme I should merely like to draw attention to some of the characteristics of a typical comic hero, that is, Desperate Dan.

'Naturally one begins with his name. I could spend a long time discoursing on this, especially on the inspired choice of the name Dan which I consider to be much superior to the word Donald or Daniel which are possible alternatives. Why it is superior is not so easy to determine. (It is not for instance as clear as the inspired choice of name by Dickens for his sullen sexton, Gabriel Grub, a name which reconciles both heaven and earth, the angelic and the mouldy.)

'Also one would have to discuss the adjective "desperate", again an inspired choice because of the connotations of menace and despair, both transfused with comedy.

'And I suppose that when one studies Desperate Dan with his unshaven appearance one could at first sight consider him menacing, especially as he is rather large. He might at first be thought of almost as domesticated Stone Age man ambling about in a world of CLONKS and AARGHS.

'He is one might say perpetually on the verge of a revelation, a being dazzled and swindled continually, sometimes by his family, sometimes by outsiders. But he always wins.

'I should like at this point to outline the plot of a typical Desperate Dan episode. In this episode . . .'

At which precise moment there was an unexpected (or perhaps expected) interruption. A slim pale bespectacled boy of the kind whose aloofness conceals a fanatical fire, whose shyness is a mask for a burning egotism, stood up and said: 'I think we have listened long enough to this ridiculous lecture. Surely, sir, you are aware that we have to try to pass an examination in a few weeks' time. As this examination will affect the livelihood of most of us . . .' Before he could proceed any further there was a brutal roar of derision and anger from the assembled multitude and expletives such as 'SHIT', 'CRAP', etc. were freely hurled.

But the serious boy though paler than before continued: 'It's possible, sir, that you may be interested in comics but that is no good reason for interrupting the syllabus. You are paid to teach us English Literature and by no stretch of the imagination can the *Dandy* and the *Beano* be said to form part of . . .'

A huge bearded student wearing a flowered shirt and tie and a brown leather jacket pushed the earnest protester back into his seat. But at that same moment as the huge hand descended on his shoulder propelling him downwards there

emerged from another part of the whirlpool a fresh-faced
curly-haired girl who shouted vigorously: 'He's quite right.
There are some of us who believe that Shakespeare and
Donne are great poets and that it is our right to be told
about them. That stuff about Desperate Dan is what we left
behind in the nursery. What do you think we are? Do you
think we are still in the primary school? Are you playing a
joke on us or something? Are you trying to take the mickey?
What sort of professor are you? Are you showing some kind
of intellectual contempt for us or what?'

'Were *you* taught about Desperate Dan when you were
in the University? Did someone decide that *you* were too
immature to know about Donne? Or about Shakespeare?
What right have you to take on yourself to judge us in
this way?'

It was noticeable that the girl who was trembling with
emotion was listened to with a certain degree of gravity and
in a reasonable silence and if she had sat down at that point
she might have swayed the meeting but as so often happens
she overstated her case: 'Even Beowulf,' she concluded
fiercely, 'is more interesting than Desperate Dan.'

Whereupon there was a universal roar of execration,
'Rubbish', 'Codswallop', 'Piss', etc. and she was forced to
sit down though battling valiantly to the end, her mouth
opening and shutting soundlessly like someone on a TV
screen when the sound has been cut off and the temporary
fault extends for minute after minute.

All this while the professor sat happily and placidly
believing that presently from the world of charge and
counter charge there would emerge some heroic figure
who would tell what the commotion really meant. It was
as if he was waiting for such a figure. Meanwhile he sat
perfectly still and relaxed while the mass seethed and
shouted, instinctively waiting for a leader, speaking for
the moment broken words like 'DONNE—OUT OUT OUT',
'TO HELL WITH SHAKESPEARE' and even 'MACDUFF FOR
THE PRIMARIES' which at that moment were being fought
in distant Florida.

But as always happens the hour produced the man and
the dialogue proceeded.

This time the speaker was a tallish bearded student who stood up with a book in his hand. His beard was of a strawy colour, his lips were red and blubbery and his cheeks had a red slightly hectic tinge. His clothes looked dirty, as if he had been sleeping in them.

'Ladies and gentlemen,' he began, 'I for one have listened to the previous speakers with amazement. What is their definition of education? I might ask this question without hoping for much of an answer.' There was an interjection from the girl who was howled down after which the students settled down to listen to what the student had to say.

'Are the previous speakers some sort of élite? Is that what they are? Let me ask you, how many of you really like reading Donne's poetry or Shakespeare's plays? It would be interesting to find out. How many of you are not bored to death by what the so-called critics call "the intellectual and imaginative, working together". How many of you believe with me that most of their work is a load of crap with nothing to say to any of us? How many of you really like these people? Let's have a show of hands on this.'

Five hands went up slowly. 'There you are. Five people. And most certainly they have been brainwashed. If there are only five people here who really like reading Donne and Shakespeare what conclusion do we draw from this? I'll tell you: we've been conned. Lecturers tell us we're stupid because we don't like reading *Troilus and Cressida*. And yet are we really to believe that we are any stupider than any previous generation? Is this feasible? Is it likely that a whole generation of stupid people has suddenly emerged? Is this a reasonable assumption? I can't believe it. It's ridiculous. A much more reasonable assumption would be that for us these people, these writers, are dead, not only physically dead but spiritually dead. And after all what's wrong with the comics? Our brothers outside read the comics. In factories, on the workshop floor, they read the comics, uncountable numbers of them. Soldiers in the army, airmen in the air force, read the comics. They read them in shops and offices. They are people exactly like us, they are human beings. Are we saying that we are better than them because we have read some of Shakespeare's plays? Are we not separating ourselves from our brothers? I say that Donne and Shakespeare are methods to separate us from our brothers, that in order to get back to them again we should return to the world of comics, that Donne and Shakespeare are divisive influences.

'And furthermore I suggest that we hold a festival. I suggest that we have an open air festival in which we will have readings from the comics, dramatic performances based on the comics, an extravaganza of joy.'

At this suggestion there was a roar of approval, which died down when he raised his arm and said: 'I think we should elect a committee here and now to organise this festival. And I mean my suggestion to be taken quite seriously. I suggest that Professor MacDuff be made Honorary President of this committee.'

The Professor signified that he accepted and rose to his feet. In perfect silence he continued with his lecture. 'I was about to outline one of the episodes in the saga of Desperate Dan . . .'

TWO

The Principal of the University was a scientist (or rather an ex-scientist) with an M.Sc. and various other degrees from other universities. His main work had been done during the war when as a member of a chosen group, he had invented a method of distinguishing between the voices of European and Japanese soldiers in the jungles of Burma. It was a well-known fact that the Japanese had used techniques of imitation to entice British (and lesser) soldiers to their deaths by training some of their people to speak good English. Professor Carstairs had put a stop to that by showing that a tape recorder with a simple attachment could easily distinguish between Eastern and Western voices. It was according to his often repeated explanations at cocktails a simple matter of breath control and pace. These two, he remarked, are very different in different races. He had once been in the same swing door as Winston Churchill but to listen to him one might imagine that Churchill had hearkened with bated breath and composed intelligence for hours to his explanations of how inferior the breath control and pace of Japanese voices were to British ones. It was often remarked that he looked rather like Churchill with his great bald head, his smallish stature, the bulldog thrust of his jaw, his habit of jumping head first into situations from which he would later extricate himself with a sophisticated cunning and especially his trick of removing his glasses when he was making a speech. He had lately taken to attaching them to a piece of tape which swung on his breast and would put them on and remove them at regular intervals.

His favourite character was the Chief Constable in *Softly, Softly* which he never missed. He liked to affect that sudden sharkish smile, the brutal physical presence, the air of decision, the ultra-sophistication and self-confidence.

He had long ago given up any pretence to creative science involved as he was in administration. After all, the university was expanding—what it was expanding to was another question—and there were so many people to see, so many people to consult . . . How could one retire to a laboratory in moments of such frantic change?

It is true that now and again he felt a certain nostalgia for his days of creativity, for the military companionship which he had so much enjoyed, for certain equations, for the marvellous randomness of the world. But though he felt this nostalgia there was a part of him which hated randomness, which felt that God must in fact be a ruler and not an artist. He used to say that Einstein was right in not accepting by intuition alone the ideas of probability.

Perhaps if he had had children . . . but he hadn't.

It was this man who met Professor MacDuff for lunch in a Chinese restaurant neighbouring the university. He had a fondness for Chinese restaurants though he couldn't have said why. Perhaps it was memories of the war when he had been busy outmanœuvring the inscrutable Japanese. Not that there seemed much difference between the Chinese and the Japanese: they both looked expressionless and were probably very cunning. He didn't really find their reading of the newspapers backwards very odd: after all he did this himself on Sundays with the *Times* and the *Observer*.

There was something churchlike about Chinese restaurants too. Or perhaps templelike. And the decor always seemed to be either lilac or red. Dragons on friezes on the walls. A moody Chinaman standing next to a telephone. You knew where you were in Chinese restaurants. It was really a business transaction. No nonsense about 'dearie' or 'love' or any of that stuff. All straightforward capitalist procedure.

It was on a Monday that he met Professor MacDuff who came in rather hesitantly not to say gingerly as he was not a devotee of Chinese restaurants, in fact hating them a bit and not liking the food very much. 'I see you're grazing already,' he said as he sat down looking with disfavour on the acres of rice the Principal was guzzling. He ordered some tomato soup and shuddered. He knew in advance what it would be like. Why did the Chinese manage to take all the flavour out of European food? What would happen if we ever went into the Chinese Common Market?

The Principal had decided to flatter him. 'I suppose you've done the Ximenes this week,' he said. 'What was that word for Six Across? I believe the clue was "Brown, that is, was Northern shall, a Highland gentleman". Eleven letters.'

'Dunie wassal,' said MacDuff with not much satisfaction since he knew he was being conned and didn't like being patronised. Nevertheless there was enough of the pedagogue in him to explain that 'dunie wassal' was a Highland gentleman (grossly anglicised) and that 'sall' was the Northern version of 'shall'.

'Of course you're Highland yourself,' said the Principal. 'I keep forgetting that. You've been here so long.'

MacDuff didn't bother to reply.

After a while the Principal said, still munching, 'Funny how we academics are always doing crosswords. I often wonder whether Kant would have been a crossword fan. Perhaps it's something to do with solving the enigma of the world by words alone.'

'O I think it's just an amusement,' said MacDuff bluntly. The tomato soup was as bad as he'd feared. It looked like blood mixed with water. And not very high class blood at that. There was also some horrible music leaking from the walls like sweat. 'Naturally,' he said aloud, 'these are Chinese from Hong Kong.'

'Yes,' said the Principal vaguely. 'Exiles.' He raised his eyes from the suey and said, 'Have you ever read any of the Charlie Chan stories.'

'All of them,' said MacDuff, 'I believe there are only five full length ones in existence. I wish people would republish the great detective classics. You never get anything but thrillers nowadays and sociological analyses. These things have no place in the true detective story, which should be a puzzle. The people should be cardboard not human beings. As in Ellery Queen for instance. Or Carr in his great period.'

'I see,' said the Principal keenly, 'a puzzle eh?' Suddenly MacDuff realised and not for the first time that this man was no fool but in fact had a very fine brain when he chose to use it.

'There was another one, wasn't there?' said the Principal. 'Van somebody or other. He did the Bishop Murder Story. I've been trying to get hold of his books for some time.'

'Van Dine,' said MacDuff briefly. 'Yes, he's good, very good.' He pushed the half-consumed tomato soup away from him. Some of it had spilt on his jacket.

'Yes, the Chinese detective stories all seem to be a bit comic,' said the Principal laying a cunning emphasis on the last word, as if he thought it would entrap MacDuff into some revealing confession.

But MacDuff at this point was holding in front of him a menu as big as a newspaper and was trying to work out which would be the least punishing item for him to choose.

'I said they're slightly comic,' said the Principal.

'Who?'

'Chinese detectives. Chink private eyes.'

'Yes, I suppose so, but then the rest of us don't have the same insight into the Oriental mind as you have,' said MacDuff. He wished he could smoke his pipe. But Chinese restaurants didn't seem to take kindly to pipes. It would be like smoking in church. He thought: The best clue I ever saw was 'Nothing squared is cubed. 'The answer was OXO. That was pure genius.

'Regarding your lectures,' said the Principal, deciding on a frontal attack.

'I beg your pardon.'

'I said regarding your lectures. Comic, I've been hearing,' said the Principal. 'I mean I've had letters. From influential parents. Complaints. Some from ministers and nationalists. Crank ones of course. But some very fierce. Some of them accuse you of being a communist.'

'I see,' said MacDuff scrubbing vaguely at the red stain left by the tomato soup.

'By the way, are you?' said the Principal.

'Am I what?'

'A communist.'

'You must know my background.'

'Yes I know. Brilliant First in English, in 1934. Member of University Socialist Party Club for the last two years of your student career. Spoke against Franco at various meetings. Why didn't you go to Spain?'

'Cowardice basically, I suppose. I should have gone. Why didn't you?'

'You must remember I'm younger,' said Carstairs with some satisfaction. He pushed the plate away and ordered banana fritters from an impassive waiter. 'Junior lecturer. Senior lecturer. Full professor. You've never been in any other university. Oh I forgot. You married in 1940. You weren't in the war of course were you?'

'I have bad eyesight as you know.'

'Of course. Your wife was a lecturer in Greek. Died last year. We were all very sorry.' He jabbed at his banana fritter. 'I wonder why you lectured on the comics. It's not really the sort of thing one does. And you of all people. What was that book you wrote, *The Theme of Resurrection in Shakespeare's Later Plays*.'

'I also wrote two on Milton.'

'Of course. I know you're a popular lecturer but you can't possibly continue with this rubbish. Desperate Dan indeed. Many people might think you were going off your rocker.'

'Do you think so?'

'No, I don't. I still don't know what the game is.'

'It's not a game. It's desperately serious.'

'I see. After all you're a scholar and you're not off your rocker as we've agreed. So what is all this about? I know

I'm only a scientist and as far as I know we haven't got the equivalent of comics in the world of. . .' He paused for a moment and then said dreamily, 'apart of course from Bergen. But that's beside the point. I should like to know what you're trying to do. Parents are protesting. You must realise that this is an odd situation. In fact I've never heard of anything like it before.'

'Well, if that's all,' said MacDuff.

'Naturally some people on the Senatus are likely to discuss it. However I'll leave it with you now. I'm sure you will see reason.'

Carstairs sat staring at his coffee for some time after MacDuff had gone. For some reason a tag kept coming into his mind, 'Lead on, MacDuff.' He couldn't make up his mind whether he was going to be Duncan or Macbeth. After thinking about this for some time he decided it didn't make much difference. He looked vaguely around him. Odd that MacDuff didn't like Chinese restaurants. Perhaps if it had been a communist restaurant he might have liked it better. Or perhaps it was all a big bluff. He got up slowly and paid his bill at the desk. Then he went out into the fine spring day, where everything was fresh and new. If one didn't have troubles like this one might even enjoy it. There was a Chinaman standing in the sunshine just outside the door staring at him inscrutably.

Professor MacDuff lived by himself since his wife had died a year before. In general he took most of his meals out, though in the evenings he made some food for himself and did a good bit of reading. He had also taken to playing chess though it wasn't until three years before that he had bought a set and was surprised to find that it wasn't quite as tormenting as he had feared. His wife had died of cancer and it had been a slow death. He had married her when he was thirty years old. He had met her in the university library where she was reading a book on Vergil. He remembered that she had looked rather like a nun, perhaps like the one mentioned in *Il Penseroso*. Her face was classical yet not cold. She was quite small.

When he came home at night he often thought about her and about the classics. The whole house seemed very empty especially in the winter time. At times however he felt that she was still there and sometimes even in his bed he would stretch out his arm as if she was present. It was a strange feeling. Sometimes he would glance up from his book thinking that she was still sitting in the chair opposite him. And then he was stabbed by the most incredible pain.

He had let the house become rather untidy though not dirty. Books were piled behind the chair in which he sat. He read indiscriminately, Science fiction, detective stories, academic books, they were all grist to his mill. Sometimes he would be reading five books at the one time. He was all right during the academic year but the vacations were difficult because they were so long. The previous year he had gone to British Columbia to see his brother who was a businessman over there. He had found the trip interesting—Fable Cottage on Vancouver Island for instance but was a bit put off by the 'stroll down Chaucer Lane in the English Village which leads to Anne Hathaway's Cottage'. However he hadn't particularly cared for his brother who had become much more vulgar and superficial than he had remembered, and who was absolutely interested in money and little else. His brother in fact was a brutal red-faced crashing bore. He would never see him again.

He sat down in the chair after coming back from his meeting with the Principal. On the floor in front of him was a bottle of Parozone, yellow, and he stared at it for a long time. It seemed in some way to soothe him. After a while he slept. Then he got up and got out his notes on Milton. In his new book which he might never complete he was trying to show how far *Samson Agonistes* was from the true Greek style of drama, how clumsy the versification was. He had always believed that Milton was strongest in poems like *Allegro* and *Il Penseroso* and that at that point there was life and gaiety and the exact elegance of true poetry.

He thought about his wife. She had a clear quick-witted practical mind but at the same time she was an idealistic scholar. She had been in far more jobs than he had ever been. For instance she had once been a waitress during the long vacation. Another time she had worked in the cinema as an usherette. She had looked after the garden which he now neglected. She also had, he thought, a purer and more zealous love of learning than he had, a combination of love and precision. Her feeling for the classics made her adore Housman whom he had always considered a bad poet. But, strangely, after she had died he had read the poems again and found that they were more piercing than he could recall. Sometimes when searching in a drawer for a cuff link he would come on a glove or handkerchief that had belonged to her and would be stabbed by that dreadful agony.

But he was all right now, wasn't he? He was even reasonably happy. At least during term time. The Logic Professor would sometimes visit him arriving at about ten o'clock at night (for he seemed to have no regard for or even knowledge of time) and they might play chess for a time. Or drink beer. Or sometimes talk. Often about Wittgenstein who after a difficult life had said that he had been the happiest of men. 'Imagine that,' the Logic Professor would say, 'an odd man. A strange man. Fine fine mind. But odd.' (He himself dabbled in alchemy and had a sundial in his garden to tell the time.) 'Something very prophetic about him. He hated the academic world, you see, and I don't blame him.' Forgetting that it was three o'clock in the morning and settling himself like a gnome on a red cushion from which the feathers were falling out as if it were moulting.

At other times the Divinity Professor would come all aflame with the latest conference he had attended and bringing along with him questions such as 'How far can we use the work of atheistic writers in studying theology?' His thin pale ravaged face showed how he was struggling against the stream.

And then of course there were his neighbours (the two houses divided by a hedge) a young couple of whom the husband was a young mathematics lecturer and his wife a teacher in a city school. They had a child of about five years old.

When he had finished his work on Milton he made himself some tea and switched on TV. A keen-eyed announcer of the type satirised by Monty Python was looking straight at him and saying:

'. . . the initiative on Ireland. To discuss what the

package may be we have brought along to the studio tonight Mr Ray of the Conservative Party, Mr Hume of the Labour Party and Mr O'Reilly of the Unionist Party and Miss Devlin.' Each face nodded modestly, mouthing some phantom unheard words which might have been Good Evening.

The announcer trained his gimlet eyes on one of the four people and said, 'And now, Mr Ray, may I ask you the following question. It has been rumoured that there is a split in the Tory Cabinet, some hawks saying that nothing should be done until the IRA have been beaten on the ground and some doves saying that there must be an initiative now. What are your views on that?'

'Well, Terence, first of all as you know very well I can't speak for the Cabinet, otherwise I would be a member of it, but it seems to me obvious speaking personally, and I must emphasise this, that we can't allow violence, the rule of violence, to prevail in Ireland or anywhere else. If you recall, an analagous situation arose in Cyprus some years ago as well as in Algeria . . .'

'Yes I appreciate that but could you be more . . .'

'I was trying to lay the foundation for an answer.'

'I understand. Can I take it then that you support the hawks? Mr Hume, what do you say to that?'

Mr Hume, a large slow man with beetling brows, leaned forward, dominating the screen like a serene basking shark.

'I think it is totally typical of the Conservative Party to take such a position. Their idea of solving any problem is to use force. The lame duck philosophy . . . We see it in UCS, in their handling of the question of children's milk, in their whole philosophy of government . . .'

'Yes but about the Irish initiative . . .'

'I was just coming to that . . . How can one believe that the IRA can be beaten when they obviously have behind them the whole Catholic . . .'

Professor MacDuff put the volume down so that the lips moved but nothing could be heard. The mouths opened and shut like those of goldfish in a pond. He went to the back of the set and fiddled about with the controls. The faces lengthened and shortened like Dali's picture 'The

Persistence of Memory' which shows watches and clocks hung like plasticine and liquorice over chairs. One could imagine cutting them up and eating them from a knife. 'The new Chinese food,' he thought. After he had played about for some time, allowing lines and dots to invade the screen, shaping faces and bodies into gluey masses, making the bodies tall and thin as the man in *Monsieur Hulot's Holiday* and fat and squat figures as in a spoon, he switched to the other channel which showed a number of girls dancing to the music of pop songs, swaying their bodies, flicking their hands, tribal people.

In the middle of this the phone rang and he went and answered it. 'Who's that?' he asked.

'BBC here. TV actually. That is Professor MacDuff, isn't it?'

'Yes this is Professor MacDuff.'

'Well, we have heard some rumours that you are teaching something to do with Desperate Dan is it and that you believe that this is as valuable as the more conventional stuff. We were wondering perhaps if you could come along to the studio and . . .'

'When?'

'When?' The voice seemed slightly disconcerted. 'Well, we were thinking in terms of this week. There's a spot called *Matters of Moment* which you may have watched . . .'

'What time?'

'If you could be along here at six o'clock on Friday night. Would that be all right? I could come along beforehand. I would handle it myself. My name is Burrow by the way.'

'On my own you mean?'

'Well, have you any other suggestions as to the format? We are always open to . . .'

'I thought I might discuss my ideas with a student perhaps if you . . .'

'Uh huh, have you anyone in mind?'

'As a matter of fact I have. His name is Mallow, Steven Mallow. I could provide you with his address if you . . .'

'That would be fine. We could get in touch with him. You would wish to discuss this issue with him, is that right?'

'That is right,' said the Professor picking up and laying

down a copy of Catullus's poems which were lying near the phone.

Steven Mallow was the student who had defended him at the lecture. Not that he knew much about him except that in one examination he had gained one mark by defining Grimm's Law.

'I can take it then that you will be at the studio for five,' said Burrow. 'We usually provide some food before you go on and then of course you have to be made up. But don't worry about that. Our girls are very expert.'

'Fine,' said the Professor, 'if that's all . . . How long would we be on for?'

'Oh I think we could give you fifteen or twenty minutes. Is that fair? Does that sound OK to you?'

'Yes, it's fine as far as I am concerned.'

'Good then. We will see you at five. Ask for me personally please. Nigel Burrow.'

Professor MacDuff put down the phone. As he looked into the darkening garden he could see the statue of the Greek boxer, arms raised in front of him, pale and trembling in the twilight.

Another short time and I shall be leaving the university, he thought. And he couldn't imagine what it would be like to be alone without anything to do. He had no hobbies at all. He did not play golf, he did not play bowls, he wasn't a committee man. He would grow old on his own, that was inevitable and terrifying. But as he stood there the line from Tennyson came into his mind, 'Old age hath yet his honour and his toil', and he was vaguely comforted by the words and their sound. They seemed to be a guarantee of something, they seemed to provide a music which he could confront the imminent chaos with. He picked up the Catullus and gazed at it absently. Behind him he could see flashes of light from the TV but no sound and he went back and switched it off completely. After some time he prepared himself for bed. As he lay down he watched the cold white moon marbling the sky, a persistent chill scrutiny, an eye of light. Forgetting, once again he stretched out his arm as if to embrace his wife and then withdrew it remembering. Turning over on his side he went to sleep.

THREE

Professor MacDuff arrived at the studio at five o'clock precisely and after inquiring at the desk about where he should go was met by Burrow who took him up to a room on the table of which there were salads wrapped in cellophane and a selection of whiskies and beer and sherry. He refused anything to drink and sat down. He felt tense as he had never taken part in a broadcast before although Burrow tried to put him at his ease. With Burrow was a man called Russell who was perhaps the producer.

'I should like to say,' said Burrow, 'that we won't discuss the subject beforehand in case you might say during the programme, "As we were mentioning before we came onto the air!" That looks bad.'

'I understand,' said the Professor looking dispiritedly at the salad and convinced that he would not be able to do more than nibble at it.

'As a matter of fact once you get started,' said Russell, 'you will forget the cameras are there and will only be concerned with what you are saying. Isn't that so, Nigel?'

'Absolutely,' said Burrow. The professor suddenly had the idea that in a short while they would forget his name and even the programme in which he was taking part and that the only reason he was there was not that he should provide information or discuss fundamental things but that he should fill up a space. Pursuing his thought aloud he said:

'Have you ever thought that producers of programmes and editors of newspapers must continue with their work because there is a space which must be filled every day? Have you ever had that feeling?'

He looked at Russell who seemed not quite to understand the question.

'I've never actually thought of it in those terms,' he said, 'but I suppose it's true in a way. Certainly we're often pressed for time.'

This wasn't at all what the Professor had meant: in fact when he tried to say what he meant he wasn't sure that he could express it. It was something to do with the fact that newspapers and programmes had been originated and

that since they had been originated they must proceed by
the force of inertia. There was another theory he had about
the relationship between space and time as far as news was
concerned but he couldn't clarify the thought. The clock
showed five past five and at that moment Mallow entered
wearing a blue polo-necked jersey and tight green jeans and
carrying a folder with papers.

'Hi,' he said raising his arm in salute. 'The communicators
are together I see.' He laid his folder on the table and
sat down.

'I think perhaps we should have something to eat now,'
said Burrow. 'It isn't much but it's the best the canteen
can do.'

They all began to remove the cellophane wrappings from
the paper plates to reveal chicken and lettuce and beetroot
and so on.

The Professor made vague dabs at it. His cuisine, what
with the Chinese food, hadn't been very spectacular recently.
His stomach was tied in knots as it always was before an
important occasion, especially one where he would have
to expend emotion. He drew in his breath and expelled it
slowly knowing that the more tense he was the better he
would perform provided that the tension didn't reach too
high a pitch. There was silence for a while till Russell said,
'I suppose Nigel has told you that you'll have to be made
up. But don't worry, it won't take long.'

'Right,' said Mallow. 'We don't get handbags do we,' and
he laughed. Russell who looked as if he had often heard the
joke smiled palely. For a moment MacDuff wondered if
Mallow had been on television before. Dearest Mary, he
said to the shade of his dead wife, please help me, it is all
for you. He tried to forget where he was by thinking of his
wife, sometimes seeing her with her head bent over a book
and at other times pruning the roses beside the Greek statue
in the garden. The curve of her back was ineffably painful
to him.

The conversation around him blossomed and concerned
itself with the chess tournament which was at that moment
taking place in Russia.

The usual banalities were exchanged though MacDuff was

surprised to notice that Mallow apparently didn't care much for chess. It wasn't the 'game for the working classes,' he said at one stage. You wouldn't see working men play it in pubs. It was too 'intellectual'. MacDuff didn't take much part in the conversation: he was thinking deeply and he was also rather nervous. To use such an instrument . . .

Eventually Burrow rose from the table and said that if they followed him to the make-up room . . . He glanced at his watch and added that he wasn't trying to hurry them but . . .

So they went into the make-up room and it didn't take very long for a young girl to dab at MacDuff's cheeks. Then they were sitting on chairs on a platform, himself and Burrow and Mallow. Burrow was in the middle.

MacDuff thought to himself, I must appear very natural, not at all crazy. I musn't move my hands or my legs, I must show conviction.

They were ready. There were some preliminaries and then the programme was stopped and Burrow told them that what they had just said wouldn't go out but they were *really* ready now.

Burrow: 'Tonight we have with us on *Matters of Moment* a Professor of English, Professor MacDuff' (he nodded towards MacDuff who moved his lips silently and nodded), 'and Stephen Mallow, a student of English in his class. Recently Professor MacDuff has been doing an analysis of comics with his students and this we hear has been causing some friction. Professor MacDuff however believes that comics have a useful part to play and those of us who had to study Shakespeare and Anglo-Saxon are I am sure wondering what he will say. First of all I should like to ask Mr Mallow if he was surprised when the Professor began to give lectures on the comics. Mr Mallow?'

Mallow: 'Not really. Perhaps I was surprised that Professor MacDuff should . . . But no I can't say I was surprised. After all lots of people read the comics, far more than read Shakespeare.'

Burrow: 'Do you mean then that you would approve of Bingo rather than Brahms?'

Mallow: 'If that is what people want. Yes.'

Burrow: 'I see. You would approve of lectures on Bingo?'

Mallow: 'Why not? What you have to understand is that most people don't read Shakespeare because they like him. They've been conned into reading him. Most people don't really like Brahms. They prefer to sit down by the fireside and read a good thriller. Or even a comic. You find spontaneous humour in a comic. It's not easy to write a good comic. You need technique.'

Burrow: 'I see. What would you say to that, Professor MacDuff?'

MacDuff: 'As a matter of fact I have brought along with me some poems which I found in a magazine, I think it is a minor magazine but the people in it, the poets, are well known, so I am told. I should like to read one of these poems. It is called 'Bus'. It reads as follows:

> Last bzz
> Izz
> drizzly
> missed.

Here is another poem:

> Mamba
> adder
> boa constrictor
> pricked her
> mam
> ba
> anaconda
> python.

The book from which this is taken, the magazine I mean, is called *Azure Blues*. The blurb reads:

'Simmons (that is the poet who wrote these verses) undoubtedly shows in this book a feeling for urban nuances which by linguistic modes he imposes on the reader. His poems in their simplicity and bizarre menace are a projection into the future.'

'I'm not quite sure,' said Burrow, 'are you approving or disapproving . . .?'

'I was wondering whether Mr Mallow,' said the Professor, 'thought that these were good poems.'

'Well,' said Mallow, 'they seem to me to be attempting something new. They seem to me to have a certain avant-garde feeling . . .'

'I was wondering,' said MacDuff, 'whether in fact the working classes would find them interesting. You see,' said the Professor, 'I think in fact they're a load of crap.'

There was a long silence in the course of which Professor MacDuff regarded with satisfaction and merciless tranquillity the expressions which crossed Burrow's face ranging from bewilderment to fear and the appearance of being hunted. He looked at that moment as if he wanted to leave the box in which he was sitting and certainly, thought MacDuff, he would have brought the programme to an end if MacDuff hadn't insisted on its being sent out live.

Eventually Burrow said out of his bemusement, 'I thought Professor MacDuff that you were in fact . . .'

'As a matter of fact,' said the Professor, 'I have also brought along with me some lines from a poet whom I admire very much. His name is Shakespeare. The speech is from Hamlet. I should like to read it. It begins as follows:

'"To be or not to be that is the question." He is of course discussing suicide. It goes on,

> Whether 'tis nobler in the mind to suffer
> the slings and arrows of outrageous fortune
> or to take arms against a sea of troubles
> and by opposing end them.'

'I am quite sure that the working men will recognise in these lines some of the difficulties that obsess us all.'

Mallow was signalling frantically.

'The fact is,' said the Professor, 'that the greater writers, the great composers, have all written about ordinary people. They were people who suffered. Shall I tell you what is wrong with people like Mallow and his kind? Envy. Pure envy. Why are they envious? They are envious because they cannot write like Shakespeare or like Sophocles or like Tolstoy. Do you think for a single moment that I could conceivably be interested in comics? Do you think for a moment that I look down on the working man? Do you think the great writers have looked down on the working man? Listen to a quotation from the comics. These sounds. "Aargh." "Yoops." They are like the sounds we would make when we came out of the slime. Aren't they? Shall I tell you something? It is the people who write the comics who look down on the working man. They are saying, "This is what the working man is like. This is what he prefers. He can't do any better than this. Give him any rubbish." And people like Mallow are the sort who try to deprive him of his heritage. Does he want us to go back to the slime?'

Burrow: 'I'm sorry, I don't understand, I thought that you were defending the comics, that you were lecturing on them because you . . .'

MacDuff: 'Exactly. And why did I do that? I did that so that I would end up here. So that I would get an audience. Why did you want me here? Shall I tell you? I'll tell you the reason why you invited me here. You don't really give a damn one way or the other. You're not really interested in this at all are you? You put me on the box because you thought I was going to be sensational, didn't you? That I would be entertaining. What the hell do you care about culture or about anything else? What do you care about all those people who have died in order to produce a poem or a symphony? You don't give a damn, do you? What can your friend Mallow say? He doesn't know enough about literature or about anything else to answer me. Does he even know enough about the comics? Does he know when the comic first started? Of course he doesn't. He's just a shallow nincompoop.'

Burrow: 'Well, Mr Mallow?'

Mallow: 'I was just about to say that this trick is what one would expect of one who is trying to defend the élite and élitism. What has Professor MacDuff ever done except to stay in his ivory tower? Can he tell us if he has in fact gone out to the people? Can he tell us that he is not defending the rotting bastions of capitalism and that in order to do that he must defend the élitism of Shakespeare and the rest?'

MacDuff: 'You asked me whether I have done anything for the working man. Yes, shall I tell you what I've done for the working man? I've spent fifty years reading books and lecturing on them. I have spent fifty years trying to separate the false from the true. I have spent fifty years trying to nurse in people's minds that love of excellence which prevents us from being animals. You may call it an ivory tower if you like. I say that I've been protecting your civilisation, the civilisation of all men. I've been trying to keep us all from being yahoos. I'm not saying that I did it alone. But I helped to do it. I'm proud of doing it. Listen to this. This is Hamlet again speaking to Horatio his friend. Hamlet is concerned about his honour and he says:

> Absent thee from felicity awhile
> and in this harsh world draw thy breath in pain
> to tell my story.

Listen to this line:

> The still sad music of humanity.

I could go on all night. When did Mallow or any of his kind ever write anything like that? Is that élitism? Shall I tell you about Mr Mallow and the rest of them? They think they know everything and they know nothing. Michelangelo and the other great painters didn't think it odd or wrong to be apprentices to painters lesser than themselves. This is the first generation we have had who think they have nothing to learn. I shall challenge Mr Mallow now. I shall ask him who wrote some great lines that I will quote. And to be perfectly fair if he can't answer these questions—since I am sure he cannot—I further challenge him to produce his alternatives.'

Burrow: 'Mr Mallow?'

Mallow: 'I haven't been a professor in an ivory tower for fifty years so I haven't got the Professor's useless learning. It would be easy for me to ask him . . .'

MacDuff: 'Please let him ask me to identify any lines that he can produce that the listeners will be able to call great. For after all I believe in the audience out there. I believe they want the best. I don't believe they are content with bingo and dominoes or whatever Mr Mallow wants them to play. I don't believe they want to read comics. I don't believe they want to be like everyone else. Even on this medium which tries to make them so I still believe with Blake and all the great writers in their potential and their individuality. I believe that they can tell which writers will set down their joys and their sufferings. I believe that they can love the best and the excellent. I do not believe in the "working man". I believe in individual men. And I say that people like our friend here are practical illiterates who wouldn't know a line of poetry if it hit them between the eyes. Our universities are full of them. But they have to make the choice whether they want to go back to the world of the comics with their grunts or forward to the best that man has ever thought. I shall be retiring after this programme is over. I am not ashamed of my lifetime's work and I want to be clear about this. I'm not ashamed of my ivory tower if that is what you call it. I have been in the firing line and a much more complex one than most. It's true I haven't fought in wars with bullets but this is another war, and I am suggesting that those great writers as in any other war should not have died in vain. Listen:

> The woods are lovely dark and deep.
> But I have promises to keep
> and miles to go before I sleep.
> And miles to go before I sleep.

I don't give a damn for this medium. And I recognise that I have to use a medium which I despise in order to say the things I have to say. I regret that I had to use subterfuge in order to get on it at all. But someone has to say the things I have said. I'm not ashamed of my life. I have done what I set out to do. And I shall continue doing it too.

'And I should like to say this to you. Always try to tell the best from the trashy. You'd try to do it when you're shopping, wouldn't you? Why shouldn't you do it for your minds? The mind surely is as important as the body. I'm not waiting for our friend to sum up. I'm leaving now. I'm leaving because I'm not going to allow them to package all this up very neatly. I say, to hell with their medium. I can step out of the box any time.'

And at that precise moment he did. He walked off down the steps, and after a long time onto the street, which was sunny and warm. He walked briskly along, meditating on how he should word his letter of resignation. He thought about his wife and felt her closer to him than ever before. She had worn out her days on Greek scholarship, practising the discrimination without which we are animals, he thought. There can be no doubt that whatever happens, we are right, he said to himself. The signs glittered all round him, the signs of supermarkets and cinemas. He felt happy and free and gay, as if new creative life had been given to him. Already he could hear the 'phone ringing or its meaningful silence. It was necessary to shed that load, to go to Spain at last . . .

By Their Fruits

MY CANADIAN UNCLE told me, 'Today we are going to see John Smith. I'll tell you a story about him. When he was nineteen years old, and coming to Canada, the minister met him and he said to him (you see, John had been working at the Glasgow shipyards before that) the minister said to him, "And I hear you've been working on a Sunday," and John said to him, "I hear you work on a Sunday yourself." So when John was leaving to come to Canada the minister wouldn't speak to him. Imagine that. He was nineteen years old, the minister didn't know whether he would ever see him again. Now the fact is that John has never been to church since he came to Canada.'

My uncle was eighty-six years old. He had been allowed to drive, I think, during the duration of our holiday with him, and he took full advantage of the concession.

'They said to me,' he told us, 'you keep out of Vancouver, you can drive around your home area, old timer. Drive around White Rock.'

Every morning he took the white Plymouth from the garage, put on his glasses carefully and set off with us for a drive of hundreds of miles, perhaps to Hell's Gate or Fraser River. His wife was dead: in the garden he had planted a velvety red rose in remembrance of her, and he watered it devoutly every day.

Once in Vancouver we came to a red light which we drove through, while a woman who was permitted to cross in her car stared at him, her mouth opening and shutting like that of a fish.

'These women drivers,' he said contemptuously, as he drove negligently onwards.

Every summer he took the plane home to Lewis. 'What

326

I do,' he said, 'I leave this lamp on so that people think I am here.' One summer Donalda and I searched Loch Lomondside for the house in which his wife had been born but we couldn't find it.

'She was an orphan, you know, and the way we met was like this. She went to London on service and decided she would emigrate to Australia, but then changed her mind when she saw an advertisement showing British Columbia and its fruit. I was going to Australia myself with another fellow, but he dropped out so I emigrated to Canada instead. One night at a Scottish Evening in Vancouver I saw her coming in the door wearing a yellow dress. I knew at that moment that that was the girl for me, so I asked her for a dance, and that was how it happened.'

He fixed his eye on the road.

'Listen,' he said, 'you can drive a few miles over the limit. You're allowed to do that.' His big craggy face was tanned like a Red Indian's. It was like an image you would see on a totem pole.

John Smith lived in a house which was not as luxurious as my uncle's. He had a limp, and immediately my uncle came in he began to banter with him.

'Here he is,' he said to his wife, 'the Widows' Delight.' My uncle smiled. 'Listen,' he said to me, after he had introduced me. 'This fellow believes that we come from monkeys,' and he smiled again largely and slightly contemptuously.

'That's true enough,' said Smith, stretching his leg out on the sofa where he was sitting. His wife said nothing but watched the two of them. She was a large woman with a flat white face.

'It may be true of you,' said my uncle, 'but it's not true of me. I'm not descended from a monkey, that's for sure. No, sir. You'll be saying next that we have tails.'

'That's right,' said Smith, 'if you read the books you'll see that we have the remains of tails. And I'll tell you something else, what use is your appendix to you, tell me that.'

'My appendix,' said my uncle, 'what are you talking about? What's my appendix got to do with it?' And he winked at me in a conspiratorial manner as if to say, Listen to that hogwash.

'It's like this,' said Smith, who was a small intense man. 'Your appendix is no use to you. It's part of what you were as an ape. That's what the books tell you. You could lose your appendix and nothing would happen to you. You don't need it. That's been proved.' His wife smiled at Donalda and at me as if to say, They go on like this all the time but below it all they like each other.

'A lot of baloney,' said my uncle, 'that's what it is, a lot of baloney. When did you ever see a man turning into a monkey?'

'It's the other way round,' said Smith tolerantly. 'Anyway the time involved is too great. Millions of years, millions and millions of years.'

'Baloney,' said my uncle again. 'You read too many books, that's what's wrong with you. You'd be better looking after your garden. His garden is a mess,' he said, turning to me. 'Never seen anything like it. All he does is read and read.'

'And all you do is grow cherries and give them to widows,' said Smith chortling. 'Did you know that,' he said to me, 'he's surrounded by widows. They come from everywhere: they're like the bees. And he grows cherries and gives them baskets of them. Did you see the contraption he's got to keep the crows away from the cherry trees?' And he laughed.

Donalda and I looked at each other. My uncle had a wire which he strung out through the window of the kitchen and on it hung a lot of cans and a big hat and when he saw any crows approaching he pulled at the wire and the cans set up a jangling noise.

'They're like the Free Church ministers, them crows,' said Smith, 'you can't keep them away from the cherries.'

My uncle once told us a story. 'When I came here first I used to drive a cab and I used to take a lot of them ministers around to conferences. And, do you know, they never invited me into any of their houses once? They would leave me sitting in the cab to freeze. That's right enough.'

'All that baloney about monkeys,' said my uncle again. 'That's because he's got hair on his chest. Mind you, he does look a bit like a monkey,' he said to me judiciously.

Smith got angry. 'You're an ignorant man,' he said. 'Just because you were on the Fire Brigade you think you know everything. Do you know what he reads?' he said to me. 'He reads the *Fishing News* and the *Scottish Magazine*. He never read a book in his life. You wouldn't understand Darwin,' he said to my uncle, 'not in a million years.'

'And who's Darwin when he's at home?' said my uncle.

'Darwin?' Smith spluttered. 'Darwin is the man who wrote *The Origin of Species*. You're really ignorant. If you kept away from the widows you would know these things.'

'Do you think the widows are descended from the apes?' said my uncle innocently.

'Of course they are, and so are you.' Smith was dancing up and down with rage in spite of his limp.

'I never heard such hogwash,' said my uncle. 'Tell me something then. Do you swing from the trees in your garden instead of digging?' And he went off into a roar of laughter.

'Oh, what's the use of talking to you,' said Smith, 'no use at all. You're ignorant.'

And so the debate went on, though deep down we could see there was a real affection between the two men. When we were going home in the car my uncle would suddenly burst into a roar of laughter and say, 'Descended from the apes. Do you think Smith looks like an ape? Eh?' And he would laugh again. 'Mind you, where he comes from on the island they could be apes. Sure.' And he laughed delightedly again.

He was really rather boyish. He was always saying 'By golly', in a tone of wonder.

'Did you know,' he told us once, 'there's a woman here who comes from the island and her son-in-law is an ambassador. If you go to their house you'll find that the children have a room of their own with a billiard table and a television and everything else. And she sits there and makes scones as we used to do in the old days. You'd think she was back in Lewis. And when the kids come in, she says, "How much money did you spend today? Did you buy Seven Up?" And if they spent more than they should have, she gives them hell. And I once saw a millionaire in her house. Sure. He was walking along the corridor with a towel round him, he had been for a bathe, and that was all he was wearing. "That's a millionaire," she said to me. "That fellow?" I said. "Yes, that's right," she said. And he looked just like you or me. He said "Hi" to me as he passed. And there was water dripping all over the floor and all he was wearing was a towel.'

He had bought himself a cine camera and the last time he had been home to the islands he had taken some photographs. He showed us them one night and we saw figures of old women in black, churches, rocks, peat cutters, all flashing past at what seemed a hundred miles an hour. 'There's something dang wrong with that camera,' he muttered. Donalda and I could hardly keep from laughing.

All the time we stayed with him—which was three weeks—he wouldn't let us pay for anything. 'I won't be long for this world,' he would say, 'so I might as well spend my money.' And we fed on salmon and cherries and the best of steaks. And sometimes we would sit out in the garden wearing green peaked caps and watching the crows as they hovered around the cherry trees.

'When my wife was taken to hospital,' he said, 'I went to the doctor and I said to him, "No drugs. No drugs," I said to him. We never had a quarrel in our lives, do you know that? She was a great gardener. When we went out fishing on Sunday she would say, "Stop the car," and I would stop, though I drove very fast in them days, and it was a little flower she had seen at the side of the road.' He smiled nostalgically.

'This is my country now, you understand. I go back to the old country, but it's not the same. I've been to see the people who grew up with me, but they're all in the cemeteries. Sure. There was a schoolmaster we had and he used to go into a rage and whip us on the bare legs with a belt. Girls and boys, it was the same to him. But there's no one left now. Canada is my country now.' And he would look out the window at the men in red helmets who were repairing the road in front of his house.

The days were monotonously sunny. There was no sign of rain or storm. It was like being in the Garden of Eden, guiltless and without questions.

The night before we left many of the widows visited him, as did Smith and his wife. The widows brought scones, cakes, and buns, and made the coffee while he sat in the middle of the living room like a king on a throne.

One widow said, 'You know what Torquil here said to my husband when he was building our house. He said to him, "I used to go duck shooting here when I came here first. It was a swamp."'

'And so it was,' said Torquil, laughing.

'He used to tell us, "The men here die young. The women live for ever. What they do is sell their houses and then they buy apartments in Vancouver."'

Another of the widows said to me, 'I saw one of your Highland singers on the TV. He had lovely knees.' All the other widows laughed. 'Lovely knees,' she repeated. And then she asked me if I knew the words of 'Loch Lomond'.

'Iain doesn't like that song,' said my uncle, largely. 'The fact is he despises them songs.' They gazed at me in wonderment. 'Iain doesn't like Burns either. But I'll tell you something about Burns. They say he had a lot of illegitimate children, but that was a lie put out by the Catholics.' He spoke with amazing confidence, and I saw Smith looking at him.

'I went home to Lewis,' said one of the women. 'The shop girls were very rude. I couldn't believe it.'

'Is that right?' said my uncle.

'As true as I'm sitting here,' said the woman.

Another one said, 'You've got lovely cherries this year.'

'Sure,' said my uncle, 'they're like the apples in the Garden of Eden.'

Smith suddenly pounced. He had been sitting on the edge of the company, brooding for a long time.

'It doesn't say that in the Bible at all.'

'What?' said my uncle, 'of course it says that.'

'Not at all,' said Smith, 'not at all. It doesn't mention the fruit at all.'

'I beg your pardon,' said my uncle, 'it says about apples as clear as anything. Do you know,' he said, turning to the widows, 'I read the Bible every year from end to end. I know the names of all the tribes of Israel. The gipsies, you know, were one of the tribes of Israel.'

'It doesn't say that at all,' said Smith, 'not at all. You read your Bible and it doesn't say it was an apple. It doesn't name the fruit at all.'

'What does it matter?' said one of the widows.

'We all know it was a woman who ate the fruit,' said my uncle magisterially.

'It might even have been a widow,' said one of the women. And the others laughed, but Smith didn't laugh. He was muttering to himself, 'It doesn't mention the fruit at all.'

'Next thing you'll be saying it was a pair of monkeys in the Garden of Eden,' said my uncle. 'You'll be saying it was the apes who ate the apple.' And he laughed so hard that I thought he was going to have apoplexy.

'Do you have a Bible here?' said Smith apologetically.

'I can't find it just now,' said my uncle.

I myself couldn't remember what it said in Genesis. My uncle started on a story about how once he had seen a black bear and it was eating berries in Alaska. 'They're very fast, you know,' he said. 'You'd think they would be slow but by golly they're not. By golly they're not.'

Some of the widows asked us if we were enjoying our holiday and we said, 'Yes, very much.'

'That's because Torquil is driving them about,' said one of the widows. 'He's a demon driver, did you know that? His wife used to shout at him and she was the only person he would ever slow down for.'

What did I think of Canada, I asked myself. There were no noises there, no creakings as from an old house. The indifferent level light fell on it. It was like the Garden of Eden uninfected by history. It was without evil. Smith was still muttering to himself. His wife was smiling.

'My friend here,' said my uncle largely, 'believes in the apes, you know. He thinks that we're all apes, every one of us.'

The women in their fine dresses and ornaments all laughed. Who could be further from apes than they were?

'Apes don't make as good scones as this,' said my uncle. 'Do you think apes make scones?' he asked Smith.

Smith scowled at him. He was looking around the room as if searching for a Bible.

'But there's one thing about John here,' said my uncle, 'by golly he's got principles. Yes by golly, he has.'

As the evening progressed we did sing 'Loch Lomond',

'. . . where me and my true love will never meet again on the bonny banks of Loch Lomond.'

I saw tears in my uncle's eyes.

'Mary was from Loch Lomondside,' said my uncle, 'but I couldn't find the house she was brought up in. She was an orphan, you know. Iain and I went there in the car but we couldn't find the house.' There was a silence.

'The only person he would ever obey was Mary,' said one of the widows.

'Gosh, that's right,' said my uncle. And then, it seemed quite irrelevantly, 'When I came here first we used to teach Gaelic to the Red Indians. Out of the Bible. And they taught us some Indian, but I've forgotten the words now. They spoke Gaelic as you would find it in the Old Testament. Of course some men used to marry squaws and take them home to Lewis. They would smoke pipes, you know.'

Smith was still staring at him resentfully.

At about one in the morning they all left. The night was mild and the women seemed to float about the garden in their dresses. My uncle filled baskets of cherries for them in the bright moonlight.

'That's the same moon as shines over Lewis,' he said. 'The moon of the ripening of the barley.'

They were like ghosts in the yellow light, the golden light. I thought of early prospectors prospecting for gold in the Yukon.

'You mark my words, you're wrong about that,' said my uncle to Smith as he pressed a basket of cherries on him. They all drove off to a chorus of farewells from myself and Donalda.

*   *   *

After they had gone, I looked up Genesis. Smith was right enough. It doesn't mention the particular fruit.

At the airport my uncle shook us by the hand briefly and turned away and drove off. I knew why he had done that. I imagined him driving to an empty house. Actually I never saw him again. He died the following year from an embolism. He dropped dead quickly in one of the bathrooms of a big hospital in Vancouver. He firmly believed that he would meet Mary again when he died.

The plane rose into the sky. Shadows were lying like sheaves of black corn on the Canadian earth which was not ours. It was still the same mild changeless weather. I hoped he wouldn't look up the Bible when he arrived home for he prided himself on his knowledge of it, and it was true that he read it from end to end in the course of a year. Even the tribes he memorized. And in the fly leaf of the big Bible were the names of his family and ancestors, all those who had passed it on to him.

I recalled the men in red helmets working in front of the house. He would drive in carefully. Then he would back into the garage and take off his glasses and walk into the house. Sometimes one could see grass snakes at the door sleeping in the sun, and Donalda had been quite frightened of them. One day my uncle had hung one of them round his neck like a necklace. 'You see,' he said, 'it's quite harmless. Sure. Nothing to fear from them at all.' At that moment the camera in my mind stopped with that image. The snake was round his throat like a green necklace, a green innocent Canadian ornament.

Chagall's Return

WHEN I CAME HOME the cat was smiling and the walls of the house were shaking. The door opened and there was my mother in front of me.

'Who are you, my child?' she asked, and her eyes were unfocused and mad. There were other old women in black with her and they nodded to me over and over. I went to see a neighbour who was ploughing, and afterwards I took buckets to the well and brought in water. But my mother was still gazing at me with unfocused eyes and she asked me again and again who I was. I told her about the skyscrapers and the man with the violin, but she could understand nothing.

She kept saying, 'In the old days there were cows, and we were children. We would take them to the grass and there they would make milk.'

'I have brought you money,' I said. 'See, it is all green paper.'

But she looked at the paper unseeingly. I didn't like the look in her eyes. In the afternoon I took a walk round the graveyard near the house, and the tombstones were pink and engraved with names like conversation sweets.

There is nothing in the world worse than madness. All other diseases are trivial compared to it, for the light of reason is what illuminates the world. All that day I shouted to her, 'Come back to me', but she wouldn't. She wanted to stay in her cave of silence.

In this place I walk like a giant. My legs straddle the ward robe, and the midgets around me speak with little mouths. My hands are too big for the table and my back for the chairs. I look into the water which I brought home from the well and it is still and motionless. But my mother's eyes are slant and the old women whisper to her. I nearly chase them out of the house but my mother needs them, I think, for they tell old stories to each other. I think they are talking about the days when things were better than they are now.

The cat's mouth is wide open and he smiles all the time as if his mouth were fixed like that.

'Who are you?' says my mother, over and over. She doesn't remember the day she stood at the door watching me leave, a bag over my shoulder, her eyes shining with tears. I used to see her in the walls of skyscrapers, a transparency on stone. My young days were happy, I think, before she went crazy. Now and again she says things that I don't understand. She speaks the words, 'Who is the man with the black wings?' over and over. But when I ask her what she means she refuses to answer me.

Night falls, and there is a star like a silver coin in the sky. I hear the music of violins, and the black women have left. But my mother's eyes remain distant and hard, and she stares at me as if I were a stone. A dog with a plasticine body is barking from somewhere and in an attic a man is washing himself with soap over and over.

One day in New York I saw that the sun had a pair of moustaches like a soldier home from the wars, and he began to tell me a story.

'I went to the war,' he said, 'and I was eighteen years old. For no reason that I could think of, people began to fire at me trying to kill me. I stood by a tree that had red berries and prayed. I stayed there for a long time till the sun had gone down, counting the berries. After that I went home and I was hidden by my sister behind a large canvas for the rest of the war. When the war was over there were no trees to be seen.'

Still my mother stares at me with her unfocused eyes. I see the whites of them like the white of an egg. She has terrible dreams. In her dreams she is being chased by a vampire, and just at the moment when he is about to clutch her she wakens up.

'Where are you, my son?' she cries. I rush in, but she doesn't recognize me. The greatest gift in my life would be if she recognized me, if the light of reason would come back to her eyes.

I wonder now if it will ever happen.

'I shall put tap-water in the house for you,' I say to her. But she doesn't answer. She only picks at her embroidery.

'And heating,' I say. 'And an electric samovar.'

'My father,' she says, 'was a kind man who had a beard. He was often drunk but he would give you his last penny.'

I remember him. He wasn't kind at all. He was drunk and violent, and he had red eyes, and he played the violin all night. Sometimes I see him flying through the sky and his beard is a white cloud streaming behind him. But he was violent, gigantic and unpredictable.

Where the sky is greenest I can see him. I go to the cemetery with the pink tombstones, and his name isn't on any of them.

What am I to do with my mother, for she shouts at the policemen in the streets. 'Get out of here,' she screams at them, 'this was a road for cows in the old days.' The policemen smile and nod, and their tolerance is immense for she cannot harm them.

The bitterest tears I shed was when she told them that when her son came home he would show them that she wasn't to be treated like a tramp. The old, black women come back and are always whispering stories about her, but if I go near them they stop talking.

'Is your seed not growing yet?' I ask my next door neighbour.

'No,' he says, 'it is going to be a hard year. How is your mother?'

'Not well,' I say, 'she lives in a world of her own.'

He smiles, but says nothing. He was ten years old when I left this place with my bag on my shoulder. That day the birds were singing from the hedges and they each had one green eye and one blue.

I begin to draw my mother to see if her reason will come back to her. I see her as a path that has been overgrown with weeds. Her apron is a red phantom which one can hardly see and the chickens to which she threw meal have big ferocious beaks. Nevertheless, she does take an interest in what I am doing, though she cannot stay still, and her eyes are beginning to focus.

One day—the happiest of my life—she speaks to me again and recognizes me. 'You are my son,' she says, 'and you left me. Why did you leave me?' I try to tell her, but I cannot. The necessity for it is beyond her understanding, and this is the worst of all to bear.

That night before she goes to bed she says, 'Good night, my son,' and in the middle of the night she tucks the blanket about me to keep me warm. I feel that she is watching over me and I sleep better than I have done for many years. In the morning I am happy and wake up as the light pours through the windows. She is sitting by my bed with a shawl wrapped round her.

'Mother,' I cry, 'I am here. I have come back.' The windows change their shape as I say it. But she doesn't answer me. She is dead. She is a statue. She is solid and changeless. All that day I kneel in front of her, staring into her unchanging face.

In the evening one of her eyes becomes green and the other blue. I take my bag in my hand and leave the house. The birds are singing in the hedges and a man is walking through a ploughed field. I do not turn back and wave. The houses are turning into cardboard and the violins are stuck to their walls. I feel sticky stuff on my clothes, my hands and my face. I carry the village with me, stamped all over my body, and take it with me, roof, door, bird, branch, pails of water. I cross the Atlantic with it.

'Welcome,' they say, 'but what have you got there?'

'It is a nest,' I say, 'and a coffin.'

'Or, to put it another way, a coffin and a nest.'